Thomas Jefferson, Rachel & Me

a novel

By
PETER BOODY

Bartleby,
Scrivener & Co.

Sag Harbor, NY
© 2013 Peter B. Boody
edition 20.0/September 2013
(second paperback edition)
ISBN 9781456347543
Library of Congress
TXu-1-705-337

Unable are the loved to die.
For love is immortality.

—Emily Dickinson

You ask if I would agree to live
my 70 or rather 73 years over again?
To which I say Yea. I think with you
that it is a good world on the whole,
that it has been framed on a principle
of benevolence...I steer my bark
with Hope in the head, leaving Fear astern.

—Thomas Jefferson to John Adams,
nine years before Jefferson's death

Chapter 1

I met the man I truly believe was Thomas Jefferson at Monticello one summer evening, when big trees cast long shadows across the west lawn of Jefferson's mountaintop.

I had booked the special tour they offer at the end of the day, after the gate on the entry road has gone down. If your name is on a list, a guard lets you through, and after you drive partway up the hill and park in the nearly empty lot, a guide tells you where to meet the shuttle for the ride the rest of the way up the mountain.

In the dying light streaming through the west windows and doorways of Jefferson's house, the evening tour makes you feel closer to him than just another tourist in the restless crowds that clomp through all day. It's easy to picture his valet, Burwell Colbert, lighting the wick in the whale oil lamp that still hangs in his library as Jefferson, stretched out on his red leather chaise longue, puts up his slippered feet with a good book, something in the original Greek.

His bed is just down a hallway, under an arched alcove that divides his dressing room from his study. If you stand beside the bed on the dressing room side, you can see the splash stains he left on the floor when he got up at dawn every day and plunged his feet into a bowl of cold water. While the rest of my evening group wandered off with the guide, I lingered to gaze at the stains and felt he could not be far away.

Why have I been so interested in this man, even as a boy, long before I began my career as a history teacher? I lack his boundless faith in mankind and the proper functioning of the cosmos.

I am no genius. I lack the brilliance, the discipline, the focus and the rigidly good habits of Thomas Jefferson — if those are the right words for a man who, like so many plantation masters, fathered children with a slave, children from whom Jefferson carefully kept his distance.

Jefferson always behaved as if he had no regrets. I have regrets. I was not a good father. I was not a good husband. Until him, I'm not sure I was ever a good friend.

After the hour-long tour, they let us wander the grounds for half an hour. I wanted the fantasy of feeling alone on Jefferson's mountaintop so I headed away from the others. I walked slowly in the grass along the foundation of the house, letting my hand glide over the walls, feeling the rough, sandy texture of the red clay bricks, each one made by Jefferson's slaves.

When I reached the south terrace — one of two elevated walkways that form wings from the main house — I climbed the steps and walked to the small brick office at the end that Jefferson called a pavilion. It was the first building he put up at Monticello, when he was a young man.

I peered through the rippled glass of its French doors and studied the room into which he had carried his bride after riding through a snowstorm. He had lit a fire and found a bottle of wine on a shelf behind some books. Nine months later, his first child was born, the only one of six — not counting the five or six more he had with his mistress — who survived beyond his middle age. The deaths all wounded him badly. When his wife, Martha, died less than 10 years later, he fell apart. He locked himself in his rooms for weeks, finally emerging only to wander his woods and grounds for hours on foot or horseback.

Maybe that's why I was drawn back to Monticello: to mourn in his company.

I turned to look across the west lawn. The glowing twilight, the silence, the sense of the man everywhere all stirred in me the complicated spirit of the place.

An aged couple, ambling along the terrace toward me, spoiled my fantasy. They smiled and nodded and went by me to peer into the brick cottage. I stepped to the handrail to gaze at the west facade, trying to imagine the elderly Jefferson on the portico steps, dropping a handkerchief to start his laughing grandchildren on an evening race across the lawn.

I was startled to see a tall, thin man standing near the north terrace, perhaps 50 yards away. He wore clothes too heavy for summer: sloppy dark corduroy knee breeches, an off-white shirt, a dark coat and red waistcoat, black slippers and dingy off-white hose. A shock of unruly reddish-white hair formed a glowing cloud around the back of his head. He stood there looking up at a majestic tulip poplar, his sharp jaw set and his chin thrust forward, holding a hand against the small of his back, as if it hurt to gaze up at the tree. He seemed curious about it. I had the feeling he'd never seen the tree before and was both puzzled and delighted to find it there.

"I didn't know they used re-enactors here," I said out loud, thinking the old couple was still nearby. No one answered. They had disappeared.

I let my curiosity draw me slowly along the terrace toward the lanky man in his Jefferson costume. I pretended to take in the glowing sky with its big, billowy clouds still catching the sunlight and went down a set of steps onto the lawn. Feigning interest in the flowers along the way, never looking at him, I moved as nonchalantly as I could.

When I let myself glance his away again, I stopped cold. He was glaring at me, 20 feet away, his arms folded across his chest. It might as well have been Jefferson himself, the commanding figure in Thomas Sully's portrait in the front hall at Monticello, painted when the man of the house was 78.

After studying me in silence, he bowed. "Good evening, sir," he said in a sullen, reedy voice that carried the hint of Virginia hill country. "I saw you from my winders."

I held back a nervous laugh. Winders?

"I thought," he said, "I'd come out to see who you might be. It's something I have not done before. I was not sure I was even able." He forced a weak, insincere smile.

I hung there, staring. "My God," I said, pointing at him, "you really do look like Mr. Jefferson!"

His slightly sour expression did not change. He turned to the tree. "It won't be long before Zeus gets to it now," he said to himself. He half-turned back toward me and looked over my head at the sky. "I'll tell you this," he said. "The lightning storms we have on the mountain pick the biggest and the best as their targets. I am surprised this specimen has grown to such a height. I'd always wished our trees by the house were as grand as this but they were not. Too little, too new in my day. But the views! We had the views! The fogs and vapors never reached us. The world lay at our feet. We watched the storms pass beneath us. It was, for a time, a world in perfect order."

I didn't know what to say. "Ah. I see. Nice," I managed.

He looked at me curiously. "Nice? Such an odd word for such a grand thing." He paused, still pondering me. "Sir, you must forgive me. I am at sixes and sevens. I have sensed the passage of time, the progress of sunlight and moonlight across my floors, the presence of passing persons, an endless parade of them, but most mere shadows to me, flickering like chimney smoke in a wind. It is strange to see you so clearly in true corporeal form. I beg you, can you please tell me what year this is?"

He was laying it on mighty thick but I played along. "Oh! It's 2010. No. 2011. Yes, 2011. I'm getting old enough to forget what year it is," I joked, even though I really didn't consider 53 so old.

He smiled and dropped his arm. "Two thousand and eleven. Oh my, oh my." He clasped his hands and, bowing his head in thought, put his two index fingers to his lips. "It must be, then, that even my grandchildren's grandchildren are long gone." He stared at the ground and looked immensely sad. He dropped his hands, hugged himself and turned back to the tree. "Aha. This one might be a century, then. I know I did not plant it." He stepped to its massive trunk, touched its gray bark and tilted his head to look up.

Strangely eager to support his performance, I said, "There was an even taller tulip tree on the other side of the portico. They cut it down last year, right? It was diseased. They were afraid it might fall on the house. That's what they told me once on the garden tour. They believed Mr. Jefferson himself had it planted, that it was the only tree left from his time, except for that decrepit cedar you can barely see out there."

I pointed to the bleached bare limbs of a half-dead tree poking up from behind green boughs beyond the lawn.

"Mockingbirds are fond of the cedar's fruit," the man said quietly, turning from the tulip tree to gaze toward the cedar. "I had many cedars planted to attract them. I always enjoyed having mockers in the neighborhood. I believe Dick did, as well."

"Dick? Who would Dick be?"

"My mocker." He must have realized I didn't know what he meant. "*Bird*," he said. "My mocking*bird*. One of them, the one I remember most fondly. I took him to the President's House with me, you know. He would take berries from my lips. Very amusing."

He dropped his folded arms and looked at me plaintively. "Do you know the last time I had any strong sense of the place my house was a ruin, with an old fool in charge, letting students in to carouse? That old inebriate raised chickens here on the lawn. He threshed wheat on my cherry and beech parquet floor."

"Good God. You do a marvelous job with this," I said.

"I beg your pardon," he said icily, fixing on me. "I do a marvelous job with what?"

"The whole Jefferson thing. I mean, what? Do you work for the Foundation?"

He stared at me blankly. "Tell me. What country is this? What do you call it? And by that I mean the country that lies beyond Virginia. Does the Union survive?"

I glanced around for the video camera.

"Well, uh, it's still the United States ... of America," I said. "The same country that Mr. Jefferson and Mr. Adams and General Washington and Dr. Franklin and all those others founded in 1776."

The man smiled. "Ah yes," he said. "I wonder if any of them linger drearily suspended between worlds like myself." He turned and looked over his right shoulder, toward the smear of the Blue Ridge as it disappeared into shadow and merged with the sky. "Well, I'm pleased to know the republic lives, very pleased indeed," he said. "And not a little surprised." He looked back at me, setting his jaw tight and knitting his brow. "But what of the South? And the new territories? What of the Constitution?"

"Oh, slavery, you mean? No. No more slaves. That ended in 1863. Well, actually later, when they amended the Constitution to ban slavery after the war. Oh yeah — did you know? We had one hell of a war over it."

He looked at me with annoyance. "Well! Of course! It was North against South," he said — a statement not a question. "And the issue was our vexing institution and its extension to the territories and quite specifically which region would control the national government. So! It seems from what you say that the coolheaded, coldhearted North with its factories and banks and stockjobbers and Abolitionists beat us. *Abolished* slavery? How could they trample on our rights of property without a war!"

He glared at me. I was a Yankee and therefore guilty. "Yes, well," I said, "the president at the time insisted, at first anyway, that the war was not about slavery but the Union." I gave him a little lesson on old Abe. Distracted by the name, he asked if this Lincoln had been related to General Benjamin Lincoln, who had fought in the Revolution, or Levi Lincoln, who had served as his attorney general. No, no, I said, this particular Lincoln was a lawyer from Illinois born to a poor family in Kentucky and now there was a massive monument to him on the mall in Washington.

"Is that so?" he asked, furrowing his brow and lifting his chin to peer. He seemed annoyed. I had the feeling he wanted to ask if they'd built a monument to him. Instead he wagged a finger at me. "I did all I could, sir, to see that slavery was never extended to the territories, including Kentucky."

"Oh. Well, let me tell you," I said, wagging my finger right back at him, "your resolutions and all the compromises that followed went out the window after Jefferson bought Louisiana from the French. The old slave states went nuts, paranoid they were going to lose control of Congress and the presidency to the North. You know, you just can't hold a country together when half of it is out of its mind, all twisted up in knots defending the indefensible."

He looked at me grimly. He seemed to want an argument but, after a moment of jaw-clenching, he let it pass. "Paranoid. I'm not familiar with that term. But I think I follow your charge. 'Demented,' from the Greek. Well. I must say. You seem well informed, sir." He lifted his chin and looked down his long, up-turned nose at me. "Tell me, do all Americans know as much as you about the history of their government?"

"Hah!" I said, feeling strangely giddy. "People today have little understanding of their government and I bet few have even the vaguest idea who Jefferson was."

His face took on that desperately sad look. "Is that so?"

I went into a rant about my frustrations with kids and the American corporate-run consumer culture, the kind of speech I never got away with at my golf club or in the classroom. My son, Ben, called me a Bolshevik. My friends at the club humor me and call me Jack the Marxist. I'm not a Marxist. I'm just an old Democrat.

"You blame the corporations," he said in a whisper, as if in a trance. "Hamilton's people. I knew they'd never cease their machinations until their systems prevailed. And you, sir, why are you not another 'brainwashed moronic consumer,' as you called them?"

"I am a teacher. Recently retired from the public schools. I taught eighth-graders American history for 30 years."

"Aha. A schoolmaster. Well. You look better fed than most, I'd say."

I looked down at myself. I was not fat, really. Just a little thick here and there. Thicker than he was, God knows. "You consume your fill of animal food, I'd wager. It shows in the jaw line. I never knew of any schoolteacher who could afford much meat."

I slapped my hand to my neck. I was an inch shorter than his six feet, two inches, but I must have weighed 50 pounds more.

The man was a stick under those bulky corduroys. I could see by his scrawny neck and tight skin.

"Well," I muttered. "My wife made the money."

He ignored my revelation. "I must tell you, sir, I do not know these terms: public school, eighth grade."

I nodded. "No. Of course not."

"I called, sir, for universal public education. I proposed the creation of primary schools on the local level, with continued state schooling for the most meritorious," he said, as if he were campaigning. "It didn't happen in my time. Not in Virginia."

"Something like it happened eventually."

"I proposed an emancipation bill. You know that, don't you?"

"Oh yes. It was in the House of Burgesses in Williamsburg, when you were a young man." I chuckled. "You had a friend bring it up, Mr. Bland I think. It would have allowed masters to free slaves without government approval. Not much of a bill but, hey, nice try. Very brave."

He ignored that remark, too, and looked me over. "Sir, I must tell you: I wonder if we might spend more time talking of these things. I wonder if there is a way you could be my guest here. Or perhaps for me to venture from the mountain." He looked at the house. "I suspect that is the purpose of my reappearance here. Through some force of nature, some continuing process of consciousness and intelligence, I may now have the chance to learn what's happened to the country and, I pray, my people, my family. I swear I've heard the voices of two of my grandchildren."

He turned and looked past me across the west lawn, toward the family cemetery out of sight below his hilltop. He seemed lost for a moment and then shook himself to attention. "Tell me. You are …"

I looked around again for the camera. I felt a twinge in my gut. This was getting very weird. "My name is Jack Arrowsmith," I said.

"Ah." He bowed. So much for the legend that he always shook hands because it was more democratic. "How do you do,

Mr. Arrowsmith. My name ... please forgive me for not having introduced myself; I am so used to strangers coming here. They all know who I am. It's Jefferson, Thomas Jefferson."

I stepped back. "Of course you are. The very author of the Declaration of Independence and the Virginia Statute for Religious Freedom and the father of the University of Virginia."

"So reads my obelisk."

"Well, you are quite dead then."

"Yes. And I long to see my family. If there is a joyous reunion in afterlife, I have seen nothing of it." He slowly shook his head. "Somehow I've been aware of you, Mr. Arrowsmith, through a certain agitation of the spirit, a nervous irritation," he said in a lowered voice. "Somehow, I know you have lost a son and a wife."

His words struck like the lightning that should have knocked down the big tulip tree. "How could you know that?" I gasped.

"I have no idea, sir, no idea at all. I speak of dreams. Forgive me for mentioning it. I understand your suffering. At least I had my daughter and grandchildren by your time of life."

I just stared at him.

"And your son, he courted quite a beauty."

I cringed. "My son *courted a beauty*? You mean Rachel?"

"Oh! Forgive me. I am not myself to gossip so. My head is in a state of flux. My head *and* my heart." He pressed his hand to his forehead, looking pained. "Oh! You are afraid, I see. Yes, yes, of course. "

"Who are you?" I demanded. "How do you know anything about me?"

He looked at me from under his strong, straight brow. He seemed about to speak but he froze into stillness and began fading away before my eyes until all that remained was a glowing vapor that lingered a few seconds in the air and then vanished.

"Holy Christ! Oh my God," I gasped, lurching backward. "What was *that*?"

Chapter 2

There was only one person I could tell about the man at Monticello.

My son's girlfriend, Rachel Carter, has green eyes, thick auburn hair that falls straight down her back, very light mocha skin and freckles. Her family, the black part of it, comes from Virginia. It has been in America for hundreds of years. She is more American than most of us. It eased my mind to think my Ben, gone forever in a car crash on an icy New England road, had loved such a woman.

Ben had gone to Columbia, where he'd met Rachel, before he went on to business school at Harvard. She was getting her master's in history and had a part-time job doing research for the historian Elmer Kant. He's the Columbia professor who makes bestsellers out of bits and pieces of American history. From the day-to-day business of slave auctions to mob violence in Kansas, he finds topics and writes them so they sell. The man's opus is one of the few reasons why anyone in America — other than a few academics — knows any history. And while Kant made millions selling books to people who didn't know they cared, I myself made a modest living trying to inspire school kids who could not have cared less, most of them anyway.

Rachel and I had become friends somehow. We'd met only a few times before Ben died. He and I had not been speaking for months but she made a point of talking to me after his funeral, at the reception. She said she needed to know I wasn't the asshole Ben said I was.

I was not offended. She struck me as the brightest, most refreshing person I'd seen in a long time. As long as she was being so direct, I smiled and leaned toward her ear and said I wasn't really an asshole. I was just very bad at fatherhood. I also didn't like Big Business Republicans much and my son had become one. "Are you one of them, too?" I asked.

She smirked. "Ben and I fought about politics all the time," she said.

"Ah! Good for you, good for you. We couldn't fight about anything. It would turn too ugly."

She smiled for a second or two then grimaced. Tears filled her eyes and she gripped my arm. "I'm so sorry. You've lost your only son. I loved him too." She looked into my eyes as she tried to control herself. I could see the struggle as it played across her face. "Can I call you?" she asked. "You're the closet thing I have left in this world to Ben. I miss him."

In the middle of a jabbering crowd of drink-sippers and hors d'oeuvres eaters, I sadly watched through the picture window of my living room as she drove off in her beat-up Saab.

She did call a few weeks later. She was working on a thesis about the few career paths that had been open to the first generation of freed blacks — something I felt a little ashamed not to have thought much about. She asked if I would read it. I did and sent her some comments.

We had coffee in New York when I went into town to sign some papers at my late wife's law firm. We talked more about history. We were careful not to talk about Ben, as if we were trying to decide whether or not we could be friends on our own.

I did some research for her on the demographics of blacks during the 19th century in my home county in New Jersey. She sent me more pages. I did more editing. We had dinner in the city, a little Szechuan place near Columbia. She loathed Thomas Jefferson for his hypocrisy — the lifelong slave owner who ridiculously blamed King George for the evil of American slavery — but she made fun of herself for it. "I'm just being my father," she said. "He *really* hates Jefferson. He hates him *too* much. It's as if he really knew him."

On my drive home from Monticello, I resisted calling her.

I wanted to let things settle down in my head. I called her the next night. By then, I had suppressed the shock of my experience, filing away the man's evaporation as a trick. There had been no other way to think about it without the world turning upside down.

"Rachel, this guy … I swear to God he was a dead ringer for the man himself," I told her on the phone. "And his act was flawless. I want to go back and find out who that guy was and what his little performance was all about and how he did that *disappearing* thing. Hey, listen! I was wondering — do you want to go along for the ride?"

She still had a month or so before classes in September and I figured her summer job with Kant was winding down anyway. There was a silence. For a moment, I thought I had overstepped my bounds.

I quickly tried to fill the awkward pause. "I need some fun," I explained. "This is an avoidance thing. I am avoiding my home. I am avoiding sitting alone waiting for my email program to chime in a new message only to find it's another Columbia alumni event, a New York Times news alert or an ad from Apple for the latest iPhone. I am avoiding Facebook and browsing the web. I am avoiding television. I'm avoiding books and my friends at the club. They're all Republicans and I'm tired of hearing them whine about Obamacare and how much his wife hates whites. I'm avoiding tennis and golf. I'd prefer an adventure, even if it's all pretend."

"Maybe you shouldn't have retired, Jack," Rachel said. "Maybe those annoying kids in the classroom with their text messages and iPods were good for your head. You're too young to quit working. I'd say a man like you is not the kind to make golf his reason for being."

I was surprised she knew me that well. I played golf every week but I could take it or leave it. "Pam was sick. We had money," I said, a bit too seriously. "I didn't have my heart in teaching anymore and those early retirement packages were irresistible."

I was afraid she was about to warn me she had no intention of starting an affair with her dead boyfriend's father.

"What happened to your heart, Jack?" she asked slyly. "Why wasn't it in your work anymore? Ben said you were a great teacher."

"He did? Ben said that?"

Rachel did not answer. She seemed to be thinking. "Well, I can't believe I'm saying this. But I like adventures," she finally said. "And maybe I need an adventure, too. I've been buried here. And we haven't seen each other in a while. So hey. Why not? Just you and me, off to Charlottesville?"

"Yeah, you and me, off to Charlottesville. I'd really enjoy your company, Rachel. Maybe we could take a week or more. You and me all over Virginia, just like the trips I used to make with Pam. Monticello, Williamsburg, Appomattox, Richmond, Petersburg … Virginia is terrific for the historically inclined."

My face felt hot, mentioning Pam again to Rachel. She had been my wife for 25 years. She had died a year before Ben, very suddenly, of leukemia. I missed her every moment of every day, even though we had gone for weeks at a time without seeing each other in the last few years. She was a corporate lawyer, always working late, always off on a case.

"Okay," Rachel said with resolve, and I could picture her nodding abruptly and making her long hair sway. "Let's go. Let's hit the road. But let's do some research. Let's make some calls about your ghost friend. And hey, listen: All this reminds me of something I'd completely forgotten until now, Jack. I want to visit the cemetery at Monticello. In your trips there, did you ever come across people dressed in old-fashioned clothes who walked around inside the cemetery fence?"

The question rang a bell. "Now that you ask, I think we did. I'd forgotten about those two oddballs."

I told her that years and years before, when we were new-lyweds, Pam and I had chatted with a couple we'd found in the cemetery. They wore old-fashioned clothes from the mid-19th century. We thought they were strange. I had asked if they worked there. No, they were Randolphs, they'd said, members of Jefferson's family. I'd wanted to ask why they were wear-ing the old clothes but restrained myself. I figured they were

Old Dominion eccentrics, all twisted up in their Jefferson roots, wandering among the lichen-stained monuments of their long-gone kin. I did not want to embarrass them.

"How old would you say they were?" Rachel asked.

"In their early 30s, probably," I said. "So weird."

"Jack," she said, "the people Ben and I saw were in their early 30s."

It's strange how things finally penetrate. I'd met a man exactly like Thomas Jefferson who had vanished before my eyes and, talking to Rachel about him, I'd turned him into a mere puzzle. Yet learning that we'd seen the same odd couple in the Monticello graveyard, more than 20 years apart, was somehow harder to swallow. I sat there, slack-jawed, until Rachel said okay, we'd figure it all out, we should get going on our research and then head down to Virginia.

We divided up the job over the next few days. From her dorm in Manhattan, she talked to somebody at the Thomas Jefferson Foundation, who denied there was anyone at Monticello who impersonated the man of the house or his grandchildren. "That's not at all what we do," Rachel was told. I called the local paper in Charlottesville, *The Daily Progress*, and talked to an editor. She'd never heard of anybody freaking out tourists at Monticello or anywhere else in town with an Old Man Jefferson shtick. "Are you sure you don't mean the guy at Williamsburg who strolls around playing Jefferson?" she asked.

Rachel talked to someone in the development office at the University of Virginia, where they still call the founder "Mr. Jefferson," as if he might pop in at any moment to see how things are going. Rachel told me the woman had laughed and said, "Try Colonial Williamsburg."

I talked to a Charlottesville police detective, who said he enjoyed my story but had never heard anything like it.

On a Saturday afternoon, Rachel drove out to my house in New Jersey and we sat on the couch, each at our own laptop, Googling over a pizza to see if anybody out there had ever claimed to see Jefferson's ghost. There were a bunch of political blogs — on both the left and right — all screaming that Jefferson was turning over in his grave about what a mess the other side had made of the country. Otherwise, the only ghost stories Google yielded had to do with a haunted town in Texas called Jefferson. None of its ghosts bore any resemblance to my new acquaintance.

Rachel had a few more chores to finish in the city for Kant before we could head south. As she gathered her things and got ready to head back to Morningside Heights, she asked if she could see Ben's room. The question shook me. I hadn't been in his room since I'd filled it with his things from Cambridge. Rachel had helped me, taking his clothes to Goodwill and some boxes of things I hadn't had the heart to look through.

Now she paused at the doorway, gathering her strength, and went straight for the large bottom drawer of Ben's desk. She opened it, slipped her hand in and pulled out a leather notebook of some kind.

"What's that?" I said.

"It's just Ben's journal," she said a little nervously. "May I have it? He used to let me read it. I feel as if he wrote it for me. I know it's obnoxious, asking you like this."

My instinct was to tell her no, it was mine. "Ben kept a journal? I thought he outgrew introspection when he gave up history for business."

She didn't answer. She stood looking at me expectantly, holding the book against her chest.

"Of course," I said. "You should have it. I'd like you to have it. Please take it. I couldn't bear to read it anyway. Why didn't you take it when we cleaned out the apartment?"

"I wasn't sure. It just didn't seem right then. Oh, Jack. I'm sorry. Thank you, thank you so much," she said, a copper color rising on her cheeks. "It means a lot to me. I've been meaning to ask you for it."

She seemed terribly uncomfortable, I realize now, but I didn't think about it at the time. I was too uncomfortable myself. It's funny. I barely gave the journal another thought after she left that day. It felt right that she should have it. Ben's secret thoughts were the last things I wanted to know.

As the days passed, I thought more about her than I did about Thomas Jefferson and the man who'd played the trick on me. This would be my first trip with a woman in the two years since Pam had died and the woman I'd be traveling with was my late son's girlfriend. My golf buddies never would have let that go if they had known.

Jefferson had a stranger relationship. Sally Hemings, his slave and mistress, was the daughter of Jefferson's own father-in-law, John Wayles. That made Sally the half-sister of Jefferson's dead wife, Martha. She would have been Jefferson's own sister-in-law, if the law had recognized slaves as human beings.

These are the oddities an old public school teacher thinks about to distract himself when he's about to get into something way over his head.

Chapter 3

It was a pretty, bright August day when we headed south from New York in my old black BMW 325, which Pam and I had bought new in 1986, when she had started to make some money. I like to keep old things going. It gives me hope for myself.

U.S. 29 from Washington to Charlottesville runs southwest, parallel to the Blue Ridge, through countryside that has been chewed up by sprawl. Rachel and I talked easily as I drove. We enjoyed watching the roadsides for evidence of days gone by. Here and there, we could see how it used to be, before a century of cheap oil and the automobile obliterated the landscape.

We could still pick out 18th- and 19th-century frame buildings every few miles, side by side with an ancient tree or two, houses and inns and general stores that once had stood alone at a crossroad but now lived on as shabby junkyard offices or UPS stores or real estate offices, wedged into a blur of auto dealers, garages, fast-food joints and the usual mix of flat, square, cheap, ugly highway business buildings.

"Look at that old place," we said to each other a dozen times.

Somewhere 20 or so miles north of Charlottesville, we passed one old ramshackle two-story frame building with whitewashed clapboard siding, its gable end to the road, its sagging front porch mostly hidden behind trees and bushes. Its paint was peeling but we could still make out the words "FOR COLOREDS" in big, faded black letters below the gable peak.

"My God," Rachel said, holding her fingers over her mouth.

"Shades of Jim Crow," I said. "The memory lingers on."

"I don't think I've ever had it brought home to me like that," she said, twisting her head to watch the place shrink away out the back window. "That was incredible. God."

"But Rachel. Surely you know institutionalized racism — segregation, I mean — became illegal only a few decades ago. No one knew they were racists back then. My family had a black maid we called Bobo, for God's sake."

"Yes, I know," she said, "but I've never seen it with my very own eyes like that. Did you say *Bobo*? Really? That's awful, Jack. Good God. Look, I'm aware of the realities of the situation, then and now. But that overt stuff, that legalized, institutional stuff — it's all in stories and books and movies and documentaries and anecdotes from old guys. Like you."

"You've only read about racists in the woodpile," I said, pretending to deflect the jab.

She twisted her mouth and stared at me as if I were an idiot, then looked away. "Yes, racists in the woodpile."

"You've never experienced bigotry yourself? I guess that's a good thing. But it's a little hard to believe it's not still alive and well and even thriving."

"I have friends who say they've experienced it. But I can't say I've ever felt that anyone hated me just because I was black. And I bet my father hasn't either. He's never talked about anything like that."

He was a real black person, the kind I used to see the Birmingham police setting the dogs on when I was a kid sitting in front of the TV. She wasn't black, really.

I knew not to express such a racist thought out loud. "That's interesting," I said. "How times have changed."

Finally I had found something about which Rachel was clueless. It seemed to me she'd been sheltered, growing up in and around New York — and not one of its white-collar suburbs. She was from Yonkers, where there's nothing odd, much less terrifying, about seeing a lot of black people walking around.

We stopped for barbecue at an old-fashioned roadside stand and ate at a wooden picnic table, talking about Jefferson and which of his slaves he had let go free. Not many — only Sally Hemings's children and one young boy who'd run off after the overseer whipped him. Jefferson had not attempted to reclaim his property.

By the time we got settled in our separate rooms at the Cavalier Inn just down the hill from the main campus of UVA, we had an hour to kill before the evening tour at Monticello. So we went for a walk to see Mr. Jefferson's "academical village" and its "lawn," as he called the central quad.

All the student rooms on the lawn, originals from Jefferson's time, were empty but the doors to several had been left ajar. I thought that was odd until we peered into one. It was barren, the battered desk bare and the fireplace cold and dark, a thin mattress rolled up at the foot of a single metal bed frame.

"It looks like something for a monk," I said. "This is what the top students compete for? To be isolated in a row of shabby old brick cells?"

"It's an honor. They even get their firewood delivered," Rachel said.

She studied the place intently. "I got a scholarship here, you know," she said. "I might have made it into one of these rooms. But the whole Virginia thing — I just didn't want to deal with it. I have relatives around here somewhere. My father knows them but I don't."

"Yeah? Anybody named Hemings, maybe?"

"Well, it so happens I might be related to them, Daddy says."

"What? No! You're kidding me!"

"Nope. I'm not kidding you." She looked at me strangely. "Hey Jack. You look upset. What's the matter?"

"Ben never told me this! I mean before he stopped talking to me," I babbled, "when he used to tell me about you. He never mentioned it!"

She reared back a little. "Why would Ben tell you such a thing? It's no big deal."

"This is big! It *is* a big deal! If you're connected to any of Sally Hemings's children, you could be related to Jefferson himself! I mean, how did I not know this? Why didn't Ben tell me?"

She watched me with a mix of amazement and concern. "Oh Jack," she said, "thousands of people are related to Thomas Jefferson. My father hardly talked about it, except to rant about bad family blood."

I didn't know why I was becoming so undone. I had forgotten how much Pam and Ben had enjoyed the place with me and how much he and I had talked about Jefferson when he was growing up. The loss of one's family requires a certain kind of denial if one is to survive intact. As part of my survival process, I had blotted out all those memories.

"Are you all right?" Rachel asked, touching my arm. "I don't think Ben kept it from you on purpose, Jack. I certainly didn't mean to. Why do you care so much about who is related to Thomas Jefferson? I mean, Jack, if I am related, it's a very distant thing."

"I don't care," I said. "Forget it. I don't know what hit me so wrong."

I thought of grasping her shoulders and telling her what Jefferson's slave Isaac had told an interviewer in the 1850s, long after Monticello had changed hands: that Sally Hemings was quite a looker, with long straight hair down her back, and almost white — just like Rachel. I didn't do it. I worked instead to pull myself out of whatever weird funk had sent me into my spiral.

On the short ride up the hill that evening in the shuttle, I told Rachel the usual things about why I found Jefferson so fascinating: high ideals, brilliant promise, great achievement muddied by flaw, failure and an ability to rationalize his way into believing whatever served his ends. He embodied all the contradictions of the USA in one man.

"There's something charming in it," I said.

"Charming!" Rachel scoffed. "It's charming to believe black women prefer orangutans to their own men?"

"Ah. His 'Notes on the State of Virginia.' Okay, there's a little problem there."

"I guess so," Rachel said. "He was a politician and a slave-holding planter who constantly deluded himself. That's why he ended up broke. That's why his daughter had to sell Monticello and go live in Boston with her son-in-law and daughter."

"I know, I know. Big, fat flaws in a life of grace, charm and beauty."

"Not to mention power and manipulation. You're such a romantic, Jack. I always wondered if Ben got it from you."

"Ben? A romantic? Mr. Harvard MBA?"

"Hey. It's time for you to admire your son, Jack." She said it carefully and watched my face, which must have gone blank. "Jack, don't you know Ben was like Jefferson?" She patted me on the arm. "A lot of contradictions there, Jack. A hard-nosed achiever fighting against his own innocence, sentimentality and romanticism."

I let a flash of anger pass. Melting, I let myself gaze at her face. "Wow," I said.

To think she knew such things about Ben. Maybe I did, too, but had forgotten much, like all those Virginia trips and chats about Jefferson.

Nearing the house, we got excited like little kids, peering out of the shuttle for glimpses of Jefferson's world. At first, we saw only woods. They thinned as we climbed and they vanished as we broke into the open atop the little mountain, pulling to a stop at the end of a tree-shrouded brick walkway. It led to the east portico, the steps of which we could just make out beyond the boughs.

Rachel and I stood smiling and looking all around in wonder. "It's so good to see it again," she said.

"It is. It's always so good to be back — but with a friend this time," I said. We grinned at each other.

During the tour, she disappeared into her own head, too busy taking in every detail of the house to pay much attention to the guide or ask questions. She probably didn't trust tour guides.

In Jefferson's dressing room, she did a strange but, to me, lovely thing. By the side of his bed, she kneeled down on one knee, bowed her head and gently pressed a palm onto the water stains Jefferson had left behind on the floor. The seven or eight people in our little group looked at her as if she were crazy.

I leaned down and whispered in her ear, "Okay, so who's the Jefferson freak now?"

Our guide stepped over. "You know what that stain is, I take it?" she asked Rachel.

"Yes, I do," Rachel said, looking over her shoulder at her with a weak smile. She shifted her eyes to me. "Ben showed me this."

And I had showed it to Ben, once upon a time.

Trying to be polite, I listened attentively as the guide theorized why the stained floor had never been refinished in all the years since Jefferson's time and Rachel lingered on her knee, looking down on the stain as she caressed it. She was in another world.

Her transfixion throughout the tour enchanted me. It made me forget about our mysterious impersonator. I was too busy thinking about Rachel and Ben to wonder if the man would show himself. I really didn't expect him to, anyway. But up in the dome room, where twilight glowed through eight circular windows that ringed the echoing, empty space, she sharply tugged my arm.

"Oh! Jack!" she hissed in my ear. "Look! Over there!"

She pointed to the farthest window on our right, its rippled glass offering a view over a Chinese balustrade and the roof to the wavelike rise of the Blue Ridge. Blocking most of the view was the man I'd seen on the lawn, peering in at us, curious and concerned. Abruptly, as if he'd heard something, he turned away and stepped out of sight.

"That was *him*!" I gasped. "Holy shit! It was him! He's out on the roof!"

Rachel's green eyes opened wide. "Oh my God I don't believe it! It's not Jefferson! It can't be Jefferson! But it looked *just like* him!" she squealed as softly as she could, hunching her shoulders.

"I wasn't dreaming!" I said into her ear, my heart pounding. "I really saw him! What the hell is he doing on the goddamn roof?"

"Oh Jack! We have to find him!" she said. "We have to talk to him! He's fantastic!"

The eight other people standing across the room's broad, green-painted wood floor glanced our way. The guide gave us a look, hesitated, and went on with her droning lecture. Rachel flattened a palm against my chest and lowered her head, looking at me from under her eyebrows. "But Jack," she said with a kind of wicked smile. "It's not Thomas Jefferson. Right? It can't be."

"Right. Of course not."

"Nobody else noticed him!"

"Doesn't look like they did."

"What'll we do?"

"Just wait. He knows we're here now. We'll find him."

We couldn't wait for the tour to end. When we finally got outside and the guide released us to wander the grounds, Rachel and I ran all around the house like a couple of nuts, peering up at the roof. There was no sign of him.

We huddled outside the west portico, our hands on our hips, scanning the grounds and roofline one more time. It was agreed I'd go to the south pavilion and take a post. She would explore. If anything happened, we'd call on our cell phones.

The trees were falling into shadow against the pale sky. Some of the high wispy clouds still caught the sunlight like tufts of cotton dipped in butter. Alone on the terrace, I felt lighter than I had in a long, long time. There was a feel to things that reminded me of childhood, when I used to play outside after dinner on a summer evening, ranging the neighborhood with my friends, tunneling under forsythia and rhododendron, crawling under porches and climbing fences. Nothing mattered except all the adventures that lay ahead of us in the twilight eternity before our mothers called us in from our haunts.

A couple browsed the gardens. Another walked the terrace and peeked into the pavilion. A teenager climbed the steps of the portico to take a picture of the west lawn. I saw no sign of our man.

My cell buzzed in my pocket. "I got nothing," Rachel said.

"Me neither."

"What do you want to do?"

"Keep waiting. Wait until everybody goes to meet the shuttle at the end of the east walkway."

Chapter 4

It was almost 8 o'clock and getting dark. The others had disappeared to the other side of the house. I began to worry we wouldn't see Mr. Jefferson after all. I began to fear there would be no more reasons for me and Rachel to be traveling together through Virginia.

I called Rachel. "Where are you?"

"I'm in the all-weather passageway under the corner of the north pavilion. It's kind of scary down here. There's hardly any light. Is it time to go?"

"They're going to start honking for us soon, I bet. It's almost 8 o'clock."

She didn't reply.

"Rachel? Hello?" I said. I looked at the phone, thinking it had dropped the call. "Rachel? You there?"

No answer. There was nothing until I heard her say, "Oh my God," very softly and muffled, her mouth away from the phone.

"Rachel? Hey, Rachel!"

No reply. Just another far-away but more emphatic, "Oh my God!"

I flew like a 20-year-old down from the terrace and across the lawn, up the steps to the north terrace and down the other side. I ran along the brick foundation to a 90-degree bend, around the backside of a built-in privy and into the mouth of the all-weather passageway. Designed by Jefferson to keep the house slaves out of sight as they worked, it ran all the way under the house and out the other side.

I ran in, passing the curved whitewashed wall of the ice-house on my right. The meager light faded as I slowed to a walk, panting hard.

When my eyes adjusted to the light, I could just make out, near the open doorway of the privy, a bench against the white-washed stone wall. I remembered it. I had a photo of Pam and Ben sitting on that bench. Now Rachel sat on it, looking fear-fully into the darkness to her right, her cell phone in the dirt at her feet.

I peered toward a dark corner of the foundation recess and could barely see a hazy cloud of something off-white, some-thing about the height of a tall man. His hair and his shirt and cuffs glowed in the gloom. My heart, still beating fast from my run, shifted gears and began to pound. He stepped forward, into the edge of the evening light.

"Aha. Mr. Arrowsmith," he said in his thin but clear voice. "Good evening, sir."

It was him all right. An aged man in period dress, too heavy for the weather, with unruly hair — red with traces of gray and white; pale, freckled skin tight to the bone; a firm straight mouth and square jaw; a strong all-business brow and a promi-nent nose with a tapered, upturned tip.

"Rachel!" I said. "Are you all right?" She sat frozen, as if he'd cast a spell on her. "Hey! Rachel!"

She closed her gaping mouth and pressed a hand flat against her chest. "He tried to put the moves on me!" she whispered in awe. "It was like the wind blowing inside my clothes!"

"I beg your pardon," Jefferson said, "but if 'put the moves on me' means what I suspect it means, I did no such thing. I would not dishonor you so, my dear young woman. You are quite mistaken."

Rachel shook her head meekly. "I don't think so," she said.

"If something has occurred which has frightened you, I beg to apologize. I assure you, miss. I pose no danger to you."

The white cloud lowered and the cuffs swung into an arc. He was bowing.

"Maybe you got carried away, the way you did with Mrs. Walker," I said.

"What? *What!* Mrs. Walker? You mean the gossipmongers and Hamilton's political henchmen haunt me still? Mr. Arrowsmith, I admitted long ago I once foolishly offered love to a handsome woman when I was a young man. I never committed such an error again."

"Handsome *married* woman," I said, surprised at my own tone. "The wife of your neighbor and *friend*." I didn't like him scaring Rachel — especially if he'd done it by making some kind of pass. I was scared, too, and the fear and anger shook my voice. I put my hand on Rachel's shoulder, to calm myself as much as her.

"Here, here, Mr. Arrowsmith. They hounded me over that awkward episode years after the fact, with affidavits and newspaper accounts intended solely to embarrass me. Perhaps it was a fair punishment for my having lost myself to the greatest of all human passions and urges. It is a powerful force of nature, is it not? My enemies dragged my youthful indiscretion into the papers when I was president. I admitted to it. So that is enough about Mrs. Walker please!"

He leaned toward me, expecting a promise to obey, I think.

I put my hand at my forehead, closed my eyes and shook my head. "Jesus. Wait a minute. What is happening?"

"I was re-elected handily to a second term despite it all, you know," Jefferson said, still leaning my way. "I think the people were pleased to know I was not made of ice after all."

The horn from the shuttle sounded: two sets of three long beeps. We gaped at the man. My eyes, adjusting to the darkness, were bringing more of him into view. He looked at us expectantly, with a pleasant smile.

"Rachel," I said, "let's get back into the light."

Slowly she gathered herself and got up from the bench to stand close beside me. I put my arm around her back.

"Your phone," I said, reaching down and handing it to her.

She took it without taking her eyes off Jefferson. "I believe it's really him," she said.

I squeezed her tightly around the waist. "Yes, yes," I said quietly. "I think so, too. It's Thomas Jefferson. It's him. He's here. We're down here under Monticello talking to the man himself."

"Wow," she whispered.

"Yeah. Wow."

"Yes, yes, my dear child," he said, "it's all very odd, isn't it? How I wish I could take it up at the Philosophical Society. Perhaps I can! Do you know, is it still there? Is the society in existence, still in Philadelphia?"

"Actually, I think it is," I said.

Jefferson clasped his hands together happily. "Oh, that is good news. We must go."

Rachel glanced at me. Our fear was fading.

"What do you mean, 'go'?" I asked.

"Pray tell me, Mr. Arrowsmith," he said, "these marvelous conveyances I've seen here on my hilltop, these painted coaches with the heavy material enclosing their spokeless wheels ... Do you travel in one yourself? They are magically self-propelled. Perhaps you can explain their operation to me."

We stared at him.

"Hmmm?" he said, leaning toward us. "What do you call those things?"

"Wait," I said. "Really. How do you do this? Who are you?"

He frowned and sighed. "Please. I must advise you to re-member our last meeting, Mr. Arrowsmith. My experience is that our connection will be broken, and I will lose my corporeal form, sir, if you insist on doubting me," he said. "It's not some-thing over which I have the least control. Neither is my pres-ence before you. I am but an autumn leaf riding on a current of air and as long as I remain suspended in the temporal plane this way I will make the most of it. Do you see the opportunity here? I wish to exercise my curiosity, in whatever time I have with you good people. So I ask you again: Do you possess one of these self-propelled conveyances? Is that how you traveled here to our little mountain?"

Rachel and I looked at each other, then back at him. "We do … Have a conveyance," I said. "It's in the parking lot down the hill. We rode a shuttle bus up to the east front."

"Ah. Shuttle bus. That's what you call the larger wagon-like machine that disgorges overfed people in strange and slovenly clothing at the path to my door? A shuttling omnibus? The women, my God, the women look like trollops from Gin Lane. The men, I swear, look like Italian clowns, creatures from the Commedia dell'Arte. What do you call the smaller wagons intended, I gather, for personal use?"

We couldn't respond for a moment. Our brains were scrambled. Rachel gathered her senses first. "Automobiles. Or cars. That's what we call them," she said. "Wait. Do you really think you can come for a ride?" she asked, a little meekly, turning to look at me with raised brows.

"Jesus," I whispered. "Would that be a good idea?"

He broke into a warm smile. "You are very kind, my dear. What is your name? Mr. Arrowsmith has not done me the honor."

"Oh!" I said. "Sorry. I was a little distracted."

"I'm Rachel Carter," she said.

"Carter! Indeed! My dear Miss Carter, you must be a brave woman to ask me the question and thus imply the invitation. Yes, yes, I would like to make the attempt." He looked at me sternly and gave his torso a slight pitch forward. "With your permission, of course, Mr. Arrowsmith."

"Can we do this?" she asked, nearly pleading.

I shook my head erratically — I didn't mean "no," I was just confused — and again failed to find words.

"It's him," Rachel said firmly. "It's Jefferson. And he's a ghost. He felt like the wind. I felt him. I felt him inside me, Jack."

"Huh?" I wasn't sure she really meant what I thought she meant.

Jefferson jerked up, as if he were shocked. "My!" he blurted. "Whatever do you mean?"

"What did he do to you?" I asked, a bit timidly.

"He tried to kiss me, that's all," she said, tilting her head at me and looking peeved. "He thought I was someone else. But it gave me a feeling." She looked from me to him and back to me. No one spoke. "Look," Rachel said. "Forget it, all right? It was like the wind. That's all."

"Well, it's true, sir," Jefferson said. "I was mistaken." I had the feeling he was trying to rescue her. "I thought for a moment I had been reunited with one from my own household," he went on, "but in strange dress. Very strange." He looked her up and down with unrestrained astonishment at her shorts and sleeveless blouse.

He forced his eyes from her to me. "I suspect such mistakes will come easy to me in these circumstances," he said.

My eyes lingered on Rachel. I sensed something changing in her expression, a new softness in her eyes.

"Was it Sally?" she asked him.

The question caught him short. "Sally? Sally who?"

"Hemings," Rachel said.

His whole head seemed to quiver. His mouth fell open. "What? You know of our Sally?"

"Of course," Rachel said. "Who doesn't?"

"Oh!" He looked frantic instead of surprised. "No, don't tell me! Does the public still know of Sally?"

"Oh yes. Everybody knows of Sally," she replied with a surprising little smirk.

He gazed at her, his mind churning. "So. You mean to say Sarah is still connected in the public's mind to me? In this year two thousand eleven?" he asked.

"She sure is," Rachel said, "probably even more than at any time since your death. There's been as much interest in you and Sally as there is in you and the writing of the Declaration of Independence."

"Oh," he said softly, his shoulders slumping. "Well … my God." He looked at the ground sadly. Then he jutted out his chin and looked up harshly at Rachel. "This is nothing less than tragic! And ridiculous!" His glare melted into a vacant stare. "Well," he muttered, lost in thought until his eyes drifted back to Rachel and his expression turned tender. "And you, Miss Carter, may I ask you what is the ancestry that produced the beauty I now behold? Are you from among the Carters of Virginia?"

She cocked her head at him sharply. "My ancestry? You mean do I have black blood?"

Jefferson instantly turned icy. They glared at each other.

The shuttle sounded three long blasts. It took a few seconds for me to open my mouth and break the spell they'd cast over me.

"Hey. You two. Look. We have to go," I said. "Rachel, you and I have to get on that shuttle. They know we're missing from the group."

"Miss Carter, I apologize for my clumsiness," Jefferson said stiffly, with a half bow. "Your racial heritage is not at all what I meant."

I had to give him credit. A full-blown racist all his life, like probably every white person in America in his time, he caught on fast. Their eyes remained locked until Jefferson turned to me with a commanding glare. "What say you, Mr. Arrowsmith? Might you and Miss Carter bring along a clumsy and disoriented soul such as I?"

Rachel and I exchanged glances.

"I don't think you should try to get on the shuttle," I finally replied. "You'll either disappear or they'll throw a net over you and call the police."

The horn sounded again. I asked if he knew the parking area down the hill, near the visitor center.

"You mean that great pile of rough lumber they put on my mountain, below our little graveyard? Yes, I am painfully aware of it."

"If you can," I said, "meet us at the parking lot to the right of the visitor center, just down the hill from it. Our car ... our motor vehicle, or carriage, or phaeton, or landau, our wagon or whatever you want to call it ... it's a small black vehicle with the letters BMW inside a small circular blue and white emblem on the back."

"What is the significance of BMW, sir?"

"Bayerische Motoren Werke. It's German."

He arched his eyebrows and frowned. "German! I never mastered German. A great mistake. But I know enough to understand it means 'Bavarian Motor Work.' Am I to take it this means your vehicle was manufactured in Bavaria?"

"Yes, yes."

"That is far away. How was it brought here? Don't Americans build these vehicles themselves?"

"It came on a ship. A very big ship. And uh ... well, they do. But look. We have to go."

"Why do you buy a manufacture that comes all the way from Bavaria when you can buy an American machine?"

"It's a better car, in my opinion. We really have to go."

He tucked his chin into his chest. "How regrettable. That is a problem for the nation." He put the back of his hand against his mouth and seemed to lose himself in thought.

I heard someone yelling for us by name. Rachel and I had to decide: take him with us? Or just go back to the Cavalier Inn and wonder about this apparition for the rest of our lives?

"Let's take him," I said to Rachel, thinking of Ben. I bet Ben would have taken him.

She didn't hesitate. "We have to," she said quietly, her eyes fixed on him. "We have no choice."

"Yes, yes, Mr. Jefferson. We should talk more," I said. "Can you meet us on the paved road, just below the visitor center?" I asked. "We'll wait for the others to drive away and then pick you up. You take the path from the cemetery down the hill and meet us. Will that work? Can you do that?"

"I have no idea. If I seem to vanish, as before, please do not ascribe it to any desire on my part to end our relationship." His expression turned dark. "You are the first people to whom I've managed to speak since my family was gathered at my bedside and, of that time, I have only the vaguest and most fragmentary recollections," he said, as miserable-looking as I've ever seen a man. "Cognac and laudanum, you see, until I told the doctor no more."

"No time to think of that now," I said. "Meet us down the hill."

We stood in silence until Rachel yanked me by the arm. "Okay. Let's go!" she said, pulling me into a run. I looked back over my shoulder and saw Jefferson watching us go.

The tour guide's scolding and the dirty looks from the others did nothing to break the spell as we rode down the hill. Our faces flushed, we whispered frantically at each other, on the verge of crazy laughter: Did you see what he was wearing? Did you see how thin he is? Did you hear that Virginia twang in his voice?

When we got to the visitor center and had walked far enough away from everybody else, we stopped, faced each other and broke into loony grins. We embraced and held each other tightly. I heard her sniffle into my shoulder and felt her quiver.

"Are you crying?" I asked.

"Just a little," she said.

Behind us, cars with headlights sweeping the woods turned from the lot and slipped down the hill. When their taillights had all disappeared, we walked silently, hand in hand, to our self-propelled conveyance.

Chapter 5

With Rachel in the back seat, I started the car and backed out of our space. Only a couple of cars remained in the lot — probably those of our guide and other staff. In the visitor center, lights went out room by room.

I drove up the hill to the end of the path from the cemetery. It emerged from a wooded slope onto a set of steps. "If he doesn't show up fast, they're going to ask us what we're doing here," I said, peering out the passenger-side window at the tunnel of darkness into which the path disappeared.

"Kill your lights!" Rachel said.

"Kill the lights?"

"Yes! Kill your lights!"

I hit the lights and the engine, too. In the sudden silence, we heard voices and a car door slam.

"My God," Rachel said softly.

"What?"

"Look," she said, nodding toward the woods. "Here he comes."

I leaned down so I could see farther up the hill. A pale, flat oval of white light the height of a man was moving through the woods at a slow, steady pace. Glowing through ghostly black branches and tree trunks, it cast tangled shadows that stretched and shifted as it floated along.

"Have you ever seen a ghost?" I whispered to Rachel.

"Not until today," she said.

I heard bluestone crunching under slow-rolling tires. I

looked over Rachel's shoulder out the back window and saw the taillights of two cars heading downhill. A third car, the last to come out of the lot, missed the turn to head down the mountain and now its headlights swept uphill.

"Whoa," I said. "What the hell are they doing?"

We held our breath, watching the car approach, stop and roll forward again. Maybe it was some staffer who was going to pull up and tell us we were in the wrong place to be exiting the mountain. We didn't move. The car rolled slowly by and continued uphill to the U-shaped driveway in front of the visitor center, which it entered and followed around to the lower exit, where it turned downhill and rolled away from us, picking up speed.

When its taillights had disappeared, we were alone with our ghost, which had paused at the edge of the woods but now floated down the steps and drifted the last few feet into a hover beside the car. Hanging there, it shifted ever so slightly up and down and side to side, like a tethered balloon nudged by eddies of air. Soon, the image of a man began to come into view inside the oval of light — our man, but motionless and flat, like a faded photo.

My right thigh bounced. The tightened muscles in my chest quivered. My heart pounded but we weren't going to run. We knew this ghost.

I gathered my nerve and lowered the passenger window. "Hello?" I squeaked. No response.

"Maybe you should open the door," Rachel said with a shaky voice, her head shivering between her shoulders. I thought she might start crying again.

The thought went through my head that my wife and son were dead so I had no more to lose and nothing to fear from anything. I leaned over to the latch and pushed open door. It swung through the apparition as if it weren't there.

"Yow," I whispered harshly. "Did you see that?"

Rachel, stiff-necked, nodded rapidly.

"He doesn't look well," I said. "I think he's still thinking about your shorts. I think they upset him."

She instantly unfroze and socked me in the shoulder.
"Ow! Hey!"

In the ghost's pale light, her eyes sparkled and her faced glowed. Her breathing and mine slowed and my thigh stopped its crazy bounce.

"Look!" she said.

The black eyes in the flat gray face moved. Its grim mouth shifted into a weak smile. The vaporous glow began to contract and fade. The image took on color and depth until the man in his heavy old clothes stood in the dark before us, lit only by the weak glow from the few security lights down the hill in the parking lot.

"Ahhhh," he said. "It has happened! I am back among the living! I had no idea I was capable of conducting this process of my own volition! It's your presence! You people affect me!"

I waved my hand at him, grimacing. "Okay, come on!" I said. "Let's get going!"

"How odd," he said, leaning down to peer at me through the open door. "One stoops down into this conveyance instead of climbing up. And these wheels ..." He leaned to his right to look at the tire. "These wheels have a very small circumference. What is the black material?"

"Rubber," I said. "We call them tires."

"Ah! Rubber! I know of it. Good for removing pencil lead from paper. I use rubber in keeping my account books tidy."

"The tires are filled with pressurized air," I said, reverting into teacher mode even though I wanted him to hurry it up.

"My," he gasped. "Pneumatic tires. How interesting indeed."

"We have to go," Rachel said. "They're going to lock the gate on us."

"It's true. We have to go," I said.

"My apologies for putting you to this trouble," he said, grunting lightly as he lifted his left foot in its heelless black slip-on into the car and gripped the top of the door to swing himself into the seat. "Is this how it's done?" he asked. "It is not easy for me. My rheumatism. I so much would have preferred returning to the earthly plane as a young man, for heaven's sake."

I reached across him and pulled the door closed, started the car and put it in drive. I was only pretending he didn't scare me but pretending seemed to work; my fear was fading. We rolled forward and started downhill. I drove slowly to follow the tight curves of the road.

At first he seemed to have trouble deciding what to observe: the interior of the car, my handling of the steering wheel or the road ahead. After he had settled on the view out the windshield and watched the road for a half-minute, he looked at me and waggled his finger. "Why, this is a magic carpet!" he gasped. "I'd believe myself to be living one of the Arabian nights if I didn't recognize my own road and its every curve!"

The gate was still up at the entry point. A uniformed guard stood there, his hands on his hips. He motioned impatiently for me to open my window. "Where you been?" he asked. "We count the cars. What you been doing up there?" He forced a smile to take the edge off the question.

"Oh, we just didn't want to leave," I said. "We wanted the vibe of being up there alone. Sorry."

His eyes fell on the man beside me. He realized something very strange was going on. "Oh!" he exclaimed.

"Ah!" I said.

The man couldn't speak. I tried to help. "He looks just like Jefferson, right?" I said.

"Lord God," the guard sang, "that is old Mr. Jefferson himself, I swear!"

"Have you ever seen him before up at the house?"

He looked at me as if I were nuts. "I never seen him before in my life except in pictures!"

"We've got to go. Sorry we kept you waiting. Goodnight now," I said and drove off before he could ask any more questions. In the rearview mirror, I saw him pull off his cap and stand in the light from his booth, gazing after us.

Jefferson gripped the rim of the dashboard as we accelerated.

"Such speed!" he whispered out loud. "By God, I might as well have been sent to the moon." He looked at the instrument cluster and shook his finger at it. "But this, this indicator," he said, trying to focus, "it is an odometer, correct?" He pointed at the little window under the speedometer displaying the mileage.

"Yes, it is. You are familiar with odometers?" I said.

"I had one fixed on the landau. It divided the miles into dimes and cents. Does yours chime out the miles as well?" he asked.

"Chime? No," I said. "No chimes. But the little computer here chimes when the outside temperature falls below 37 degrees to warn you there may be ice on the road."

"Is that so! Ingenious!"

He leaned my way and peered at the speedometer. "That pointer … it appears to show we are traveling at 40 miles per hour!" he said.

"It does indeed, yes."

He snapped his head to the right to look out the passenger window. "We are flying!"

"It's nothing. This old rig can do 100 easy."

"No!"

"Um, hey," Rachel said, gripping the back of his seat to pull herself forward. "Did you actually say 'dimes and cents'?"

He looked ahead at the roadway in its tunnel of light. "The wonder of it! What a great boon for civilization!" he said. He tightly held the parking brake handle with his left hand and the door's armrest with his right.

"Don't pull on that," I told him about the parking brake.

"Mr. Jefferson?" Rachel said. "Dimes and cents?"

"Yes, yes! Dimes and cents!" he barked, his head pushed back against his seat. He sounded a little frantic. "Tenths and hundredths, tenths and hundredths, my dear young lady," he said, trying to calm himself. "And it would chime them out. It shortened the long ride to Poplar Forest by dividing it into manageable increments, you see."

He looked around. He tentatively ran his long fingers along the plastic liner of the passenger door. He rolled his hand into a fist and rapped his knuckles against the window glass. He leaned forward to study the lighted dial and colored LEDs of my old FM radio and CD player. He poked it with his index finger.

"What is this strange illuminated instrument?'

"It can play music," I said. I was going to put something on for him but a warning bell went off.

"I thought you said it didn't chime," he said.

"Seat belt," I said. In my old car, the warning sometimes went off when the belt of an occupied front seat was not latched and sometimes it didn't.

"Pardon me?" He turned and looked at me with deep concern.

"Seat belt. That strap over your right shoulder. I forgot to tell you. You have to put it on to make that gong stop. It's designed to protect you in a crash."

He seemed stupefied. "Seat belt," he whispered, his face blank.

Rachel stirred. "Here," she said, leaning over the seatback to grab the belt and extend it. He turned to look at her over his left shoulder. "No, other side," she said. "It's to your right."

He looked the other way and I glanced at the jumble of hair on the back of his head hanging over the collar of his coat. He was real.

"You take this strap," Rachel told him gently, reaching across him, her lips close to his ear, "and you pull it across your chest."

He seemed flustered. He reached for the belt with his right hand, the wrong one for pulling it across his chest, and feebly tugged at it.

"Wait, wait," Rachel said, leaning further in front of him to reach for the seat belt and pull its clasp to the latch. Her face was very close to his. "There," she said as she clicked the latch into place.

Jefferson pressed his head against the headrest and clenched his eyes shut. "Oh, such an agitation of the nervous fibers!" he whispered in some kind of pain. "It is so terribly unhealthy without release!"

"What?" I asked. Was he really talking about sex? Was he really as horny as a goat?

Rachel, poised beside him, seemed oddly oblivious. She held still, very close to him, and studied his face with angelic tranquility. "You're so real," she whispered.

"Please, young woman, I ask you. Please withdraw." She did not move at first. She looked at him with growing concern. "Oh," she exclaimed, her brows furrowed. "Oh," she repeated quietly, her face softening. She folded herself back through the gap between the seats and plopped backward. In the rearview mirror, I saw her staring straight ahead, wide-eyed.

"My apologies, my apologies, my dear child," Jefferson said with exasperation, his eyes still shut. He opened them and drew a shaky hand across his tired face. "I am not at all myself. I have much thinking to do."

Rachel and I eyed each other in the mirror. "Are you all right, Mr. Jefferson?" I asked after a long silence.

He did not move at first. Finally he rolled his head and looked at me. "I was not one to believe in the existence of an actual hell but everything has changed and now I fear that may be where you are taking me in your fantastic illuminated carriage. Perhaps this was not such a good idea."

"No, no, we're headed to Charlottesville," I said. "And this thing is called a car. Or automobile. As we told you."

He was silent for a time. "What," he finally asked, "is the source of its vitality?"

I tried to explain.

"Petroleum," he repeated dully. "From the earth."

"Yes. Whale oil went out a generation after you were gone."

He stared out the windshield for a while. He was thinking. He brought his hand to his chin and asked, "This petroleum, being so efficient ... is it used to illuminate your lamps?"

"It's refined petroleum. We call it gasoline. And no, no. It is far too volatile for that."

"So what produces the light that emanates from the front

of the carriage and shows our path ahead? What produces its concentrated brilliance?"

"Electricity," I said, launching into a short treatise on the battery, the alternator and the sealed headlight.

"Ah," he said, tugging at his chin. "A headlight. The brilliance of lightning contained in glass. We could have used this invention for our carriages and, I should say, our lighthouses. It turns night to day ahead of us. It is fantastical. Dr. Franklin would be thunderstruck, as am I."

"Are you, uh, still in touch with Dr. Franklin somehow?" I asked, glad he'd recovered from his episode. "I mean is he going to pop out of the woods and need a ride?"

I was half hoping he'd say yes but Jefferson shook his head. "That would please me very much," he said. "Dr. Franklin would be good company right now." He paused to think. "Actually he might pretend it's all nothing to him. I think I'd prefer Rush, or Priestly."

I saw the trace of a smile on his lips but it quickly faded. "But alas, I've had no contact through my twilight with anyone I knew in life, Mr. Arrowsmith," he said, half-turning his head toward me with a slight tilt. "I've heard voices. They seemed to come from two of my grandchildren looking for me, as I have mentioned. A terrible thing to hear."

"Which two grandchildren?" Rachel asked.

He looked over his shoulder toward her. "Geordie and Cornelia," he said. "Why ever do you ask?"

Rachel thought for a moment. "Geordie and Cornelia," she repeated. "Those were their names! The people Ben and I met at the cemetery! I thought they were eccentrics."

He reared back and stiffly turned his head further toward Rachel. "Oh dear!" he said. "In corporeal form, you mean? Like myself now?"

"Yes, yes! It seemed so!" she said. "And Jack met them there, too, we think, but 20 years before Ben and I did. How amazing!"

"Oh dear," Jefferson said, rolling his head away, pained. "I hope they are safe. I hope they are happy. However do I find them?"

He seemed lost in thought, his face twisting with grief. I felt very bad for him. "Oh Mr. Jefferson. Do you want to go back?" I asked. "Perhaps tomorrow we can look for them."

He looked ahead. "Yes, yes. I must. I must look for them," he said, "but not just yet, not just yet," he added after a pause. He took a deep breath. "Time wastes too fast, I fear. Who knows how much of it we have together, you two and I? I wish to continue our adventure. Perhaps I can document it for the Philosophical Society. I'll need paper and ink. Perhaps you can help me with that. But it pains me to think my family is nearby. It pains me deeply. I am in severe conflict."

"They seemed very content," Rachel offered.

"Yes, yes, it's true. They did," I said. "They seemed perfectly fine."

"Ah! That pleases me greatly to hear. Thank you, thank you."

I stared at the road and flexed my fingers on the steering wheel. Maybe we were saving him from becoming the kind of ghost that haunts places, a lost soul forever searching. For someone so torn about his loved ones, I thought, he'd moved on quite easily.

"So, Mr. Jefferson," I asked, "tell me, how in the world did you know my son was courting a beauty?"

"Ah! Yes, Mr. Arrowsmith. I am so sorry to have startled you with that. I seem to lack common sense in this odd state of mine. I saw them at Monticello. I saw this charming young woman with us, Miss Carter, and your son, whom I remembered having seen before somehow —— perhaps 'sensed' is the better word — with you yourself, Mr. Arrowsmith, and the lovely woman I take it was your wife. You were so fine with your son, telling him about my eight-day clock and my triple-sashed windows and my dumbwaiter and my polygraph. You both so carefully studied the water stains on the floor by my bed. I believe that's what woke me from oblivion. And in another dim moment of consciousness, I saw that same young man with Miss Carter, just the two of them. He was instructing her as you had instructed him! She was a sight to behold!"

He sighed deeply. "You, Mr. Arrowsmith, you and your family were the few people whose faces took on life for me through my disembodied trances. I do not know why. But I did dream of a son, long ago. I did dream of a son."

I wasn't sure what he meant. He unfolded his arms and looked at me carefully. "Oh, Mr. Arrowsmith," he said, shifting his hand to my knee and patting it in a fatherly way. "We share great loss. It is the nature of life to lose those you love. Loss is inevitable. Love is not. It is therefore precious. I lost too many of my family too soon to eternal separation. My wife, my infant son and daughters, my beautiful grown daughter Polly, that poor child, she resisted my many admonitions so. I loved them all."

For a few seconds more, he kept patting my knee, lightly and mechanically, using the tips of his fingers rather clinically, as if the gesture did not come naturally to him. I wiped my eyes and tried to get a grip. He leaned toward the windshield and stopped patting me. "Tell me, now. What is this pavement employed for the roadbed? Such speed would not be possible without this amazing ribbon of unobstructed and completely uniform pavement."

Rachel sat silent and still as he and I talked and we came off the mountain road onto the modern approach to the interstate, passing through an intersection under a bank of traffic lights. He dipped his head to study them as they passed overhead and then watched intently, calmer now, as we curved up the ramp and merged onto Interstate 64.

"Why, it's a mighty river," he said to himself. "How I could have used such a pathway in my day! My endless travels on muddy roads and across swollen rivers and streams were such a dreary and dangerous chore. But tell me, why the bizarre colored lights we passed back there?"

"It's a stop-and-go signal," I said. "To control the flow of traffic."

"Stop-and-go signal! To regulate the flow of vehicles! And it is electrical, I take it."

I smiled and leaned his way. "I can't tell you how fun this is going to be, showing around a Founding Father."

He did not respond. He was lost in the experience. After moments of silence except for the rush of wind and the rumble of tires, he looked at me, cocked his head and announced he was hungry. "It's the oddest thing," he said. "It's almost over-powering, I'm so famished."

"Really?" Rachel asked, gripping his seat to pull herself forward.

"It seems so! It's a marvel, isn't it? I feel it greatly. But oh!" he said, distracted. "Inns require ready money! I fear I lack ready money." He fidgeted with his pockets, grimacing. "My grandson Jeff would take care of these things for me." He stopped fidgeting and stared straight ahead. "I do wonder what became of my good Jeff. You didn't see him anywhere, did you?"

We both assured him we had not. I was not in the habit of touching men on the knee but he'd done it to me so I did it to him. "He lived to a ripe old age, defending your memory to the end," I said. "Served in the Confederate government." His ratty brown corduroy pants felt thick and heavy, the knee inside barely more than bone. I added a bit hoarsely, "Please don't worry about money."

"You are most kind. It troubles me …"

"You are our guest."

He bowed his head and closed his eyes. "Well, you are very kind. I thank you. I dislike this position of dependence."

I stopped patting but left my fingers on his knee. I felt sorry for him. I suspected he needed human contact as much as food and I was not surprised he did not like being the guest instead of the host.

I put both hands back on the wheel. We hit 70. He held onto the dashboard, as if he were on a roller coaster. "Great heavens," he said, his head stiff on his neck. "Does this speed have some effect on the digestion?"

We were coming up on an old, big, beat-up Pontiac sedan riding low and cockeyed in the right lane with a burned out taillight. We could hear a loud, rhythmic thumping, the bass of its CD player or radio. As we floated past, we could make out the heads of five young black men inside, wearing do-rags. They looked a little scary to me. Jefferson stiffened at the sight of them and turned to follow the tank of a car sliding past his window. Its occupants stared back blankly, without hostility, except for a man in the back, who calmly gave Jefferson the finger.

Jefferson reared his head. "Ah! The insolence!" he said. "Are those people field hands? That one who made the gesture should be whipped!"

"I don't think so," I said, glancing in the mirror at Rachel. I did not catch her eye. She was staring at Jefferson's head.

He asked who was responsible for overseeing those people and expressed surprise that they would have their own self-propelled carriages.

"They are free people," I said. "No one oversees them. One of them is president of the United States. Cars are fairly cheap, old cars anyway. Everyone has a car in America," I said, "even poor people, except in the big cities."

He looked at me hard. His mouth fell open. "What was that you said?"

"Uh … oh … You mean that a black man is president? Yes, yes, a black man is president. Must be one hell of a shock for you. I guess it still is for a lot of people."

"No, it cannot be. How can it be? How can a negro win election at all, much less handle the rigors and the demands of such a position? You are joking, of course, Mr. Arrowsmith."

"No, no. I wasn't joking at all." I had to peel my eyes off his stricken face to watch the road. I glanced in the mirror at Rachel. She looked pissed.

"Yes," Rachel said, leaning close behind his head. "A black man is president. He went to Columbia College and Harvard Law School. He's a brilliant man."

"Maybe too brilliant," I chimed in, "and too much of a philosopher, to be a really great president." I thought of adding, "Kind of like you," but held my tongue.

Rachel fumed silently, glaring when I glanced at her again. Jefferson looked out his window. "My God. What is this world into which I've been transported? Does he dress like those people?" He gestured rearward with his head. "My field people wore those wraps on their heads. Such lazy people. One had to brandish the whip to inspire some of them. I did not like brandishing the whip."

"He wears a suit to the office," I said.

"The office?" Jefferson asked.

"The Oval Office," I said. "The White House. The President's House."

"I don't know what you mean by Oval Office," Jefferson said. He seemed to be getting annoyed.

"You shouldn't say they were lazy," Rachel scolded the back of Jefferson's head. "Those fields belonged to you. They weren't paid to tend them. You gave them a few clothes and blankets and a little food just to keep them alive. Why should they work hard for you? Your overseer would whip them, even if you wouldn't. And you could sell them off like cattle and separate their families forever, anytime you wanted. The black race is still suffering from the scars of that treatment."

Jefferson sat up and looked straight ahead. "Never! I never did such a vile thing!" he said as if he were talking to a voice in his head. "I never, never broke up families!"

I wasn't so sure he remembered that entirely correctly. We rode in silence. Light from outside the car lit up Rachel's face. She was thinking, staring past us out the windshield.

"Your president. A black man. I just don't believe it. You tell me it's so but I cannot believe it," Jefferson said, breaking the spell.

"It's true," I said.

"Not for long, if the economy doesn't get any better," Rachel said.

"I must meet this person," Jefferson said, yielding to the unbelievable.

I told him there was no way he was going to meet the president.

"No?"

"No way in hell."

"Not in hell? Ah, well then," he said. "Why ever not?"

I tried to explain as we slowed for the exit ramp that presidential security was impenetrable. The days when common citizens could walk into the executive mansion for an open house had ended long, long ago.

Jefferson shook his head in silence and spread his hand over the bottom half of his face as he pondered the impossible. Rachel put her hand on his shoulder, as if she wanted to make up for snarling at the back of his head. "We'll talk about it. It's a lot to take in, isn't it? I'm sorry I got a little snappy back there. You said you were famished, right? You must be tired too."

He brightened, eager to change the subject, perhaps. "Oh, yes, yes, thank you, my dear. I am far hungrier than fatigued. I'd say I am not fatigued at all. And the hunger is a delightful sensation. I'm so sorry we could not dine at Monticello." He searched in his coat, as if he were looking for money again. "I would have been pleased to serve you there. A proper dinner at 4 o'clock."

"No, no, I'll be the host. This will be on me," I said. "Please allow me. You spent years feeding strangers at Monticello."

He sat back. "Yes, yes, that is exactly so! It distressed my poor daughter at times but I could not turn those people away."

Rachel checked her iPhone and found a restaurant called Fleurie. She called and made a reservation. The phone, of course, intrigued Jefferson. He gave us the etymology of "cell" and "phone," from Latin and Greek, and asked if he might inspect the device. She leaned forward to show him how it worked. I glanced at the two of them sideways. I swear he was smelling her neck and closing his eyes. She had no idea.

She declared he needed decent clothes and did another search to find a Target in a mall out on Route 29 north of town. When we parked in its vast floodlit parking lot and stood beside Jefferson as he grimly surveyed the alien landscape with a superior and disapproving air, it hit me: He was no longer a ghost, at least not in his own mind. He was a great and famous man, a retired president of the United States, a founder of the country. We minions were about to take him on a tour of something he never would have imagined, a big box store in his native territory, once the frontier of Anglo-American settlement at the foot of the mountains and now a world built for the automobile, a sprawling tangle of jammed highways and monotonous shopping malls.

"This is an incomprehensible sight. It is ghastly. You say we are near Charlottesville?" he said.

I assured him we were. "Are you ready?" I asked.

He took another look around, turned to me and nodded. Rachel and I guided him to the automatic glass doors. He watched with a haughty, even angry look as they opened by themselves. "Clever," he muttered. "A bit like the entry to my parlor. But these are self-activating. Electrical?"

"Electrical," I said.

"What triggers them to open?"

"I don't know. An electric eye, we used to say, but I don't know what that is, really. Do you, Rachel?"

"Infrared or motion sensors, probably," Rachel said.

Jefferson glanced at her with surprise. We entered and, after passing through the second set of doors, he halted just inside the store. His mouth agape and his eyes wide, he stared at the rows of towering shelves full of merchandise receding into the distance, the weird scene awash in a white light as bright and flat as the noonday sunlight on a beach. Speechless, he panned slowly from the shelves to the bank of checkout machines on the left to the electronics section on the right with its big TVs silently playing a scene from "Ice Age 3: Dawn of the Dinosaurs."

He cocked his head and frowned. "Vivaldi," he said. "'Summer.' There is an orchestra somewhere in this freakish place." He peered into the distance, looking for the musicians. I told him it was a recording, a performance captured in time and preserved so it could be played over and over for years to come.

"Oh my word!" he grumbled. "You must tell me how. But for now, let us proceed."

He strolled along with us at his sides, his hands clasped behind his back, stopping to ask questions, sometimes looking from the goods to the people who passed by. Many returned a curious stare. The clothes and his imperial air drew their attention, I think. There was no shock of recognition in their eyes, no amazement. He was merely an oddity, as they were to him.

The first product he stopped to ponder for more than a moment was a toilet, part of a display intended to show off an étagère. He knew what it was and he spoke of the privies at Monticello and the indoor plumbing and water boxes he had seen connected to commodes in France. "I never installed them at Monticello," he said. "They wasted water and we had no water to waste on our hilltop."

In the toy section, he spotted a SpongeBob cuddle doll and a Yoda pillow. "These monsters," he said, handling the Sponge-Bob, "what are they for? Not playthings, are they? They look like African idols. They would have frightened my daughter Polly. Her sister Patsy would have seen to it that they were burned in the forge at the nailery."

At the back wall filled with Schwinn bicycles, all leaning at the same angle side by side on two elevated shelves, he squeezed a tire. "You mean to say a man can ride along upright under his own power on those two wheels?" He shook his head. "The simplicity of the machine embarrasses me. I should have thought of it." I rolled my eyes at Rachel.

A hefty woman in too-tight jeans and a fat young boy stopped in front of us, the kid in baggy below-the-knee shorts, sideways baseball cap and a gigantic University of Virginia T-shirt.

"Whoa!" he said, looking at Jefferson. "What *you* got on?"

The woman apologized and yanked the boy away down the aisle. "Don't you be bothering people," she scolded him.

The father of the University of Virginia watched them go, tall and straight and brittle. "I'm extremely pleased to see the university survives but that outfit … It is hideous. And please don't tell me that negro boy is a student there."

Rachel shook her head with annoyance. She said he was too young to go to UVA but if he had good enough grades he could be a student there one day. Jefferson flicked his eyebrows, shook his head with irritation, clasped his hands together behind his back again and went on with his tour, wandering slowly among the power tools and cleaning supplies, the auto accessories, the kitchen gadgets and the computers and printers. I gave him quick explanations. "Merveilleux, merveilleux," he said, shaking his head. "There's a kind of madness to this dream. I am overwhelmed." He asked if these manufactures had been made in the United States.

When I said most came from China, he said, "Oh my. China! I see," and flicked his eyebrows.

Rachel herded us to men's clothes and picked out khakis, a blue button-down shirt and a lightweight gray cotton sports jacket. She held up a pack of underwear. "Do you think he's going to be a boxer man or a BVD type?" she asked me.

"Not those," Jefferson said, pointing at the three-pack of briefs in her hand. "If that illustration is an accurate depiction of what they look like unfolded, no, no, no. It's a wonder the population is able to reproduce if that's what your men wear."

She held up a pack of boxers with blue and yellow dots.

"Aren't they made in white?" Jefferson asked.

There didn't seem to be any plain white boxers. He had to settle for blue and yellow dots, which he proclaimed "an affront to decency if not civilization itself." I think he was being funny. There was the hint of a smile on his lips.

At the checkout, he wanted to know about the "foreign" woman — she was Pakistani, I guessed — and the scanner and credit card reader at her station. I explained as best I could.

"Baffling. You mean to say there's no hard money for everyday transactions? It is all calculated telephonically on credit?" he asked. He shook his head slowly. "So the bankers control everything," he muttered. "That cannot be good for Republicanism. I fear for your country."

Outside, as we walked to the car, Rachel and I, like hyperactive aides, lectured him on the banking system, the Federal Reserve and the national debt, the real estate bubble and the personal debt crisis that had thrown the country into recession. His whole face twitched and his head shook in confusion. He stopped, eyed us with steely disapproval and turned to look back at the store.

"I should not be so surprised at all of this," he said to himself. "I should not let it trouble me. It's not my concern anymore."

Rachel stepped closer and put her hand on his shoulder. "This all must be very hard to take in," she said.

He studied her face. They looked into each other's eyes for what seemed a long time.

"I forget myself," he said quietly. "I forget my circumstances."

"Hey," I said. "Remember the hunger thing? Food? Let's think about that. We'll be too late for dinner if we don't hurry it up."

He peered at me, confused, then smiled quite warmly. "Yes, yes, Mr. Arrowsmith! We'll be true Parisians, dining so late!" He clasped his hands and rubbed them. "I must not spoil this good company. Let's see what your generation has done to French cuisine!"

Chapter 6

We got ready for dinner as fast as we could in our rooms at the Cavalier Inn, Rachel alone in hers and Jefferson with me. He carefully inspected the room and its fixtures, asking questions. When I turned on the TV, he plopped at the foot of the bed in wonder and gazed at CNN, one gangly leg crossed almost effeminately over his knee.

"This light box is fantastical! What a world! You people have invented everything we ever dreamed of, even in or wildest imaginings," he said. "I pray I have the time to comprehend it all."

I told him about pixels and phosphorous dots that glowed in different colors when stimulated by an electrical charge — I was mixing up my TV technologies from the pre-digital era, I admitted, and told him I really had no idea how the thing worked.

"We must disassemble one and determine its workings ourselves," he said absently as he watched the Aflac duck enduring its torments. "What the devil ..." he muttered, barely moving his mouth. He asked for an explanation. I did my best and he took it in silently with a puzzled, impatient look.

"It's getting late," I said. "They won't serve us if we get there after 10, Mr. President."

But just then a piece came on about a news conference at the White House, and there was the familiar image and voice of President Obama at the lectern. Jefferson bolted over his knees and pointed at the screen with a waggling hand. "Why, that's him, then! The negro!"

"Yes, that's him. The negro. Pardon me, Mr. Jefferson, sorry to be blunt, you wouldn't know this, but really, I have to tell you that you can't talk like that these days."

"Talk like what?"

"Making an issue of somebody's race like that. I thought you were catching on."

His face took on a strange look, a twisted mix of disgust, anger and frustration, but he didn't say a word. "Whatever you advise, Mr. Arrowsmith," he said ominously and looked back at the TV. After a moment, he commented, "The man speaks well. I see he has white blood."

I wanted to tell him, but did not, about another president, Ronald Reagan, and the famous line from his TV debate with Walter Mondale in 1984: "There you go again."

I helped him take off his clothes and work the shower, which might have embarrassed me if he hadn't been so completely at ease with it himself. Servants had attended him since childhood and he was just an old man, after all, which I had trouble remembering. He was, I must say, a very well-endowed old man. No wonder he'd gotten himself into fixes all his life.

With his wild hair draped over his collar, he looked like an eccentric UVA professor in his khakis, shirt and sports jacket. With only minutes to go before Fleurie would stop serving dinner, we went out to collect Rachel. At her door, he shot his cuffs, scrunched his shoulders, and looked down at himself. "So peculiar," he said. Turning to the right, he clasped his hands behind his back and studied the décor and the view out the glass wall of the hallway: a lit-up gas station and quick mart across the street three stories below and headlights sweeping through the busy intersection.

"Your electricity has turned night into day. Where are we exactly?" he asked.

"That's Emmet Street right out there," I said, pointing.

"Ah! Emmet Street! Something I can understand, finally. Named for our first professor of natural philosophy! My guess is this was the Warrenton Road in my day."

Rachel's door clicked open and we turned around. For a moment, we couldn't speak or move; we could only stare at her like a couple of old fools. She didn't seem to mind, beaming back at us in a summery floral dress with bare shoulders and a tight waist above the skirt.

"Oh my," Jefferson said.

"Good evening, gentlemen," she said, reaching for Jefferson's arm with one hand and extending the other to me.

"What a breathtaking vision you are," Jefferson said, taking her hand and lifting it to his lips. She smiled shyly and blushed.

We careened in the BMW to the pedestrian mall in the heart of town, Jefferson laughably chatty. He kept turning his head Rachel's way and managed to turn far enough around to look at her in the back seat several times despite obvious jolts of rheumatic pain. He told us — her, really — about the rustic Charlottesville he once knew and the land on which the university was built, land that his friend, Mr. Monroe, had owned at one time.

He fell silent and stared up the hillside on our right as we passed a beautiful Greek revival building of red brick with towering white columns, illuminated dramatically in floodlights — the Rotunda, the centerpiece of the university.

"How is it to see your building again?" Rachel asked. "That's a statue of you in front on the terrace."

"Indeed," he said, without answering her question. He seemed lost in his thoughts.

He recovered after we parked and found Fleurie on a side street just off the mall. It was a cozy little place, a candle and slim vase with a single flower on each table. Only two were occupied. The room had exposed brick walls, dim lighting, a dark wooden bar. Diners could see into the kitchen through a portal in the back.

After we were seated at a round table for four, Jefferson between Rachel and me, he identified the flower in our vase as alstroemeria, native to Peru and first introduced to the world by a Baron von Alstroemer, a friend of Linnaeus. "It can be found in a few English greenhouses and, it appears, here in Virginia in your day," he said, then leaned to my ear and touched my arm. "Somehow I am going to repay you for this meal and everything else," he said softly.

"Please don't even think about it."

"I insist. I'll devise a way. I assure you, sir."

"All right, then. Thank you," I said, just to humor him.

He sat up straight. "I would be delighted if you both would consider me your host tonight," he announced. "Credit me for the expense. I pay my debts, Mr. Arrowsmith."

"Certainly, certainly."

"So, my dear child," he said, "Mr. Arrowsmith says you attend what we once called King's College. Tell me, what do the academics of New York in this day and age consider the great moments of American history?"

"Well, there's a big subject," Rachel said, unfazed. "The Revolution, of course. The adoption of the Constitution. The emergence of parties. The Louisiana Purchase. The War of 1812. The Era of Good Feeling, the Jackson presidency."

"I had a fine bust of the general," Jefferson said. "I am not surprised to learn he became president. Like me, he lost first to an Adams before his turn to be tortured came."

"Oh my God," Rachel said. "So you knew him."

"Oh yes, yes. I met him. He and his entourage stopped by Poplar Forest, my little retirement house near Lynchburg, you know, to pay their respects on their way up from New Orleans. There was to be a celebratory dinner for him in town. He showed up unannounced and insisted I join him to share the honors. A rough, tempestuous character. So terribly opinionated. Now tell me, what is this 'Era of Good Feeling'? What a quaint reference."

They huddled, eagerly trading questions and answers — Rachel in giddy wonder, Jefferson basking in her attention. He ordered wine for the table. I called for a martini. "Strong spirits?" he asked when the drink came in a rather large up-glass. "And such a goodly portion."

I shrugged. "Blabbermouth soup. Is it a lot by your standards?"

"My standards are antiquities, I know, but yes, yes. Keep your wits about you, Mr. Arrowsmith. You are our coachman." He lifted his brow at me before returning to Rachel, who eyed me and smiled, as if she might be worried. I did feel left out, a little, but I wasn't making much of an effort and really didn't mind. I was very tired.

Jefferson asked for spectacles when the menus came. The waiter produced a pair of drugstore cheaters. He looked them over and put them on. "Very comfortable. What is this material?"

"Plastic," I said. "Both the frame and the lenses."

"Plastic. In the sense that it is highly moldable in some way?" He took them off and studied then. "Plastic," he repeated and put them on again. "Do you mind if I do the honors, Mr. Arrowsmith?" he asked perfunctorily, barely waiting for my answer before ordering, firmly and clearly, no lonely lost soul caught in the wrong age. When he had finished, he snapped off the glasses and handed them back to the waiter.

He ordered five entrées from the menu. Once he'd questioned the startled waiter to determine that the ingredients were on hand, he also ordered some things that weren't listed — a roast quail with onion sauce, braised artichokes and asparagus with an herb vinaigrette — and explained their preparation. He chose four appetizers the menu did list: lobster bisque, braised short ribs, shrimp risotto and foie gras. He asked a lot of questions about the foie gras. The waiter told him it came from France in a tin. He asked what a tin was, where in France it had shipped from, by which importer, and by which merchant it had been sold to the restaurant. The dumbfounded waiter tried to explain what a tin was — "A metal thing that's sealed up. I don't know. With a label on it. Whatever. You really don't know what a tin is?" — and said he couldn't answer the other questions.

The chef came to the table and, clasping his hands together, protested apologetically that it was too late for him to take special orders.

"Oh my dear sir," Jefferson said, "this is such a special occasion for us. We're so sorry to be coming in so late. It has been quite a day. Couldn't you make an exception for us tonight and show us your legendary talents? We've heard so much about you."

The chef, whose face had been fixed in a polite smile as he had listened, tilted toward Jefferson slightly from the waist, flicked his eyebrows, straightened up and began rubbing his palms together. "Well, I … I would like to," he said in a heavy French accent. "Yes. I will." He gave a sharp nod, abruptly turned on his heel and strode back to the kitchen.

"My, my. Well done, Mr. Jefferson," Rachel said, beaming at him.

"I'm feeling a little at home here," he said.

When the waiter returned, Jefferson ordered more wine as Rachel and I eyed each other: a Frontenac, a Bordeaux and a Cabernet and, for dessert, a Madeira and some vanilla ice cream and ginger cake.

Plates, bottles and glasses jammed the table with far more food and wine than we could ever eat or drink. He joked about his big appetite and the odd time of the meal, so long after the usual time, but he barely ate a thing and, for all the wine he'd ordered, he took only a few sips. We peppered him with questions and he told stories about Franklin, John Adams and Patrick Henry, trying his best, I thought, to speak well of them. "I can't tell you how delightful it is to taste good food and wine again," Jefferson said. "I have been in purgatory. Now I am truly restored to life. I can feel it. I feel a nervous excitation, a new vitality. What are we to make of it?"

I was thinking more about the bill, and his grand way with my money, and the ridiculous spread he'd piled before us, than what to make of a world in which the dead came back to life.

I glanced at Rachel, probably with the look of disapproval Ben accused me of wearing most of the time, and Jefferson noticed. He lurched forward. "Oh, my new friends. You have been excellent hosts and guides for me. I hope I have not overwhelmed you. My manners do not travel well to this United States of the 21st century. You must forgive any missteps."

"There have been no missteps, Mr. Jefferson," I said. "It has been a delight." But I swept an arm over the jammed table and added, "It's just all this food. More than we could ever eat. All ordered by a man known for his sensible eating. Didn't you write that no one regrets the food one leaves on the plate?"

"I wrote a lot of things. I cannot remember them all. But this is a special occasion, Mr. Arrowsmith, a celebratory dinner with new friends, a celebration of my adventure with you. A proper meal is only fitting." He seemed to consider the issue settled and changed the subject. "So tell me, Mr. Arrowsmith and Miss Carter, how have you managed to maintain such decorum in the face of the supernatural?"

Inelegantly, I had my elbow on the table, my chin resting in my palm. "What else can we do?" I said. "Life is full of mysteries. As Mr. Adams wrote you, insects shouldn't expect to comprehend the workings of the cosmos."

"I believe Mr. Adams was quite wrong. We are not insects," Jefferson said. "In the best part of our hearts, we are divine. From where else can a Locke, a Newton, a Galileo or a Handel spring?"

He turned to Rachel. "You are a remarkable young woman," he said, reaching over to pat her hand. "You are so conversant in the politics of your time and the history of your country. Do you speak French?"

"I do. I do speak a little French. I'm way out of practice, though."

"Eh bien, il faut que nous parlions le français ensemble, ma chère," he said.

"Bien sûr, très bien, je l'amerais," Rachel said with a shy smile.

"Miss Carter, you are a sparkling jewel. You would have taken them by storm in Paris."

Her smile brightened. She glanced down at his hand. "Thank you," she said, more coquettishly than I would have expected of Rachel.

"I take it you are legally white," he said as pleasantly as he'd said everything else.

Rachel cocked her head and squinted at him in surprisingly good-humored disbelief.

"Legally white? You must be joking," she said.

He shook his head. "No, why would I be?"

She looked at me, then at him, and let out a restrained little laugh. "We don't have that distinction in the law anymore, Mr. Jefferson." Her face flashed with anger, a bolt that came and went as fast as lightning.

"Oh!" he said dramatically. "Yes, yes. My, how things have changed. A negro president. Field hands roaming about in their own self-propelled carriages making rude gestures at their betters. Well. You seem so to me, my dear. Mostly white, I mean."

I wondered if he'd more wine than I'd thought. She lowered her chin and eyed him from under her brow with a rumpled smile. I expected an explosion.

"I'm so glad," she said.

"You do have some negro blood, then."

Rachel looked at me in a slow burn. "Well, yes, I do," she said with strained patience. "My father is black. Well, partly so. But unlike me, Mr. Jefferson, he is not *bright*, as you'd call it. Or high yellow, as you Southerners used to say. He looks like the real thing, a real live black man."

"Oh! Well, I look forward to meeting him. What does he do? Is he pleased about the president?"

"He's a chef with his own little restaurant. Coffee shop, really. Yes, yes, he is pleased about the president, as a matter of fact. But he's disappointed in him. And suspicious. He doesn't like politicians, no matter what color they are."

"Good for him, good for him. Neither do I. No use for them at all," he chuckled.

He asked where the coffee shop was and, when she told him Yonkers, New York, he fell into a rhapsody about the scenic beauty of the Hudson River valley and the charm of the old Dutch houses he'd seen on a tour to New York and New England that he'd made with his friend Mr. Madison. When he and Rachel gabbed eagerly in another huddle, I didn't mind. She was beautiful and charming and smart — and maybe a bit dangerous if you crossed her — and I didn't blame the sprightly old man for finding her so engaging.

It was well past midnight, the restaurant empty except for the waiter and the chef and his assistant in the kitchen. They did not seem to mind that we showed no signs of leaving. They kept glancing at us, talking excitedly.

The bill came to more than $1,400. I consoled myself that it was a bargain for a meal with Thomas Jefferson. "Remember," he said in a stage whisper. "I will reimburse you, Mr. Arrowsmith. I will find a way. I will reimburse you for everything, I assure you."

My attempt to reply was cut off by the chef, who appeared at the table and gaily asked, in his heavy accent, if we'd found everything satisfactory. When Jefferson answered in French, they broke into an enthusiastic chat about the Loire Valley, which attracted the waiter, who joined in, the three of them jabbering excitedly. I couldn't help noticing that Rachel was watching Jefferson with a peculiar look of angelic affection and wonder.

The chef broke into English. "But I must tell you somezing. Pierre here pointed ziss out to me and eet eez so true! Do you know you look so much like Mr. Thomaz Jefferson himself? Eet eezs crazy, just crazy how much you look like Mr. Thomaz Jefferson!"

Jefferson smiled and nodded. "I'm so pleased to know at my age the resemblance still holds," he said. At that, Rachel tore her eyes off him to smile at me — as if to ask, "Do you see how crafty and clever he can be?" I grinned.

Back at the Cavalier Inn, when Jefferson and I said our goodnights to Rachel at her door, Jefferson kissed her hand again. To my amazement, she curtsied.

"My, my, Rachel, where did you learn that trick?" I asked.

"I learned it for a play in elementary school," she said. Then she leaned over to peck Jefferson on the cheek. His face broke into swirls of red. I noticed that his hair looked redder but did not think much about it at the time.

I was beyond exhaustion but he and I stayed up for hours Googling things and listening to music on my Mac. He was still at it, stretched in a chair with the computer on his lap, when I got into bed and fell instantly to sleep.

When I woke up, it was morning and Thomas Jefferson was gone.

Chapter 7

I looked in the bathroom. I looked in the hall. No Jefferson. I took my room key and went out to look over the intersection of Emmet Street and University Avenue, bustling even at 5:30 in the morning. Beyond it I scanned the sloping hillside at the corner of the University of Virginia's main campus.

There, just about to disappear around a bend, strode a tall man in khaki slacks and a gray sports jacket. He didn't have crazy white hair. It was all red. I stared at him until he was gone then bolted in my boxers and T-shirt for Rachel's door.

"Rachel, " I whispered loudly, knocking lightly. "He's gone!"

"What?"

"He's gone! I think I just saw him walking up the hill toward campus."

She came to the door in a white terrycloth robe, tightening her sash, her long hair spread across her shoulders. I told her what I'd seen. She crossed her arms and shrugged, closing her eyes in a long, slow-motion, sleepy blink.

"Okay. But wouldn't he know where he is, pretty much? He just wants to see his university, maybe." She looked down. "Nice shorts, Jack. What are those? Little fish? You have legs like Ben." She smiled a little sadly.

"You're not worried about him?" I asked, wondering why she seemed so calm while I felt so panicked. "I'm responsible for him. He's helpless."

"That man is an Alpha Male, Jack. I think he'll be all right.

He knows where we are." She looked into my eyes.

Was she trying to tell me something? Of course I wanted to explore that Alpha Male remark but, for the safety of my own fragile ego, I knew enough to skip it. "Hey!" I said. "Do you believe this? We had dinner with a ghost, the ghost of Thomas Jefferson!"

"I know, I know," she said, her eyes widening. "I think I've been treating it all as a dream. I slept as if I were dead."

"He Googled all night," I said. "He got pretty good at the keyboard." I held up my index fingers and repeatedly stabbed one then the other in her direction. "Hunt and peck, hunt and peck."

She gaped at me. I gaped at her. She slumped, looking exhausted, and waved at me to follow as she turned into the room and dove onto the bed. I plopped into a wing chair between the bed and the window.

"He was real," she said from her pillow. "Why did he order all that food?" She closed her eyes. "He was so at ease, so comfortable with himself."

I told her we'd listened to an old Scottish reel I knew he used to play on his violin called "Money Musk." I'd found it on iTunes and played it on my Mac. He'd been delighted to hear it again.

"Wow," she said, her eyes still closed. "Playing a reel for Thomas Jefferson. What is happening?" There was no urgency in her question, just a dreamy resignation.

She was quiet for a long time before she opened her eyes, studied me with a sweet, curious look and asked me to tell her how I'd met Pam and where we'd been married and if we'd been happy.

"Why do you want to know all that, Rachel?"

She shrugged. "I've always been fascinated by other people's parents. Ben didn't reveal much. Pam was a big lawyer, right?"

It did not feel right, telling Rachel about Pam, but I did anyway. I told how she had landed the job with the big firm in the city when Ben was a little kid. She worked late, stayed overnight in the city, went off on long trips and started making buckets of money. We hired a nanny for Ben until I came home each day. I made his dinners most nights. I helped him with his homework. I lured him into American history, taking him off to see the Liberty Bell, Bunker Hill, the Capitol, Mount Vernon and Monticello —Pam managed to come with us on that trip, which had delighted Ben. He wasn't used to his mother being along.

We never fought, Pam and I. We had some talks. We were both so very reasonable and understanding of each other's concerns, but I started to feel a little lost when Pam got so busy.

Ben was devoted to her. All their separations seemed to strengthen their bond while mine with Ben began to fray. I thought I was the only one who tried to be tough with him. He was flippant and cocky — not toward me so much but about life. He needed a little humility. We had fights. When he went to Columbia, he and Pam often had lunch in the city. They went to dinner and shows sometimes. Pam never met Rachel, whom Ben was just beginning to see when Pam got sick. By then he and I were barely speaking, except when he came to the house to see his mother there. We'd merely acknowledge each other.

"How did it all go so wrong?" I said. "It think it was mostly something in me. You must know better than I do what Ben thought."

"No, no. Ben didn't talk about it." She lifted her eyebrows but otherwise didn't move or make a sound. "Kind of like a war veteran."

"Huh? There was never any war."

"I'm sorry about you and Ben, Jack," she said. "It wasn't fair to you."

"Thank you. Something went wrong. I thought it was my job to guide him. He thought he didn't need me. Maybe he didn't."

"I don't think that's true at all. Stop thinking that, Jack. I didn't mean to make you sad. And Mr. Jefferson ... he'll be back. I just know it. He wouldn't just leave us like that," she said, nestling into her pillows and closing her eyes.

She fell asleep quickly. I could tell by her breathing. I watched her for a while, lowered my head against the back of my chair and nodded off myself.

We woke up two hours later. I jumped up to check next door. He wasn't there. Now Rachel was as worried as I. We dressed quickly and went down to the car and drove around the campus. At the little business district called The Corner, near the Rotunda, I called out my window to a group of students sipping lattés at a sidewalk café. I asked if they'd seen a guy who looked exactly like Thomas Jefferson in a sports jacket walking around like a tourist. They laughed and didn't bother to answer.

We thought he had to be nearby, exploring what had become of his creation. We parked the car, walked to the terrace in front of the Rotunda and looked up at the statue of him there. It had a strange effect on both of us. We looked at each other, sharing our amazement at knowing the real man, a man who, before the previous day, had always been a statue, a painting, or a mere re-creation from words on a page.

We made our way up the steps. The front door was locked so we went to the back and found a door that was open. Inside we came upon another statue of Jefferson. This time we refused to let it mesmerize us. I ran up the stairs while Rachel looked around the first floor and then downstairs. School was not in session; even when it is, UVA uses most of the Rotunda's unusual curved spaces for meetings and ceremonies. The place seemed deserted, except for a few people in tucked-away offices.

On the terrace outside the back door, overlooking the famous central lawn of Jefferson's campus, we found a guide assembling a tour group. I asked if she'd seen our man. I was prepared for more laughs — the tourists standing behind her did chuckle — but, practically flapping her arms like a duck, she exclaimed, "Oh, yes! Yes I did! He did look like Thomas Jefferson!"

She was a pleasant Virginia girl who had a nice, soft Tidewater accent, nothing like Jefferson's sturdy and slightly clipped western twang. "What's the deal with him?" she asked.

"Actor," Rachel said. "He does Jefferson for a living."

"Really!" She wrinkled her nose and lowered her voice. "You know, he seemed a little disoriented. I was wondering if he were drunk. He asked where the privy was. I showed him the men's room inside."

"I think he was just exhausted," Rachel said. "We'd been up all night, working on a script."

I raised my eyebrows. There's something both repellent and enchanting about a woman who lies so easily.

We knew he wasn't in the building anymore so we turned, looked out over the lawn, then at each other, and started down the steps. "Okay. You take the right side, I'll take the left," I said. "I'll meet you at the end, then we'll check the gardens and the ranges," as Jefferson called the two facing rows of brick student rooms and faculty apartments that extended from the Rotunda along each side of the lawn.

I walked from the hot, bright summer sunlight bathing the lawn into the cool shade of the colonnaded portico that protected the big, old-fashioned doors and windows of the rooms and apartments. I pressed my face against the glass and found each room empty. I had looked into several by the time Rachel called from across the lawn. She was almost exactly opposite me, about halfway down from the Rotunda, looking through an open door into a student room.

I trotted over and peered over her shoulder to see into the room, where a tall man, in khakis and blue shirt, lay with his back to us, stretched out on the skinny bare mattress of a single bed, the gray jacket I'd bought him draped on a desk chair.

"Look! He's got red hair," Rachel whispered.

"I know."

"Is that *him*?"

"Look at the clothes. It's got to be him."

We stepped into the room and stood there gaping at him. We held still, watching the rise and fall of his side. He was out cold, breathing slowly. Rachel leaned back and whispered into my ear, "I hate to bother him. He hasn't had a good night's sleep since 1820-something, right?"

She stepped forward and quietly sat down on the edge of

the bed. She looked at me questioningly. I nodded. She leaned to him, put her hand lightly on his shoulder and whispered, "Mr. Jefferson, Mr. Jefferson …"

He stirred slightly and took a deep breath. "Patsy dear?" he mumbled.

"No, sir, no. Not Patsy," Rachel said.

"Sally," he said, more firmly this time. "I've had the most astonishing dream. I visited the future."

"It's not Sally, Mr. Jefferson. It's Rachel. Rachel and Jack. You're still there. You're still in the future."

He seemed to hold his breath. "Oh dear," he finally said, very softly. He didn't speak again for what seemed a long time. Neither did we.

"Oh! Forgive me!" he croaked, still motionless. "I am suddenly filled with an immense sadness."

Rachel and I exchanged grim looks. She patted his shoulder. "I'm sure you are missing your family and your friends. We're your friends, your new friends. We won't let you down. I promise."

Even before the arrival of Thomas Jefferson in my life, I'd become oddly prone to getting a little weepy at the drop of a hat, usually alone, in the dark, at a movie or watching TV. What she had said to him made my eyes well up. I quickly wiped them before Rachel could see.

"You are so kind," he said softly. Still with his back to us, he slowly brought his hand to his face. He seemed to look at his fingers, flexing them, turning his hand over and back.

"My poor old wrist! It no longer aches with rheumatism. Nor my fingers. How very extraordinary. My hands appear to have … changed."

"Your hair," Rachel said. "It's red again."

"Truly?"

He lifted himself on his elbow and turned to look blearily over his shoulder at Rachel.

"Oh man!" I whispered. He looked to be about 40 or so, Thomas Jefferson in his prime.

"My God," Rachel said, rising halfway up. "Your skin, it's

so rosy and freckly, Mr. Jefferson. And the wrinkles are gone."

He swung his feet to the floor, sat up and pushed the fingers of one hand through his hair. "What has happened?" he said, peering at Rachel, as if he were looking into her eyes to see himself.

Rachel stood up and stepped away from him, pressing a hand against her chest. He looked around the room. "A water bucket!" he said. "For my feet!"

Rachel and I gaped at each other. "I don't know where we'd find you a bowl of water at the moment," I said.

"It keeps colds away," he said. "Very important, Mr. Arrowsmith. Perhaps more so now than ever."

He ran his hands through his hair again, trying to sweep it back behind his ears. After each sweep, strands fell forward across his ears and along his sharp jaw line. "I am in need of a ribbon," he mumbled. "I have not worn my hair this long in years."

He looked around again curiously and broke into a smile, his blue eyes shining. "You know, I know this room! This was the one inhabited by two of those loggerheads we expelled after the disturbance on the lawn during our first term in operation," he said cheerfully. "Oh, I forget his name, the instigator. A local boy, the fool son of a rich man."

"So Mr. Jefferson," Rachel said, flustered, trying to compose herself. "How do you feel? Do you feel as well as you look?"

"I do! I believe I feel remarkably well!" he said, gripping his knees. He stood up easily, with a look of happy amazement. The hint of the stoop I'd seen in the old man was gone. He stood straight as a ramrod.

"Oh yes, I feel remarkably well indeed!" he said.

He tested his wrists, pressing each with thumb and forefinger. "Drat. The right still seems troublesome. I injured that one when I was in Paris. But the left! The left is completely without pain. I broke it in old age."

He rolled his shoulders, stretched out his arms and interlocked his fingers to crack his knuckles. "My, my, my, what a gift is this! What a gift!" He lifted one knee, pulled it with both hands as high as it would go and did the same with the other. "I'm young again!"

He looked at Rachel, then me, puzzlement erasing his smile. "But what is happening?" he said, gazing into the middle of the room. "I have passed through to a true afterlife. But I had hoped to linger as a spirit over the heads of my daughters and my grandchildren. A kindly sylph and no bother to anyone. Now I am a full-blooded man again, not a spirit, and of an age when my grandchildren did not yet exist. What new torment is this?"

He sat lost in thought, finally peering at us quizzically as if he'd forgotten we were there. "Oh my friends, my friends, my dear new friends," he said, standing up, gangly and tall. All of a sudden he bowed to Rachel, one foot forward, his right arm curving across his lowered chest, his face toward the floor. Then he turned and bowed to me. "Allow me to present myself at the court of Miss Carter and Mr. Arrowsmith," he said. "I am Thomas Jefferson, an able-bodied man again, at your service."

I don't know what Rachel was thinking but it came into my head that he was back at the age when — some people think — he'd first started having sex with Sally Hemings, when he was envoy to France and she was a 14-year-old companion and maid for his younger daughter Polly. Sally's older brother Jamie, Monticello's cook, was there, too, taking lessons from French chefs so he could serve a proper meal to company in Paris and back in Virginia when they returned.

"Well," Jefferson said, removing his coat from the chair, "I shall make the most of this phenomenon as best I can. I haven't finished taking a look around the place. Let's see what they've done with it."

Chapter 8

We walked down the hill into the business area. Rachel told us to wait while she popped into a gift shop. Jefferson and I stood chatting about the weather in that part of Virginia. He said Albemarle County was well known for its cloudless blue skies, which I wanted to argue about — how were its skies any bluer than Washington's or Wheeling's? — but I held my tongue. She came back pulling a wind-blown strand of hair from her eyes and holding up a blue ribbon. "It's for your hair, Mr. Jefferson," she said happily.

"Ah! I must be a sight. Thank you, Miss Carter. Haven't worn a queue in ages. It will take me back to high times, when I was young and richer than Croesus."

This time a few people passing by seemed startled then amused at the sight of him. Jefferson did not notice. He seemed to ponder something and raised a finger. "It was the Fourth when I died, you know! Even in my fog, I knew it was the Fourth. I had waited for it before letting go. The fiftieth anniversary of the signing!"

"Yes, and not only that," Rachel said, "did you know that John Adams died in Braintree the very same day? His last words were, 'Thomas Jefferson still survives!'"

"No!" Jefferson said, gaping at Rachel. "Is that so?"

"Actually, there's evidence he did not say it quite so clearly," Rachel explained. "He muttered a lot of things in a kind of fog himself and somebody picked out the words and put them together and that's how the newspapers reported it. But anyway, Mr. Jefferson, your friend Mr. Adams was wrong," she said, touching Jefferson's sleeve. "You'd been gone a few hours by the time he died."

For a moment, he seemed lost in thought with a slight smile on his lips.

Rachel chattered on about July 4, 1826. The news spread across the country that the "North and the South Poles of the American Revolution," as his friend Dr. Benjamin Rush had put it, had both died on the 50th anniversary of the Declaration of Independence, a cosmic acknowledgement that the brave new country had been chosen for special attention by God.

Jefferson's face reddened. "By God? Well. I doubt that. But I see you are a fine historian, Miss Carter," he said, looking troubled — not by the God reference so much, I suspected; he may have been thinking of Adams and Rush, wishing he could see them again, or at least write them. As if to distract himself, he looked around, asked if there were a tavern or inn or coffee shop nearby and suggested we find some muffins and coffee. It seemed he was hungry again.

We found a small luncheonette. No one paid any particular attention to him as we came in. He and Rachel sat side by side across from me in a booth. She held up the ribbon and he turned his head as if on cue to let her pull his hair into a ponytail. Her eyes calm, her face a peaceful blank, she tied the ribbon into a bow at the back of his head as if she'd done it a thousand times.

"We'll need to go shopping for you again," she said. "You need more clothes."

"Yes," he said. "It vexes me, these money concerns." He turned to me. "I must find a way to repay you, Mr. Arrowsmith."

I waved my hand. "Please. I have a pension. And my wife was rich."

He was silent a moment. After thinking a while, he said, "I beg your pardon, but might there be a tailor nearby, someone who could prepare a proper wardrobe for me? Just a few things?"

It took me a moment to dismiss the idea of lecturing him about the expense of custom-made clothes. "Yes, yes," I said, "I'm sure we could find a good tailor. Definitely in Washington."

He sat up and cocked his head with a grin. "Washington City?"

"I was thinking maybe we could take you there. Just to see it. What do you think, Rachel?"

"Unless," she said to Jefferson, "you'd like to see more of the neighborhood here in Charlottesville."

"I am fascinated by all. But to see what time has done to our new federal city, why, that would be a grand expedition."

The idea of it started me thinking. "Hey. What about an even longer trip?"

Rachel seemed startled. "How long do you mean?"

"Maybe a ride on a train. All the way out, to the coast. What about that?"

Jefferson gasped, incredulous, a wide smile brightening his face. "The coast? You mean the Pacific? Are you serious, Mr. Arrowsmith? The Pacific? Can it be done?"

Why not the West Coast, I thought. He could see the country from the train. We couldn't fly because he had no passport, no photo ID, no legal identity at all — which made me wonder, in the back of my mind, what we were to do with him after the fun was over. How long did we have with him? Would he disappear any minute? Or was he now immortal? Would he outlive me and Rachel and everyone else, for the rest of time, like a vampire?

Security, I said, was a little more relaxed at train stations than at any airport. All he needed, Rachel chimed in, was a fake driver's license to get on the train and she knew people who could make him one.

"You have criminal friends?" I said.

"Hey. I went to college in New York. It's easy," she said, "and it works as long as it's just to get into a bar or past a quick security check, I guess."

We huddled, thinking through an itinerary. We could take Amtrak from D.C. to Chicago and then ride the Southwest Chief to L.A. — Pam and I had taken the Chief before Ben was born, back when she indulged, and even enjoyed, my love for the American landscape. And then we three could drive up the coast and catch the Empire Builder for the ride back. I'd never taken the Empire Builder and always had wanted to. A lot of its route followed the same path as Jefferson's Corps of Discovery, the 1803-06 Lewis and Clark expedition to collect specimens of flora and fauna and find a trade route across the continent to the sea.

Rachel fretted that she didn't have all that time. She had seminars coming up soon and Professor Kant wanted her back on the job in September.

"Maybe you could fly back from California. My treat," I said.

She considered the idea with a kind of thoughtful pout. "That could work," she said.

"Fly!" Jefferson exclaimed. "I've been aware of your flying machines! I've seen them or sensed them, from the roof. They were high in the air over Monticello! Astounding! Positively astounding! The air has true substance, does it not, like water? Water can support a boat; the air can support a barn door carried away in a storm."

Rachel bit her lip at him. "You like it up there on the roof, huh?"

"Oh, I do. There was much trouble getting it all correct, you know. It has quite a complex design, and there were many problems in its construction. I like to keep my eye on it, to see that it's holding up. But Mr. Arrowsmith," he said, reaching a hand across the table to grasp my arm. "You say we could *not* fly? You say it has to do with these security concerns you've spoken of?"

I explained the problem. If I bought the train tickets, only I would be required to show my ID. When we boarded the train, he might or might not have to show his fake driver's license; I'd been to Philadelphia recently on the train and security seemed a little haphazard. But I did not want to chance it at an airport with a fake ID. They'd lock him up.

"Appalling," he said, letting go of my arm and sitting back to stare at the table. "An American needs *papers* to travel? Like a *negro*?"

"The real problem," I said, "is you're not legally an American. You're not legally anybody."

He looked down for a moment, then lifted his eyes glumly. "Penniless as well."

Breakfast brightened his mood. He had been delighted to find English muffins on the menu. His proved "perfectly adequate," he said, but it couldn't compare to those made by young Peter Hemings, his chef for a time at Monticello, after Sally's older brother James, his previous chef, had been given his freedom. "Muffins were Peter's one great skill. He was never very good at much of anything else. Certainly never as good a chef as Jamie had been, poor soul."

Rachel and I exchanged looks. We knew the story of James Hemings and his sad fate. We'd talked about it. It was a story Rachel's father had told her when she was a kid during one of his Jefferson rants. Professor Kant had once told her he was considering a book with James's story at the heart of it but "The Hemingses of Monticello" had come out, won a lot of prizes and taken the wind of Kant's sails.

Jefferson talked absently about all the training he'd paid for in Paris so Jamie could become an expert French chef. I could barely listen. I was too busy watching Rachel, who seemed very angry. She fidgeted with her fork and kept glancing from her plate to Jefferson to me.

"This is a slave, you're talking about," she blurted out, stopping Jefferson cold.

He stared at her with a weak smile. "I beg your pardon, Miss Carter?"

"A black man, a mulatto like me, held in bondage. A piece of property. In service to you, his master, until you let him go as part of your deal with him. You treated him quite badly in the end, withdrawing your offer for him to come cook for you at the White House."

"What?" Jefferson squawked. "Miss Carter! My heavens! Forgive me, but I don't believe you know the facts. I am astonished you even refer to the matter."

"I considered doing my thesis about Jamie Hemings," Rachel said defiantly. "He and his sister had you over a barrel in Paris. You couldn't force them to go back to Virginia with you and they knew it. Slavery was illegal in France. They were free! So Jamie made you promise to let him go free after you all returned to Virginia, as soon as he taught his brother to cook for you. And then when he was out on his own, struggling to make it, his former master is elected third president of the United States and entices him with a great job offer to cook for him in Washington, which he soon withdraws, just like that, because Jamie doesn't say 'yes' fast enough. What happens next? Jamie kills himself! Boy oh boy, there's a lot about you to ponder in that story, Mr. Jefferson!"

"About me?" Jefferson repeated with otherworldly calm. "You blame me for Jamie's tragical end? That is absurd. And I signed that agreement with him of my own volition. I suggested it myself. It was not his idea."

"Oh sure," Rachel said. "And what about Sally? Why didn't you let her go free, too?"

"She was a child," he said, still without a hint of defensiveness or anger but his expressionless face flushing deeply. "Listen to me, please," he said coolly, even as he jabbed his finger onto the tabletop. "She was a dutiful and devoted servant. She did not ask to be released from service. That was Jamie's desire, not hers. It was most unfortunate for us all that the neighbors went on to spread lies about her all over Charlottesville."

Rachel squared her shoulders and leaned toward him. "Mr. Jefferson, the story of you and Sally Hemings remains important because of the legacy of slavery, a legacy that still plagues the nation you founded in ways most people cannot or will not acknowledge. In some places, it's all still going on, the suppression of blacks. It's just gone underground. For God's sake, now they've even taken the word 'nigger' out of 'Huckleberry Finn' to help them make believe we've all gone so far beyond that. We're all so sensitive now," she said mockingly, puffing herself up and wagging her head.

He blinked. "Huckleberry Finn?"

I raised a finger. "Uh. It's a novel. But Rachel!" I said brightly. "You know, Rush Limbaugh and that Glenn Beck guy, they say ..."

She ignored me. So did Jefferson. "You worked your whole life with Madison and Monroe," she scolded him, "to maintain the power of the South over the federal government, a power guaranteed by the three-fifths clause. Imagine it! The Constitution of the wonderful new republic dedicated to the rights of man making blacks worth three-fifths of a white man! That gave you extra voting power against the North!"

She hunched low over the table. "You know, some people think you founded the University of Virginia just so you planters would not have to send your boys to those bastions of abolition, Harvard or Yale or Princeton, where you thought they would be indoctrinated by agitating professors. Freedom of speech! Enlightenment thinking, bullshit! Mr. Jefferson, you condemned slavery for show and all the while maneuvered to protect it as an institution. You lived off the sweat and tears of slaves until the day you died."

"'Bullshit?' You sound like my overseer Bacon! Miss Carter, I've heard all this before."

As much as I admired her fire, I wished she'd stop. It was way too soon to be dressing him down for his sins. "Rachel," I said, "hey, could you relax a little. Let's just get to know each other for now."

"You do not understand my times, Miss Carter," Jefferson said patiently. "And you are not so fine a historian as I thought. You are forgetting everything about the politics of the Constitutional convention, everything about the delicate balance required to establish and maintain the union. The times were not right for the catharsis of emancipation. You don't hack out a cancerous organ! It will kill the patient! There were many questions to be resolved — economic, legal, political and ethical. We needed time."

She tilted her head and closed her eyes. "You needed time. Right. I guess so," she said. "And a war and then lynchings and then civil rights marches and then little girls dying in fire-bombed churches."

Red swirls rose like fireworks on his skin but still he kept his voice and his expression imperiously neutral. "Well now, I will not defend myself, Miss Carter, for the evil of slavery or household matters at Monticello or my staffing decisions in the year 1801," he said.

"Maybe you should," she said. "You should hear my father rant about you!"

"You are mistaken about me. I treated my people well. I did all I could. And I served my country in good faith and with honor. A few of my colleagues and I gave it the dream of liberty."

Rachel bowed her head at him. "You could have done more, as did your neighbor, young Mr. Coles. He set his slaves free and gave them farms to tend out west."

"He was very rich. He could afford it. And he was young. The fate of the world is for the young to determine," Jefferson said. "And now, today, in your time, these people are free. We were on the right path after all."

"Yeah, if a grotesquely bloody war and a century of legalized racism can be called the right path. And these people are not truly free, not all of them, not by a long shot."

We fell silent. The whole place had turned still. People were glancing at us. I marveled that a woman who claimed never to have experienced bigotry herself could be so angry about it. She and Jefferson looked at their plates.

He picked up his knife and fork and laid them neatly on the side of his plate. "I believe, Miss Carter, that arguments about contentious matters never clear the air," he said. "I apologize for my offenses and those of my times. Yes, yes, you are right. There is much to explain. Perhaps you'll allow me to compose my thoughts on paper before we continue this discussion. I do my best thinking with pen and ink."

Rachel looked at him, a little abashed. "I think you're right about never being able to clear the air."

"Explain, not justify," he said, the blotches on his face fading. "You know, I am coming to understand why I've been allowed back in this world." He looked at the tabletop, wearily let out a burst of air. "You challenge me."

She nodded feebly. "I didn't mean to be rude."

"No, no. I appreciate your frankness. Quite admirable. I especially admire it in the young — and a young woman at that."

She let that one go. No one spoke. I had the feeling, once again, that something had happened and I had not been part of it.

With the storm over, he said he wanted to take a stroll on his own. I gave him $40, my watch and a piece of scrap paper with my cell number on it in case he ran into trouble. We'd be packed and ready to go when he returned, I told him, so we could hit the road for Washington.

Rachel was quiet on our drive back to the inn. I asked if she were all right.

"Not really," she said.

We stood close together in the elevator, our shoulders pressing against each other. I put my arm around her back and gave her a gentle sideways hug. "Yow. You really let him have it, Rachel."

"He really pissed me off."

In the hall, she stopped and turned to face me. "I'm not sure I should go on this trip of yours. This is all crazy, Jack!"

"Hey, you've got to come," I said, grasping her shoulders. "I have to share this with someone. No one will ever believe a word of it. You're my witness. And it will be fun!"

"Fun? I don't know if 'fun' is the word for it," she said, slumping her shoulders and tipping herself against me, resting her head on my chest for a moment. Then she stepped to her door, opened it and, with a little wave of her upturned hand, disappeared.

My son Ben sure found himself one fine and fiery woman. I burned with pride for him as I stared at her door.

Chapter 9

Jefferson was back in an hour, very chipper and brimming with commentary about his university. As he jabbered, we finished packing up and went down to the car. Before we left Charlottesville, we drove downtown and found a bookstore, where he picked out a pen and a notebook: a Mont Blanc Starwalker Cool Blue ink cartridge number that cost me close to $500 and a fine leather journal from Venice that cost $95. He called the pen a "technological wonder" and a "fine instrument."

"Moneybags," Rachel whispered in my ear at the cash register. I didn't mind. I was willing to spend every dime I had on our time with Jefferson and, when it was over, play a little golf and then lie down and die.

With Rachel in the back seat and Jefferson beside me, we covered a lot of topics on the way north — including 9/11, which he'd already come across during his overnight Googling. I think it was too much for him to fully comprehend, even though he said he'd watched an "animated picture" of the planes hitting and the towers imploding. "The Muslims caused us no end of troubles in my day as well," he said, and leaned toward us to listen carefully when we explained the phrase "politically incorrect."

Crossing the Potomac, he sat up and peered out the window but the bridge structure blocked any view. "We are hemmed in. How odd of the designers to prevent the spectator from observing the marvels of nature and man," he said.

We navigated around Washington Circle Park and turned

off to the southeast. "This is Pennsylvania Avenue," I told him. "We're headed toward the President's House but we can't drive past it anymore because they closed off the street." I gave him a brief lecture on car bombs.

He scanned the buildings along the way, most of them nondescript modern office boxes. "Strange edifices," he said. "I do not comprehend these fantastic, oppressive designs. In their great height, they are marvels of construction to me, yes, but they do nothing to lift the spirits."

He leaned toward his window to peer at a few antebellum brick buildings, three-story walk-ups with shops and bars on their first floors. Lincoln would have recognized them but Jefferson did not.

"You're not surprised how built-up it is?" Rachel asked. "Wasn't it woods and stumps and swamps when you were president?"

"It's very changed, yes, but I am not surprised. The plan of the city was intended to accommodate improvement and a great increase in population," he said, gazing out his window. In the rearview mirror, I caught a glimpse of Rachel looking at him, intently studying his hair and his profile.

At H Street, we stopped at a light. Jefferson looked over his shoulder at a massive building of shining steel and glass, broken into vertical and horizontal elements, with a stylized globe on the wall near the entrance. It was the headquarters of the World Bank.

"Great heavens," Jefferson muttered, looking it up and down. "My God, what has become of us? There is no art, no humanity in it. Just the raw power of the construction itself. It looks evil. How telling that it's a bank."

Across the intersection he spotted the Renwick Gallery, an elaborate 19th-century brick pile with a mansard roof. He dipped his head at it. "That's a ponderous thing. Does it lay claim to a French style?"

"Yes, Second Empire, they call that. It's an art gallery," I told him. "Part of the Smithsonian, a network of national museums."

"So it is a property of the national government? I would

have preferred consistency with the classical forms for our federal buildings," he said. "I wish they had kept to the plan."

I had booked us two rooms at the best small hotel in town, the Hay-Adams. Pam and I had stayed there. We had loved looking over darkened Lafayette Square at night to the floodlit White House, as bright as a sugar-coated confection in a baker's display.

We swung into the hotel's circular drive just off 16th, pulled under the porte-cochère and parked, leaving the car to the valet, and walked in to the cozy, darkly gleaming oak lobby. A few people sitting in overstuffed armchairs and sofas looked up at Jefferson. I didn't sense they recognized him; I think they simply found him striking: a tall, bony, good-looking man of intelligence and power with a ponytail and ribbon.

After we'd gone to our rooms and the bellhop had left Jefferson and me to ourselves, I opened the French doors onto the balcony to reveal the view. "Mr. President, there it is. Your former home away from home."

He stood straight and tall and looked through the great boughs of Lafayette Park's trees to the White House. The Washington Monument rose behind it and, farther in the distance and partly hidden by trees, the white dome of the Jefferson Memorial.

He lifted his head high, looking down his nose at the place he probably had hated most on earth, at least during his last years as president, when the country had turned on him for his disastrous trade embargo.

"I can't even guess what you're thinking," I said.

He blinked at me, said nothing and looked back at the house. "I'm thinking, Mr. Arrowsmith, of all the men who have lived in that house since I left it. I'm especially thinking of your negro man. I'm wondering how they manage their post in a world with its terrorists and ballistic missiles and billions of souls across the globe competing for its resources. It seems too much for any man. But never mind. Tell me, what is that massive obelisk in the distance?"

"A monument to George Washington. Built in the 19th century."

"Of course." He nodded slowly. "And beyond that, the ala-baster copy of the Pantheon, it appears."

"A memorial to you. Built in the 20th century."

There was a flicker of a smile. "Oh? Why so long?"

I folded my arms over my chest, like him, and gave a lec-ture on the politics of Jefferson denial and Jefferson worship. For decades after the Civil War, Republicans had considered Jefferson — the founder of the Democratic Party, the party of the vanquished rebel South — a problem. And Republicans had run the country. It was an aristocratic Democrat like Jefferson himself who pushed for the monument as World War II loomed and the Nazis threatened to roll over Europe. FDR was a Jeffer-son fan who saw the memorial as a symbol of America's com-mitment to the rights of all mankind.

"So the Republicans, as you call them, suppressed my lega-cy, and it took this man Roosevelt to restore it," he said. "A New Yorker?"

"Yes, that's right. A New Yorker." I didn't ask how he'd known that; I guessed the Dutch name must have been familiar to him.

"A patroon from the Hudson Valley?"

"Well, yes, that's right."

"My entry in the Wikipedia had not a word about all this," he said.

"Well, this wasn't about you so much but the mood of the country and the nature of the times."

There was a knock. I opened the door for Rachel as Jefferson stood to greet her. "Ah Miss Carter! So good to see you! Mr. Arrowsmith has been giving me a very compelling history les-son," he said.

"What did you think of that view?" she asked. "Is it good to see the White House again?"

"Oh, of course, yes, it's good to see anything again that has survived from my times. It was a perfectly good country house in my day, really," he said. "We made some improvements — the colonnaded dependencies for one. I am glad to see the house well preserved and in use. I only wish I could meet the man inside."

He wanted "some good exercise before dinner" to ward off hunger, he said. We also needed to find him more clothes. So we went out, Jefferson striding in the lead, as if it were still his city and we were the first-timers.

Venturing out into the warm, humid air, the thick summer haze a creamy bronze, he hummed cheerfully as we walked behind him, Rachel and I grinning at each other and hopping an extra step now and then to keep up.

He looked both ways up and down 16th Street, to the left, then right, as if he were an old hand at traffic dodging, and led us directly across the street from the hotel. We stopped on the sidewalk, Rachel and I on either side of him, while he studied St. John's, the "Church of Presidents," a stucco building with yellow walls. "It's a handsome little structure," Jefferson said, his hands on his hips, "but I was not pleased to hear they had put up this church on the edge of Federal Square. I felt that any church in the district, except in the old commercial centers of Alexandria and Georgetown, would be an affront to the essential principles of the republic."

"We're still fighting over your wall of separation," Rachel said.

"I'm sure," he said. "Such conflict is our lot. So many zealots in the land."

We crossed over to what Jefferson had called Federal Square. It had been renamed after Lafayette, I told him.

"Oh yes, I was alive. It happened in 1824, Mr. Arrowsmith. The marquis paid us a visit, you know, in 1825. He came to Monticello during his grand tour. It was in anticipation of the 50th anniversary of the Declaration. He'd grown quite portly. Unrecognizable, really, with a much younger woman in tow whom we were all told to consider his daughter."

Standing in the park, he looked over its trees and flowers and peered at the black equestrian statue at its center. "And who is that?" he said. "Is that meant to be Jackson?"

I told him it was.

"You'd think they'd have put Lafayette here. Politics, no

doubt. The rearing horse is quite remarkable. There must be a very carefully calculated system of internal weights. I knew horse races to be conducted here. I vaguely recall a zoo as well," he said. He did not mention the slave market I knew had been there, too.

"You know," Jefferson said, "we created this square out of the President's Park by running Pennsylvania Avenue through. We did that in '04."

He looked at the people sitting in the park and passing by on its walkways. Most were office workers, I guessed, well dressed in suits and skirts. There also were a few little flocks of tourists in droopy shorts and T-shirts.

"Where are your blacks?" he asked.

"Pardon me?" I said.

"There were always blacks in the streets of this city in my day. Servants, mostly, but many free. I see none at all. It strikes me as quite peculiar. Your blacks are all free now. And one of them toils there, in the President's House. So where are all his kin?"

I shook my head. "I don't know. I hadn't thought about that."

"They're all working," Rachel said. "Some in offices, many in service jobs. Waiting tables. Driving the buses and cabs we see going by. Working for the city. Washington's black people live in Northeast, on the other side of Rock Creek, and in Southeast, on the other side of the Capitol. I did a paper on the history of black settlement in D.C. once."

"Ah! I would be pleased to read it, if you have a copy," Jefferson said. "And we must investigate further. Perhaps tomorrow. It is as striking a change to me as the self-propelled traffic and the blue pavement and these massive edifices that loom against the streets."

Jefferson led us out of the park across Pennsylvania Avenue. He barely glanced at the White House as we walked along the perimeter fence. He seemed more interested in the grounds and the old trees than the building. Up ahead, a dozen protesters shook signs with pictures of torn fetus parts, shouting rants we could not hear at first. I made them out as we neared the little throng.

"We want a krees-chyun in the White House," cried a large woman in a tight T-shirt with an image of Obama sporting a Hitler mustache. "Washington, D.C., is the District of Corruption!"

"Ah," Jefferson said, approaching the lady we'd just heard yelling. "You believe the president is not a Christian?"

"He's a Muslim!" another one shouted.

"Ah Muslim!" Jefferson said, rearing back a little. He looked at Rachel. She shook her head. "No. Wrong," she said.

The protesters flocked toward Jefferson like metal shards to a magnet. His interest excited them. I had the feeling they hadn't had anyone to talk to, except each other, for a very long time. Clustered in front of him, they tried to outdo each other, loudly assuring him that yes, indeed, Obama was a Muslim, a Socialist, a Hitler, a dictator and a baby-killer.

"Great heavens," Jefferson said. "What does your loathing of the president have to do with abortion?"

"He's a lee-beral," the fat woman yelled. "Lee-berals are baby-killers!"

"I see," Jefferson said. "But what does the presidency have to do with the taking of a fetus before quickening in some private house?"

A skinny man pushed through the cluster in front of Jefferson and leaned toward him.

"Obama's pro-abortion, isn't he? Abortion is a greater evil than taxes or slavery, and if we do not repent, will we not be judged? Have we not been warned? Nine-eleven was our warning! Repent! Turn back to God!"

He wore a queer smile as he waited for Jefferson's response.

Jefferson merely smiled back at him. "I am puzzled. Are you a preacher, sir?"

"Thirty-five percent of the abortions are had by black American women," he blurted, "women who make up only 12 percent of the population. The Jews have nothing on this. Abortion in this country is truly the greatest holocaust!"

"Holocaust! A burnt offering of dead babies?" He turned to Rachel. "What is this man talking about?"

Rachel stood with her hands clasped behind her back, unfazed by the crazies. "The word now refers, generally, but not always, to a mass killing of the Jews by the government of Germany during World War II," she said. "Six million European Jews were murdered by the Hitler regime."

Jefferson staggered back a step and pressed his hand to his forehead. "What?" He looked at me. "This is a matter we have not yet covered."

"That's nothing compared to what Obama allows to happen here to those black babies!" the skinny man said, dark and murderous. "His own kind! He does it to his own kind! These Africans!" His crazy stare shifted to Rachel. "Hey! Are you a black woman? You look like you might be. You should care about this! They'll make you kill your babies! You shouldn't be hanging around with these egghead liberals!"

The others began shifting toward him, gathering around to put Rachel at the center.

Jefferson and I stepped close to her. He held up his hand at the man who'd shouted at her and was about to speak but Rachel beat him to it.

"I'm not telling you a damn thing about what I am," she said. "Who the hell do you think you are asking me such a thing, you creep?" She put her hands on her hips, her face that earthy red I'd seen before.

He froze for a second and then bolted at her, letting his protest sign drop to the sidewalk. His crowd of allies fell back with a collective gasp. Before I could react, Jefferson, who was closer to the man's line of attack, stepped forward to block him and shove him violently away.

"Keep your distance, you cur!" Jefferson shouted, his eyes on fire. "By God, I wish I had my pistols," he said. "I'd shoot you dead!"

Two White House cops burst through the little crowd around us. One of them grabbed the skinny man as he was lurching backward from Jefferson's shove. "Hands behind your back!" the other cop shouted. The man tried to break free but the second cop twisted his arm to force him to the sidewalk. They handcuffed him, the man grunting and gasping and barking, "Nazis! Police state Nazis!"

The cops pulled him up so he could put his feet under himself, which he managed to do despite a lot of kicking and squirming.

"Are you all right, miss?" a third cop asked Rachel. There were a half-dozen of them now, pushing back the protesters, holding out their billy clubs as defensive bars.

"I'm fine. He never touched me," Rachel said, flustered but pretending not to be.

"Miss Carter!" Jefferson said. "What an outrage! Are you well? Might you faint? I'd say not, looking at you."

I put my arm on her back and, with my other hand, held his arm.

"It was rather rousing," he said to me. "These black men in uniforms! They were marvelously efficient! Who are these people?"

He was amazed to learn there was such a thing as a White House police force and that it included negroes. One of them asked for our names. "Thomas Jefferson," our hero said, watching the cop write it down on his pad, stop and look up.

"Thomas Jefferson?"

Jefferson nodded gravely. "It is my name."

The cop looked at him and broke into a big smile. "Well, all right, all right. That's good!" he said, nodding rhythmically. "You look like him, too!"

"Yes, yes," Jefferson said, eyeing us.

"Do you have some ID?" the cop said pleasantly.

"ID?"

"Identification," the cop said. "Driver's license? Library card?"

I stepped forward. "No, no, he's our guest, and he left his wallet in the room. By mistake. We're staying at the Hay-Adams. " I pointed toward it, as if that helped.

"Oh," the cop said, a little startled. "Well, okay. No problem.

I don't really need it. I just wanted to see it in print." He widened his eyes and held up his hands at us. "I mean, 'Thomas Jefferson' all spelled out. I'd like to see that! For a guy that looks like him, too! That's funny!" He twisted his head from side to side as he looked at Jefferson's face. "Man! That's wild!"

"Wild? Wild indeed," Jefferson said.

We thanked him, waved at the others and started walking side-by-side down Pennsylvania Avenue toward the Treasury. Rachel took Jefferson's hand and offered the other hand to me. I came alongside and grasped it.

"Wow," she said. "I'm still all shaky."

"No fears!" I said. "We'll save you, Nell! At least he will," I said with a nod to Jefferson.

"Who's Nell?" he said.

My rush was giving way to a happy dreaminess when Jefferson stopped us. Something had caught his eye ahead.

"My God no!" he muttered. "Is he back, too?"

"Who?" Rachel asked, still holding his hand.

"A man dressed in the fashion of my day," he said in wonder, raising his free arm to point. "His walk, his form, they were familiar."

"Who was it?" she asked.

"I can't believe it. I fear it was my nemesis during my early days in the new government. I fear it was Hamilton!" Stricken, he looked at Rachel, holding her hand tightly. "Could it be? Can he walk the earth again as do I? While my wife, my daughters, my friends remain lost in eternity?"

We didn't know what to tell him. We shrugged and shook our heads, opening our mouths to speak and finding nothing to say.

Not as happily as we'd walked before, we went on to the Treasury Building — a monstrous abomination in Jefferson's view; a vast, ugly symbol of the worst of Hamilton's pro-banker policies — but we never saw anybody who looked like Alexander Hamilton until we took Jefferson to see his statue on the south side of the building. The color rose in his cheeks as he read the bizarre, overwrought anti-Jeffersonian prose on a plaque on the statue's pedestal:

"He smote the national resources and the abundant streams of revenue gushed forth. He touched the dead corpse of the public credit and it sprang upon its feet."

It was strange language, twisted and defensive. A Republican administration had erected the statue, not long before the Crash of 1929 and the Great Depression. As we walked back toward the hotel, he lost himself, obsessively explaining his economic policies, waving his hands, looking up to the heavens and pleading that we "must understand" him. We assured him we did.

"And any man fool enough to get himself shot in a duel is no man to trust with your country's faith and credit," he said of Hamilton.

"Absolutely," I said, not wanting to go into it with him any deeper just then. He must have known that Hamilton had won their battle over the nation's future. All he had to do was look around.

At the hotel desk, we asked where we could find the nearest men's clothing store. I went upstairs while Rachel took him off to Brooks Brothers, just a few blocks away, with my credit card. I took a shower and lay down on the bed in a robe and fell asleep watching TV. A knock at the door woke me. I had been so dead to the world it took a few seconds for me to remember where I was. At the door stood Jefferson with a big smile, carrying a tan leather satchel in one hand and a clothing bag draped over his shoulder.

"Mr. Arrowsmith! My friend! Thanks to your courtesies, I am properly outfitted for the road! Finally! After we dine, I must write tonight! I must get to work on my notebook for you!"

He laid the clothes bag on one of the twin beds and the satchel on the rack at its foot, as if he'd done such things before. I took the cue about the notebook and dug it and the fancy pen out of my suitcase for him.

"No sign of Hamilton for you, was there?" he asked. He wasn't kidding. I told him no, Hamilton had not paid a visit.

As he unpacked his new clothes, he said Rachel had planned

to take a hot bath in her room. He questioned the very idea of immersing "the whole body in water for reasons other than health, particularly with heated water. My experience with warm baths was quite unfavorable. It produces boils, you know. On the buttocks." As for himself, he'd liked his shower the night before and wanted another one.

I raised my hand toward the bathroom. "Enjoy your shower," I said. "There are robes on the back of the door, by the way."

"Excellent," he said, disappearing from view into the bathroom. "Oh, Mr. Arrowsmith. How would I obtain a bowl of cold water for my feet? For the morning."

I told him I'd call the desk and arrange it.

Feeling a weirdly urgent compulsion to check on Rachel, I went out to see her as Jefferson hummed tunes in the bathroom. "How are you?" I asked when she answered her door in her robe. "Just thought I'd check. You're okay? He's okay?"

She nodded and stepped back to let me in.

"He's showering again," I said. "I just felt like coming to talk to you. Alone. I don't think I'll get many more chances for it."

"I know," she said. "Jack. Come sit down." She plopped like a rag doll at the foot of her bed. I took the wing chair.

"What's going on?" I said.

"I'm glad you came over. You're pretty tuned in, Jack. Somehow you knew."

"Knew what?"

"I feel I should tell you something."

My stomach tied itself into a knot. "Oh. This doesn't sound good."

She twisted her fingers together and fumbled with them absently, staring at the floor, thinking. "He asked my permission to kiss me," she said. "I let him."

"Oh," I said. I tried to figure out what to think. "When was this? You mean just now? When you went to get the clothes?"

She nodded.

I put my hand to my chin and shook my head, confused. "He's not real," I said. "Are you saying you like him, this spirit, or whatever the hell he is? You want my blessing? I mean why tell me? I'm not your father."

She looked at me wearily. "I just want to be honest and open and I don't want to hide anything from you, Jack."

I stood up. "Okay. This is crazy. He's a *ghost*. Or *something*. But you don't have to tell me stuff like this. I don't really want to know."

She smiled primly. The thought crossed my mind she wasn't going to let my clumsiness and confusion hurt her feelings. "Don't be upset with me," she said.

"Okay. I guess I am upset. Hell." And tired. We were both tired from the strain of pretending all was right with the world. I ran my hand over my head. Rachel watched me sheepishly.

"I find him intensely attractive," she said. "Powerfully attractive. It's like a weird spell."

"Oy," I said.

Rachel crossed her legs and leaned back, propping herself on her hands. "Jack, Jack, I need a friend. I'm a little bit scared," she said.

She didn't look scared to me but she sounded very serious. "I'm scared, too, Rachel," I said, "but I'm having fun at it. I think I am, anyway. I'm having fun being scared. It's very refreshing to feel something again."

She nodded rapidly, as if I'd just hit on something. "Yes, it can be fun to be scared. It can be good, I think."

What were we talking about? I didn't know. I was still trying to find my footing when I caught a glimpse of something in her open suitcase across the room, something I recognized but didn't place right away. I was too distracted to think about it.

She asked me to be her friend, no matter what. The question surprised me but I said, as calmly as I could, of course I would.

When I left, I stopped in the hall to let the image of the object in the suitcase come into focus through the muddle in my head. I knew where I'd seen it before. It was Ben's journal.

Chapter 10

I did not bring up Rachel with Jefferson. I didn't bring up the journal with Rachel. I was never very good at being direct with people when it came to weighty matters of the heart. I did not want things to get complicated between us. It had all felt so light. I did not want it to turn heavy with trouble and regret.

For dinner at the Hay-Adams, he was decked out by me, his creditor, and by Rachel, his fashion stylist and fellow profligate shopper — and prospective new girlfriend, I feared — in a blue blazer with gold buttons, a silk white shirt with French cuffs and cufflinks of onyx and gold, a yellow paisley tie, stone-washed Egyptian (she told me later) cotton chinos and cordovan loafers. He still wore Rachel's ribbon in his queue. She had over-dressed him a little, I thought.

He also wore a faint smile of self-satisfaction, and looked off into the middle distance, not at either of us, as he told of the deal that he, as secretary of state under Washington, and his Virginia ally, Congressman James Madison, made in 1790 with Treasury Secretary Hamilton to locate the "Federal City" on the Potomac.

I wondered if Rachel didn't like seeing him so happily lost in his own head. "You know I can't help adding my father's two cents," she told him firmly. "You're leaving out the fact that this district was carved out of slave territory. That's what you and Madison wanted. This was slave territory, and slave labor built it."

He seemed unruffled, which hinted to me of their new bond. Whatever it was, they now had an understanding, or so

I sensed. "Yes, yes," he said. "You are correct. There were sectional considerations — there always were in a republic divided between North and South by custom and economic interest. "

"I know you were aware," she said, angling her head toward him, "of the irony of people in bondage helping to build a new nation founded on the principles of liberty and equality. But was anyone else aware of the irony then? It seems now as if no one gave it a thought."

"Well, Miss Carter," he said, spreading a thin sheen of butter on a piece of crusty bread, "the fact that slaves would perform manual labor, especially in the South, was so much an accepted practice that it really was no cause for commentary at the time. But our institution had its critics, of course, even in Virginia. Abolitionism was taking root in the North above the Ohio and here and there in the South. But no, no one gave a thought to the daily sight of workers in the field or at labor digging foundations or some such, even at the Capitol. I certainly did not. It was as common a sight as the passing of clouds in the sky." He put the bread in his mouth and kept his eyes on his plate. It wasn't shame that rattled him, I thought; it was Rachel's power.

He changed the subject to Lewis and Clark and the expedition on which he'd sent them. That led us, eventually, to a discussion of the rise of the railroads, about which Jefferson was enthralled, and the railroads led us to our train trip. It was worrying her, Rachel announced. "Should we really take Mr. Jefferson so far from Monticello?" she asked.

"Oh, Miss Carter," Jefferson said. "You are kind to fret for me. But I feel the pull of the continent." He reached for her hand and patted it. "I feel there may be a kind of redemption in it for me."

In our room after dinner, I sat at the desk and opened up my Mac to book our train reservations: three coach seats on the Capitol Limited from Washington to Chicago because the roomettes and bedrooms were sold out; three roomettes from Chicago to Los Angeles on the Southwest Chief, and two eastbound on the Empire Builder from Portland to Chicago and the Broadway Limited on to New York.

Jefferson, wearing drugstore spectacles so h(
his notebook, draped himself in a nearby armcha
upholstery, one long leg thrown over the armrest.

"I want to show you something," I said.

"Very well, Mr. Arrowsmith. I'm always eager .ᵤr your instruction."

It was late August, the month that Martin Luther King had
made his "I Have a Dream" speech on the steps of the Lincoln
Memorial in 1963. I had always played it for my students. I
found it on YouTube for Jefferson. He stood and leaned over
my shoulder, watching silently.

I wondered what he was thinking as King declared that the
negro, 100 years after emancipation, was "still not free, still crip-
pled by the manacles of segregation and the chains of discrimi-
nation," living "on a lonely island of poverty in a vast ocean of
material prosperity, an exile in his own land."

For a long time, Jefferson did not move. When King spoke
of "the architects of our Republic" and the "magnificent words"
they had written in the Constitution and the Declaration, Jefferson leaned toward the screen and put his hand on my shoulder.

"Rousing," he said when the video was finished. "A remarkable speaker. There always seem to be such negroes who have
the power to enthrall the others."

He sat down in an armchair and told me neither he nor many
of the wisest men on two continents had believed whites and
blacks could live together in peace, and if they could it would
have been to the detriment of the white race. He was coming
to realize, he said, that time had greatly changed the circumstances. He had been startled and troubled by many things he'd
already seen: a black president, for one, and black men in uniform, exercising civil authority on the public streets outside the
President's House. He was glad emancipation had come; it was
inevitable. As for its long-term effect, he remained anxious.

"I fear for my country," he said. "I am not at all sure the
great Civil War you fought settled anything for good. I wonder
if blacks and white can truly share this country; and I wonder if
certain forces are undoing the North's ugly, bloody victory. Not

nuch to re-establish the Confederacy, perhaps, but rather an inevitable segregation of people into their correct classes and racial blocks."

Through his Googling and our chats, he said, he had come to suspect that strict constructionists and states' rightists had been slowly breaking the bonds of northern federalism, and at an accelerating pace ever since the Reagan presidency. Profound political divisions would always threaten so vast and complex a republic, he said. There may have been a "pax borealis" for a little more than a century but it was truly over, he said. "Your autocratic Supreme Court, a power unto itself we never meant the court to be, will see to it. At least, that's what I sense after reviewing what I can find so far in my effort to gauge the state of the nation."

That night, I half awoke to hear our door click closed. I listened for his breathing in the other bed and heard nothing. I never opened my eyes and soon fell back to sleep. When I awoke in the morning, he was there, already up, writing in the chair with my laptop open beside him.

I went off to pick up the train tickets at Union Station and take the car to long-term parking at the airport. I met them for a late lunch at the Smithsonian Air & Space Museum, under the Spirit of St. Louis suspended from the ceiling. They greeted me as if we hadn't seen each other in ages, especially Rachel. She hugged me and Jefferson shook my hand. "Look what I have secured, Mr. Arrowsmith!" He showed me a driver's license, which looked real, but he called it "an abomination. It troubles me as well that Ms. Carter has her connections among a criminal element."

She had called an "old college friend," as she put it, whose younger brother made and sold fake IDs at Columbia, CCNY and all over the city. She had sent him an iPhone headshot and he had sent the license overnight to Rachel at the hotel.

"I don't feel good about it," Rachel said, "but it's the way things work."

"You sound like one of us wicked plantation masters, Miss Carter," Jefferson said with a smirk.

"I know," Rachel said matter-of-factly.

We strolled the mall down to the Jefferson Memorial. He studied the big statue of himself, and his words inscribed on the curving interior walls, with arms crossed over his chest and a satisfied little smile. He said there were errors in the transcriptions, that liberties had been taken with his words, unless his memory failed him. "And what little use this sort of public immortality has been to me or the country," he added, shaking his head slowly.

At the Lincoln Memorial, he looked cross as he gazed at the gigantic seated man. "They've made him into a god," Jefferson said. "I was simply oversized in my rotunda down in the marshes. Mr. Lincoln's pose here is fitting for Zeus, not an ambitious lawyer and politician who happened to preside artfully over our inevitable upheaval."

We stood on the spot where King had given his "I Have a Dream" speech. "This place was filled with blacks that day," Jefferson mused. "And yet I haven't seen one on our walk today except in service, emptying one of those public trash receptacles or guarding some doorway."

As we walked up the mall to the National Archives, I noticed that he had been right. There were no blacks in sight. In the cool, dark rotunda, we were the only people except for the guards. They were black.

Jefferson stood silently, his hands clasped behind his back and his head bowed, reading over the Declaration of Independence in its gas-filled bulletproof frame. He looked serious and grim, like a man at a graveside.

"It was merely an assignment," he said quietly. "A job I carried out. I was pleased later in life when it took on such symbolic value for the new nation. But it contained nothing new. There was no new thinking in it. And what flare I brought to it, the Congress extinguished."

Rachel touched his shoulder. "They are beautiful words, far more accessible to the world than Locke's or Hume's or Adam Smith's. It's brilliant."

Jefferson turned and smiled warmly at her. "You think the

changes Congress required me to make did not detract?"

"No, as I told you, Thomas, I think they were good edits. Everyone needs a good editor. Even you."

He looked back at the parchment sealed in its case. "Well, I'm pleased you like it. I never imagined as a young man, when I wrote it, barely in my thirties, that it would turn out to be the best work of my life. I thought my friends in the Congress had ruined it. And it's troubling to see it. It does not feel revered to me locked in its case. It feels imprisoned. It's reminding me quite powerfully that I am dead and perhaps all that I had stood for is dead as well."

He rubbed his brow as if in pain. I watched Rachel pat him lightly on the back. "Do you have a headache?" she asked.

"No, no, not yet," he said.

Jefferson was somber at dinner that night. He spoke of his "people," his closest servants — Jupiter, Great George and Ursula, James and Bob Hemings and Burwell Colbert and all the others, except Sally. He never mentioned her.

When he pulled from his coat pocket a pair of old metal-framed spectacles to read the menu, Rachel sat up straight. "Where did you get those?" she asked.

"I had misplaced them, my dear," Jefferson said, pulling them off to smile at her. "They were in my old clothes. I made sure I transferred them for dinner tonight. To read the menu and the wine list."

He put them back on and returned to the menu. Rachel put her hand over her mouth and stared at the glasses on his nose.

"What's the matter, Rachel?" I asked as Jefferson looked at us over the metal rims.

"Oh! Nothing!" she said.

"It's something," I said.

She slid her fingertips from her mouth to her chin. "The glasses. They reminded me of something, something I'd forgotten all about," she said. "There was a box in our house when I was little. I think it had a pair of metal spectacles in it just like those. I don't know. I think there was something else but I can't remember."

"What was so special about them?" I asked as Jefferson listened tranquilly.

"I don't know," Rachel complained. "I don't know. I haven't thought of those things in years."

"If it's important, it will come to you," Jefferson said.

It came to me first, not Rachel. I was certain that I knew why she had reacted so strongly to the spectacles. I went to bed after dinner but did not sleep well. I was waiting for Jefferson to finish his TV news watching, his Googling and his writing. When he finally went to bed himself, he conked out like a rock.

I got up, put on a robe and went out, closing the door softly behind me. I had second thoughts about going to see her — I knew I'd had too much claret — but before I could stop myself I rapped lightly on Rachel's door. She came quickly, wearing no robe, just her big blue T-shirt. Her face, so happy at first, broke into near horror.

"Jack!" she cried in a loud whisper, obviously expecting someone else.

Her distress was unnerving. "Oh! Sorry!" I hissed back. "I couldn't sleep and he's out cold. But the thing is, see, I thought of something I had to tell you. With him not here."

The awful look on her face melted into one of troubled concern and, if I read it right, a kind of sad sympathy, which I did not like. "Jack," she repeated softly.

"It's about the spectacles," I said. "Don't you know about the spectacles?"

She looked toward my room. "You said he's asleep?" she said.

"Out cold. Conked right out as soon as he hit the sheets."

"Really?" she said. A flash of anger sparkled in her eyes. "Let me get my robe on."

She let me in, wrapped and tied the robe and sat down on the foot of the bed. "So. Okay. What is it about the spectacles?" she said.

I plopped into the wing chair. "Hey. Forgive me for asking," I said, "but is this for real? Is something really going on between you two?"

Rachel looked down and pressed her hands together into the crease of her robe between her knees. She nodded. "Well, I don't know," she said without looking at me. "Yes, yes, maybe there is. A little something." She looked up. "Please don't be mad at me, Jack."

I wasn't mad. I was something else. Worried? Jealous? Lost? "Two's company. Three's a crowd, you know?" I said, even though I was not at all sure that was my problem.

"No, no, it's not like that. I love you, Jack. He loves you, too. He's very free with the word. 'I love that man Arrowsmith,' he told me. 'He is a true and steady friend, the kind one must treasure in life. Like dear Mr. Carr.' He said that, Jack, I swear."

I gave a look of surprise. "I didn't know he could be so affectionate. We're still quite formal with each other." I didn't want to show her how much her news had touched me.

Rachel snorted. "Whatever," she said. "You men always have issues. Such delicate creatures."

"Yeah, right. I know. Okay," I said. "So I love him and you love him and we all love each other. That's why I don't want anything bad to happen to you."

She smiled weakly, dropped her gaze and seemed to think of something. She looked anxiously at her suitcase. It was closed now.

"What is it?" I said.

She shook her head. "Nothing. I just …" She held out her hands to either side, turned up her palms and shrugged. "I don't know."

"Okay. You're a grown woman. You know what you're doing. You even know a criminal, which amazes me. I'm not going to let myself get all twisted up just because I wish I were 40. Or 29. But he is a little old for you, isn't he, Rachel? What is he? Forty these days? But I know, I know, it's just a fling, right? A meaningless fling."

She smiled. "Jack, I know it's nuts. But I can't help myself. It's a strange thing but I feel compelled to love this man." She leaned toward me, the smile cracking, her eyes almost fearful.

"Compelled? Compelled by what?"

"Compelled by everything in my heart and soul. Compelled by history, Jack."

What could I say to that? Before I could react to that strange revelation, she sat up straight and recovered herself. "So Jack. What's this about the spectacles?"

I took a deep breath and told her this story:

In 1938, a black woman from California wrote the Thomas Jefferson Foundation to say she had a pair of spectacles, an inkwell and a shoe buckle that had belonged to Mr. Jefferson. She claimed these things had been given to Sally Hemings soon after his death and had remained ever since in the Hemings family, of which she was a member. She offered to sell them. She wished she could donate them but she needed money, she wrote.

"The Foundation declined," I said. "Can you believe it? They said they already had plenty of personal items that had belonged to Jefferson."

The reasons for their indifference were undoubtedly far more complicated than that, I said. Rachel listened with a strangely bland, empty look. "In those days," I went on, "when Jim Crow had ruled for generations, no one had talked about the fine-featured yellow children at Monticello for generations. Something that once had been a great national joke, known by everyone across the country, had been taboo so long by 1938 that no one even remembered it except a few historians. They chalked up those silly old Jefferson miscegenation stories to political hyperbole, wild tales spread by rabid abolitionists before the Civil War, or fantasies dreamed up by pathetic black people trying to make themselves feel important. Just about every plantation master in the South had been screwing slaves and making yellow babies for sport — but oh no! Not Thomas Jefferson! He was much too dignified!"

"I bet," I said to Rachel, whose look had become almost glassy, "the Foundation did not want to revive and legitimize the claim of a person of color. No, no, that's actually not quite it. I bet it wasn't that subtle. I bet the Foundation actually believed there was no way an old black woman in California could possibly have owned anything that had ever belonged to Thomas Jefferson. The very idea was preposterous. The rewriting of history had been so complete that no one had to lie or delude themselves or suppress anything to feel totally righteous and correct about the decision to reject her."

Rachel lifted her eyes from the floor and looked at me.

"So I've been thinking," I said. "Maybe your father's stories about a Hemings connection are right. Maybe he has that old lady's things in a shoebox somewhere. I just have a hunch that you've seen them. Somewhere, sometime, someplace, when you were a kid."

She looked down at the floor again. "Oh!" she said. After a long silence, she looked up at me as if she'd forgotten I was there. "Oh, Jack!" she blurted. "My father is so weird." She leaned over her knees. "Maybe, maybe I do remember something."

"Okay. I'll go now," I said, standing up. "I just wanted to see you. In private. I just had this hunch and I had to tell you about it."

She watched me sadly, her chin rising as her eyes followed me up. Then she stood, too, and, after a moment of doubt, put her arms around me and pressed her head on my shoulder.

I hugged her. "Rachel, Rachel, you be careful now," I said.

She sniffled, nodded and said she would.

I returned to the room, stopped to listen to Jefferson's slow breathing and slipped into bed. I heard him move. "Oh, Mr. Arrowsmith," he said. "Have you been to see our Rachel?"

"Oh! Yes, yes, I couldn't sleep," I said. "I just remembered something I wanted to tell her."

"Aha," he said with a little laugh.

"No, no, we're just friends; she was my son's girlfriend. I really just wanted to mention something to her."

"Yes, yes, I know, I know," Jefferson said, unconvinced and apparently unbothered. "The spectacles, I suppose. She is a beauty. So intelligent and so bright."

"Bright?" I couldn't believe my ears. I knew he did not mean smart.

"I believe she is the child of octoroons," he said in a clinical tone, "with a very bright negro mother who abandoned the family."

"I don't know, I never asked."

"She told me," he said. "As a kind of confession, I think. It came as no surprise."

I didn't know what to say.

"Well, I return to my reveries," he said. I heard him rolling over. "I haven't slept so well in ages. I'm surprised I awoke. Goodnight, sir."

I could not sleep for hours. It was dawn before I somehow drifted off.

Chapter 11

When I woke up, it was almost 8:30 and someone was knocking on the door. I opened it to find Rachel dressed and ready for the day.

"What are you two lazybones doing?" she asked.

"What are we doing? Isn't he with you?"

"No."

"Oh brother. Here we go again. Maybe he'll be 12 when we find him this time."

Rachel's face froze at that thought. The phone rang. We looked at each other. "Who the hell is that going to be?" I said.

It was a Sergeant Somebody from the Metro Police who asked if I were Jack Arrowsmith. "And you are a friend of a man who goes by the name Thomas Jefferson?"

"Yes, I am," I said, covering the mouthpiece to say to Rachel, "Oh boy. The cops have him." She gasped.

I asked where he was and if he were all right.

"He's a little shaken up. Some bruises but we think he's okay. We're taking him over to the clinic in Southeast. He was wandering around near the Navy Yard and someone gave us a call about him."

"Wandering around? He's okay? He's all right?"

"As I said, Mr. Arrowsmith, I think so. We're taking him over to the clinic, United Health Care in Southeast, just to have him checked out. He has no ID except what appears to be a fake driver's license. We've confiscated that. He said 'highwaymen' attempted to rob him. That's the word he used. This man, is he handicapped in some way? Or a mental patient, Mr. Ar-rowsmith? Why does he carry a fake ID? We could charge him for that."

I cringed. "I have no idea! I didn't know he did! He's ... just very unusual ... he's brilliant, a little odd. He's a relative of my son's girlfriend, actually." Rachel scowled. I slapped my hand over the receiver. "It sounds like he got mugged," I told her.

The sergeant told us to meet him in the emergency room. "And Mr. Arrowsmith. Is this man's name actually Thomas Jefferson?"

It occurred to me a lie might work better than the truth. I couldn't think of a good one. "Yes, it is, it really is," I said.

In the cab, Rachel and I rocked and bobbed in unison to the sways and bumps of the bad city roads as we entered a part of Washington I'd never seen, far from all the monuments and shrines and tourists. The city stretched out around us, low and shabby, with brick multi-family houses and low-rise apartment buildings and no one on the sidewalks and no cars moving on the streets.

We went into Southeast on Southern Avenue, the straight-as-a-rail southeast boundary road of the District of Columbia, laid out in Jefferson's time, and pulled into a big parking lot that surrounded the hospital, a glass-fronted multi-story insti-tutional box from the 1970s. In the ER, we told the woman be-hind the desk we were there to see a man recently brought in by the police, a crime victim with minor injuries, by the name Thomas Jefferson.

The woman didn't even blink. She lifted a phone receiver, said, "I have the people here for Jefferson," and hung up.

"He be right out," she told us. "You can have a seat over there."

We waited. People in varying states of illness and injury slunk in their plastic chairs around the room. The head of the woman next to me hung down on her heavy chest. I watched her for a minute.

"Rachel," I said, "is this woman all right?"

She peered at her. "I don't think so."

"Ma'am, ma'am?" I said, nudging her shoulder. She didn't react.

I rushed to the counter. "Hey! I think this woman is in trouble here!"

The attendant stood halfway up and leaned out from her counter to look. "Her again," she said, and picked up the phone. In 20 seconds, a team of paramedics and nurses burst through the ER double doors and surrounded the woman. Rachel and I stood and stared. One of them called her by name: "Sarah? Sarah?" I thought Sarah was dead but apparently not. She groaned once. They put her in a chair and wheeled her into the ER.

"There's no one here with her," I said to Rachel.

"No," she said.

"Diabetes, maybe," I said.

"I guess."

We sat holding hands like a couple of frightened tourists. It must have been 20 minutes before the double doors into the treatment area swung open to reveal our man rolling out in a wheelchair pushed by a nurse. He had a purple eye and a square bandage on the back of his head. His queue was gone and his hair a mess. Dirt and blood streaked his blue blazer and gray flannels. A tall man in a white coat with a stethoscope draped over his shoulder walked beside him and two cops followed.

"There are my friends!" Jefferson said brightly, pointing to us.

Rachel and I exchanged looks. "Christ. They beat the shit out of him," I said.

Her eyes filled with tears. She put her palms together and pressed her fingertips against her lips.

"I found your black citizens of the Federal City!" he said cheerfully with a sweep of his arms as he rolled to a stop before us. "They're all here in the Southeast quadrant!"

Everyone in earshot laughed and the laughter soon broke into bubbled words: "He got that right"; "You oughta come more often"; "Somebody put that man on the news"; "Oh, they will, honey."

"Are you Mr. Arrowsmith and Miss Carter?" one of the cops

asked, his hands on his hips, his black leather holster creaking. We nodded.

"I understand all three of you are staying at the Hay-Adams?"

"That's right," I said.

"Well, he was wandering a little far from home, down by the Navy Yard, and he got himself mugged."

"Robbed by brigands!" Jefferson exclaimed. "I had a hundred dollars in my pocket, Mr. Arrowsmith. I took it from your wallet, to be put on my account. Five portraits of General Jackson on Federal Reserve Notes, with the President's House on the obverse. I must ask: Are there no notes that feature the author of the Declaration?"

"You're on the two-dollar bill, Mr. Jefferson," I said, looking at the doctor and the cops. They all looked down at him with a mixture of amusement and contempt.

"He really ought to have ID on him at all times, especially if he tends to wander off," said the other cop. "A real ID. Where did he get that fake one?"

"We don't know," I said.

The doctor bent toward us. "His name is actually Thomas Jefferson?"

"Yes, it is," I said. "See, when he was an infant, even then they all thought he looked just like him. Red hair, that nice square jaw, prominent brow, his body long and bony even as a baby. Very intelligent eyes."

At that moment, Jefferson's eyes looked a little frightened, gazing at Rachel. He wasn't listening to me.

"Do we need to know anything in particular about his injuries?" I asked.

"Looks like somebody kicked him in the face," the doctor said. "He was very lucky there was no damage to the eye or the orbit. He caught the worst of it on his brow and as you see he has contusions. He's going to look like a prizefighter after a big bout for a while. And he's got a good bump on the back of his head. We had to shave him back there. Had to get rid of his pony tail."

"Did you save the hair?" Rachel asked. They had not.

"This man of science answered many questions for me, Mr. Arrowsmith, about the ointments and salves in use now and the array of devices around us in that room," Jefferson said. "Dr. Rush would have taken much more blood, I told him. They took just a small vial here. And what was the name of the machine that reveals the bones? They showed me the image of my skull, Mr. Arrowsmith. Extraordinary!"

"X-Ray, Mr. Jefferson," said the lady attendant behind him, patting on him the shoulder. "This is a real nice man," she said to us. "He's got class. Not feeling so hot but treats people nice anyways. That's what he does. You's about the only white man I think I seen in here in months, honey, who wasn't near dayd or all broke up anyways," she said, leaning toward him. "Except for the people from wrecks on the highways, this place is for people who can't pay the beel."

"Are your people from Virginia? You speak exactly like some of my field workers," Jefferson said.

"What? I ain't no field worker, honey," she said. "I am in the health care field. I ain't no field worker. What trash you talkin' about?"

Rachel rolled her eyes at me.

"Oh! I apologize!" Jefferson said.

"Humph. I forgive you," the woman said. "And yes, my family is from Virginia. That's pretty nearby so that shouldn't be no surprise, now, should it?"

"Yes, Mr. Jefferson is a nice man," the doctor said. "Although he did ask me what schooling I'd had as a physician. He seemed quite shocked when I told him UVA. He wanted to know how long they had been admitting negroes," the doctor said with raised eyebrows.

"Yes, I should have said 'blacks.' Isn't that right? No offense intended," Jefferson said.

The cops gave us a lecture on keeping a better eye on him but seemed rushed. I had to show them my driver's license and give the hospital a credit card to pay the bill. It came to more than $3,800. The paperwork took half an hour. It was as if I had to sign my life away.

The attendant wheeled him outside, where the sun was now well up and the air stank of car exhaust and hot blacktop. She patted Jefferson on the shoulder and told him to take care of himself. When the cab came, Jefferson got up from the chair without difficulty, but cringed and held his head before slipping into the back seat. Rachel followed him in.

"Headache," he explained, his eyes clamped shut. The bruise was the color of liver. "I am prone to these attacks and I fear I am starting one in earnest today. They can last for days, weeks."

Rachel put one hand on his knee and the other on his shoulder. "What happened?" she asked piteously.

"I've never experienced criminality of this kind, in Paris or Rome or London, in New York or Philadelphia, and certainly not in this city! This was a country town. I had burglars in Paris, beggars and thieves everywhere. There were urchins and knaves in the dark corners of New York. But this kind of violence! No!" he muttered bitterly, squinting with pain. "The effrontery! In broad daylight, *in broad daylight!*"

"You were out pretty early," Rachel said. "It's empty on most city streets at dawn. You were an easy target. You stuck out like a sore thumb in your blue blazer."

"Are you so sure that whole race is not plotting to make victims of the whites?" Jefferson cried.

"No, no, Thomas. It's not about that."

"No? Are you sure? How can you be sure?"

"Calm down," she said softly, a hand on his shoulder.

He seemed to gather his resolve and turn himself to stone as he told us about five black men who had attacked him as he walked to the Navy Yard. "I used to walk there through the bogs and marshes from the President's House. People along the way knew me," he said. "Just as I did then, I wanted to walk. I am not getting enough exercise. Exercise keeps away the headaches and many other ailments!"

Walking past the Capitol, he became aware that he was in an area with a black population, he said. "I had hoped to find someone along my way to engage in conversation. I wanted to ask about the nature of the community there. What work do these people do? Do they vote? Are they pleased with their black president? But the streets I followed were deserted even as the light came up, which I found most odd. Don't people rise with the sun? Isn't there much to be done?"

He said he'd passed through a different area, a small section where the houses looked new. They were on rectangles of strangely lush green lawn and there was a sign by the street. It read "Navy Villas." He saw white people in a paved area getting into their shiny vehicles. As he had walked on, the housing became old and decrepit again, with boards in windows and clutter in the weedy yards behind metal fencing.

"I was on L Street when the young negroes appeared ahead of me, turning the corner toward me in a pack. One rhythmically beat a stick of some kind on the walkway as they strode toward me. They wore very strange clothing, heavy and drooping, and tightly wrapped skullcaps like those of my field workers. I was curious, not alarmed. I thought I would speak to them. As they neared me, I said good day.

"They jabbered at me in a tongue I could not understand. There were English words mixed into their peculiar vocabulary and I made out the question, 'What you got?' That's what they asked: 'What you got?' They surrounded me. It dawned on me it was a robbery. I told them quite plainly that I had no possessions, that I carried no purse, that I was a visitor with no business there except to satisfy my curiosity. They became even more agitated. They used strange, violent motions of their arms and hands when they spoke to me in a peculiar rhythm and they intermixed their diatribe with foul language. I distinctly heard myself called 'bitch.' They demanded the cufflinks I wore. I turned them over. One of the men — boys really — shoved me; I fell back and the one behind me caught me and shoved me forward. The one before me displayed what I took to be a pistol, a dark metal object with a strange square shape but it had a trigger and a barrel and he held it oddly on its side, with his arm extended toward me, and pointed it at my face. He said he was going to kill me and again called me a bitch.

"I was then struck from behind. My knees buckled. I went down on my side. Their hands were on me, seeking my purse. They took the bills from my pocket and cursed me. One kicked me in the face. They walked off at an easy pace. I could hear them go, with their hellish jabbering.

"I was in some pain. I lay there for a time. I was trying to get up when a vehicle stopped and a man, a black man, came to my assistance. He used his telephonic device to call the police. He was dressed like the office workers we've seen, with a cravat, like the white people getting in their vehicles in that newer section of housing I'd passed. He instructed me to wait with him. I said I could walk back to the hotel. He said no, that I should not attempt it, the wound on the back of my head was bleeding. So we sat on the edge of the street until the police came. He said he was a lawyer who worked in the Department of Justice. It was quite confusing to me, a black lawyer assisting me after those black devils had robbed me."

Rachel took his hand. "Mr. Jefferson. Don't go out without us. These are different times, different places from those you knew. Stay with us."

Jefferson said he'd never traveled without a servant before and, depending on the nature of the trip, he might have been armed in case of trouble. "I see now there is violence abroad in your country, as I expected there would be. There is danger. We knew that allowing the free blacks to remain at large would lead to trouble." He pressed his hand to his head. "Jamie would have prevented this ugly scene. Just by his presence, he would have prevented it. I must say I thought of him."

Rachel turned away to stare out the window, leaving a hand on his knee. We bounced along in silence. I finally said, "You're getting it all wrong, this thing about black violence. It's endemic. There's plenty of white violence, too. What about that creepy protester who attacked Rachel?"

Rachel kept her gaze fixed out the window. "Oh, that was politics," Jefferson said, rubbing his head.

At the hotel, she helped him out of the cab, her arm around

his back and his arm over her shoulders. We went to our room —
Jefferson's and mine — and Rachel helped him onto the bed.

"I will recover, I assure you," he said. "The headache is not
from the brigands' work. It is my old affliction. It comes on in
times of nervous agitation."

She gave him Advils, pressed his forehead with washcloths
soaked in cold water and asked me to get him ice. She leaned
over him, stroking the back of her fingers along his cheeks.
When he fell asleep, I was still standing by the side of the bed,
watching them.

I slept alone in Rachel's room that night, smelling the scent
of her hair on the pillow.

Chapter 12

His headache had passed by morning, which he called a miracle wrought by Miss Carter's kind attention. "Onward to the Pacific!" he declared, insisting there was absolutely no need to delay our journey west. But we did move our reservations ahead a day just to get his clothes cleaned and let him rest.

In the room, Rachel introduced him to Beethoven, downloading his symphonies on my laptop and putting them on her iPod for him. He'd heard of the man but had never heard his music. I bought a book about the Lewis and Clark expedition for myself. Jefferson eagerly reviewed it. "Barely scratches the surface, it appears," he said, handing it back to me. As for the magical pictures of the western lands through which the explorers had passed, he'd already studied many of them on the computer, he said, and looked forward immensely to seeing them for himself, even if from the distance of a railroad carriage.

We went for a walk in the afternoon. Before we could stop him, Jefferson leaned into a guard booth at the White House west gate to ask how one made arrangements to see the president. We grabbed his arms as two White House police officers emerged from its doorway on full alert, silently staring at us as we hustled him away.

We had dinner in the room, watching CNN and "Saving Private Ryan" on a DVD.

All he could do was repeat, "How is it done, how is it done?" Eventually, he settled into what seemed a hypnotic trance and didn't say anything more for half an hour, when he remarked out of nowhere, "We are all so proficient at making war, and the engines of destruction to wage it, are we not? I'm not surprised about the aggression of the Germanies, united as a single nation. There is an ominous undercurrent in some of Mr. Beethoven's strange and mighty music. It's all brutish power and dogged perseverance."

We'd decided to take the risk of attempting to board the train without any ID for him. Earlier in the day, I'd gone to Union Station to exchange the tickets for a set that reflected our new departure date and I'd studied how the security process worked. I came back and told Rachel and Jefferson that it seemed to me he just might get on board without a problem, as long as I showed all the tickets and my own ID.

After we'd dropped our bags at Union Station the next morning, she took him for another shopping trip. I met them at the station. They seemed quite the pair when I spotted them coming toward me: Jefferson in sunglasses, like some movie star — the kind who prefers Tribeca to Bel Air — with his young trophy wife in designer jeans and diaphanous white blouse with spaghetti straps.

He held out the iPod Rachel had bought him. "Look, Mr. Arrowsmith! Now I have my own! Miss Carter said I must have one of these miraculous instruments!" He had a very slight limp but otherwise seemed fine, except for the bandage on the back of his head and the bruised eye hidden by the shades.

They didn't check driver's licenses at all when we boarded. As I'd hoped, all I had to do was show the three tickets.

He and I sat side by side in our coach seats and Rachel sat across the aisle with an empty seat next to her. Jefferson was not as bedazzled by the train as I'd expected him to be; he marveled at the "vast capacity of the carriage" but not the scenery whizzing by: his car rides with us must have prepared him for motion and speed. Instead, he was curious about what he saw out the windows: old brick factories and warehouses; back lots, ramshackle slums and junkyards; clanking, flashing grade crossing signals and backed up traffic. "What a busy, busy country you have," he muttered. "And such great swaths of hellishness. But where are the people?"

It was true. We almost never saw a human being, even when we passed tiny backyards jammed behind dirty brick houses into concrete and cyclone-fenced warrens.

I loaded his iPod from my laptop and showed him pictures from my photo albums. There were many of Ben and Pam. I had not looked at them in a long time and really did not feel ready for them but Jefferson insisted; he said Rachel had told him there might be family photos on my laptop. She stood in the aisle as we rocked along to see them herself.

I treated it as an exercise in self-control, a kind of therapy. Jefferson simply enjoyed himself, as if there could be nothing sad about looking through pictures of my dead family, two people I'd loved and lost forever. "So charming," he muttered about Pam. "And such a fine young man," he said of Ben. His ease with them cheered me. I liked that their deaths did not seem to matter just then, at least to him. Death, in his day, was understood to be a member of the family.

"Oh! Monticello!" Jefferson whispered when pictures from a Virginia trip came on the screen. "There's the tulip tree I planted outside my rooms!"

That night, the windows black as we rolled northwest, Rachel slept tipped against the side of the car while Jefferson and I chatted for hours. It was the middle of the night when he asked what I remembered best about my wife. Her illness, I answered. He nodded. "That will fade. It will be the last thing you remember one day soon," he said, patting my knee. I felt a kind of release, telling him how smart and pretty Pam was and how hard she worked.

He told me his wife was a beauty, too, with many talents and charms. A fine musician, an excellent hostess, a firm keeper of the household. She was strong-willed and highly competent but he left her alone too often. And when he was home, he tested her strength again and again trying for a son.

"I am to be blamed for her early death," he said. "I could never have acknowledged it in life. Somehow I am free to do so now."

He pressed his hand to his head and excused himself to listen to his iPod. Above the rumble of the wheels, the clang of crossing signals and the explosive wallop of another train roaring by the other way, I could hear him softly humming as he sat with his eyes closed and his head pressed against the back of his seat.

In Chicago, we boarded the Southwest Chief. Each of us had our own little bedroom with a seat big enough for two that converted into a single bed, a second narrower seat at the other end of the compartment and a fold-up sink and toilet in the corner.

Jefferson kept himself busy investigating every nut, bolt, switch and handle in his room. I sat down with Rachel in her compartment, directly across from his. When Jefferson poked his face in, I pointed to the seat facing us. He sat down and crossed his legs, his hands folded in his lap, and watched the countryside as we crossed Illinois, heading toward the Mississippi and the empire he had bought from Napoleon for a few cents an acre.

He chatted about the Mexican war, about which he'd read on my laptop, and the "theft" from Mexico of the Southwest territories and California 20 years or so after his death. He called it as inevitable and as problematic as emancipation. The landscape turned flat. The little towns shriveled to bleak outposts with wide main streets running perpendicular to the tracks. Jefferson sat up and peered at the fields, trying to identify the crops. The harvest was under way, big green combines moving in staggered phalanxes across the fields. He asked what operation those machines performed and I did my best to tell him. Without WiFi on the train, we could not Google.

"I don't see a single laborer across that wide view. Only the great machines," he said in wonder.

"Cheaper," I said. "Cheaper than slaves."

"I should hope so. I assure you, slaves were not cheap. In the end, there was no profit in them."

At dusk, we got small bottles of wine with twist-off caps and some plastic packets of crackers with fake cheese. I offered a toast as we approached the Missouri River in the darkness, not too far from the place where Lewis and Clark had launched their expedition.

"To the intrepid explorers," I said, "and the brilliant president who inspired their mission of discovery."

Jefferson smiled and gave a little bow. Rachel and I raised our cups and sipped our Inglenook. He grimaced at the wine and cheese and reminisced about the months he and the whole country had waited to hear from his Corps of Discovery. Fur traders and Indians, he told us, had carried letters, logs and journals back "to the Spanish posts at Saint Louis, opposite Cahokia, or to Sainte Genevieve, opposite Kaskaskia, where our couriers could retrieve them."

He knew the country we were crossing better than we did. He told stories of the French, Spanish and English posts in the "far west," the Indian tribes and their startlingly eloquent chiefs, the settlers pushing across Tennessee and Illinois, the American flatboat traffic on the Mississippi bound to New Orleans with loads of tobacco, flour, pork, bacon, lard, cider, butter and cheese. "Better cheese than this orange paste, I'm sure," he said with a scowl.

In the dining car, we ate at the same table with an elderly black lady dressed in a hat and dark suit who seemed intent on speaking to us as little as possible. Still wearing his sunglasses to hide his black eye, Jefferson introduced himself to her. She gave him a sour look when he said his name and nodded at Rachel and me but otherwise kept her eyes on her plate and never told us her name.

Jefferson tried to draw her out. She was going to Los Angeles to see her daughter, she told him in a sullen, low chant. It was a shame, he told her, that she had to travel across the country alone. She did not react except to make a brief humming sound.

"Forgive my curiosity, but is your daughter in service to a family there in Los Angeles?"

"Oh boy," I said.

Rachel lowered her head at him. "No, no, you didn't mean that. You are using old language and old ideas and it sounds very offensive, Mr. Jefferson."

"Yes?" he said. "Is that so?"

The woman glared at him. "She's a professor at the University of California at Santa Barbara," she said.

"A professor! My! Ah, I see, very nice, very nice. Tell her to come to Virginia. We always can use good professors there."

She flashed her eyes at him and went back to her dinner.

Jefferson pressed on with questions. What did her daughter teach? Books and writing. Where did she obtain her education? Chicago schools and a scholarship to Harvard. Is such a thing common, for a black girl to go to Harvard?

"My, what a question," the woman said with a slow, pained laugh. I thought she was giving in to him a little.

Was her daughter's father still living? What was his work? Had his forebears all done the same work — barbering — since emancipation and before? She looked at him, no longer surprised by anything he said.

"Emancipation," she repeated flatly. "You're mighty nosy, ain't you?"

Rachel stopped him with a short lecture on the few lines of work open to blacks after slavery. She told the woman she had been researching the topic for her thesis. She succeeded in distracting Jefferson — now he asked Rachel the questions — and allowing the woman to finish her trout amandine in peace.

After settling her bill, she excused herself, glaring at Jefferson, and we wished her goodnight.

"Such an unfriendly person," Jefferson said. "Did I offend her in some way?"

"Too many questions," Rachel said. "It was rude, as if she were a specimen. And I think she was put off by your whole Jefferson act."

"Yes, my act." He looked at me. "People think I'm an eccentric playing myself. So Miss Carter theorizes."

Late that night, we rolled into bad weather. As I watched from under the covers of my narrow bunk, lightning in rapid flashes revealed a low, gently rolling landscape of woods and fields, captured in flashes of icy blue light.

An hour after we had all gone to bed, there was a light knock at my door. I figured it was the porter. It was Rachel in a robe. She poked her head in. "Hi," she said.

"Hi," I said, propping myself up on my elbow. "What are you doing?"

"I don't feel like sleeping," she said. "Can I come in?"

"Sure, you can come in. What's up? Lonely, huh?"

"Exactly," she said. "He's asleep. I tapped on his door. I bet he has his ear buds in, with Vivaldi playing. Or Beethoven. Anyway, he's doing his own thing."

"There's not much room," I said, patting the bed.

She shrugged and stretched out behind me, on top of the covers, and rested her chin on my shoulder. We watched the lightning. It came in multiple bursts, trees thrashing violently in a wind we could not feel or hear. A few drops of rain jiggled across the black glass. It was tornado weather out there.

She let out a long breath. "God. He thinks I'm her."

"That you *look* like her," I said.

"No. That I *am* her. He says she was beautiful, and sweet, and kind, and strong, and extremely capable, and if he can walk the earth again, so can she."

I didn't answer. She fell silent for a while. "Jack, he thinks you've been sleeping with me. He says he believes me when I deny it but I don't think he really does. And he doesn't want you to know I've been with him."

"Sounds like a silly novel," I said.

She laid her head on my arm. She was asleep in a little while and I held still, trying not to disturb her, as the wind stirred up the Louisiana Territory and I wondered when Pam and I had last lain in each other's arms.

Chapter 13

For a full day and another night, we rolled across the country, watching for hours as snowcapped Pikes Peak emerged from the plains and the wagon ruts of the Santa Fe Trail weaved over the scrubby grassland from one side of the train to the other. Ratty towns appeared, fringed by mobile homes plopped every which way on the dry brown earth, until we climbed into the barren hills of New Mexico, our pace barely more than a crawl passing Uncle Dick Wooten's ranch, a famous stop on the Sante Fe Trail. There we watched a coyote in the high, dry grass slinking from spot to spot as it tracked a cowboy on horseback. Neither the cowboy nor the coyote paid attention to our slow-rolling train.

Jefferson followed our route on a map and took notes, moving around the observation deck to catch better views. He told us of the Comanche and the Navajo, how different they were from each other, and chatted with other passengers, asking where they lived and what they did for a living, but pressing no further. They chatted with him eagerly and must have found the tall, angular man in his Brooks Brothers jeans and a black pullover interesting, maybe even a curiosity, but no more than that. He seemed a little bored with them. They were all white people; the black people on board did not sit in the observation car or come through the sleeping car section.

In Los Angeles, we stayed at the Beverly Hilton, Jefferson and I as roommates. I sensed no secret assignations. We were all together almost all the time. He did decline to sit by the pool with Rachel and me. "It's madness, this lying naked in the sun," he said, heading off to sit in the lobby because he wanted to "observe the fashions."

The glitzy shops on Rodeo Drive and the spectacular displays of food at the Farmers Market delighted him. At the La-Brea tar pits, he peered intensely at the mastodon, sloth, bison and saber-tooth tiger bones trapped in their petroleum matrix.

"I am so much better off than these specimens," he said. "I have living companions!"

We ate downtown at Campanile and in Beverly Hills at Spago. Our conversation flowed, our friendship reaching a level of comfort and ease I had not enjoyed with anyone else in many years. These two had become my family.

We turned quiet on the drive up the coast, spellbound by the cliffs, coves, canyons and unworldly rock formations towering above the Pacific surf and the low layer of soft haze it created. Jefferson, breaking one of our reverential silences, expressed regret that he had no time to sketch, collect specimens or take notes.

"Even in this afterlife, it seems life wastes too fast," he said quietly, almost to himself.

We spent a night in Santa Barbara browsing around and, the next day, headed north again, stopping for a picnic at one of the dirt redoubts atop the cliffs on the ocean side of the road. He asked about the barking sounds. Seals, I told him. He stood beside Rachel with his hands on his hips, the afternoon sun shining on his high forehead, and listened.

"How do the Californians live with such spectacular beauty?" he asked. "How do they define their cosmos so that such a sight as this can be taken for granted?

"I think there's a point," I said, "at which one can't be amazed anymore. If we have to live with the amazing, we always find a way to make it mundane."

He folded his arms over his chest. "Yes. I'm so very glad you both have found a way to accept my return. You are the only difference between heaven and hell for me."

I often have thought of that comment when I ponder my

own circumstances. It reminds me to be thankful for the friends I keep.

We spent a night at the Ventana Inn in Big Sur, our dinner talk quieter and a little sad because we'd be losing Rachel the next day. In the morning, we walked up a dirt trail into the hills to see the redwoods. I was a few yards behind them when I saw Rachel reach for his hand as he tilted his head up at a gigantic tree. He showed no sign of his old arthritis pains. I envied him. He'd been given another chance at life.

We drove our last leg later that afternoon, Rachel and I mostly silent as he went on about the great size of things in America compared to Europe.

At the San Francisco airport, he was either speechless, staring skyward in awe, or nearly frantic with questions as he tagged along after us on the way to the terminal. Airplanes undid him. He seemed almost appalled, watching them roar into the air. All the distractions made us forget to be sad. We said our goodbyes, a hug for each of us from Rachel. She pulled a package from her carry-on and handed it to me before breaking away to join the line for the security check. After she passed through, she waved at us from the other side of the barriers, looking as though she might cry, and disappeared into the crowd.

If Jefferson ached to see her go, as I did, he didn't show it. He was too busy managing his amazement and awe, not only with the airplanes, but the seething crowds, the security checkpoints, the flight monitors and the architecture. As we went back to the parking lot, I said nothing about the package and neither did he. As he got in the car, I opened the package standing near the trunk. It was Ben's journal. Rachel had taped a note on its cover:

Jack—
I could not decide how to handle this. At first I wanted to save you from ever having to see it. I finally decided that would be wrong and no time would be better than any other to give it back to you. I've learned you are a good friend, the best anyone can have. Forgive my presumption in writing that I think you must have been a good hus-

*band and a good father. I don't have to ask you to take good care of our
friend. I know you will.*
   Love,
   Rachel

I stood staring at her note. Finally I tossed it and the journal
into the trunk. Something made me angry. Fear, probably. Driving off, I took Jefferson's silence to mean he knew all about the
journal, which gave me a target for my anger. He was complicit.
   My silence seemed to rattle him. He began making eager
attempts at conversation. He wanted to go to Napa and see the
great wine region. He chatted about its history, about which
he'd read on line. Eventually I gave in to his jabbering, agreeing
we should go, and our equilibrium seemed restored. How easy
it is to pull out of a nosedive if you do it in time.
   Napa was lovely, of course. For a while, I nearly forgot
everything except him and me, the rolling vineyards and the
fine wine and that clean, clay-hard California sun. Perhaps the
wine is why I remember so little about Napa except my sense
of peace.
   He also wanted to spend some time along the Columbia
River, exploring Lewis and Clark sites in Oregon and Washington. It was not something I ever would have dreamed of doing
before I'd known him. I did not care for the Pacific Northwest.
Too wet, too full of pines, too gloomy. Jefferson's enthusiasm
cured that. It was almost insane. If he hadn't been so articulate
and precise about things, I'd have thought he was an overgrown
child, delighted by everything he saw — from rain showers and
rainbows to totem poles and Mt. Shasta.
   At his urging, we found a stable on Long Beach, just north
of the mouth of the Columbia River, where they offered riding
lessons, pack trips and guides. Before they would let Jefferson
take a horse, he had to sign up for a lesson. I bought him a pair
of Levis at an Astoria department store and a pair of used western boots we found in a thrift shop not far from our hotel. They
fit him well.

"I'd employ you at Monticello, Mr. Arrowsmith. I'd pay you a fine salary," he said, as I acted as his valet, holding the boots between my knees while he worked them on.

"I would have been your first white valet, I think. Right?"

"Yes, yes, indeed," he said. "I'm thinking in terms of these post-emancipation times of yours."

Once again, he apologized for depending on me — for money, he meant — and promised to repay me one day.

I watched his lesson from the side of the ring. The western saddle didn't faze him. He grabbed the pommel, lifted his left foot into the stirrup and smoothly hauled himself aboard.

The guide, a mid-40-ish woman with short gray hair, was about to tell him to do something when Jefferson twitched his feet and started the horse into an easy gait around the ring, stroking its neck and leaning forward, talking softly into its ear.

"My, you do know what you're doing," the woman said. "I guess you didn't get that black eye from a horse."

The next day they let him take the horse out with the woman as our guide. I ambled along on a packhorse as we headed down the beach toward the river, Jefferson trotting in ever widening loops around us. As we neared the cape, he took off into a full gallop like Lawrence of Arabia galloping over the desert.

The guide seemed not to care when horse and rider disappeared far up the beach, around a gentle bend to the east.

"He's good," she said. "Do people tell him he looks one hell of a lot like Thomas Jefferson?"

"Oh yes. Not as much as you'd think, but it's happened."

We passed the bend and came upon a sweeping view: the very end of the beach, where the sand meets the river and the river meets the sea. A hundred yards ahead of us, he stood holding the reins, close to the water's edge, as still as a statue. He was looking to his left — eastward, back the way his devoted explorers had come.

Chapter 14

We rode the Empire Builder back, crossing the northern tier of the country from Portland to Chicago in two days. Moonlight tinged the deep snow in the mountains on our first night out. It made me think of my coming winter, alone in the house, my adventures over.

I spent most of the time sitting with Jefferson in his roomette, dozing or staring at the rugged mountains and the monotonous plains. Between glances at the country and checking his map and timetable, he kept busy writing in his notebook as he listened to his iPod.

When there was a cell tower nearby — whenever we were stopped in a station — he would ask to borrow my phone and with two fingers hunting and pecking he'd write Rachel messages that he would delete after they had been sent, not realizing, I guess, that they remained in the trash, easy for me to find and read if I wanted to. I never did. I did not want to know their secrets.

"She asked me to report my impressions of the passing scenery," he explained. Although he carefully observed my lesson in how to use the phone, he was not interested in calling her. "Conversation should be reserved for company," he said. "It's unnatural to converse with the empty air — and rude when someone else is present."

"Well, I'd agree with that second point," I said.

I called her a few times. We were all cheery and chipper. I would report what we'd seen from the train, which she already knew from Jefferson's messages. She'd report on work and school, telling me she was taking a new seminar run by Professor Kant on the Revolution. Whenever Jefferson came up during the discussions, she had to control herself because she so badly wanted to tell them things Jefferson had told her. She never asked if I'd read Ben's journal and I didn't bring it up. I supposed she understood it would take me some time.

She did ask me to put him on the phone once. "Oh yes, yes!" he said in an unusually loud voice. "It is you! I hear your voice, Miss Carter!"

He listened uncomfortably, constantly shifting the phone against the side of his head and then holding it out to look at it impatiently.

"Oh yes, it is most pleasant. Mr. Arrowsmith and I make excellent traveling companions. We have much in common. Many interests!" he boomed.

He listened again, glancing at me and then reflexively turning away. "I beg your pardon? I'm not sure I heard that."

He hunched down his head and lowered his voice only slightly. "Ah … yes, of course, I do, I do. We are so busy, I must say … What? I beg your pardon?" His fidgeting stopped. He held very still.

"Oh, you mustn't fret, child," he finally said. "All will be well. Trust in providence. How much pain they cost, these sorrows we dread but which never happen."

He handed the phone back to me with an oddly blank look.

"Is she still on?" I put the phone to my ear. "Rachel? Still there?" She was not.

"Is she all right?" I asked him.

"Oh, yes, yes, I'm sure. She confesses to missing us too much. She finds it disturbing, she writes, missing us as she does," he answered with a placid smile.

He went back to his notebook. I stared out the window. I could understand Rachel making love to him. He was youthful and handsome. He was kind, courteous and steady and not the monster her father had trained her to believe. But why would

Rachel let herself fall in love with a man who had no prospects or money, a freak who might disappear at any moment?

We were nearing Chicago when she sent an email reporting she had found an apartment that Jefferson could use for free near the Columbia campus. An assistant professor was taking a sabbatical and needed someone to water the plants and take care of the cat in his one-bedroom walkup on Claremont Avenue. It was a harebrained idea. How could he manage on his own? I showed Jefferson the email. I told him he should come stay with me in New Jersey instead. It was a roomy house and he could stay forever as far as I was concerned. "If you're going to live forever, Mr. Jefferson, I'll leave it to you," I said. "I'll leave you everything I've got."

His face showed no expression. I don't think he liked me saying such a thing.

"Oh, you are most kind, Mr. Arrowsmith," he said dutifully. "I would enjoy your company immensely but I feel I must not burden you or Miss Carter further. It pains me to be your perpetual guest. You would have no escape from me."

"I think you will find New York a cold city, Mr. Jefferson, if you are alone and without money."

"I'll have you and Miss Carter nearby. Perhaps I will get to know some of the faculty at Columbia. I would like to meet Miss Carter's Professor Kant. All I know, Mr. Arrowsmith, is that I cannot continue as your charge."

Changing trains in Chicago, I called Rachel while Jefferson and I were sitting in the sun on the steps of the Chicago Art Institute, watching people. I reported what time our train would arrive the next day. She reported we were invited to dinner in Yonkers to meet her father the night after our arrival.

"Rachel," I said, turning away from Jefferson, who wasn't paying attention to me anyway, "I wish we could talk about this apartment thing. I don't think it's a good idea at all. And you're introducing him to your father? The Jefferson hater?"

"I have to. I told my father about him. I want them to meet. It's important to me. He'll be good. He promised."

"You didn't tell him the man was a ghost, did you?"

"No, I didn't. He's not a ghost. Not anymore."

I didn't know what to say to that. I just stared into space. She told me Professor Kant wanted to meet Jefferson too. "He thinks he may be able to help him," she said.

"What on *earth* did you tell *him*?"

She'd cooked up quite a tale, I suspect with Jefferson's help. She had told Kant that I knew this interesting guy who lived in Albemarle County —an eccentric but brilliant man named after Thomas Jefferson who'd been living off the grid. He didn't even have a driver's license.

"Kant bought that?"

"Well, he didn't challenge me."

I listened with astonishment as she explained her plan. She would introduce Jefferson as a descendant who looked quite like his namesake — the last line of an eccentric family, a man who'd lost all his papers and personal possessions in a fire and had suffered a head injury in a fall escaping the blaze. She would say I had known him for years and was taking him under my wing to help him get his feet back on the ground. He was smart and charming but all alone in the world and a little lost. A little strange. Perhaps even autistic. He'd led a sheltered life.

I didn't say a word and looked warily at Jefferson. She asked me to hand the phone to him. I got up and walked down the sidewalk and back. During that brief stroll, I decided that all I could do was relax, accept whatever was happening between them and do whatever I could for them.

Jefferson and I rode all night sitting up in coach seats with our twist-off Inglenooks. He barely touched his, having pronounced it "even more vile than I remembered from the journey west." I guess I had too much. I said at some point in our rambling conversation that when I'd had the chance I'd avoided resolving the ill will between my son and myself and my failure would haunt me until I died.

Jefferson more or less ignored my overwrought confession, which was kind of him, I thought.

"One of the rules by which I lived, Mr. Arrowsmith, was to be astonished by nothing. I am attempting to follow the rule now. Let nothing rattle you. Meet adversity, upsets and challenges of every kind with perfect sangfroid. It prevents bilious attacks and regrettable behavior."

Chapter 15

Striding in a torrent of people from Penn Station, we spilled out into glaring sunlight and air that stank of hot asphalt, brine, exhaust, cheap perfume, Sabrett hot dogs and garbage. Yellow cabs screeched, honked and angled into every nook in the jumble of traffic on Eighth Avenue. People jostled by on the sidewalk in ragged streams, like opposing schools of fish that broke and re-formed in the current.

Jefferson stood still in his shirtsleeves, taking it all in, his blue blazer hooked on a finger and slung over his shoulder, as if he were just another white-collar guy. He still wore his shades.

We grabbed a taxi. He peered quizzically at the hack license of our Pakistani cabbie, who took 10th Avenue uptown. Its apartment buildings struck Jefferson as "hulking and oppressive."

"Wait until we take you downtown," I said. "You can't see the sky down there."

"The value of real property has driven this city to grow upwards," he said. "That comes as no surprise to me. Considering the physical barrier to lateral growth imposed by this island location, the commissioners should have given more thought to the unhealthy effects of height when they drew these upper streets," he said. "They imposed no limit, as we did in Washington. There should have been more parks as well."

Rachel was waiting for us in front of 125 Claremont, a block west of Broadway, in the same shorts and top she'd worn on her ride to Charlottesville with me, which felt to me like something from the very distant past.

"Hello, gentlemen!" she called as we got out of the cab.

"Miss Carter! Ah, my dear Miss Carter! So good to see you again!" Jefferson said, rising to his full height and striding to the sidewalk with his hands extended toward her. "Mr. Arrowsmith has been excellent company but we are a trio and your absence was deeply felt." He looked over his shoulder at me. "Was it not, Mr. Arrowsmith?"

I finished up paying the cabbie. "Very deeply," I said as I slid my wallet in my back pocket.

Rachel hugged him and then me. "Jack," she whispered in my ear as we embraced. "I missed you."

"I missed you, too," I said, letting her go, "but I had Mr. Jefferson's company, which never ceases to amaze me."

"It's my turn to have him," she said happily.

"So it seems."

Carrying our bags into a handsome walk-up beaux-arts apartment building next to the Manhattan School of Music, we followed Rachel upstairs. On the way, she chattered about all the work Professor Kant had her doing for a new book he was planning about none other than Thomas Jefferson. Annette Gordon-Reed's success with her book about the Hemings family had inspired him, Rachel said, "to prospect the Jefferson gold mine himself."

"Gold mine?" Jefferson said. "Hah! How I wish it were so for my own benefit." He asked about the Hemings book and I told him I'd give him my copy. I never did. It slipped my mind and he never reminded me. For all I know, he read it on his own and never mentioned it.

When she opened the door to the third-floor apartment, I peered in. "Wow," I said. "Cozy."

Jefferson, barely giving the place a glance as he went in, zeroed in on a row of books on a shelf and stood inspecting the titles and authors' names on their spines.

The apartment was in the back of the building. A dingy brick wall a few feet across an airshaft filled the view out both living room windows. "Isn't it great?" Rachel said, showing off the place with almost manic enthusiasm. "The School of Music does concerts and recitals. You can go. They're open to the public. Isn't that great? And it's a very quiet building, with a lot of Columbia people. The kitchen is simple to take care of and you have this nice living room with an HDTV and the parquet floor, like the one in the parlor at Monticello!"

"Well, not quite the same," Jefferson said, looking down at his feet.

She looked at him for a moment with a kind of nutty panic. "It is cozy, isn't it?" she said. "The professor who lives here is single. He's on sabbatical in China for six months. The place is full of books, which I thought you'd like, but so many of them are in Chinese." She raised her brows and giggled nervously.

"Oh my," Jefferson said mildly. "Chinese. How interesting." He looked at me and flicked his brows.

It wasn't a bad little place. There were bookshelves across one wall above a leather couch and a square, brushed-steel coffee table; to the right of the couch, a hallway led to the bathroom and bedroom. Between the two windows, a Chinese landscape hung on the wall, and below that there were low built-in cabinets with stereo speakers, an iPod dock with no iPod and a flat-screen TV.

A leather chair with a modern chrome reading lamp, a leather ottoman and a side table took up most of the wall on the right beneath another Chinese landscape. Like the other one, it was eerie, with otherworldly yellow mountains shaped like sugar loaves. Each bore two vertical rows of Chinese characters in the sky between the mountains.

In the corner, behind the leather chair, stood an antique grandfather clock, probably late 18th century. On its face were painted a couple of thatched cottages and two sailing ships, the wind billowing their sails. It was simple and handsome, probably of pine, with a neat cherry inlay around the casing and a small golden eagle clutching a ball at the top. It wasn't ticking.

I noticed Jefferson gazing at it with a look of relief, as if he'd just spotted Monticello beyond the next hill.

"I wonder if it works," he said.

The assistant professor's flattop desk, which he appeared to have cleared out, was in a corner beside the front door, with a black file cabinet beside it and more shelves full of books on the wall above it. There was a phone on the desk but no computer. In the corner, there was an alcove containing a tiny but modern kitchen.

Jefferson looked around, his arms folded tightly against his chest, a weak smile on his face and a worried tilt to his brow.

"How far away do you live, Miss Carter?" he asked.

"Oh! It's just a 10-minute walk across campus. Off Amsterdam Avenue."

"Very good." He turned to me. "And Mr. Arrowsmith, is this place easily accessible to you?"

"If you need me, I could be here in half an hour, if the traffic is light."

"Good, good."

We looked into the bedroom. It was a dark box with a king-size bed with no headboard. An antique wooden night table and a large wooden wardrobe were crowded into the space between the bed and the wall. The room had one window at the foot of the bed with a yellowed shade. Beyond it was the same dirty and graying brick wall across the airshaft.

We peered into the bathroom. It was tiled in tiny white ceramic squares, with a sink and a tub with a shower. Under the sink was a large cat box, with several turds tilting in the kitty litter.

"What is that?" Jefferson asked.

"The cat box," Rachel said. "It's your only chore. It will be nothing for a man who owned horses and dogs and cattle and sheep."

He offered a placid look and vague smile. "We did not keep their excrement in the house."

"Oh, it's nothing, you'll see," Rachel said.

"My heavens," he muttered as we turned to go back into the living room.

"There's no computer, I see," I said to Jefferson. "You take my laptop. Keep it here. I have a PC at home."

"Oh, Mr. Arrowsmith, are you sure? That would be most

kind," he said, leaning toward me.

"Don't give it a thought," I said. Where, I asked Rachel, was the cat.

"Hiding under the bed," she said. "She's been a little spooked since I took over feeding her and cleaning the litter box."

"Pray tell, Miss Carter," Jefferson said with a diplomatic smile, "what does one do with the contents of the litter box?"

"I'll have to show you how to clean it," she said nervously. "You just drop it into the toilet with a tissue. Every few days the litter has to be changed. But you know, really, I can come and do it for you."

"Ah. How kind of you to make that offer."

Rachel, I suspected, was going to be doing more than cleaning up cat turds for him. I looked at the floor and shook my head.

"What?" Rachel said. "What are you shaking your head at?"

"I understand it's a good deal, a temporary solution to Mr. Jefferson's housing situation, and I understand his strong desire to be independent," I said, turning to him and bowing slightly. "Forgive me for talking about you as if you weren't here." He nodded. "But I am worried, Rachel, that Mr. Jefferson will find this place very dark and claustrophobic and very difficult to adjust to. It's not his style."

"I know. It will be a challenge, Jack," Rachel said. "We'll help. You'll visit often, won't you? And I'll be nearby. He'll have the chance to study and read and write and get to know the city a bit and it won't cost anything, not for the apartment, anyway. Until we figure this all out, it's just a place for him to have his things and be on his own."

I rubbed my cheek and looked around the room. "You'll need some books, Mr. Jefferson. Of your own, I mean."

"Oh yes," he said. "By all means. I cannot live without books."

Rachel and I sat side by side on the edge of the couch while he put his few things in the bathroom and the bedroom wardrobe. He placed his journal and pen on the barren desk and set up the laptop there. I felt as if I were watching my son on his first day at college and I was not doing much to help him.

"Is there internet here?" Jefferson asked. "Any WiFi?"

"Oh yes," Rachel said. "Cable. Right there," she said, pointing to an Ethernet port in the wall.

Another bill, I thought, as Jefferson bent over to study it.

We went out and walked the neighborhood for an hour as evening fell. He remembered riding through the hilly countryside on the Bloomingdale Road when New York was the capital and he lived there as Washington's secretary of state. "It was all woods and fields and farmhouses up along these heights," he said. "Very pretty country. Its tall hardwoods reminded me of Virginia."

We showed him Grant's Tomb, into which he stared with a worried look; Riverside Church and the main campus at Columbia. I thought of Ben as we stood before Hamilton Hall. In our own times, Ben and I had spent many hours in that building as undergraduates, passing by the statue of Hamilton on his pedestal in the courtyard a half dozen times every day.

Jefferson studied the statue. "I swear I saw that man near the Treasury. Well ... Good men came out of this college, I'm sure," he said, not very convincingly. "After all, here's Mr. Arrowsmith. And Miss Carter. I will try not hold Mr. Hamilton or his monarchist conspirators against this old Tory institution."

For dinner, Rachel had stocked the fridge and bought wine. She wrapped him in an apron and tried to make him follow the recipe for coq au vin from a cookbook. He didn't know where anything was. He didn't know how anything worked. Rachel had to help him constantly. As he followed along, he talked about his own recipes collected in France and followed at Monticello by James Hemings.

We sipped wine while dinner simmered and watched the beginning of "Gone With The Wind" on a pile of cushions on the floor. She thought it would be fun and instructive for him. I can't blame her for the choice. I didn't think twice about it myself. Still distracted by the equipment and technology at first, and then by what he considered the "interesting use of horns" in the theme music, Jefferson fell silent and still as he read the

introduction — about the knights and cava
fair of the old South — as it scrolled over sh
working the fields and magnolias in full bl
Technicolor-fake spring day.

"How very sentimental this is," he muttered.

In the beginning, Rachel and I peeked at each other behind
Jefferson's back and rolled our eyes at the film's references to
"darkies" and its depiction of slavery as the foundation of a
benign civilization in which grace, gallantry and gentility
reigned.

"How about rape, incest, sloth, poverty, political paranoia,
exhausted tobacco fields, debt and economic collapse?" I whispered to Rachel.

She punched me hard in the arm. "You're talking pre-cot-
ton. The South was the Saudi Arabia of cotton for the world, Mr.
History Teacher."

"Hey! Ow!" I said. "Not the political paranoia part. The
richer they got and the more important slavery became after
the cotton gin, the crazier those planters and politicians got trying to defend it."

Jefferson ignored us, transfixed.

At the intermission, we rushed through dinner, Jefferson
talking excitedly about the medium, now that he'd seen two ex-
amples of Hollywood films: how vividly a moving picture rec-
reated life; how much more intense and riveting it was than any
play he'd ever seen. "It seems to focus the attention so fixedly
that it tricks the mind into believing completely in the scene it
portrays," he said eagerly. "Perhaps there is some explanation
in it of my re-creation!"

Before we could ponder that idea for long, he exclaimed
that much of the world re-created in the film had been quite familiar to him, in spite of the different fashions and the technical
innovations of the "mid-century," as he called it, a generation
after his demise. He asked about the scenes of Atlanta. He wondered how they had simulated such a great conflagration, and
how a city that hadn't existed in his lifetime had sprouted up
and turned so quickly into a metropolis that would have been

..1 a target for the Union invaders.

We watched the rest after dinner. The spell did break a few mes: "Such silly people," he said once. Later he sneered, "Why, this is a mere romance, a melodrama for women."

But soon he fell into a dark rapture. The dead South, dead wives, dead children and, finally, the family's deathwatch for the noble Melanie undid him. He held himself so rigid that his head shook as we watched the O'Haras file one by one from the hallway into Melanie's darkened bedroom to say their good-byes. And at the end of the film, after Rhett Butler walks off into the fog and Scarlett collapses on the staircase vowing to rebuild her life at Tara, Jefferson dropped his head and sobbed.

"Oh my God!" Rachel gasped, reaching for him. He lay his head on her breast and clenched shut his eyes, tears streaming down his flushed cheeks. She stroked his hair and told him she was sorry, she hadn't thought it through, she shouldn't have brought that film.

"My dear Mr. Jefferson," I said, resting my hand on his shoulder and feeling him quiver. "You have a lot to take in. I can't imagine what it's like."

I could see him struggling to control himself, wiping his eyes through clenched teeth. "Forgive me," he said in a thick voice. "I am not myself. My nerves have reached their limits. We are not meant to live on amidst the scattered debris of our own ancient times. This world is for the living, not the likes of me."

We both stayed with him that night, Jefferson in his tomb of a bedroom, Rachel and I under a blanket on the couch, our heads at opposite ends.

"Go in there with him, Rachel," I said. "He's so alone."

She said no, she knew there were times when he did not want her or anyone's company.

Chapter 16

We took Jefferson to meet Professor Elmer Kant at his office in Hamilton Hall the next morning. Jefferson had been a little quiet and glum. As we walked toward campus, he very softly hummed a tune that I guessed was an old ballad. Perhaps he was trying to gird himself for Kant. Rachel had abashedly told him that the professor, in the book he was planning, would argue that Jefferson had led a Virginia cabal that bore the blame for making the Civil War inevitable.

I asked him what tune he was humming.

"It's 'Broom of the Cowdenknows,' Mr. Arrowsmith. A lovely thing, but a rather plaintive song about lost love and exile," he said with a kindly smile. Later, we'd all find out that Rachel's father knew it, too, much to Jefferson's delight.

At Hamilton Hall, we stopped again in front of Hamilton's statue. Jefferson looked up at it with a smile that was nearly a grimace. "I feel as if I'm heading in for another meeting of General Washington's cabinet," he said. "Time for another cockfight."

"He promised me he'd be polite," Rachel said. "He promised to listen to you. If anyone can steer him away from his new project, or reshape it, it's you. I want you to try."

He patted her lightly on her back. "An eccentric with the name Jefferson? Surely he will humor me, not listen. But thank you for your faith in me, and your guidance, my dear Miss Carter."

I hadn't been inside Hamilton Hall in 35 years. It rattled me. Thoughts of my son overshadowed whatever fond memories I

had of my college days, which had not been all that pleasant —
demonstrations all over campus, enraged red-faced police with
billy clubs driving students from the quads, swinging away at
any of them clumsy or panicked enough to have fallen down.

Rachel knocked on Kant's door on the third floor. Opening
it when he called us in, she revealed a trim, graying, bespec-
tacled black man in a bow tie and tweed jacket with a red handkerchief in his breast pocket. He rose from behind his cluttered
desk.

"Aha, Rachel! You've brought your remarkable Mr. Jefferson!" he said as he came from behind the desk. "Good morning,
sir," he said, extending his hand to Jefferson, who shook it.

"I'm honored to meet you, Professor. I look forward to reading your works. I'm sorry to say I have not yet had the chance,"
Jefferson said.

"Well that's all right, I can give you a copy of the last one."

"And what was the subject?" Jefferson asked as they let go
of each other's hand.

"Oh, it's a short work on the decline of the whaling industry.
I looked at the impact on New Bedford and Nantucket and tried
to show how the changes that occurred in those small places
reflected all the ways the country itself was changing."

"Ah. Interesting, interesting," Jefferson said. "What era
would that have been?"

"Oh, you know, the early second half of the 19th century."

"With the advent of petroleum as a fuel," Jefferson said.

"Yes, that, and the decline of the fishery due to over-har-
vesting."

"And the war. I presume the war had an impact."

"Well that's very interesting. The Civil War, you mean, I
take it. Yes, the war did encourage the use of petroleum as a
lubricant. It was readily available by then in the vast quantities
required."

Kant turned to me and Rachel introduced us. "What a name,
Mr. Arrowsmith, what a fine name," Kant said. I looked at his
face and decided he wasn't mocking me. Academics sometimes
get into the Sinclair Lewis thing with me. One asked me once if

my middle name weren't "Babbitt." I'd felt like slugging him. Kant invited us all to take a seat. Rachel and I went to a green leather couch and Jefferson took the worn cordovan leather armchair angled in front of Kant's desk.

"My God, you do look like your namesake, Mr. Jefferson. How absolutely remarkable," Kant said, staring at him.

"Yes, so they say. I'm descended from the family, through the Randolph line," Jefferson said, without missing a beat.

"And I gather your parents were big fans."

"Fans?"

Kant tilted his head. "Fans. Fanatics. About the original Thomas Jefferson. Otherwise why would they have given you his name?"

"Oh, the original Thomas Jefferson was my great-grandfather, actually. From Wales, near Snowdon."

"No," Rachel said, shifting forward on the couch and reaching toward Jefferson. "That was the Founding Father Thomas Jefferson's grandfather. Right?"

"Exactly," Jefferson said with a glance toward Rachel.

"It must be easy to get confused," Kant said with apparent sincerity.

"No, I'm never confused about those matters," Jefferson said politely.

I was getting the impression that he and Rachel had not prepared for this so well. No one spoke for several seconds.

Kant broke the silence. "Well, Rachel says you have a vast knowledge of all things Jefferson," he said, leaning back in his chair comfortably, like a judge in his chambers settling in for a good off-the-record chat with a defense attorney. Rachel and I sat upright and rigid, like parents watching a shrink testing their child.

"Oh, I'm quite familiar with his history," Jefferson said, "and the events and great issues of the day in which he played a role, yes. Merely one of my hobbies," he added, looking toward Rachel with a smile.

"Aha," Kant said. "What others hobbies do you have, sir?"

"Natural philosophy, agriculture, gardening, architecture,

classical and contemporary literature, history, both ancient and modern, music of all kinds, politics though I really do hate politics, I really am most interested in the rights of man, and there's also good food and wine, tinkering — I patented a very useful plow, you know.

"Yes, yes, just like your namesake," Kant said a little impatiently. "And what do you do for a living?"

"Nothing. I'd farm if I had any land. I devote my time to observation, study and reflection."

Kant raised his eyebrows again. "How lovely. Sounds like my job."

"Yes? Are there more such positions available here?"

Rachel and I held very still, as if we might crack into a thousand pieces and fall in a heap on the floor.

Kant skewed his mouth and glanced at Jefferson sideways. "Well, there are, now and then. There's quite a competition for professorships. Would you like to teach?"

"Quite possibly. I've known many fine teachers and admired them. Our great Scot, Professor Small, was the most influential for me. Of course, I assembled the faculty at the University of Virginia." Jefferson glanced at Rachel then looked at Kant. "I mean to say Jefferson assembled the first faculty there."

"Yes, one of his many great achievements."

"Yes. I think so."

"Too bad he did not follow through on slavery. And too bad he promoted the notion of nullification. As much as he claimed to dread the failure of the Union, he led the way, really, don't you think?"

Jefferson smiled. "I knew you'd mention that. There is a difference between believing in the rights of the states and the claimed right of secession."

"I would argue that one leads to the other."

"You have hindsight, sir, which makes everything obvious. Mr. Jefferson was living in a time when the republic was a very bold experiment. There were no precedents. It was all a test."

"Jefferson's political descendants — and his own family descendants — were secessionists," Kant went on.

"They lived in a different era from the one i̶
triarch lived. Their circumstances were not his
decried secessionism. As he did in his own ti̶
one of those fools who bellowed for it. Blame the New En̶g̶
ers for threatening to play that card during the embargo."

"How can one argue for nullification without leaving the Union vulnerable to collapse with every crisis?" Kant asked.

"We had a Constitution that established our national bonds. Rejecting an act of Congress if it is illegal can do nothing to change a word of the Constitution, or any aspect of its application. With your view so complicated by hindsight, you are failing to grasp the freshness of the elemental issue of my day, sir."

"And that is?"

"The balance of power between the states and the national government, of course. To be in favor of a limited national government did not mean that Jefferson preferred to see the Union collapse and the states go their separate ways. Far from it, far from it."

Jefferson was calm and polite. Kant was getting irritated — not with the argument, I suspected, but with the nut he'd been made to waste his time meeting.

"A historian," Kant lectured, "looks not only at the circumstances of a particular moment in history, but also its effects over time. An effect of Jefferson's constant drumbeat over state's rights — not to mention his lifelong machinations to preserve and promote the political advantages of the slave states in the operation of the federal government — was to nourish the cult of secessionism and the paranoid resentment that an economically powerful and yet vulnerable one-crop South felt toward the rising industrial and political power of the North as its population grew. Taken with his failure to provide any leadership or example on the emancipation question, Jefferson must be regarded as the de facto father of the Confederacy, the man who, with his friends, planted and nourished its seed. The South certainly looked on him that way itself, didn't it?"

"Is that so?" Jefferson asked, honestly surprised.

'It's such a fascinating notion," Kant went on. "A Founding ather who was, in fact, a secret secessionist, a man who plotted the federal government's death at its very inception. It will make a good book. Good Jefferson books always sell."

Kant was playing, I thought, at being outrageous, the way star professors love to put on shows.

Jefferson did not move. "That is your thesis?" he whispered.

"Well, okay, that's pushing it too far," he said. "Just kidding."

"Kidding?"

"Joking."

"A strange thing to joke about."

They fell silent. Rachel and I looked at each other. Maybe, I thought, it was time to bring this show to an end.

"Oh, I have a question for you," Kant said, lifting a finger in the air. "This is a mystery for all biographers of Jefferson. What was his relationship with his mother? Do you have any thoughts on that? He apparently adored his father. At least he left behind a few admiring words about him, but the absence of almost any reference to his mother in his voluminous records, except for a little sneer about her fancy English ancestry, raises the suspicion he had some sort of problem with her."

"I have no further thoughts on that," Jefferson said.

"I have a hunch," Kant went on, "that his mother was a nag, a haughty nag, without much in the way of education or intelligence, but much breeding and pride; an unloving woman who drove her husband and her eldest son a little mad because she looked down on them for being provincial Virginians. She was, of course, born in London and I'll bet she was always complaining about their rough existence among the riffraff there in the Piedmont, always talking of her England-this and her Randolph-that. I wonder if she wasn't a blithering fool and that her snobbery was the source of that great chip Jefferson had on his shoulder toward people who were rich, powerful, aristocratic and entitled — people just like himself. It was all mixed up with the pain of her coldness and her distance as a mother."

Rachel and I gazed wide-eyed at the two of them. Kant waited proudly for Jefferson's response, a smug grin on his face. Jefferson sat ramrod straight but with a calm, almost beatific expression.

"I must ask, my dear sir," Jefferson said, "if all professors in this day and age indulge in the pursuit of such piffle. The state of Mrs. Peter Jefferson's mind, and the effect of her behavior on her eldest son, is a matter that can never be proven, and so it can have no bearing on anything. It was not a concern anyone thought about in those days and it cannot be now. Even if some theory such as yours could be proven, what's the use of it? We all have our little burdens, and we all succeed or fail in spite of them, or because of them."

Kant, listening respectfully now, had put his elbows on his desk and brought the tips of his fingers lightly together. After a pause, during which the two smiled at each other, he tilted back his head and opened his mouth, making no sound for a moment, until finally he spoke the words, "Well said. You get an A."

Jefferson cocked his head. He didn't know what that meant.

Kant leaned forward, as if he were speaking to a dunce. "Oh. You don't know what an A grade means, I suppose. It means very good," he said, speaking the words "very good" very slowly, with an absurd emphasis on each syllable.

Rachel was blushing. I wanted to tell her she was working for a major asshole. Jefferson never waivered in his serenity. He turned his head and looked at us, without expression, then looked back at Kant.

"Well, my good professor, it is most kind of you to give us some of your time. I look forward to reading your work over the coming season."

Jefferson stood up and bowed. Kant watched him, then stood up, too. I thought for a second that a flash of fear flickered over his face.

"Well then, Mr. Jefferson. It's an honor to meet you," he said, extending his hand, which Jefferson took and shook with a warm smile.

"Goodbye," Jefferson said.

Kant lifted his eyebrows and turned to look at Rachel

"Oh," she said. "Thanks so much for meeting him."

We got up.

"A pleasure, Rachel. For you, anything," Kant said, "anything at all."

"Miss Carter, Mr. Arrowsmith," Jefferson said, after going to the door, opening it and stepping aside for us to pass.

"I'll see you, professor," a rattled Rachel called back through the doorway. "Thank you so much."

"Bye-bye now," Kant said.

Jefferson leaned in to grab the doorknob. He said nothing to Kant as he pulled the door closed, turned to us and, striding forward toward the stairwell, said, "Let's move right along, then, my friends."

Rachel looked panicked. Jefferson's cheeks blazed with his now familiar crimson flush. "What a peculiar man," he said with an air of exasperation. Rachel looked at him as we started down the stairs, surprised, I think, that he wasn't angry or miserable. She broke into a smile of relief.

"You told him," she said joyfully.

"I think so," Jefferson said.

"I'm so sorry I did not see that coming," Rachel said. "I'm going to tell him I couldn't believe how rude he was. So … he thinks you're odd. You *are* odd. I'm sorry I dragged you in there to meet him."

"No, my dear. Don't you remember? I insisted. I'll win him over. Do you really consider me odd?"

Chapter 17

Rachel drove us up to Yonkers in her battered Saab, making a stop at Broadway and 116th Street to pick up her best friend Sandra, a senior at Barnard who played on the varsity basketball team and was majoring in American history; Sandra's boyfriend Sam, a medical student in preppy crewneck sweater and khakis; and Chris, Sam's best friend, a grad student in English with a beard and glasses wearing a black T-shirt and black pants.

James Lewis Carter lived in a faded two-and-a-half story, 100-year-old Queen Anne row house on Buena Vista Street, a section of Yonkers hard on the railroad tracks and the Hudson River. It was where Rachel grew up after she and her father had moved north from Virginia. A small, compact black man with short salt-and-pepper hair met us at the door dressed in gray flannels, a blue button-down shirt and a gray cardigan sweater. He greeted us a little wearily, the whites of his old brown eyes yellowed and the irises rimmed by milky rings.

After introductions in the hall, the house smelling deliciously of whatever he was cooking, Mr. Carter invited us into a gloomy living room with stucco walls, dark oak trim around the windows and doorways and an oak floor visible between a couple of well-worn dark cinnamon-colored Persian rugs. There was an upright piano against a wall and Jefferson went straight for it.

"Ah! A fine spinet!" he said.

Mr. Carter paid no attention to him. He leaned to me and

told me he was sorry about my boy Ben. "He was a fine young man. Helped me out around here."

"Really? He did? Ben? You mean fixing things? Chores?"

"Replaced all the insides of the upstairs toilet. Fixed a leak in a faucet. That sort of thing. He liked my black-eyed peas and molasses, Ben did."

"Oh! Good!" I said, trying not to seem startled.

"Where did you find this lovely instrument?" Jefferson asked excitedly, caressing the top edge of the piano.

"That's my upright," Mr. Carter said. "Brought it up with us from Virginia. That was my mama's. She played mighty well."

"Really?" Jefferson asked, a little troubled. "Well, well! I had a portable grand at one time," he added with enthusiasm, "made by young Mr. Hawkins of Philadelphia. Do you play, Mr. Carter?" he asked, holding one arm cocked behind his back as he leaned over to investigate the keyboard. The hair was still shorter and thinner on the back of his head, not quite covering a slight bump and a bruise.

"I do," Mr. Carter said, "now and then, when the mood strikes me. It's not often. Not much point in playing alone. I play the church piano on Sundays and that's enough for me."

The younger people took their places in the living room, Sandra and Sam perched on the couch, attentive but not entirely comfortable. Chris sat in an armchair, looking bored. Rachel had brought them for cover, I guessed, to make the evening less likely to erupt into something ugly with her father.

Still standing, I studied the slightly frayed and faded floral upholstery of the heavy couch and matching armchairs. I imagined they and all the furnishings had come down through his family, like the piano, from the early part of the 20th century. It didn't look as if he'd bought anything new in decades. There was no computer or iPod dock, no TV or stereo, no artwork on the walls, no photos on tabletops or the mantel except for one small cluster on the upright, which Jefferson called me over to enjoy with him — all snapshots of Rachel at different ages, from toddler to college graduate. The only other sign of life was a recessed nook across the room two steps up from the floor. It contained bookshelves, and an armchair, side table and standing lamp for reading.

"I hope you might play for us later," Jefferson said as he went to take a seat in an armchair. I went to the couch to join Sandra and Sam. Mr. Carter remained in the hallway with Rachel, ready to go to the kitchen, I guessed. "If I had a fiddle," Jefferson added, "I'd join you in something."

"A fiddler, just like the Jefferson of old," Mr. Carter said.

"I have a fiddle upstairs, Mr. Jefferson. I play, or used to. You could have the use of it."

"Is that so?" Jefferson said. "How kind!" He held out his right hand, exercised the fingers and tested his wrist. "I'm terribly out of practice. It has been a very long time, but I must say my rheumatism has never been less of a bother."

"Mr. Jefferson," Mr. Carter said, "just how do you pass in this world, looking so much like the old master of Monticello?" He squinted one eye and tilted his head.

Jefferson looked at Rachel and me. "Oh. I've had no trouble." He bowed to Rachel's friends, one arm crooked behind his back, one leg forward. "I thank you all for accepting it."

They tittered. "No problem," Chris said. "We see a lot of weird people around Columbia."

The others glared at him. He looked puzzled then hunched his shoulders and slapped the side of his face. "Oh. Sorry."

"I am related to the man," Jefferson said, ignoring Chris and sticking to the script he should have used with Kant. "I assume my parents saw some resemblance in me even as an infant. My, isn't that strange?"

"Oh yes, very strange," Mr. Carter said. "And what do you do, Mr. Jefferson?"

Rachel's complexion was darkening by the second.

"I have an income," Jefferson said. "I am a dilettante and a philosopher."

Mr. Carter emitted a wordless exclamation of wonder, a two-noted hum that rose then fell, like "My, my!" without the words. "Philosopher! And an income! Wouldn't that be nice," he said, shaking his head. "Though I doubt you're a dilettante.

Dilettantes don't generally know what they're talking about."
Jefferson smiled. "Aha! Thank you, thank you, Mr. Carter,
for your confidence in me. I hope it isn't misplaced. And what
about yourself, sir? I hear you have a profession."

"Is that what you hear? Yes, I've been a cook all my life. It
goes way back in the family," he said, "all the way to slavery
time."

"Slavery time!" Jefferson said with his fixed smile. "Well.
Not many slaves were skilled chefs."

"That's true," Mr. Carter said with a grin and a tilt of his
head. "Not many at all. But some."

"And you yourself still practice the art?" Jefferson asked.

"Yes, I do. I'll keep at it until I drop dead. Or whatever it is
I'll do." He laughed wheezily. "I have a little coffee shop here in
town. We feature some favorite Southern items. I keep surprising them with a little French twist here and there." He chortled.
"I have to keep the money coming in for this girl of mine, even
with her scholarships."

"French twist? Is that so?" Jefferson said.

"Oh, desserts mostly. I make a nice meringue. No one here
in town knows what it is but they like it. The yuppies wrote me
up once in The New York Times. You know, telling white people
to come up and try out the crazy black man's little dive in Yonkers. We had a good bump for a few months but it didn't last.
Rachel helped with the waitressing."

"I didn't know all this about your father," I said to Rachel.
"I didn't know you worked for him as a waitress."

She shrugged. "Had to. My dad's business."

Jefferson gazed distractedly at the recess full of books. He
asked if he might go look at them. "Of course," Mr. Carter said,
and Jefferson got up and stepped into the nook.

"Mr. Carter," I said, "you came up from Virginia, right? How
long have you been here in Yonkers? What brought you here?"

"Oh, I came up 15 or 20 years ago," he said, taking an armchair close to the fireplace. "Rachel was just a child. We were in
Emporia. Business was no good. My customers were all dying
or disappearing. The whites were moving into the countryside

around the city. They didn't go to me for a meal. They went to Cracker Barrel. They thought Cracker Barrel was real country cooking. The black people downtown, well, they didn't bother much with my food either," he said, "not the younger ones anyway. I just had the lonely old folks to feed, white and black."

"Did you have some connection that brought you here?" I asked.

Jefferson was bending down to peer at the shelves, pulling out volumes and reading the spines.

"I did. I had a sister up here. This was her house. Her husband passed and I moved in here with Rachel. Rachel went to school here. I started the coffee shop from scratch over on Hawthorne. My sister passed five years ago. She had the sugar and a bad heart. I've done pretty good and I've been able to take good care of my little girl." His eyes took on a vacant shine and he smiled glumly. "I miss Virginia, though."

"I, too, miss Virginia," Jefferson offered, looking up from a book. "It's my country, as well. At least the Piedmont is. Tell me, do you find this World Book Encyclopedia a useful reference? It is full of marvelous color pictures and some very elaborate typefaces," he said, holding up one volume and flipping through the pages. "I can see the printing process was one I do not understand at all."

"Oh, that's old. I got that for Rachel a long time ago. But I use it. It's good enough, if you want a white man's view of the world at the time, you know."

"That's for sure," Sam said. "Your pre-internet version of reality, too."

"You should be Googling, Mr. Carter," Jefferson said. "I Google, but with a healthy skepticism." He peered at a low shelf. "I see you have some works of American history," he said, taking another book. "Ah. 'The Ideological Origins of the American Revolution' by Bernard Bailyn," Jefferson read aloud from the cover. "Is this good?"

"Interesting, yes, yes. It was more about money than he thinks, though. It was all about money."

Jefferson looked at Mr. Carter. "Money! It certainly was.

What is *not* about money?"

"Well now! I thought it was you, Mr. Jefferson who wrote otherwise in 1776," said Mr. Carter with a strange, almost wicked smile. "Some things are about honor. Some things are about human rights and human dignity, not bailing out a pack of spendthrift planters in debt to English bankers at the public expense."

Jefferson blanched. He fumbled for a reply but he was tongue-tied, his eyes fixed blindly on the table, the color rushing to his face.

Rachel, ignoring the conversation with a hostess's smile, brought two chairs from the dining room, one for herself and one for her father. "Come on, Daddy, sit down," she said, motioning him to sit. After he grumpily took a seat, she went about serving everyone wine.

Handing Jefferson a glass, she whispered loud enough for everyone to hear, "Please don't mind Daddy when he gets testy."

Jefferson blinked and looked at the wine.

"Before dinner?" he said. She ignored the question and continued to deliver wine.

Jefferson soon seemed fine again, eager — I suspected — to pretend that Mr. Carter had not touched a nerve. He drew out Rachel's friends about their classes. When he learned of Sandra's European history courses and her plans to go to the School of International Affairs at Columbia, Jefferson brightly challenged her to give us a "seven-minute summary of European history from the 18th century to the modern day."

She bashfully protested but then rose to the challenge like a brilliant contestant on a game show, firing out her facts like a machine gun and blurting out a last sentence about the wavering stability of the European Economic Union — just as Rachel called "Time!" Sandra collapsed into her seat with a jubilant laugh. We all applauded, including Jefferson.

Mr. Carter excused himself and, heading into the kitchen, said over his shoulder that we were having something he was sure Jefferson would like.

Jefferson kept the students buzzing about history, politics

and life on campus. He asked each for an assessment of President Obama and each expressed disappointment with him "for being so centrist," as Sam put it. "Oh, that's the way it always is with one's constituents," Jefferson said. "Once you try to govern, many of them damn you as loudly as your enemies had been doing all along." That stopped the conversation cold. The kids gawked at him with silly grins.

"I only mean," Jefferson said brightly, "it's a fact of history." They nodded and let it go.

When Rachel announced that dinner was served, we ambled in, spreading around the table as she instructed each of us where to sit. Jefferson stood frozen, ignoring her instructions and looking ashen. "How did you know?" he asked Mr. Carter, who was standing in the kitchen doorway, wiping his hands with a dishtowel.

"Oh now, anyone can read books about Mr. Jefferson and what he liked."

Rachel took his arm and gently nudged him to the head of the table. "Daddy wants you here," she said. "He says it's only right." Jefferson, speechless, let her maneuver him to his place.

The entrée was boeuf à la mode, a favorite from his days in Paris and the White House: a beef eye round baked for hours in an iron casserole like a pot roast, with salt pork, cayenne pepper, cloves, allspice, carrots and onions, served with "mushroom catsup" gravy. We all learned from Mr. Carter that "catsup" did not refer to anything made of tomatoes, originally; it simply meant a kind of relish.

For side dishes, he served fried asparagus and mashed potatoes and, after the meal, a green salad with a dressing of vinegar and sesame oil. For dessert we had gingerbread, lemon curd tarts and ice cream — all favorites at Monticello long ago.

Jefferson insisted on tiny portions but ate enthusiastically and talked almost manically, especially after the plates had been taken away and we lingered over our wine. He offered catty character studies of Patrick Henry, Benjamin Franklin and George Washington. He claimed that long ago the temperature in Paris for days and days one winter did not rise above 20 degrees below zero, a peculiar assertion I think we all found very hard to believe. He asked if anyone had ever seen a mastodon or at least knew of anyone who had seen one and he grilled the students on their lives, their studies and the rules they had to follow on campus and in the dormitories.

Sometimes, as the dinner conversation rose and fell, I thought I saw a hint of worry in his eyes.

Back in the living room, he drew us out on the Civil War, Lincoln, the Emancipation Proclamation, Dr. King and the civil rights movement, World War II and "our more recent military engagements." There were no awkward moments this time. Jefferson created so much conversational momentum we all lost ourselves in it — all but Mr. Carter, who seemed reserved, listening with a slight frown and at times glaring at an obliviously cheerful Jefferson. I knew Jefferson was too keen an observer to have missed Mr. Carter's odd distance and strange looks. I wondered if his enthusiasm and good cheer were an act.

A weird thing popped into my head during the after-dinner chatter. I had to fight off an overwhelming urge to tell everyone about a kind of firecracker I'd known when I was a kid that was called a "nigger chaser."

No, don't do it, I kept telling myself. Don't do it.

Nigger chasers were little tubes, about three inches long and a half-inch in diameter, wrapped in red paper with a fuse protruding from a skirt at one end. Light the fuse and run away and, in a few seconds, the thing shoots into the air with a whistling shriek, emitting sparks as it screams at high C, zigzagging in frantic loops for three or four seconds before exploding. Apparently, its flight seems to have reminded us white people of a negro trying to evade the hounds or a mob.

As a little kid, I had thought it was very strange that someone could walk into a gas station along the highway in North Carolina and buy something they called a nigger chaser, right out loud. It was proof to me of Southern "prejudice," as we referred to it when I was a boy. Such a quaint word, "prejudice." "Racism" and "racist" were not in the lexicon, except as technical terms for what the Nazis practiced. Nazis were racists and there were none left after World War II. They had all been killed or they had surrendered and reformed themselves and there weren't any of those mad-scientist Jew-killers left anymore. So I believed in fifth grade.

What can we make of the "nigger chaser," I wanted to ask the group. Had anyone heard of it? Could anyone imagine a time when a product with those words printed on its side would have been sold to people who didn't give the name a second thought, travelers on their way home to New Jersey and Connecticut from the South, that crazy far-away land where fireworks were legal and black people were made to sit at the back of the bus?

I managed to keep my mouth shut, busying myself with Jefferson and Mr. Carter, watching them for signs of trouble. As Mr. Carter's glares became obvious, I worried that the party might end with a scene or at least a sour note. If Rachel was worried, too, she gave no hint of it. She was a good soldier. Or waitress, I should say — doing her duty, puttering around pouring wine, cleaning up the kitchen.

After she brought out Madeira, Jefferson said — for no reason that I could fathom — that the country had "successfully integrated its black citizens into society," or so it seemed to him. Mr. Carter smirked. Sam and Chris looked at each other almost sheepishly. There was a long silence that Mr. Carter broke, snarling that the country owed its black citizens an apology and the payment of reparations.

After another silence, Chris shrugged and looked anxiously at Sam, who averted his eyes. "Well, you know what?" Chris said bravely, "I think we're past all that. I think black people now have every opportunity to succeed if they work hard and have the right attitude. Success in the system is reparation enough."

Sandra nearly jumped out of her seat. "You've got to be kidding me!" she scolded. "That's what you believe? Have you looked at any of the statistics? Things like income, life expectancy, education levels, rates of illiteracy and unemployment?"

She shoved Chris's shoulder. "Just because your family broke out, you think everybody can if they just *try hard*?" She said the last two words loud and slow and shook her head. "Man. You boys sure are some stupid niggers."

Mr. Carter sat up straight, raised a finger in the air and fixed his eyes on her. "Don't use that word in my house," he said.

Sandra froze. "Oh. I'm sorry, Mr. Carter. I apologize."

No one moved except Jefferson. He leaned forward, holding his chin and squinting, seemingly oblivious to the tense moment. "Mr. Carter, perhaps we could try working toward your goal," he said.

"My goal? You mean an apology and reparations? How's that?" Mr. Carter said.

Jefferson leaned back and crossed his long legs. "Perhaps," he said after a moment, "we could undertake a campaign to win at the very least an acknowledgement of the nation's debt and perhaps the construction of a monument to the bondsman's labor in the federal city. I have some experience in these things. I would be happy to meet with your congressman and senators, if it could be arranged. I could establish contacts with the press. Finding writers to take up a good cause cannot be too hard these days. Perhaps the president would be interested. I'll write him."

Rachel and I glanced at each other. Jefferson, I feared, had lapsed into some kind of delusional state to which perhaps ghosts were especially prone. Everyone stared at him dumbly except Mr. Carter, who grinned.

"Well, now, Mr. Jefferson," he finally said. "Sounds like you have connections in Washington!" He chuckled, letting his gaze fall to his hands, which he folded together on the edge of the table. "Well. Isn't that friendly now. Thank you for your offer. I'm too grouchy and too disillusioned an old man for all that. I don't believe it could be successful."

Rachel stood up. "I have to go to the kitchen," she announced. "You just be nice, Daddy." Sandra, who hadn't said another word since "nigger," rose abruptly and followed her.

I started to get up, saying something about seeing if the ladies needed another hand in the kitchen, but Mr. Carter waved me down. "They got it," he said.

"No women's lib here," I quipped.

Jefferson turned to me. "Women's lib?"

"Women's liberation. We'll Google it," I said.

Jefferson smiled and looked at Mr. Carter. "That meal. It was remarkable to me. It might as well have been prepared by Jamie Hemings, our chef in Paris."

Mr. Carter lifted his brows. "Well, now. How about that? You know," he said with the same kind of fixed smile that Jefferson sometimes wore, "there's a story about Jefferson and James Hemings that came down through my family."

"Oh?" Jefferson said, giving no sign this topic had come up before, over muffins back in Charlottesville.

I slowly sat down again.

Mr. Carter made a small grunt. "Yes, yes, indeed. James Hemings was a difficult man," he said, leaning forward. "Gave old Massah Jefferson a lot of trouble. Worked in the house at Monticello, always close to the man. Great servant for him in Paris! A fine chef! But he had Jefferson over a barrel. He could have gone free in France and taken his sister with him. So he made that deal for himself with Jefferson about going free when they all got back to Virginia. Jefferson, gentleman that he was, signed a paper and when the time came he kept his word and let him go off the mountain. He kept Jamie's sister Sally for himself, of course. She didn't want to go anyway."

Jefferson raised his chin and offered a grim smile.

"Now, can you imagine what it was like in those days for a free black man trying to scratch out a living as a cook? Jamie didn't make it any easier on himself, I know. He was a drinker. I myself don't drink, Mr. Jefferson. Used to. But no more. Jamie did. He was what you call today a *prima donna*, too, I guess. Always expecting something special from the Jeffersons. But that's because he was so good at whatever he chose to do and always so close to them. And trusted. And don't forget. He was pretty darned white. He'd been given a taste of freedom and dignity, too, not a common thing for a man born into slavery.

Just a little taste of it, like a Jew at Auschwitz who's allowed to shine the commandant's boots because he's so good at it. Gives a slave a big head, you know?"

Jefferson cocked his head, his smile fixed. "Auschwitz?"

"But the same man," Mr. Carter said, ignoring him, "who gave James Hemings that dignity, he took it away, just when James Hemings needed it most. See, what happened was Jefferson made him an offer and then as fast as you can say 'Jimmy crack corn' he took it away. No sir! No job for him at the White House!"

Chris and Sam lowered their faces and peeked from under their brows at Jefferson, who never flinched or let his expression change.

"My, my, all things flowed from Mr. Jefferson, didn't they?" Mr. Carter went on. "Not from God. Or any natural order of things, as he had so eloquently told the world they did. They flowed from no one and nothing else but Mr. Jefferson. The Master."

I took Rachel's absence in the kitchen with Sandra as having been calculated. She had known this was coming. I wondered if she'd even prepared Jefferson for it.

"Mr. Carter," Jefferson finally said, "I believe you read too much into whatever traces of that matter were left to history. As does your daughter."

Rachel came to the kitchen doorway, holding a dishtowel and a plate. Sandra stood behind her. "Daddy," Rachel said.

"Well now, it's just a story," Mr. Carter said. He leaned back and chuckled. "Just a little story I know. Not many people do. And there's more to it. They found him hanging by the neck, you know. Naked as a jaybird, twisting under a meat hook."

"Well, that's enough," Rachel said.

He eyed her a while then abruptly nodded. "Well. Sorry to get carried away," he said. "Your name and your resemblance to the man himself warm my blood, Mr. Jefferson."

"Quite all right," Jefferson said quietly, his eyes fixing at the table before him.

Rachel's friends mumbled about schoolwork they had to

get back to.

"Well," Jefferson said, folding his arms. "It has been a long day for me."

"Oh! Everybody just wait a second!" Rachel exclaimed. She ran upstairs and came back down with a battered violin case. "It's old, but I keep it in tune," Mr. Carter said, looking at it wearily.

Rachel gave it to Jefferson, who had warmed at the sight of it, opening it reverently. "Just go play something with him on the spinet, will you, Daddy?" Rachel asked.

Mr. Carter reached for her from his chair. She stepped toward him and put her hand on his shoulder. "I will, child," he said, trying to smile but rattled and tired all of a sudden.

"Very nice," Jefferson said as he studied the violin. "This is quite old indeed, isn't it?"

"It's been in the family a long time," Mr. Carter said, grunting as he got himself up out of the chair.

"You wouldn't by any chance know 'Broom of Cowden-knowes,' would you?" Jefferson asked.

Mr. Carter nodded. "Sure I do. Who wouldn't?"

Jefferson grinned. "Well now, I'm so pleased to hear it. Will you join me in it?"

They went to the piano while Chris, Sam and I took our seats in the living room. Rachel sat down on the staircase, a few steps up, where she seemed to study Jefferson like an art student taking in every detail of a Michelangelo.

An old Scottish ballad, it was a simple tune, not a challenge for either of them to play, I supposed, but sad and beautiful. At a point near the end, Jefferson lowered his violin and, letting Mr. Carter continue to play, he sang in a clear, fine voice: "*Adieu ye bonny yewes, adieu; farewell all pleasures there; to wander by her side again is all I crave or care.*"

He gave a little bow and looked up at Rachel with a cheery smile. Mr. Carter turned from his piano bench, smiling, too. We all clapped, except for Rachel, who watched in a kind of happy trance as her father got up and shook Jefferson's hand.

She stayed with her father that night, telling us she'd take the train into the city in the morning. I took the Saab and, with Jefferson riding in front, drove her friends to the Broadway gate of the Columbia campus. After they got out and Jefferson was settling back into his seat, they crossed in front of the car heading off to their dorms. It was a cool night but I had the driver's window open so we could hear him when Sam said, "Damn, that was wild. What a creepy weirdo that red-headed freak is."

Jefferson patted my hand. "It's nothing. I'm well used to contempt and mockery. Don't worry about me, Mr. Arrowsmith. I understand my dilemma."

We sat together on the couch until 2 in the morning, watching "It Happened One Night" on AMC. Jefferson said "Oh my!" and laughed at Claudette Colbert showing her leg to get a ride. I slept on the couch and, in the morning, shook his hand, promised to see him soon and took a cab out to LaGuardia, where I grabbed the shuttle to Washington to go fetch my car.

Chapter 18

Before our trip, I had established a simple, well-ordered world for myself and now I tried to restore it. Ben's journal was not part of it. When I got home, I put the notebook back in the drawer where Rachel had found it.

That did not keep me from thinking about him. I had loved Ben, beyond all measure, but liking him had been a different matter. Something happened after he'd reached a certain age. Money was everything for Ben. His goal in life was to have it in quantity. I worried he did not have much of a soul and wondered how I'd failed him.

If Rachel had loved him, I must have been wrong. He was tall, handsome, athletic, smart, happy and gregarious. He succeeded at everything he did. He was the magna cum laude captain of the baseball team, with pretty girlfriends before Rachel who would last a year or less. What made Rachel different I did not know. Somehow she had found a way to make him love her. Now she seemed to belong to Jefferson in some mysterious way. But I was not at all sure she had aroused anything in him but the desire for sex with a beautiful and doting attendant.

I ignored all the mysteries. I worked on the house, my old car and the yard. I sat in the hammock after lunch, reading. I played golf at the club and I went to the gym. At night, I looked at the news and DVDs. Now and then I went out for dinner with friends from the club. Whatever I did, Jefferson and Rachel were always in the back of my mind in a troubling way.

She kept me up to date by phone. He wanted to buy a mockingbird and had been shocked to learn there were laws against keeping wild birds as pets. He had been hanging around bookstores and going out for dinner whenever Rachel could not cook for him so he needed more money. I sent a cashier's check for $38,578.76, the balance left in Ben's college fund. She used it to open an account at a Chase branch on Broadway. Until he somehow acquired a legal identity, she would have to dole out the money and pay his bills.

I bought myself a new laptop and soon began to receive email notifications of his purchases on iTunes: Mozart, Vivaldi, something called "The 50 Most Essential Pieces of Classical Music," the original soundtrack to "Gone With The Wind," the "Grand Canyon Suite," a blues album called "Blue Highway" and, of all things, "Remember Al Jolson, Vol. I."

He'd asked me to avoid calling him during his "trial of independency" so I emailed to ask why Al Jolson. He replied in a tone that, to me, read as if I had bothered him: "Dear Sir: I discovered this performer while Googling musical topics. I was struck by his use of the blackened face. Late in life I heard of musical shows in which white actors and dancers appeared as negroes. Blacks had a great sense of rhythm, you know. I was most curious. With every sentiment of friendship. Th:J."

When friends and their wives had me to dinner, I talked about Monticello's beautiful sky at dusk, the water stain on the floor by Jefferson's bed, the incredible scale of the territory he'd brought into the Union with the Louisiana Purchase and the charm, confidence and calculated reserve I sensed in the man when I read his letters to John Adams. I also talked about his courtliness and dignity. I drank too much wine but never made a scene.

"He's a great man," I said to the bafflement of one set of hosts.

"Well, I don't know," said my friend Jim Hudgins. "You really think so? Slave master and all that? Abuser of his housemaid?"

"Damn right, I think he was a great man," I said, too loudly. "He didn't abuse anybody."

I was among a small group of retired men who met for lunch every Thursday at the Bergenfield diner. We talked politics, books, movies, history and assorted diseases and orthopedic conditions. I sometimes made them talk about Jefferson. They all seemed to believe he had fallen from the Founders' pantheon because of his hypocrisies, which annoyed the hell out of me. "You all should move to Texas and run for the school board," I told them. None had ever been to Monticello. None had any sense of the man. And none, including myself, could count a single black person as a close friend.

When the weather turned warm again, I thought even more about Monticello and the stuffy Dome Room where Rachel had spotted him in the window. On the golf course, I asked my partner if he knew that Sally Hemings was actually the half-sister of Jefferson's wife. No, he didn't know that. "Isn't that something?" he said vaguely as he kneeled down to assess the slope of the green for his putt.

I received a letter from Jefferson, written on fine paper. It was another apology for his dependence on me and more thanks for my support. He reflected on the oddity of his situation and his determination to reconstruct himself as best he could.

"Dr. Franklin believed in resurrection and the afterlife," he wrote, "and I had my hopes for it, but cannot fathom what the purpose of this vestigial existence can be, other than lashings from Miss Carter and her father for all my transgressions. But I perceive a conviction of design, consummate skill and infinite power in every atom of the universe. There must be a purpose that is beyond our powers to comprehend."

He wrote that he'd been doing a lot of reading. Our war in Iraq had been a grave mistake, he'd decided. We'd had no choice in Afghanistan and should not have divided our attention from it with the Iraq invasion. He wondered about the "shockingly pervasive" influence one man, "Cheney, the vice president before Mr. Biden," seemed to have had in the operation of the federal government.

Jefferson was a very fast learner indeed. "No system of government can be devised which will rule out the ascension of a dictator, if the mass of people are deluded," he wrote.

He was attempting to address "the great question of slavery and the failure of myself and my fellow Virginians to remove this stain on our country," he wrote. "It is my hope to assist historians in their thinking about my role in those times."

Good luck with that, I thought.

Rachel came out one weekend. I had promised myself I'd begin reading Ben's journal by then — I'd decided I'd been wrong to ignore it — but when she called to say she was coming I decided to wait a few more days.

I was on the porch in my jeans, a T-shirt and old sweater reading a Shelby Foote Civil War book when the Saab pulled into my driveway. I stepped down onto the lawn and she walked straight into my arms — I opened them just in time — and wrapped me in a hug. Feeling a silent sigh escape from my chest, I kissed her forehead.

"Where is himself?" I asked.

"He couldn't come right now. He's sick. He's got to stay in," she said.

"With what?"

"Diarrhea. And terrible headaches."

"Oh wow. Those are old afflictions for him. He must be stressed out," I said. "Poor bastard."

We sat at the kitchen table and talked over coffee. "He studies and writes in the mornings," Rachel said, hunching forward over the table with her arms tucked hard against her sides. "He walks all over the city in the afternoons. He keeps pestering people, complete strangers on the street, black people, about their family histories. So I've been told by some of the music students he knows from next door."

So the ghost of Thomas Jefferson was haunting people in Morningside Heights. I said I hoped he was all right. "You know, I've been wondering," I added, "if Ben and Pam are going to peek into my windows one night. I haven't been sleeping too well."

"You haven't read the journal," Rachel said. "I can tell."

"I am afraid to read that thing. I had gotten myself settled down about Ben and Pam. Then we found our Mr. Jefferson and now I don't know what the hell I'm doing or how anything is supposed to work. How can I open those pages and bring Ben back to life on top of it all? It's too damned painful."

"I know," she said, looking sadly at the table.

"And why do you want me to read it? That notebook would have sat in that drawer forever if you hadn't dug it out."

She bit her lip, hesitating. "I was afraid you'd find it. I wanted to make sure you didn't. But then I began to think I'd made a mistake, that it wasn't my place to keep it from you. It's yours. He was your son. You have unfinished business with him. You two were all screwed up."

"Oh brother. This doesn't sound good," I muttered. I got up to make a couple of sandwiches. Neither of us spoke. I put the sandwiches on plates, brought them to the table and sat back down. "All screwed up. Yeah, okay. So. Hey. Speaking of screwed up, what are you doing with this man? I mean, are you there with him all the time, Rachel?"

"No, not all the time. I come when he needs me."

I gave her a look. "When he needs you? That doesn't sound right, Rachel. What are you? His servant? It's been driving me a little crazy trying not to think about whatever the hell it is you two are doing."

"It's driving me a little crazy, too," she said. "I don't know what the hell we're doing. We're all screwed up, too."

"Maybe you need to figure that out."

"I know, Jack. You too. Figure your thing out. For Ben's sake."

I considered saying, "Ben's dead," but, of course, so was Jefferson. It seemed a touchy subject.

We ate our sandwiches and lapsed into small talk about Elmer Kant and her coursework and after lunch we went for a walk. It was a hazy end-of-summer New Jersey day, almost Southern in its languor. We passed my neighborhood's sprawling ranch houses and postwar colonials with their perfectly manicured yards and turned onto the old main road, laid out in colonial times. Treading on old slate sidewalks tilted by the roots of ancient maples, we headed down the hill toward the village.

We ran out of things to talk about. "Thomas is very high maintenance," she blurted to break the silence. "He leaves everything in piles. He throws his clothes on the floor. He's got newspapers and magazines and books everywhere."

"He's used to a big staff," I said, "people buzzing around him all the time to meet his needs. Have you and he seen your father again?"

"No, no. He's angry with me. He doesn't understand why I've befriended this man. I think he knows it's really him, Jack. I think he knows that man is Thomas Jefferson himself." She stopped walking and stared at the sidewalk. "There's something strange about the way my father speaks of him to me. As if he's been expecting him to show up in my life."

I put my hand on her shoulder. We started walking again, our arms across each other's backs. "I like your father. He just wants to watch out for you," I said.

She ignored me. "He's going to go through that money you sent in a few months," she said.

"I know. He's like having a kid again."

We browsed through a couple of shops. She bought him a wide-brimmed straw hat meant for gardeners. Back at the house, we sat and talked on the couch as the shadows reached across my yard. After an hour, we hugged and I stood on my front lawn watching her drive away.

Chapter 19

Rachel called me that night from her dorm room to say I had to read Ben's journal. She'd intended to tell me so that afternoon but she'd failed to gather the courage. Jefferson had convinced her to try again.

"It's that bad? Then I'm sure I don't want to read it," I said.

"Is he there now? With you?"

She said he wasn't. He was at his apartment, probably, or at the School of Music next door, or visiting with Kant, or strolling Broadway to look into the bookstores near campus. Or down in Harlem, talking to black people, which she wished to he wouldn't do so aggressively.

"Talking to black people? What the hell is that? He's going to get beat up again or worse. Did you let him read the journal?" I asked.

"No, no, Jack. I just told him a little about it. He called it a tragedy, a son's misunderstanding of his father," she said.

Her sniffle broke our long silence. Her voice thicker than before, she said Ben had known I'd cheated on Pam and that's what started the whole mess in his mind.

At first, I had no idea what she meant. "What? Cheated?" I squawked. And then the memory slowly came back to me.

"Oh! Oh, God almighty," I said in a low groan. "The teacher. The *teacher*. Oh for Christ's sake! Are you kidding? Ben *knew*? That was nothing. It was one night. It didn't matter! It was a terrible mistake! It never affected my family, it caused no harm!"

"Ben knew. He believed you drove Pam to find another

man," Rachel said.

I was so distracted I did not process what she'd said. The forgotten memories of my adultery were coming back in jagged pieces and I struggled to put them together like a man hit by a wave trying to find his footing.

Ben had been about 16. The teacher was a sad young woman who taught English in the middle school. It was after a party Pam did not attend. She was traveling, handling a case in Washington. The teacher was a newlywed who'd had a fight with her husband. He'd walked out.

We went to her place. I can't remember her name. Cheryl, Sherry, Sheila. She cried afterward. I felt old and mean. I apologized — probably the worst thing I could have done — and left. I never touched her again. I would say hello to her politely in the halls, my smile a death's head grin. It felt like one, anyway. She left school at the end of the year and I never saw her again.

"Oh Christ," I said to Rachel as those shards were still falling into place. "I'd forgotten all that. Shit. It was a very minor crime compared to your man Jefferson's."

"Jack ..."

"Okay, look, I'll read it. I'll read the journal and we'll talk about it if you're now in the personal catharsis business."

"Jack, I didn't mean ..."

I hung up and went to find the journal. I took it outside and sat on my deck. I needed some time to gather my wits before I opened it. I could almost hear the air roaring out of my life.

This is what he wrote:

My father and I have barely talked in months. I've been angry with him because I blame him for my mother's death. I know he cheated on her. For a long time, I have believed his cheating is what drove her to cheat on him. Why didn't they just get a divorce? My mother loved my father, I understand now, and he loved her. That was hard for me to see until I had a very strange experience after my mother died and I took Rachel on a trip to Monticello.

Mom and Dad taught me to love Monticello. They took me there a few times as a kid and I always remembered the visits because they seemed so happy together. I never saw them like that except there. So it seemed. I'm not the kind of person who is sentimental about places and things, like my father. But Monticello does get to me: it's beautiful, balanced, orderly, and it has this glow for me. In my mind, it was always sunny there.

Our trips to the mountain had been Dad's idea. He was the Jefferson fan, which I came to consider a little silly when I started to study history seriously. I think Dad's attraction for Jefferson was a little creepy. Forget slavery and the "Notes on the State of Virginia," forget even the Declaration of Independence and the Kentucky Resolves. For Dad, it was all about Jefferson's house and gardens, his French mirrors and Philadelphia harpsichord, his monogrammed shirts, his blooded horses, his wine and fine food and his unmitigated gall. Dad didn't have those tastes in life. He was just a regular middle school history teacher — okay, he was WASPy, which was unusual and kind of old-farty for a public school teacher — with an aging car he loved and a couple of tweed jackets he never got rid of. When Mom started making us rich, it didn't change anything about him, except I think he was a little lost when we moved to the bigger house and got a maid.

I thought of going to Monticello after Mom died because it was there Dad seemed to love Mom most. It was the warmer, easier way they talked to each other, holding hands as we walked on Jefferson's garden paths. Somehow those memories made it easier for me to grieve for Mom without feeling so bad. Monticello cleared away all the clutter and made things simple again.

I looked up from the notebook and out across my lawn. Had I known Ben could think and write like this? No, I hadn't. It was a shock.

When I took Rachel there, and we walked the same paths Dad and Mom had walked from the house down to the family cemetery, I started to think maybe my father didn't deserve the anger I felt toward him, no matter what he had done.

I knew he had cheated on Mom because I'd seen it with my own eyes. I was sitting in the back seat of a car with some friends waiting for a girl to come out of her house one night. We were parked on a street in Bergenfield near an old brick apartment house. I saw Dad's car down the street. I saw him get out with this teacher I knew from school and I saw them go in the doorway.

I never told him that I'd seen him. I should have. Instead I started sassing him all the time. I just gave him a lot of crap and I had as little to do with him as possible. It went downhill from there and things got pretty bad between us. He'd sit me down and say let's work this out and I'd just clam up. I didn't tell Mom either, of course. She thought I was going through a phase. He thought I was just an entitled prick for whom life had been way too easy. That's what he said once when he tried to pick a fight with me, right before I left for college. I didn't bite even though some of the things he said hurt me pretty good. There was some truth in it.

Maybe it all would have blown over eventually but I avoided going home when I started at Columbia. I'd see Mom in the city. We'd have lunch or dinner. She'd tell me I had to clear up this thing with my father. She said he was depressed. She also got on me about how fast I went through girlfriends. I made some joke, I don't remember what. Dad was right. I was a smart-ass.

We had truces. At Christmas, I'd go home and Dad and I would be polite to each other. But that was it. He had no idea why I hated him. I think it drove him crazy. It started to make me feel kind of sick and ugly when I started going with Rachel and she started talking to me about the problems between me and Dad. She said I should stop acting like some Sicilian with a vendetta and go talk to him. She'd never met Dad but she saw a picture of him at the house — I took her out to Saddle River to see the house once when both Mom and Dad were away — and she said he looked kind, which annoyed me.

When I decided to get my MBA and got into Harvard, he tried to be nice about it. He said I was smarter than he'd ever been. "No, no," I said. "You have to do what feels right for yourself. You're a teacher, Dad, a great one." I don't know where that had come from but I believed it. It didn't clear the air. He nodded and clammed up. What a jerk he could be. He thought I was bullshitting him.

Then I started to notice bruises on Mom's hands. She said some guy in a plane had shoved a suitcase into the overhead rack while her hands were in the way and banged them up. It sounded a little weird to me. Some other time when I saw bruises on her arms, she said she had fallen during a tennis game. I wondered if she was getting into fights with Dad. Real fights, punches and smacks. Nothing like that had ever happened before, not when I was at home. Dad was not the type to hurt anybody. But she kept saying how worried she was about him, and how she wished he and I could talk and work things out.

She was looking pretty tired, as if things weren't going so well, and all I could think was that Dad had flipped out and was hurting her. I started to think I had to go home and confront him. I dreaded that. I have to admit I was scared. I was having trouble sleeping. Rachel said she was worried about me. She kept telling me to go home and work it out. That only made me nuttier. I didn't understand what was happening to me: I was afraid and that seemed to paralyze me. I'd never been afraid like that before.

I looked up. I couldn't remember when we'd told Ben about Pam's cancer. I looked back down at the page, took a deep breath and forced myself to read on.

I was at Grand Central one day with Rachel and some friends. We were going skiing and taking a train. She didn't know how to ski but we were going to teach her. We had some time to kill before the train so we hung around in the station just watching people. We were all kidding around near the clock at the information booth when I saw Mom come down onto the floor of the station, out of the escalator from the MetLife Building. She looked so tired. She was walking straight toward me. She put on a big smile but she looked worn out and the smile looked all wrong. I didn't move or say anything to anyone around me. I just watched her. At first I thought she'd seen me. I started to walk toward her but then I realized she wasn't looking at me, she was looking at someone behind me. I got this panicky feeling and I stepped behind Rachel, who looked at me funny. Mom never saw me. She walked right by us and a few yards away she went up to this tall, well-dressed black man, a good-looking guy in a suit, and put her arms around him. He looked pissed. He didn't put his arms around her. I couldn't believe it. I felt dizzy or sick, I don't know what.

But it got worse. He kind of grabbed her and walked off with her by the arm. I told Rachel to wait, to stay there, I had to go, I'd be back, and I headed after them into the crowd. I didn't realize it at first but Rachel followed me. She saw everything I saw. The man, holding Mom by the arm, led her down a concourse to one of the dark dirty platforms where there was no train and no people. He stood there yelling at her. I couldn't hear what he said because of the hum and noise from nearby trains but he held her by the arms and he was shaking her.

I hate writing this. It hurts to think about it and it hurts even worse to write it down. But it's my assignment, part of the therapy deal.

All of a sudden he slapped her hard and even over the noise of the other trains I heard her crying. I just stood there, paralyzed, freaked out and stuck to the floor. I can't believe I didn't do anything for her. I should have killed that guy. Rachel said "Oh my God" behind me and took my hand. She pulled me back. That's why I didn't do anything, that's why I didn't go down there and beat the shit out of that asshole. But I know that's crap. I think I made that up as an excuse. I was stuck, frozen. And when he started to turn her around and take her back up the ramp toward us, the only thing I could think of was getting away. I did not want Mom to know I'd seen it.

My mother was not the sort of woman to take abuse and beatings. She just wasn't. It made no sense to me. This story just did not fit. It made everything feel like even more of a mess. Rachel and I did not go skiing. We went back to her dorm. I was a wreck. As time passed, I turned it into something I could understand: It was all about being mad at myself for not having gone down the ramp and shoving that guy onto the tracks. Rachel tried to calm me down. When I stopped ranting, she said we had to help my mother. A day or two later, we were trying to figure out what we should do when Dad called to tell me she was sick. She had leukemia and it was bad.

I know leukemia can cause bruising. I still don't know if the bruises on her hands and arms had been from that guy or from the disease.

I could not read more for a long time. By the time I could go on, dusk had fallen and I read in the light from the kitchen windows.

I went home to see her. She was in bad shape. Dad had taken a leave from school to stay home and take care of her. They had nurses, too, full-time. Mom did not want to go to a hospital. I kept asking how it all happened so fast, didn't they know something was wrong, couldn't they have done something before it got so bad? They wouldn't answer me. They'd say pointless things like, "It's no one's fault" or "There's no reason to go into that, Ben."

"Ben, your father doesn't need this from you now," Mom said when Dad was out of the room. "He's got his hands full with me. Go back to school and come back when you calm down, all right? I'll get better. This happens in waves."

I was so twisted up that I guess anger was the only thing my brain could come up with. I was so pissed off at both of them for fucking things up so royally I couldn't think.

I just left. I went back to school and just lost it. Crying, smashing stuff, staring at the wall like a 14-year-old. Rachel couldn't help. I stopped seeing her. She would call and I'd let it ring but one day eventually I picked up and let her talk to me. She said I needed help handling all this, that I should see someone. I thought that was a load of crap. But I did it, finally, after Mom died. I don't know if she really expected to go into remission. Maybe she just didn't want me around when she died.

In my first session on the couch, the idea came up that I should go down to Monticello. I was feeling bad about Dad, which was something new, and we talked about that and pretty soon I decided I wanted to go.

It really did help when I went down there with Rachel. I was a little better by then anyway but it cleared away some of the clouds. I can't explain it. Somehow that place up on Jefferson's hilltop helped me think better. I'm a Hamilton man. Jefferson was a Pollyanna. But I love him because Dad loves him.

That's not the end. Rachel and I met a man and a woman at the Monticello cemetery — first the man. He was inside the black wrought-iron fence, which meant he had to be family. He said good day to us and tipped his hat and introduced himself through the fence as George Randolph. He was tall and skinny with reddish hair and when he spoke he always wrapped his arms across his chest. He wore the damnedest clothes, a longish jacket and a skinny ribbon bowtie and tapered slacks, very tight at the calves and something like a Confederate cavalryman's Hardee hat with a blue cockade and feather in it. When I asked him if he was a re-enactor of some kind, Rachel shoved me a little, like I'd been impolite. He smiled and said no, he was not a re-enactor, whatever that was.

"Have you come to see Mr. Jefferson's grave?" he asked.

I said we had.

He studied Jefferson's obelisk. "This wasn't what he designed. This is much larger. The original was so defiled by tourists that this monstrosity was erected by Congress here and the gates have been kept locked ever since."

Rachel asked where he was from.

"Oh, I'm from here. I left it for a time and it broke my heart to do so."

That shut us up for a minute. He seemed to forget about us. He looked at the obelisk and started walking. His legs were moving but I swear he kind of drifted more than walked as he slowly circled around it as if he were in a trance or something. We stared, both of us getting pretty freaked out. We didn't notice for a while that a woman — a young, very beautiful woman in an old-fashioned dress and bonnet — was standing in the enclosed area too. She must have been behind a cedar or stone at first. I don't know.

She walked straight toward us with a happy look. "Why, you are a beauty," she said to Rachel.

Rachel sort of reared back. "Oh! Thank you!"

"Are you one of our Hemingses? I'd swear you are one of our Hemingses."

Rachel looked at me and I looked back at her and laughed a little. "I don't know. My father says we may be related to the Hemingses but I never really believed him."

"Is that so? Well, I say you are one of our Hemingses and I swear I can see our Sally in you. I have to picture her because, of course, I didn't know her in her younger days, but when I do picture her, you are what I see."

"Really?" Rachel said, "You knew what she looked like when she was older?"

The woman looked all surprised. She had elegant, fine features and she this adorable forehead. I know that sounds weird but I'd never noticed a woman with such a pretty, high, gently rounded forehead. Her dress was low-cut and it showed off her collarbone and her neck and her modest cleavage. I don't know. She looked about 25. She was amazingly pretty.

"My name is Cornelia Randolph," she said pleasantly, as if that explained everything. "I never married, you know."

We didn't know.

"Hello, Geordie dear," she said as George drifted alongside her.

"We're family, you know," he said. "I had no children. We didn't have our own families, so the old one binds us forever. We hope you have children. They will free you from yourselves."

"Geordie, you were too young to know Sally well but perhaps you can see the likeness in this lovely yellow girl."

"Oh, I think I do, now that you mention it," he said cheerfully, peering at Rachel.

"Okay," I said, "This is pretty weird. Who are you people really?"

"Well! Who are you? You haven't said, which is not very nice," Cornelia said sweetly.

Rachel and I looked at each other again. We told them our names.

"A Carter! My goodness!" said Cornelia.

"Oh, now, that name," George said, holding his brow, "Arrowsmith, Arrowsmith. I swear I know it. Have you been here before?"

"Yes," I said, "a few times. With my father and mother."

"Do you know, I remember that?" he said. "We had a chat, I believe. It seems as if it was only moments ago. Just before you two came by. Did you see them? How are they? Lovely people, for Yankees."

I couldn't speak for a second. "They're not too good. My mom passed away."

Both said they were sorry to know it. "Ah. Gone in a flash. Yes, yes. But death is no tragedy," George said, "unless there are unresolved matters that bear on the soul. That's what we've found. My poor grandfather. I believe he had many unresolved matters, unbeknownst to himself — and for all his goodness to us. They were matters of the heart and soul that might not trouble a lesser man at all."

"My, I do wish we could see him," Cornelia said quietly, looking

off toward the house.

"I too, sister," George said. "One day, perhaps, we will. We have time on our side."

What these two strange people had said about death and unresolved things did not make much of an impression on me then. I thought they were creepy, eccentric Virginians who had an obsession with the past, a couple of wacky Jefferson descendants — they must have had the key to the graveyard gate — who dressed in old clothes and pretended to be his grandkids. I wanted to get away from them.

We said goodbye but for the rest of that trip Rachel and I couldn't stop thinking about them. It almost made me happy, having those strange people at the cemetery to talk about with Rachel. I figured they had given me a good excuse to call Dad. I could ask him if he and Mom had really talked to those people once. Maybe from there we could start to patch things up.

I've had a hard time doing it. I keep letting it slide. I don't know why. I'm afraid of him. I never was before. I didn't used to care if he disapproved of me. All of a sudden I seem to care a lot. What's up with that? Maybe I can find out next time I'm on the couch.

I cannot explain how lost I was, sitting out there in the dark, swept away by my own tears. We shield our souls in this life so well from life's tragedies. It is a rare thing to feel the full force of all one's sorrows in one terrible moment.

Chapter 20

The tall, well-dressed black man haunted me. I pictured him hitting my wife and thought about buying a handgun and hiring a detective to find him. I took the train to the city and stood in Grand Central for hours watching tall black men in suits as they strode across the polished marble floor. It was a sickening exercise.

After the weeping and the rages and all the fervid schemes to find the black man, I eased into a stupor, exhausted, sleeping until noon, eating old cans of beans or hash that had been in the pantry since my old life, when I had a wife and a son. I did not see Rachel or Jefferson for weeks. I did not see anybody. I ordered a new bed, box spring and mattress. I got it into my head that I could not sleep in the same bed in which I'd slept with Pam.

Life required a façade of perfect sangfroid, Jefferson had once told me. I kept hearing those two words in my head.

Rachel called a few times. I would not pick up. She left brief messages, asking to see me, saying we had to talk, telling me she was sorry and asking for help with Jefferson.

She said he had hired some young black boy as his "assistant." His name, she reported, was Sam but Jefferson called him Pip.

"Jack, I think he's losing his mind," she said in one message.

I felt a glimmer of interest but let it go.

Jefferson sent me a few short emails, asking if I were ever coming to see him in New York. I did not reply and after a few weeks he gave up. I'm sure he didn't like typing; he made a lot of mistakes. But then his handwritten letters began to arrive, one almost every day, on heavy Crane's stationery, with his name and address embossed on the back of the envelope and mine written on the front in his neat, angular, nearly vertical script. I let the letters pile up unopened. I don't know why.

Jefferson did not like using a telephone. He called and left a message only once. By then, I'd paid a backlog of bills, his and mine, and the leaves had turned brown and the weather had turned chilly. I was asleep on the couch when he called at about 11 o'clock one night. It felt like 3 a.m. to me. I was slightly drunk or hung over, as I was most of the time then.

Jefferson's voice sounded thin, patrician and far away, as if I were hearing it through the centuries instead of my phone line.

He apologized for being "an awkward speaker when using the telephonic instrument" and said he hoped I was well. "Your two friends think of you often, and most fondly, with good memories of our time together, but with heavy hearts and hopes for a reunion at your first possible convenience," he said haltingly.

He coughed lightly and hesitated. "Our dear Miss Carter is very busy with that pompous buffoon Kant; he continues to press her into service for his absurd account of my many great transgressions against the Union. Have you received any of my letters, Mr. Arrowsmith? I myself am well, my time spent in several endeavors that I hope may bear fruit. I have constructed a device with which I intend to capture a near-tame mockingbird I have found living in Riverside Park. I am surprised to find him this far north, especially as we approach winter. I believe he needs to be saved from the coming cold weather. He would make an excellent companion. I will name him Dick, after the bird I took with me to the White House. Do you know how I might find berries of cedar here in the city? Oh! I have received a letter that indicates it is from the White House, thanking me for my own recent letter to the president. It was on the reparations question that Mr. Carter and I spoke of. The White House reply contains no references to it at all, so I suppose it is some clerk's work. I hope ..."

The message machine beeped and cut him off. I did not call back and he did not try again.

I played golf a couple of times. I did not enjoy it. My partners asked me if I were all right and I said I was fine, just a little preoccupied lately with a book I was working on. I made that up just to satisfy them. I told them it was about Thomas Jefferson and it was not yet a good time for me to be revealing much about it. Talking took too much away from my skittish commitment to writing, I said.

As Christmas approached, I received some party and dinner invitations. I ignored them. But Nancy Steinberg, a neighbor for years who had raised three kids on her own after her husband had left her, forced the issue by coming to the door. She looked at me in my bathrobe and beard at 11 o'clock in the morning and said, "For God's sake, Jack, what the hell is going on with you?" Without waiting for me to conjure up a reply, she held out an envelope and said, "Here, you're coming to this."

I selfishly wondered why Rachel and Jefferson hadn't come calling to save me from myself. Perhaps they had their own troubles. Perhaps they were afraid I'd lash out at them. Perhaps they felt I'd made my decision to keep my distance and they had to respect it. Nancy, on the other hand, had nothing to lose walking over and knocking on my door. I pulled myself together and went.

She had gone all out for the bash. There must have been 50 people at her house, standing shoulder to shoulder all over the living room, dining room and kitchen. She did it just the way Ted, her ex-husband, would have insisted, as if his departure hadn't mattered: a catered affair, cocktails, hors d'oeuvres and dinner, with people sitting all over after dinner had been served perching plates on their thighs. Ted paid for it all, anyway, one way or another, I'm sure, and I was happy to drink his booze and pretend I was just fine chatting with old cocktail-party and golf-course friends. She was quite the good sport, Nancy was. Perhaps it was a fantasy inspired by my desperation but, to my surprise, I had fun, in a hazy sort of semi-drunken way.

Standing in a group of men who carpooled to jobs in banks and brokerage houses in the city, I said, "Hey. Here we are, happy bastards in our nice New Jersey suburb, and I just want to ask you: Doesn't it seem really, really odd that 145 years after the Emancipation Proclamation, we could be at a big party like this and there is not one single black person in the crowd, even in the kitchen?"

I didn't know where that had come from. They didn't get it. I didn't get it myself. For a few seconds, they stared at me in disbelief.

"Oh, Jack, come on. You know the blacks all live in Englewood," said Doug McCall, a stocky duffer who worked at Morgan Stanley. "Even the rich ones. Up on the hill. Doesn't Eddie Murphy have a mansion up there?"

"Yeah, Eddie's up there," said Stan Lynch, a tall guy with a spectacular second wife. "Or he used to be anyway. He got divorced again years ago. It's one of those Spanish houses with the clay roof tiles from the 1920s. I think the wife got it."

"Some WASP tycoon builds it back in the Twenties," Doug said, "then some Jew buys it from the WASP's lazy grandkids in the Seventies and then you get a black man like Eddie Murphy in there in the Eighties and Nineties. What a progression. And now no one knows who's in there. Some Mexican drug lord or Russian crook."

"You history teachers," snorted Don Klein, a CPA with an office in the Seagram Building on Park Avenue. He had taken no notice of Doug's Jew reference. It was all in fun and everyone knew the rules allowed for some fun. "Jack, you are always thinking about the strangest things. That's why we love you. But it's good your dear wife made some bucks working with that pack of jackals in the MetLife building or you wouldn't be here either. You'd be off with the blacks in downtown Englewood."

Everyone laughed. Don was such an outrageous asshole. He was known for his Don Rickles obnoxiousness. We hated and loved him for it. I grinned, not at what he'd said but at his ridiculousness. It was my first grin in months.

That night at home, I started reading Jefferson's letters, in the order in which they had arrived. They all began "Dear Sir" and ended with a sentence that always transitioned into the same final phrase, "As I am now and will always be, your most fond and affectionate friend, Th:Jefferson." It choked me up, seeing that, which I now suppose meant that my spirit was healing somewhere way down under all the scabs.

The poor man wrote me about his wife, Martha. He had been mindful of the need to protect her memory from political foes and from biographers for all time, he wrote, so he had instructed his daughter in the last weeks of his life to burn all their correspondence. It "had been full of the most intimate details of our domestic life as well as our expressions of love and devotion for each other," he wrote. "None of it was the public's business, nor any historian's."

He confessed there had been self-interest in his instruction to Martha. Some of his letters did not "paint the most flattering picture of myself. I freely expressed my frustrations and resentments to her, and these feelings are always unflattering to the person who expresses them."

He wrote me about slavery, too, all rationalizations for his failure to lead any campaign for abolition. It was all the same stuff I had read before in his published letters and papers. More surprising was the attention he gave to the medical benefits of sex, which he described as "the most irresistible of the motivating forces in man."

"For all the trouble it can cause us, it has its benefits. It is a natural palliative for the male of any species," he wrote.

He revealed that, before he'd gone to Paris to replace Franklin as the American minister, his friend Dr. Rush had told him he had better find a way to satisfy his needs without resorting to Paris prostitutes. Franklin had told him the same thing in so many words. He'd taken their advice, Jefferson wrote, and as a result his spirits had been very good when he was in France. He did not offer details.

He was troubled about the United States.

It would take him some time, he wrote, to comprehend "this idea that women have the capacity for public service. It is as fantastical to me as a black man serving as the president. But I am aware that times have changed without me and I have much to assimilate before rendering any public judgment on these matters."

He was certain about one thing: "A cult of selfishness," he wrote, threatened the bonds of civil society right down to the family level, "the basic societal unit of a republic." It was even common now for educated people to "establish common-law relations, living as husband and wife and having children without marriage," which he considered a threat to social order. "But ironically, perhaps, it is less grievous," he said, "than sodomites being recognized by the state as legal spouses allowed to adopt children. General Washington's head must be spinning in his vault!"

He thought there was something very wrong with a people who talked into their pocket telephones in public places and whose children would not tear themselves away from electrical devices on which they played games and wrote snippets back and forth to each other. "The people seem unaware of any common interest," he wrote, except as "mere consumers." As a result, they do not interact with the world. They live in a fog of delusions, he believed.

"I hope for the best. It can't be as bad as it seems. I still trust in the people to recover their senses, but it may have to come at great expense, perhaps even bloodshed. Such a revolution was required to end English rule and nearly a century later the sin of slavery."

He added a postscript about his "changed circumstances." He realized that he was "no longer a master in any sense of the word. In fact, I am now the slave, bound by chains unbreakable, except by the love of friends."

As I reached his most recent letters, those that had come near the holidays, his handwriting changed. It was crimped and compressed. Some letters were nearly illegible. They were about people he had met on the streets of Harlem. He said he felt a compulsion to learn their stories and write them down. He took to cramming postscripts into the margins. He clipped articles from newspapers and magazines and included them with his letters. He insanely underlined every line of some. I sometimes could not connect the enclosures to anything he had written.

His most recent letter had come early in the New Year. I could read very little of it, except something about Obama and the Tea Party people. Near the end, I could decipher the phrase, "The art of life is the art of avoiding pain," but whatever came next I couldn't read at all.

I finally sat down at my desk and dug out my old box of stationery to write him. I apologized for my mean-spirited withdrawal from the world. I told him I'd enjoyed all his letters and asked if he and Rachel would accept a visit from their spiritually frail and abashed old friend.

In the dead-of-winter days that I waited to hear from him, I noticed an article in the Colonial Williamsburg Journal, which Pam and I had been getting for years because we'd been donors ever since our honeymoon stay. There was a big feature about the brilliant man, Bill Barker, who had been their Jefferson interpreter for many years. He was retiring.

I had an idea. I'd been thinking of calling Rachel to talk to her about it when her father rang me up one morning. He asked me to come right away. Rachel and Mr. Jefferson, he said, needed me.

Chapter 21

Mr. Carter came out of his house as soon as I pulled up to the curb. He walked grimly toward the car in a blue parka that seemed too big for him, vapor puffing from his mouth in the cold air. He pulled open the passenger door and leaned in.

"We got to go downtown to Bellevue. Rachel and Kant are there trying to get him out. She asked me to call you. He wants us to come, she says."

"Hop in," I said.

Mr. Carter was not a hopper. He carefully folded himself into the car and closed the door.

"Kant?" I asked. "Why would Kant be involved in this?"

"Rachel couldn't reach me at first. I was out walking. I don't have a cell phone. She was afraid to call you, afraid you'd hang up on her. What's wrong with you, anyway?"

"Nothing. I'm fine. I had some bad news I had to get over."

"Hmmph. You've got two friends who need you and they won't ask you for help? That ain't good. What kind of friend is that?"

"Right. You're right, Mr. Carter," I said.

"I know I'm right. Damn right I'm right."

He told me that neighbors in Jefferson's building had called the police. There had been some kind of scene in the hall. The police decided he was crazy. It didn't help that he said he was tired of pretending and insisted he was the real Thomas Jefferson.

I rubbed my chin with one hand as I drove, thinking. I asked how Rachel was handling it. "You'll see," he said grumpily, staring ahead.

Mr. Carter limped slightly as we walked from the parking garage to the hospital and, after asking directions at half a dozen reception desks and nurse's stations, finally found our way to the place where they put people for observation in the psych ward.

We stood at the end of a long hallway in front of two green doors and announced ourselves through a speaker. Far-off moans, shouts and occasional screams echoed through the walls.

First one, then two and finally three creatures peeked at us through the crack between the doors. They grunted and vanished just before a bolt clicked. One of the doors swung open to reveal a large black man in a white uniform. "Who you here for?" he asked.

"Thomas Jefferson," I said.

"Uh-huh. He's popular. He already got two visitors but okay," he said, pushing the door open wide.

We followed him in and headed across an open area to a common room. Disheveled people in bathrobes and paper slippers shuffled slowly along, glancing at us and quickly looking away. Some talked to themselves.

I heard him before I saw him.

"You people should consider yourselves the true Americans! You and our aboriginal friends, the Indians of our frontiers. Such orators, those people! And such an abiding sense of honor and pride! Don't mind the Declaration, all that about the wild men of the frontier. They truly were wild men, they killed indiscriminately, but, well, friends, the Declaration was a political document, purely for effect, and it was a reflection of the times. My heavens, the native-born American is so rare these days. The Indians, as I understand it, are reduced to selling tax-free tobacco and fleecing gamblers. Astonishing! And terrible! You negroes, yours is a meritocracy of labor and service; you may be the only good Americans left, our only true republicans. I never, never would have expected it."

"I ain't no Republican," someone said.

We rounded a corner and there he was, lounging in a plastic

armchair in the corner of the room in bathrobe and slippers, one long leg folded at the knee over the other, smiling pleasantly and holding a finger in the air as he made his points. About a dozen patients — black, brown and white, men and women — had pulled their chairs toward the corner, facing him, listening with smiles and grins. As he went on about negroes carrying the economy of the South on their backs and building the great edifices of the federal city, some of the black people called out "Amen" and "Hallelujah" and "You right on, Mr. Jefferson."

Rachel sat on one side of Jefferson, leaning back in her chair, gripping each armrest, looking pained and worried. Sitting on the other side of him, looking bored, was Professor Kant, his elbow on the armrest, his chin propped in one hand. I barely noticed him. I could not stop staring at Rachel's lap, where a spherical shape stretched the buttons of her blouse.

When she saw me, she broke into a rapturous smile and her eyes filled with tears. "Jack! Oh Jack!" she cried, springing up to make her way toward me through the jumble of Jefferson spectators. "Jack! Oh I'm so sorry Jack," she said, wrapping her arms around me and sobbing into my shoulder. "I should never have made you read it. I shouldn't have done it, I shouldn't have done it."

"It's all right, you sweet girl. I'm the sorry one," I said, hugging her, feeling her belly hard against me. Into her ear, I whispered, "Rachel, what on earth? Are you ..."

She lifted her head, looked into my eyes and nodded slowly. "I must have missed my pill one day. Or two. I guess." She bowed her head. "It's not like me to do that."

"And it's ... his?"

She seemed unable to speak for a moment. Frozen with a crazed expression, she opened her mouth and shook her head to force out her words. "Yes, yes, of course it is, Jack. But he thinks it could be yours." She emitted a weird little embarrassed laugh.

It all was reminding me of "Rosemary's Baby" but I held my tongue about that. "God. He's not just a supernatural piece of work. He is nuts," I whispered. "Jesus. Are you going to keep it?"

She was supposed to get her degree in May. She was supposed to go find a teaching job. She was supposed to be young and free and smart and on her way to a great academic career.

She looked wounded. "Jack! *It's Thomas Jefferson's child!* A son! He never had a son, not one that lived. How could I do that to him? I wouldn't, I couldn't, Jack," she said, wiping her eyes. "I mean, if it were yours or Ben's …" She looked in horror at me and stopped herself. "I only mean it would destroy him — even if he thinks it's yours. He wants the child! He's vowed to raise him!"

I could see she knew it was ridiculous to expect a penniless ghost of a man to support anybody. She didn't believe her own words. And yet she'd ignored the fact that he'd had sons. Only a *white* son had not survived. There'd been three boys with Sally Hemings, all set free, along with a daughter.

"Ah! Mr. Arrowsmith! My dear Mr. Arrowsmith!" Jefferson called cheerfully, rising from his seat. "My heavens, sir! How very good it is to see you again! I feared we'd lost you, my friend! You've come back to us! You've rejoined the living! I am so glad!"

I turned to Mr. Carter. "You knew?"

"I knew," he said. "I was expecting it. I've seen this kind of thing before."

I gaped at him. He shrugged his shoulders. "What's there to be surprised about? I saw it coming, didn't you? You know the man. From books, I mean."

I tried not to smile at Jefferson as he approached but he was so inanely cheerful I couldn't help it. I'd missed him. And there he was, the fine-looking man in the Houdon bust come to life in a hospital gown. "Mr. Jefferson," I said with a bow, "I'm pleased to see you. But good God, what have you been up to?"

"Oh, I have been terribly busy. Overwhelmed. I would have written more often but there was so much to attend to."

"So I gather," I said. I turned to Rachel. "How are you going to do this? What about your career?"

"I'll help with that," Kant said, peering from behind Jefferson. "Rachel's friend here has provided me with a great deal of entertainment. He's really a very interesting man. He's really got Jefferson down cold. I don't care how crazy he is."

"Why is he here?" I said. "He's not really crazy." I looked from Kant to Rachel to Mr. Carter. "Is he?"

"Just a misunderstanding, Mr. Arrowsmith," said Jefferson. "Just a little confusion with the armed men your city government has roaming about. This institution, I must say, is not so bad. It is quite an improvement over Bedlam and even Dr. Galt's hospital in Williamsburg. Oh! I forget my friends!" He stretched his arm toward the seated spectators who'd been watching us with mouths agape. "Here! Let me introduce them."

He put an arm over my shoulders as he addressed them. I was his dear friend, he said, and Mr. Carter was the lovely Rachel's proud father.

The people smiled and nodded. "All right!" one said.

"Mr. Arrowsmith," Jefferson said, "there are many interesting people here. Would you like to meet any of them? It's strange how our black friends are just themselves. That is Willie, there, and Ellie here, and then we have Bob, Jackson and Alverta. But many of the white gentlemen and ladies seem to believe they have come to us from history, much like myself. I wonder. Why would the negroes be exempt? Could it be because they have no history except servitude? I think there may be some connection. In any case, let me see ... Napoleon Bonaparte is somewhere in the vicinity, I believe, drifting about. There's Jesus Christ over there beside Joan of Arc. Mr. Beethoven is here. That's rather nice because I have been enjoying his dark, forceful, modernistic music in spite of myself."

"Tell me, are there any other Thomas Jeffersons here?" I asked.

"None. I am the only one," he said. "I seem not to be a very popular figure these days. Oh, Mr. Carter," he added, turning to him, "I have acquired a violin of my own. I had hoped you and I might play again."

Mr. Carter looked at me with a blank face. I couldn't help holding back another smile. All of a sudden an oddly pleasant feeling was coming over me as I stood there at Bellevue with Kant, Mr. Carter, Rachel and Jefferson. I realized I was feeling myself to be part of one big, boisterous, insane family — and I liked it.

"So," Jefferson said, turning to me. "What do you think? Are you able to affect my escape?" he asked.

"I don't know ... I don't know what's going on here, Mr. Jefferson." I looked at Rachel. "I am confused, as usual; in more ways than one."

Kant folded his arms and smiled at me. "We'll straighten this out," he said. "I have made some calls of my own."

Later that afternoon, a psychiatrist told Rachel and me that Jefferson wasn't violent or suicidal and that the hospital needed to make room for people who were.

"He is delusional and probably bipolar and if you are supervising him I hope you have plans for his treatment," he said. "You know, I myself am a Jefferson fan. He's really *good*. I talked to him about Poplar Forest. I was just there with my wife. It is a charming retreat, architecturally simple, or should I say perfect, where Monticello is quite contrived, you know."

In his thirties with a trimmed beard, the shrink grabbed his chin as he looked past my shoulder into space. "His knowledge of Poplar Forest's design and construction was intimate and richly detailed. He talked of a trip there from Monticello in a coach with two granddaughters and a servant and stopping for picnics along the way. I suspect his intense fixation with Jefferson is connected to his really striking similarity in appearance to the actual man. It might inspire a troubled person to acquire the personal history to match it."

He released Jefferson into my custody after I gave the hospital a credit card to cover the bill and we'd endured a lecture from a detective about keeping him under control and off the streets without supervision.

Chapter 22

Jefferson's high spirits vanished in the car, as if they had all been for show. Sitting in the front seat beside me, he barely spoke, turning his head only occasionally to study a building, a person or a taxi driver's face.

Rachel, Kant and Mr. Carter sat wedged in the back, silent, too. I dropped Kant at the Broadway entrance to the Columbia campus. He had a class. Mr. Carter insisted on getting out, too. He said he'd take the train and a bus home and brusquely rejected our pleas — mine and Jefferson's; Rachel kept quiet — to let us drive him home.

"What's up with him?" I asked as we headed for Claremont Avenue.

"He's mad at me," Rachel said quietly.

As we neared his apartment building, Jefferson spoke up.

"I fear you will be distressed when you discover the condition of the apartment," he said. "Rachel has been admonishing me not to abuse your trust. That is not at all what I meant to do."

"Oh no," I said. "You haven't been tearing down and building up, have you?"

Jefferson rotated his head to look straight at me. "Oh my goodness. How well you know me," he said. "Perhaps I have been too quick to react to eruptions and spasms of the nervous fibers."

We found a small crowd of students sitting on the front stoop of Jefferson's apartment house. Several had brought cases that obviously contained musical instruments. "Hey, Mr. Jefferson," said one, standing up before the others.

"We waitin' for some more work today," said one of the men without a case, a young black man in jeans and a sweatshirt, his hood up, hiding most of his face.

"We thought we had a date to play today," said the woman, a young Asian.

We stopped in front of the steps and Jefferson raised his hand in a motionless greeting. "I'm sorry, my friends, I was detained. Is Pip inside?"

"He's exercising the bird," the girl said.

"Ah. I told him not to let Dick out when I am not at home," he said, starting up the steps. The group parted to make way for him.

"Can we come up?" someone asked.

"If you would please wait for me here. I will have further instructions," Jefferson said as he continued into the building. "I apologize to you, my friends. I regret the disruption."

At the foot of the steps, I looked at Rachel quizzically.

"He's taken over, Jack," she said in a whisper. "He's unstoppable, exhausting. The neighbors want him out. There's been a lot of damage."

"Damage?"

"Well, he took out a wall."

"What?"

"That's what a couple of these kids are here for. They're his laborers."

"Good God. A wall? He took out a wall?"

She just looked at me, bracing for the worst, I suppose.

"Who are the musicians? What is he, the Pied Piper?"

"They practice with him. He's a regular at their concerts. He invited them over. The dean has spoken to Kant about him. Kant vouched for him."

We followed after Jefferson, who stood impatiently at his door. "Rachel," he said testily. "I believe you have the key, my dear. They made me empty my pockets at that hellhole."

Rachel fished it out and handed it to him. When he unlocked the door and pushed it open, we heard a commotion and a young boy's voice: "No, bird! This way, bird!"

"Oh no," Jefferson muttered as he went in. "Pip, Pip! I told you never to let Dick out in my absence!"

We followed him in. Rachel stepped away from me, hiding half her face with her hand.

"Pip! These windows must be closed!" Jefferson yelled, lurching over books, newspapers, magazines, plants, broken plaster, pieces of wood and scattered seed trays to reach the windows.

I stood frozen at the sight before me. A black boy, about 13 or 14, chased a lean, gray bird around the room. Its wings flashed a blurred pattern of black and white stripes as it fluttered along the ceiling like a moth, avoiding the boy's net.

"Why were these open, Pip?" Jefferson shouted, failing to control his anger as he struggled to get the sashes down.

"I didn't do it! I didn't open the windows! It got hot in here for them working! They opened them!"

My jaw dropped and I held out my arms in wonder. A plastic shower curtain covered the couch. What had been the wall behind it lay broken in scattered shards of plaster and splintered two-by-fours. I could see into the bedroom, where the books that had been on shelves over the couch were now stacked on the floor beside the bed.

A cylindrical wooden birdcage, its hatch open, hung from the ceiling over the couch in the new space between the living room and bedroom. Potted plants covered the windowsills, with more plants crowded onto cheap plastic tables along the wall. He had set up UV lamps over them, with wires all over the floor connected to extension cords that stretched in a strained web under the tables.

"Damnation! They'll kill my plants, letting the cold air in like this!" Jefferson said frantically.

By the television, DVDs in uneven stacks gave way to newspapers and sheet music spread across the floor in an arc toward the corner armchair, where books lay stacked in unsteady piles. Others had been left open on the floor, including big coffee-table books about the ruins of Pompeii, the architecture of Greece, the Palladian tradition in England.

I looked at the grandfather clock. The top casing and the face had been removed to expose the movement. A violin lay propped in the corner beside it.

"Jesus H. Christ," I whispered. "What on earth were you thinking, Mr. Jefferson?"

"The design was intolerable. I have been improving it," he said as he pulled on the sash. "Pip! Stop chasing him now!"

"But it's not yours," I said. "You're not even a legal tenant. You have no right. And what about the money? You must be close to broke!"

His face broke into swirls of red blotches. His head shook. For an instant, he seemed defiant. Then he clenched shut his eyes, squeezed each hand into a fist and spat out the word: "Shit!"

A thought crossed my mind, filling it with a new horror. "Where is the cat?"

"I have it, Jack. She's all right," Rachel said. "She's with my father. He likes cats."

"Pip!" Jefferson said, looking insane with rage. "Stop chasing the bird! And help me close this window! Now! Instantly!"

The moment he said it, the bird dropped from its momentary perch on the frame of the Chinese picture behind the desk and dove straight across the room and out the window.

"No! Oh no!" Jefferson shouted. "Dick! Come back, Dick! Oh no, he'll die in that cold!" He stared out the window for a moment then spun around to face Pip.

"I didn't let him out, Mr. Jefferson!" the boy said, rearing back. "One of those boys you had working in here did dat. They all left for lunch."

"If I had a whip, you'd be worked hard for this!" he shouted. He picked up a newspaper, rolled it into a tube and lunged at Pip.

"Mr. Jefferson!" Rachel exclaimed. "Stop!"

Jefferson swatted at the retreating boy and caught him hard across the side of the head. Pip cried out, clutched at his face, looked at Jefferson in amazement and ran sobbing for the door. Jefferson followed on his heels, swinging at him with the newspaper. "You little fool! You knew the rules! You did not follow the rules! You've lost my bird! You've lost Dick! We cannot love a child who will not follow our rules!" He chased him out into the hall, Pip's footsteps receding down the stairwell. Jefferson leaned over the railing, yelling at him to never come back, he was too much of a fool for household service, his had been entirely unworthy of his master's trust and love and now how was his master to manage with no servants, no servants at all. He sounded close to tears.

The downstairs door slammed shut, followed by dead silence. Rachel pressed her hands over her face. Jefferson, after a long time without making a sound, muttered something and started down the steps.

Rachel and I stood paralyzed, looking at each other until she shook her head at me. "Jack, we have to get him out of the city. He can't live here. It's a disaster," she said.

The downstairs door slammed shut again. We stared at each other for three seconds and then bolted in unison into the hall, down the stairs and out the door. At the top of the entry steps, we slowed to let the little crowd of Jefferson workers and musicians part for us with quizzical looks. Across the street, we could see Jefferson's head bobbing above the line of parked cars as he loped uptown.

Pip lived in the General Grant housing complex on Amsterdam, Rachel told me. "That must be where he's heading," she said.

"What's going on?" the Asian girl with the violin asked. "We had a practice!"

"I don't think it's going to happen," Rachel said.

With Rachel and me following behind at a fast walk, Jefferson turned onto LaSalle and headed east. He crossed Broadway and stopped at the far corner to talk to two Hispanic women with a baby carriage. We nearly caught up with him before he strode off again. As Jefferson passed him, a Korean man sorting vegetables in sidewalk racks waved at him. "Mr. Jeffah-sahn,

Mr. Jeffah-sahn! How you today? Got fresh peas! Peas from
Carifahn-nya!"

Jefferson raised one arm in a half-staff salute as he passed
the man. "Did you see Pip?" he asked.

"Yes, yes, Pip go by. Just now, head home," the grocer said,
pointing east. He spotted us trekking after Jefferson. "Hello,
Miss Rachel," he said. "Fresh peas today! Mr. Jeffah-sahn like
fresh peas! From Carifahn-nya!"

With Rachel and me right behind, Jefferson headed for a
complex of tall, brick apartment buildings, ugly things from the
1960s or 1970s. He waved at a group of young black men as he
passed them.

"Hey Boogz, there go you white friend," one of them said
as Jefferson passed.

"And there goes his bitch," another said. "Man, they crazy."
They leered at Rachel as we approached. "Sistah, you bettah
watch yo'self with that load you carrying."

She ignored them. Jefferson veered off the sidewalk and into
a parking lot. We loped behind him toward the covered entry-
way of one of the buildings. A woman coming out the door held
it open and nodded at him. We came right behind and caught
the door as it was closing.

"I must explain to Pip's guardian this will never happen
again," he said to us over his shoulder. "I am not cruel to my
servants, nor to children!"

It was dark, dingy and deserted in the foyer. Cigarette butts
littered the floor in front of the once-shiny elevator doors.

"Mr. Jefferson," Rachel said, catching her breath, "this
woman just might call the police on you for hitting him. Just to
get money."

"I am well aware, well aware, Miss Carter," he said as he
stepped into the elevator after two young Latinos had stepped
out. "Hey, man," one said to Jefferson.

"Does he know everybody?" I asked Rachel.

She nodded with wide eyes.

We rode to the 12th floor. The long, barren hallway with
its rows of green metal doors showed no signs of life. Smells

and muffled sounds mixed in the stagnant air: cabbage and hot fryer oil, the syncopated thump of bass beats from a jumble of salsa and rap.

He led us to a doorway halfway down the hall and knocked. "Miss Jamison? Miss Jamison? It's Jefferson," he said, putting his ear to the door.

In a few seconds the door burst open. A short, heavy woman glared at him. "What you want!"

"Pip. Is he here?"

"He ain't here. What he be doin' here? He never here. I can't keep track of that child."

Jefferson attempted to peer past her into the apartment.

"What you got him doin' for you now?" the woman said. "You owe me a hundred dollars."

"Yes, yes, tomorrow. I'll go to the ATM tomorrow."

"You better. I get Andre on yo' ass."

"Well, where is Pip?" Jefferson asked.

In a high singsong voice, with a huffy tone, she said, "You know he not named Pip! He named Quentin. Sam Quentin, after my cousin."

"Yes, yes, I Googled it. I don't like the name. It's ridiculous. I've named him Pippin. It's the best of my apples. In a crate of bad apples, he's the good one. Where is he?"

"I don't know where he is! How should I know? He probably over at them other white folks he took up with. He's probably cheatin' me out of that money. Seen none of it yet."

"What white people? He's working for other white people?"

"They treats him like a pet dog, the way them white people do. They got a *brownstone*, you know." She emphasized the word, as if to make fun of it, and rolled her eyes. "Shit."

"Where?"

"It's up there 'round 140th Street. I keep track of my kid. Welfare ain't gonna catch me bein' a bad guardian." She turned her head and called over her shoulder, "Hey! Hey Mama! Where dat brownstone with the white folks that Quentin go to help sand the floors at or whatever?"

We could just hear the wobbly voice of an elderly woman.

"It's 141st Street, number 413," the woman said. "I have it written down."

"Four-thirteen. See? We do keep track. And don't forget. You owe," she said, pointing her finger at him before slamming the door.

We followed Jefferson to the elevator.

"Why isn't this kid in school?" I asked.

"The schools here are filled with criminals. I'm teaching him now," Jefferson said. "His guardian prefers it."

"Mr. Jefferson here is going to get in trouble for *that*, too," I said to Rachel as he charged into the elevator. We followed like scurrying aides.

He bolted from the elevator ahead of us and charged outside. As we headed up Amsterdam, Jefferson called over his shoulder, "You should not be exerting yourself this way, Miss Carter. You people do not need to assist me. You should return."

"I'm staying with him," Rachel said to me.

"Yes, yes, I'm staying with him, too," I huffed.

It was just about then that I noticed, out of the corner of my eye, a black SUV, its darkly tinted windows reflecting a distorted streetscape as it rolled slowly along Amsterdam a few lengths behind us, inches off the line of parked cars.

"Rachel, I think that car is following us."

"Really?" She peered over her shoulder at it.

We loped after him for blocks. At 141st Street, we turned right, the black SUV still trailing us. It didn't have a New York plate. It had a white one with small blue letters or numerals, like those on government vehicles. That gave me hope they weren't drug dealers that Pip or Jefferson had somehow wronged.

"The house must be beyond that church," Jefferson said, pointing toward the far corner. "I don't understand what he is doing with other employers. It was not the arrangement."

The brownstones we passed looked shabby and run-down except for the last one in the row. Its stones were cleaner and brighter, the dark green paint on its window and door trim fresh. We were so busy following him, and he was so focused looking across the street to the left for number 413, none of us noticed that a wooded, grassy park had opened up on our right, sloping uphill from behind a chain-link fence along the sidewalk. "Hey," I said to Rachel when I finally noticed it. "Look at that beautiful old house!"

Perched on a knoll in the middle of the little park stood a big, wood frame federal mansion, its porch, shutters, trim and big brick chimneys white, its walls a mustard yellow. A sign on the fence read: "Alexander Hamilton's home, The Grange, National Park Service. To open 2011."

Jefferson seemed to have become aware of the changing prospect across the street and had turned to look at it himself. He halted and stared. His face dropped.

"My God," he said.

"It's your best friend's house," I said as we came up beside him. I glanced over my shoulder. The black SUV had stopped, too.

"They have maintained his private home as a public monument?" Jefferson asked.

"I think they moved it here recently. A couple of years ago," Rachel said. "I didn't know until now exactly where they put it; I never come up here. It used to be around the corner. There's a garden there now. I remember reading about it in the paper."

Jefferson emitted a guttural sound of disgust. "The man got himself shot before he'd lived in it for a year or two," he muttered. "Why has it survived? Why do they preserve it at public expense? He was a confessed adulterer. The house is nothing, a pile, a mere copy. Today, you would call it ... what is the term I've seen in my readings? You'd call it a McMansion! Just another arriviste's ugly assertion of wealth."

Rachel watched him with a look of worry; she seemed about to reach for him. But something caught Jefferson's eye. "No!" he hissed.

"What?" Rachel said.

"There he is!"

We followed his gaze. Standing at the top of the steps on the porch, leaning with one hand on the railing, one knee cocked, was a small, trim man in formal 18th-century dress. Even from across the street, the prominent nose, strong jaw and broad forehead of Alexander Hamilton were unmistakable. He smiled defiantly as he looked down at us.

"I saw you at the President's Park," he called.

"I have no time now, Hamilton!" Jefferson answered, as if they'd just battled it out at a cabinet meeting in front of George Washington that morning.

"Stirred up more trouble, have you, Mr. Jefferson? You womanish prig," Hamilton blurted. "No need to attempt courtesies anymore! The general isn't in the room!"

"No, he wouldn't be here with us now, would he?" Jefferson said. "You deserve this hell as your haunting place, you ass-kissing Caribbean bastard."

"You're still mucking with the slaves, I've noticed, eh, Jefferson?" Hamilton yelled.

"And you with other men's wives!"

Jefferson flinched as he said it; he'd given Hamilton the perfect opening for a dig about the Walker affair. Hamilton only smirked. Jefferson shook his head, spat "Bah!" and started off. "Why him, of all people? He's the last of my contemporaries I care to see again. He makes me lose my composure!"

We followed, looking over our shoulders at the man on the porch. "That was *him*? That was Hamilton?" I asked Jefferson. Hamilton stood fixed in the same pose on the porch but raised one hand after us in a mock salute of farewell.

"It certainly seems so," Jefferson said over his shoulder. He stopped and looked at Rachel with sudden concern. "Heavens! Are you all right, Miss Carter? Why did you insist on following me like this? You should not be exerting yourself so!"

She was about to answer when Hamilton called out after him.

"Have you noticed, my great friend of liberty," Hamilton sneered, "that you damned Virginians lost every argument? This is not your republic. It is the one I envisioned, a nation state in which the people thrive because of my policies! I dealt with reality, Mr. Jefferson. I dealt with the world the way it really works, a world driven by the twin motives of fear and greed, and I believe I have been rewarded with the pleasure of seeing you humiliated for your girlish delusions about the nobility of mankind!"

Jefferson pretended not to have heard him. He looked at Rachel, his face flushing, waiting for her answer. She looked back at him anxiously and said nothing. He turned and started off again.

The black SUV was rolling again, just behind us now. "Jesus H. Christ, what did I get you into?" I said to Rachel, slapping my hand on my head. "Uh, hey, Mr. Jefferson," I called to him, "what about this black vehicle that has been following us? Why do I have the feeling you know who that is?"

He turned and looked as he walked. "Yes, those people."

Rachel looked first at me then at him with a new wave of worry. "Thomas! Why haven't you told me about this?" she said.

"I did not wish to alarm you. It's nothing. Pay no attention to them."

"Who are they?" I asked.

"Young men with wires that connect into their ears. Like the device you gave me for my iPod."

The SUV stopped at the curb by the last brownstone. We climbed its steps and Jefferson leaned down to peer at the nameplate above a single buzzer. "Weitzman," he said. "Germans, I suppose. Like your car. Perhaps his ancestors were Hessians." He pressed the buzzer.

After a few seconds, a woman's voice came through the speaker. "Yes?"

"Good afternoon, madam, I beg your pardon. My name is Thomas Jefferson. I am looking for a young man I call Pip whose guardian tells me is now in your employ."

There was a pause. "Well … you mean Quentin? Or Sam, I mean? He prefers Sam."

"Yes, that's the boy I refer to. I understand the peculiarity of my calling him Pip. His name is ridiculous, you see, so I gave him another."

"And you're who? Did you say Thomas Jefferson?"

Jefferson, who had been bending toward the speaker, stood

up and sighed with annoyance. "Yes, yes, that is my name. As disturbing as that may be to the world, that is indeed my name."

"Well, I'm sorry. Sam is helping my husband with the floors. We're redoing the floors."

Jefferson bowed his head and grimaced. "Well then. Would you please tell him that I regret having lost my composure and that I do not blame him one bit for the loss of my bird?"

"He can hear you right now."

"Ah. Pip! My apologies to you! I ask you to forgive me for my loss of composure. I need your good services. I am not myself."

Silence. Finally, the woman came back on. "I think he's upset. About losing your bird. He says you hit him with a newspaper."

"Yes, yes, I did. So?"

"We're concerned about him," the woman said. "We've called Social Services. He should be in school. We normally see him only on weekends."

I leaned to Rachel. "Yeah. To sand your floors for five bucks an hour," I whispered.

I realized someone was coming up the sidewalk behind us: three men in dark suits and sunglasses. Just as Jefferson had said, each one had a plug in one ear with a coiled wire leading behind his neck. They stopped at the foot of the staircase and looked up at us.

"I have this feeling that what we have here," I said, "is the Secret Service. Or the FBI. Mr. Jefferson, have you been writing more letters to the president?"

My question annoyed him. "Yes, yes, Mr. Arrowsmith. I have. He never replies." He leaned down to the speaker. "Excuse me, madam, isn't that a matter for his guardian to decide? She is the responsible party. I've just come from her. She told me I'd find him here. May I see Pip?"

There was a pause. "My husband is coming down," the woman said. "Hold on."

We waited a long time. The three men in suits stood patiently on the sidewalk, hands clasped behind their backs as if they'd been ordered to stand at ease. Rachel and I glanced at them nervously while Jefferson completely ignored them. A window opened above us on the top floor. A dark-haired young man poked his head out. "Uh ... Who are those people in the suits?" he asked.

Jefferson stepped back and, holding his hand over his eyes for shade, peered up at him. Then he finally turned to look at the three men. Neither they nor Jefferson altered their blank expressions. "Oh," he said, looking back up at the man in the window. "These people are federal spies. They insist on following me about."

"Why would that be?"

"Well, they tell me I am a person of interest. That's their phrase for it."

I leaned into Rachel's ear. "You didn't know anything about this?"

She looked at me and shook her head.

"What has our friend done?" I whispered.

One of the men in suits stepped closer. "Excuse me," he said. "Are you a friend of Mr. Jefferson's there?"

I took a breath and said, "Yes. I am. What's the deal? Are you Secret Service?"

He was. He held out a wallet with a badge. His name was Turner. He asked if I were Jack Arrowsmith. I told him I was. He said they understood I was supporting Jefferson, that I had provided the funds for Miss Carter to open a bank account for him.

I said that was true.

Jefferson ignored the impromptu interrogation going on behind him. He asked the man in the window if he could talk to Pip. The man mumbled, "I really don't think so," and closed the window.

"Mr. Arrowsmith," said agent Turner, "we'd like you and Miss Carter and Mr. Jefferson to join us. We'd like to talk. You are under no legal obligation to come with us. It's your choice. We are making no arrests here. We could give you a ride back to Mr. Jefferson's apartment."

"What is it, gentlemen? What now?" Jefferson asked, turning around to face us from the top of the steps.

"We'd like to talk to Mr. Arrowsmith about you, Mr. Jefferson," Turner said. "It's time for a chat."

"Would you stop following me if we granted your request?"

"Very possibly," Turner said. "It all depends on you."

We heard the front door locks, bolts and chains coming undone. Jefferson turned around. The young man from the window, a clean-shaven, square-jawed thirty-something fellow with well-trimmed black hair, held the door ajar and peeked out at him.

"What's going on out here?" the man said.

"Oh, sir, are you Mr. Weitzman?" Jefferson asked pleasantly.

"Yes. And you are ..."

"Thomas Jefferson. I believe you know that." He extended a hand toward Weitzman, who looked at it, looked at Jefferson's face and opened the door slightly to shake the hand.

"Yeah, hi," Mr. Weitzman said. "So. Thomas Jefferson. Isn't that the name of the, um, Founding Father?"

"Yes, yes, that's correct," Jefferson said with a slight bow and a smile. "That is I."

"Really? Now, he was the one ... let's see ... the one who said, 'Give me liberty or give me death.' Right?"

I couldn't tell if the man were serious. Jefferson tried to keep his courtesy smile in place. "Why no. That was another person," he said. "That was Mr. Henry, sir. Patrick Henry. A very great orator but a man of little reading or education. A lazy dolt, in fact. I am surprised not to have come across him, too. I suppose he'll turn up somewhere."

"Really?" said Weitzman.

I looked at Turner. He was in a huddle with his one of his colleagues. "We'll be right with you," I told him.

"Oh, take your time," he said.

"Okay, so then," Weitzman went on, "which one was Thomas Jefferson again? What did he do? Was he the Louisiana Purchase guy?"

Jefferson reared back. "You mean to say, you do not know?"

"I'm in banking. I was economics at Trinity. Then Wharton

for business." He smiled warmly, as if he didn't have a thing to be ashamed of. "I don't know much of that American studies stuff. I haven't taken American history since sixth grade." Jefferson's lower jaw jutted forward. He had to unclench his teeth to speak. "I see," he said.

"So who was he again?" Weitzman asked.

Jefferson shook his head slightly, more a tremble than an expression of bewilderment. "Are you familiar with the Declaration of Independence?"

"The Declaration of Independence? Oh! I knew that! 'We the people' and all that."

"No, not 'We the people.' Please, may I see the boy?"

Weitzman winced. "I don't think it would be a good idea. He seems a little ... afraid of you. You hit him. What are these people in suits here for?"

"Don't mind them. Pip is distressed because I gave him a little whack with a rolled up newspaper. It's not as if I had him whipped."

Weitzman's face darkened. "So you hit him, right?"

"Well, yes, of course, I ..."

"You probably shouldn't do something like that with somebody else's kid, you know? Or any kid. Jeez."

Jefferson stared. "Yes, well, all right. I understand."

I think he was pretending. I think he didn't understand at all.

"You know, if you want to see him," Weitzman said, "you should deal with his mother, not with us. Or whatever she is. That woman. Okay? Is that all right ... Mr. Jefferson? That would be more appropriate, don't you think?"

Jefferson realized there was no hope. He held still, hiding his misery. "Ah. Yes, yes. Of course. Very well," he said.

After the door closed and Jefferson had turned around, Rachel and I, on either side of him, extended an arm across his back and gently guided him along behind the Secret Service trio to the SUV. He moved like the old man we'd left behind in Charlottesville so many months before.

Chapter 23

At Jefferson's apartment building, Turner and another agent climbed the stairs with us to Jefferson's apartment. As Jefferson fumbled with his keys outside the door, a round little man in a sweat suit accosted him.

"We've all had enough. If you don't stop all the disturbances, we're calling the police again!" he squealed.

Jefferson stared at him coldly. Turner watched placidly, maybe even bored. After a panicked silence, the man erupted into a diatribe about all the banging and ripping and the hordes of people coming and going. Whatever was going on in that apartment had to stop, he said, his voice rising higher, his body set to flee even as he struggled to stay on the offensive. There was no permit for any renovations, he said, and everyone in the building was fed up.

"So I was told this morning," Jefferson said. "I have this information, sir."

I held up my hand at the man and told him that whatever had been going on in the apartment was over but everyone would have to put up with the noise of repair work for a while. "I'm sorry," I said to Jefferson. "That wall must go back up."

He raised his eyebrows at me, hesitated, nodded and returned to the locks. He opened the door and we followed him in. Turner stopped and looked around. He asked Jefferson why he had taken out the wall.

"To create an alcove for my bed," Jefferson said diffidently.

Turner slowly nodded, as if that explained everything. He

asked if he could sit. Rachel and I pulled the plastic shower curtain off the sofa for him. Pieces of plaster clattered to the floor and Turner waved a cloud of white dust away from his face. As his partner stood at military ease by the door, one hand clasping the other below his belt buckle, Turner — addressing himself to me — said that "my friend Mr. Jefferson" had sent a dozen long, involved letters to President Obama offering his thoughts on many subjects, including reparations for blacks and an analysis of the diatribes, speeches and public statements of his foes. Turner said that Jefferson had found in them a common pattern of veiled threats and a possible code to communicate with "foot soldiers in the field."

"He used a numerical formula to analyze certain word patterns," Turner said. "There were pages of numbers handwritten in columns and rows. It must have taken him days and days to produce them. We assumed he was a disturbed individual. His allusion to the danger of assassination is what really got our attention."

"I am disturbed, indeed," Jefferson muttered.

"You wrote that you had been studying presidential assassinations, correct?" Turner said to Jefferson.

"Indeed. It is a phenomenon of our history, a tradition born in the hatreds and fratricide of our unending civil strife."

Turner turned back to me. The correspondence, he went on, included an elaborate diagram of the White House, showing access points and possible routes of attack. The idea that an assassin could gain entry to the White House was "more than a stretch," Turner said, but Mr. Jefferson had been so persistent with his letters, and the diagram so well done and detailed, albeit out of date — it seemed to have been based on plans drafted soon after the War of 1812 — that he'd set off alarm bells in the Secret Service.

"We have since learned he is not a danger," Turner said. "It has been concerning to us, however, that he is a person with no identity and almost no paper trail — access through Ms. Carter to a small bank account, an episode with some protesters outside the White House perimeter, a couple of talking-tos from the police in Manhattan, a brief incarceration at Bellevue. And then there was the guard at Monticello who claimed to have seen a man who looked for all the world like Thomas Jefferson, riding out one night as a passenger in a small black coupe, like your 1986 BMW 325, Mr. Arrowsmith."

Jefferson listened wearily, slouching in his armchair in the corner, a blank look on his face. Rachel sat sadly at the desk in the corner. I stood in the front of the room, near the ruins of the wall. I could see into his bedroom. He had a large, plastic, aqua tub beside his bed, ringed by ragged water stains on the floor.

I looked at Rachel. "Wouldn't Ben have loved all this?" I said.

It startled her but, after a moment, she smiled at me warmly. "I think so, yes."

Turner leaned forward and said directly to Jefferson. "You must stop writing letters to the president. It would be best for you to avoid any activity that might be perceived as demonstrating any unusual degree of interest in him."

Jefferson held his head high. "I am to be censored then. My suggestions and observations are not welcome."

"I think you may not realize, Mr. Jefferson," said Turner, "that there are many people working very hard to study every aspect of the president's security every day and to take every precaution. By the way, you do not seem to realize the president does not go for strolls to Georgetown or the Navy Yard. That's not a security issue. You don't need to worry about that."

"I would like to meet the man. Can it be arranged?"

"No," Turner said.

"And this is so because I am perceived as a danger to him?" Jefferson said.

Turner put his hands on his knees as he leaned forward. I had the feeling he liked Jefferson. "Yes, you are on our list. We'll be watching for you. Consider this a warning. Don't go anywhere near the White House. And don't go anywhere near any place the president might be, no matter where it is in this country or any other. Is that clear?"

Jefferson looked glumly over Turner's head. "Ridiculous," he said. "This cannot be legal. Except perhaps in Mr. Hamilton's great nation state."

"I ask again: Do you understand?" Turner said.

Jefferson looked at him icily. "I understand perfectly. Thank you."

Turner studied him. "Where were you born, Mr. Jefferson?"

"At Shadwell, in Albemarle County."

"Where did you go to school?"

"I went to the local English school at age five and the Latin school at age nine. I studied with a clergyman from Scotland, Mr. Douglas. I went later with Dr. Maury, a correct classical scholar, and then down to the College of William and Mary, where I studied the law with Mr. Wythe."

Turner slowly shook his head. "And your parents?"

"Peter Jefferson was my father, a surveyor and mapmaker and farmer, and Jane Randolph, of the Virginia Randolphs, who trace their pedigree far back in England and Scotland, to which you may ascribe whatever merit you choose."

"So, what would it be? You must be about 260 years old then," Turner said.

"I am a ghost, Mr. Turner, a circumstance that has created an array of problematical situations. I met these two friends at Monticello as a mere spirit," he said, holding out his arm toward Rachel and me. "I acquired a corporeal form, obtained renewed vigor and youth and went off with my new friends in their self-propelled carriage to see your country."

Turner leaned farther over his knees, looked at me with a small grimace and squinted.

"It's all true," I shrugged. "I don't know what else to tell you."

"It is true," Rachel said.

We all just looked at Turner and he looked back at each of us, one at a time.

"It's a crime," he said, "to provide false information in an investigation such as this." I sensed he was reading from a script and didn't take the threat too seriously.

"Nobody's providing false information," I said. "I met this man last August on the west lawn at Monticello. I brought Rachel to meet him soon after that. He was kind enough to make an appearance for her under the house in the all-weather passageway."

"I really had no control," Jefferson interrupted.

"No, you didn't, did you?" Rachel said slyly. Jefferson glanced at her and nearly smiled.

"We took him away with us," I went on. "One thing has led to another. Hey, would you have any pointers on how to get a Social Security number for a person in his shoes so we can get him a job?"

I had the feeling Turner was holding back a laugh. He kept a straight face and shook his head. "I think you're out of luck," he said. He studied Jefferson thoughtfully. "We know everywhere you've been with him and Miss Carter since your visit to Monticello, Mr. Arrowsmith. We know what they've been doing in the city, what you were doing in New Jersey. Mostly."

I guess that news didn't surprise any of us. "This is worse than King Louis and his spies," Jefferson grumbled.

Turner abruptly shook his head, got up and turned to me. "He's going to get himself in a lot of trouble if someone doesn't keep him under control," he said, handing me his card. "Here's my number. We're calling off the investigation but keep us posted if you think there's something we should know." He pointed at Jefferson. "No more letters, Mr. Jefferson!" he said.

"Do not point at me, sir," Jefferson said calmly.

When Turner and his mute partner had gone, Jefferson folded his hands together and pressed them against his forehead, closing his eyes. Rachel got up from the desk chair, went to sit on the ottoman at Jefferson's feet and rested a hand on his knee.

"This hasn't worked," Rachel said to Jefferson.

"I would disagree," he answered, his eyes still closed. "I was progressing toward an orderly new world for ourselves. Until I struck Pip. That was a great mistake. I was not myself."

"No, you were not yourself."

He opened his eyes and attempted to smile at Rachel. "I have always meant to be kind," he said.

We sat in the rubble and dust and talked as the room darkened. There was something about the three of us being alone together that soothed me. Rachel poured wine. Jefferson brightened eventually, chattering excitedly about the stupendous bridge he had noticed up at Fort Washington during a walk in Riverside Park. I brought up the retirement of the Jefferson interpreter at Colonial Williamsburg. I had seen on the Williamsburg website that they were still looking to fill the position. We had to act quickly, I said. We had to get him down there for an interview and worry about the Social Security problem later. As odd as it might be for him to live and work in a kind of museum of his own youth, I told Jefferson, it might be a solution to his troubles with the 21st century.

"I have no troubles. I've been quite content," he protested. "I am enjoying my visit immensely. It is a struggle but there has been much to learn and it has been a bracing experience. Now," he said, turning to Rachel, "my dear, would you put on my music? It is the time of day for it."

She went to the cabinet between the front windows, where an iPod had been mounted in the absent professor's player.

"Put it on shuffle, my dear," he said.

The volume was low. I could just hear a slightly tinny old recording of Charles Trenet singing "Que Reste-t-Il de Nos Amours?"

Jefferson listened, his chin high. "Hmmmm," he said. "Lost youth. Lost love. I find it charming." He clasped his hands and tilted his head. "Well! Shall we have dinner together?" he said, a little of the sparkle returning to his eyes. "It has been far too long since the three of us enjoyed each other's company without some horrific commotion."

"Yes," Rachel said softly. "Like old times. Shall we go out or stay here?"

I looked around the room. I wanted to go out but Jefferson said he preferred to stay in "if you can pardon the mess." He asked Rachel to pick up some things at Mr. Kim's and at the D'Agostino on Broadway. "Mr. Arrowsmith, what would you like? I am thinking of a cod simmered in wine with fresh peas

from Mr. Kim and a bottle of good Pouilly Fumé. I happen to
have an excellent one handy in the icebox."

"That's what he calls the refrigerator," Rachel said.

Rod Stewart came on, singing "Long Ago and Far Away."

"Did you put this on the iPod for him?" I asked her.

She nodded. "Yes, but he found most of them on his own."

Jefferson raised his chin again, listening. "Ah! Mr. Stewart's
rendition of a delightful tune, Mr. Arrowsmith. It was one from
a period of great brilliance in American popular music. Pithy,
witty, charming lyrics. Just wonderful. There are better songs;
Mercer and Porter and Loesser, they were all nothing less than
geniuses, but I am fond of this one."

"He thinks of me when he hears it," Rachel said quietly,
"but he'd never tell you that."

Jefferson looked abashed for only a second. "Oh! Well, of
course. Of course I think of you. I'd already learned the search
process on iTunes, however, before Miss Carter came to my assistance."

Rachel looked at me with a crooked smile. "He's so sweet,"
she said.

He was about to say more when I heard a tapping and a
fluttering sound. We looked to the windows. A gray bird with
a blur of white and black markings under its wings was at the
window nearest Jefferson, lightly beating its breast at the glass.

"Dick!" he shouted. "It's Dick!"

He sprang from the armchair, threw himself at the window
and struggled to lift the sash. Rachel and I leapt up to help. The
window popped open and we raised it as high as it would go.
Jefferson leaned out into the airshaft.

"Dick! Dick!" he called.

The bird was gone. I feared it had hurt itself. But as Jefferson
leaned out calling for him, Dick reappeared in the air before
him, furiously beating his wings in a hover. Jefferson held himself still and erect. The bird disappeared, then returned once
more, this time landing on his shoulder. Jefferson drew himself
back into the room, the sleek, handsome mocker on his shoulder. Its yellow eye — intelligent and strangely human, with a

sharp black speck of a pupil — was fixed on Jefferson's face.

"Rachel, some berries for Dick! And a dish of water!" he said, easing himself back into his chair. "Dick! You are a fine bird, Dick! You have returned. What have been your adventures? Do tell us!"

He sounded bright and gay but there was an odd twist to Jefferson's mouth and terrible pain in his eyes.

I closed the window. Rachel put a small dish of berries and saucer of water on the windowsill. As she stood by, Dick jumped from Jefferson's shoulder to the windowsill, dipped his beak into the water, lifted up his head and drank.

"Good bird," Rachel said.

"Wait 'til you hear him perform," Jefferson said to me. "It's my fancy that he's full of melodies from the hills of Virginia. He specializes in the cardinal, you know," Jefferson said.

Rachel put on a parka and, heading out for the groceries, smiled at us from the doorway.

"Can I go with you? Need help?" I said.

"I'm fine. I'm so glad Dick's back," she said, fixing her gaze on me and smiling. "He's a rare bird."

Staring out the window at the airshaft, Jefferson said when she'd gone, "Mr. Adams would be pleased with me, eating his Massachusetts fish."

He got up wearily, took the berries and saucer of water and walked with Dick on his shoulder to the large wicker cage suspended from the ceiling. "Time for a rest, Dick," he said. The bird fluttered from his shoulder, landed at the open hatch of the cage and hopped in. Jefferson put in the water and berries and locked the hatch. "You're safe again," he said. "All is well."

Jefferson asked me to please pardon him for a few moments. He put on his old metal-framed spectacles and fussed at his desk with papers and books. My old laptop was open on the desk, running a slideshow of my photos on the hard drive. I saw Pam by the roses in our backyard. I saw Ben and Pam on skis at Stratton. A tune came on that I didn't know. I lowered my eyes and focused on the music. It was an old Celtic song, or seemed to be. A woman with a sweet, pretty voice sang it:

Where are you tonight, I wonder?
Where will you be tonight while I cry?
Will sleep for you come easy while I alone can't slumber?
Will you welcome the morning at another man's side?

Distracted, his face set with a hard and worried look, he took off his spectacles after a few minutes and got up from the desk to go into the kitchen. I wondered if it was the right time to tell him I had never slept with Rachel, and to ask him where they planned to have the child and what in God's name they thought they were doing. I decided not.

He came back with a bottle. "I've gotten so used to modern ways, eating late, drinking early," he said. "Would you like some Madeira, Mr. Arrowsmith? It has been a vexing day, has it not?"

"It has and I would," I said, realizing how tired I felt. I asked him if he'd mind closing the lid of the laptop. "Those photos. I'd rather not see them right now."

He glanced at it. "Oh! I always enjoyed those pictures of yours. But yes, of course, I'll close it. I'm sorry. And I'm sorry for the shock you have endured, Mr. Arrowsmith. We have been thinking of you with great anxiety. We are so pleased to see you again."

I smiled. "Likewise, likewise. Sorry for the long absence. I did not want to be wandering around with my wounds showing."

"Ah yes, yes, I know what you mean. Your withdrawal was a necessary part of the healing process required after a great shock to the soul."

He poured us each a glass, put his on the windowsill and collapsed into the armchair. "Things have changed," he said, taking a sip of his drink.

I sat back on the couch with my glass in hand. "I know," I said.

"Well, I mean these times," he said with a flourish of his hand. "For one thing, you people now take music so much for granted. It's everywhere in your lives. On the television, the radio, the iPod, the computer. This ubiquity relegates music to a kind of atmospherical role, like the wind and the weather," he said, shaking his head. "In my time, to hear one of the ladies play the pianoforte in the parlor after dinner was a particular pleasure. Well, *usually* a pleasure, I should say. And to hear a full orchestra perform Bach or Haydn! Why, my heavens, that was a grand experience one remembered forever. I myself had not heard such a demonstration of the divine until I escaped the provinces and went to Paris."

"The past seems better," I blurted.

Jefferson arched his brows. "Do you really believe that, Mr. Arrowsmith?"

The Madeira blossomed in my throat. "No. I suppose not. I don't know."

He protested. "How could you not know? You people live so well. You are not threatened by bilious fevers or plagues. You all take pills that reduce the incidence of apoplectic fits. What are they called? Statins! Your wives do not die in childbirth, the way ours did." He turned grim at that thought and stared at the floor.

"Yes," I said. "Nostalgia is an illusion. It is the absence of pain. That's what it means in Greek, right?"

"No, not at all. It means a return home. It refers to a longing to return home."

"Oh! Well, whatever," I said, sounding like one of my eighth-graders. "But the point I wanted to make is this: We are not wired to remember pain. We remember pleasures vividly but pain only faintly, and only as an idea, not an experience. We cannot conjure up how the pain itself actually felt. Hence the past always seems better than it really was because the painful parts are left out. I think it is a product of Darwin's natural selection. So women do not dread another childbirth and men do not run away from battle or the dangers of the hunt."

"Hmmm. Interesting," he said, thinking on it, tapping the tips of his fingers together. "Natural selection. Yes, yes, I've read your Mr. Darwin." After a while, he folded his hands together, touched his knuckles to his chin and looked into the middle of the room. "The past was cloaked in darkness, ignorance and exploitation, Mr. Arrowsmith. I cannot imagine thinking of the past as a better time. But you know," he said, bowing his head sharply, "it is so impossibly frantic and irritating, this modern life of yours. There is too much to master. There is too much to choose from. It is all a jumble. Everyone walking around staring at or listening into their instruments."

"I think you're right," I said.

"The center cannot hold," he said. "I recall that phrase from a poem I discovered somewhere." He looked over my head and stroked his chin. "Too much information. Too many gadgets. Too much selling, everywhere, all the time … or marketing, as they call it," he mused.

We sat silently for a while.

"Mr. Arrowsmith," he said, "I must ask — forgive me please — if you might be angry."

I angled my head. "Angry?"

"With me. And Miss Carter."

I looked at the floor, a little surprised. Their relationship had never angered me. It baffled me. I told him so.

"Ah," he said quietly. "You know, I always wished for a son."

"A legal son. A white son, you mean," I said, surprising myself again. I had not meant to go on the attack.

He lifted himself up a bit, straightening his back and shoulders. "Well. As you say: Whatever." He thought for a while, then went on: "Do you wonder, Mr. Arrowsmith, whose child this is? I do."

"No, for God's sake! Not at all!" I said, tensing up, my nerves and muscles ready for a fight. I was surprised as well as angry. Jefferson, his biographers will all tell you, hated confrontation, but with me he had gone directly to the point. "Look. It's not mine, if that's what you're asking," I said, "and I don't believe Rachel is the kind of young woman to have been with anybody else but you. You should know that about her."

He calmly listened and slowly nodded. "I know human nature, in spite of what Hamilton believes," he said. He pressed his fingertips together again. "Mr. Arrowsmith, I am aware now of the great leaps of knowledge and understanding that have been achieved in, oh, what is the word again — *genetics* — since my day. I am aware of the operation of deoxyribonucleic acid in the transmission of hereditary information. I've read Watson and Crick's original paper. And let me say the double helical structure of the DNA molecule is, by the way, more proof of a cosmic intelligence," he said, emphasizing the point by aiming his index at the ceiling.

"I think so," I said.

"I am well aware," he said, "there is something called the Y chromosome that is passed through the male line. It is how they showed that a Jefferson male was 'almost certainly' — as I see it put in the academical papers on the subject — the father of at least one of the children of my servant Sally Hemings."

He looked out the window. "You know, I have refused to give Professor Kant the satisfaction of an answer on your so-called Hemings question. As obvious as it may be, he craves hearing it from me. I think he secretly knows I am Thomas Jefferson and not the deranged freak of nature we have pretended myself to be."

"I wondered about that."

"Well," he said, swiping at his sleeve to brush off some plaster dust, "I correct myself. I *am* a freak of nature, but I'm not deranged. Kant and I have had many long and enjoyable discussions and debates. His enmity toward me was entirely superficial, I think, unlike Mr. Carter's. That strange man dislikes me quite sincerely. But Kant! I rather like Kant. He has assisted me in learning more of the history of the country since my own time. He has guided me through his class syllabi. He's working on my identification problems as well, you know."

"No, I didn't know. That's good. I suppose he has some connections."

"Apparently so."

Jefferson paused and looked at me with a weak smile. "On my desk," he said, "I have for you my confession on this matter, Mr. Arrowsmith. I hope somehow it can be of value to you. If the handwriting can be shown to be my own, and the factual details verified or at least supported by all that's known, per-haps it will fetch enough at auction to repay some of my debt to you."

"Oh!" I said, realizing what he was talking about. "My goodness. Well, thank you! But won't it be obvious the paper and the ink are modern?"

"Yes. That is a problem. That is why I have included in the letter a secret about Monticello that I believe no one knows ex-cept me and a long dead mason, who was a member of my fam-ily, and my valet, Burwell. You once asked about the letters my wife and I exchanged. Mine to her were destroyed. But there is, hidden in the foundation, near the spot where I met Miss Carter, a lead-lined sealed box containing my wife's letters to me when I was away in Williamsburg with the Assembly and in Philadelphia with the Congress. My confession gives its lo-cation with some specificity. Its discovery might tend to sup-port these documents and your account of meeting the ghost of Thomas Jefferson, wouldn't you say?"

I didn't know what to say. I gaped at him.

"My God. So you did have children with Sally?"

"Do not forget, Mr. Arrowsmith," he said, after studying me for a moment, "that my country — by that I mean Virginia — was not settled by Puritans, nor did we suffer with the absur-dities of your Victorian era's many hypocrisies, which I have learned still affect this country.

"Sally's brother James taught her to be quite assertive of her rights, you know," he went on. "Both could have left me in Par-is as free persons. Which only served to intensify her appeal to me. I had no control over the attraction. I would have quashed it if I could have." He looked up, thinking. "You know, I must say, Miss Carter's charged defense of Jamie soon after we three first met was quite enchanting to me. It was as if she'd known and loved him, too, as Sally loved her dear brother."

He leaned forward toward me. "I have been astonished to find this matter is still an issue. More than it ever was in my day, really! And now all the fuss over this! All the dust that dreadful newspaper scribe stirred up, and it's still settling down like the ash that fell on Pompeii. Dig me up and this is what you find: the whole sorry thing pickled in time."

There was a sudden silence from the iPod.

"Did you love her?" I asked.

"Oh! That is a very personal question but I'll allow it, for you, Mr. Arrowsmith. Sally? Certainly not; not as I had loved my wife, no."

"What about Rachel? Do you love her?"

The mockingbird began to chatter lightly, emitting soft squeaks, clicks and little whistles as if it were speaking to Jefferson. He cocked his head and looked toward the bird. Dick broke into a rendition of the loud angry call of a blue jay.

"Old Dick likes to perform in the dark," Jefferson said. "It is warm in here so he thinks it's spring in Virginia, a lovely time."

"Your relationship with Rachel. Is it purely therapeutic? For convenience? Do you love her?"

"Just as you do, Mr. Arrowsmith," he said absently, "I'm sure. Just as you do."

Dick kept at renditions, offering up a crow, a cardinal and a robin. Jefferson watched him with obvious pleasure. On the iPod, something familiar, something strange — a mournful electric guitar solo, accompanied by electronic strings, a tinkling sound and the murmur and rising roar of a crowd — came up in volume like smoke rising from a smoldering fire. "Don't tell me. Is that Pink Floyd?" I asked, thinking I'd have to ask him about Rachel again when the time was right, and I'd tell him that if he didn't love her and promise to stay by her forever he was a heartless manipulator and I wouldn't stand for it.

"Well, it's Roger Waters," he said. "Formerly of Pink Floyd. English fellow. They split up, you know. Years ago."

I grinned. "Ah, yes. I do."

"Mr. Arrowsmith, do you feel we should seek a DNA test? I understand this is possible in utero." He pressed the tips of his fingers together and tapped them lightly as he waited for my reply.

My God, the man could make your head spin. I blinked and forced myself to focus. "Does Rachel want a test?" I asked. "It's entirely up to her, isn't it?"

"You mean legally?"

"Yes, and morally and ethically and everything else."

"Of course, of course," he said. He flattened a hand against his chest. "I myself ... I would like to know. The child is a boy. That has been determined with the, what is it, the ultrasound machine. I would like to know if he truly is my son, as long as that is now possible."

"Well he's not mine, Mr. Jefferson. I keep telling you. He could not be. I have never touched her."

He smiled at me patiently. "So you wouldn't mind the test, then?"

"Why do you want the test so much if it's not mine?"

"I simply want to be sure it's mine, a proven thing, through science."

He thought I was a liar or Rachel was a slut or both. "As I said," I said, trying to hold back my anger, "it's her decision. Not yours or mine."

He rubbed a hand over his mouth and stared at his knees. "Well. She resists. I had hoped to recruit you into my cause ... that is, if it were your cause also."

"Rachel knows it's yours," I protested. "You should be satisfied with that."

He smiled and tapped his fingers. "I suppose it is difficult for me to forget the old days. My apologies. I will not press the matter."

"You should love her. As you did your wife," I said.

At that moment, the mockingbird pretended it was a crow and Jefferson's faint smile disappeared. He looked at me coldly. "I will be very frank with you, Mr. Arrowsmith, because the circumstances are so extraordinary. But more so because you are my friend. I must tell you I am not capable of the kind of love I think you speak of. The loss of my wife left a part of my soul an empty vial which I have forever lacked the spirits to fill up. I thought once or twice I had escaped the veil of my mourning but I was mistaken."

He looked at the ceiling to recite the poem from Homer he'd

inscribed on his wife's tombstone at Monticello: "*Nay, if even in the house of Hades, the dead forget their dead, yet will I even there be mindful of my dear comrade.*" He looked back at me. "I gave her my promise. She asked me for it, for the sake of the children. There was no need, no need for her to ask."

The mockingbird fell silent. On the iPod, the drums came in on Roger's guitar solo, very bluesy, very Mississippi Delta. As tears came into my eyes and blurred my sight, Jefferson startled them away: "What about you, Mr. Arrowsmith?" he asked. "Does your love for your lost wife leave room for Rachel? Or any other woman?"

I allowed him the question. I'd had the effrontery to ask him mine. After thinking, I said it did. "I find one does not exclude the other. I find one intensifies the other. And Ben, too. She's all about Ben in my head. "

He considered my answer and acknowledged it with a monotonic hum. "Yes, I'm sure your love for your son is at work in all this, my dear friend."

He seemed a much stronger man than I at that moment.

On the iPod, Roger's number gave way to "Ashokan Farewell," the theme to Ken Burns's documentary about the Civil War. The mocker started in again with a round of imitations, even with the room in near darkness. Keys jangled at the door. It swung open and Rachel came in with two plastic grocery bags. She asked what we were doing sitting in the dark.

"Just talking, my dear," Jefferson said.

We ate by candlelight around the coffee table and settled into easy banter. Rachel helped me try to convince Jefferson that Williamsburg would be a good place for him. He listened politely but shook his head. "It is not my nature to go back in time," he said. "I have no interest in it." Rachel urged him to keep an open mind. She said she could find work in Williamsburg, at the college, and that she'd like it there.

The talk of his situation wearied him. He formally thanked us both for all we had done for him that day and told us he had some writing to do before retiring.

We had been dismissed, both of us.

I drove Rachel to her dorm. On the way, I expressed surprise that she hadn't wanted to stay with Jefferson at the apartment. "Oh, I never stay with him," she said, pretending it was all perfectly reasonable. "He must have his own space, you know? He's Thomas Jefferson, Jack." She hunched forward and said it again. "He's *Thomas Jefferson*. I'd do anything for him."

"You're kidding," I said after glancing at her. "That's just weird, Rachel. It's not like you to be a sap. You would do anything for him? Whatever he asks?"

"That's not what I meant." She put her hand over her face and closed her eyes.

"Do you actually love that man? Or whatever he is?"

She lowered her hand, clenching shut her eyes in pain. "Yes," she whispered. "I do. I've fallen in love with him. I believe he loves me, too."

She'd been hard on me, leaving me alone with Ben's journal, but I could not bring myself to tell her what Jefferson had told me.

Chapter 24

Jefferson had to move out in early April, when the contractor got to work putting the Claremont apartment back together. He came to stay with me in New Jersey, where I finally convinced him to call Williamsburg about the still unfilled job there. He gave in, I suspect, because he did not want to spend the rest of his life — and who knew how long that would be — as my permanent houseguest in "this strange, artificial landscape" of suburbia.

Rachel stayed in the city. She had fallen behind on her thesis for Kant and wanted time alone to finish and get her degree. After the wall had been restored, she moved to the Claremont apartment to put things back in order for the professor's return.

She had a fight with her father when she went up to Yonkers to retrieve the cat. She told me on the phone he had stood in his doorway, yelling at her that Jefferson didn't love her, he was using her, she was a fool to be stepping and fetching for him and having his child. He slammed the door on her as she stood on the porch with the cat carrier. She was about to drive away when he burst out of the house with something under his arm. Rachel, in tears, drove off before he could get to the car, leaving him standing at the curb shouting after her.

As she was telling me about it, she started sniffling on the phone. "How does he know anything?" she said. "He doesn't know."

I told her I was sorry to hear it, even though I felt the old man was right.

A few days later, Mr. Carter called me. All business, he asked for my address. He said he had something to get rid of. It came in the mail a few days later. I unwrapped the brown paper and opened the cardboard box to find a small, polished walnut case with brass hinges and latch. It looked old. I opened it and found inside an inkwell, a tarnished silver shoe buckle and a pair of old metal spectacles.

There was a note: "These are for Rachel. I don't want them in the house any longer. I'd forgotten I had them. Give them to her for me please."

I put the box in my desk and, distracted by Jefferson's presence, forgot about it.

I installed Jefferson in Ben's room. He laid low. He did a lot of reading, writing and listening to music. He kept Dick on his shoulder and let him fly in the living room, always after asking if I'd mind. He watched DVDs and went for long walks. I joined him sometimes. We went to movies at the multiplex. He loved going to the movies. The big-screen experience dazzled him.

I liked having Jefferson around, especially in the evenings, when we'd share a few glasses of wine and talk politics — his politics, mostly: John Adams, John Marshall, Madison and "that adulterer Hamilton." Jefferson was good company, even though I sensed he was a little ill at ease in my house.

As the weather turned warm and the trees popped their buds, I started getting calls from friends to play golf and to come for dinner. They asked what had happened to me all winter, where had I disappeared to, what the hell was going on. I told them I had been hiding in my study, working on a book about Thomas Jefferson, trying to make myself into a real historian.

There must have been talk that a tall, red-haired man had been seen coming and going on foot from my driveway, taking long walks down the winding main road. For a long time, no one said anything about him to me, not even my neighbor Nancy Steinberg. Our houses were well hidden from each other by a line of young spruces but there were some gaps and I could see her now and then in her Mercedes, going by on her long driveway.

Jefferson and I ran into her at the Pathmark. Jefferson loved the Pathmark. He was always calling for me to come look at an artichoke or an avocado or a pineapple. He leaned over the displays and studied the onions, corn, tomatoes and potatoes, picking one up with breathless awe and, agitated, putting it down to scratch notes in a little booklet he kept in his jacket pocket.

One day Nancy came wheeling around the corner of the fresh produce aisle, her wildly curly hair bobbing around her head. "Oh my! Well, hello boys!" she said, as if she'd caught us at something. "Shopping for dinner? So Jack, for God's sake, who's your new friend here? You haven't introduced him. Everyone wants to know."

"Oh hi, Nancy!" I said. "This is Thomas Jefferson. Mr. Jefferson, my neighbor, Nancy Steinberg."

"How do you do, madam," said Jefferson, with a half bow. He was holding a cantaloupe.

"Thomas Jefferson, huh? You're not serious! Any relation?" she asked, playing along.

"Very directly," Jefferson said. "I have the selfsame Y chromosome. Tell me, how do you like this melon, madam? Have you ever seen such a giant?"

"Well, yes, I see giant melons all the time," she said after a pause. Nancy had quite a rack. She looked at me with arched brows and turned back to Jefferson. "Huh. You even look like him. Are you serious about the chromosome? What are you? His great-great-great-grandson?"

"No, I'm his ghost. I'm the man himself, restored to flesh and bone through some mysterious process that appears to have nothing to do with the usual operations of nature. But I ask you *this*, madam: How could we be surprised by such a thing in a universe of black holes and anti-matter and honeybees that follow a lead bee by the thousands to a new nesting site and make their descents and landings all in perfect coordination? I saw that on PBS, I believe. Did you see it? It's all miraculous! Nothing should surprise us!"

"Bees? Ghost?"

"Yes, yes," Jefferson went on, "I was a decrepit ottamy of 82 when I began this adventure into your times. Now I feel myself to be a man of 40 or less!"

"What the hell is an ottamy?" she said.

"A skeleton, my dear woman."

"Oh." She stared at him, her flash of scorn turning into vague wonder. Breaking into a grin, she said, "Oh! Oh, you are so very good! Oh, Jack. He's fun. My God. Very, very good. Well, how about that? You don't meet a ghost every day in Pathmark. You, Mr. Jefferson," she said, driving her finger into Jefferson's chest, "must come over one night with Jack and tell me all about yourself. I want to hear about Marie Antoinette. You met her, right? Was she really such a stupid bitch? Are you just visiting, Mr. Jefferson? Or have you moved in with Jack?"

"Just visiting my old friend Mr. Arrowsmith. Moving on to Virginia soon, I hope."

"Back to your roots. So Jack. You haven't turned over a new leaf? Because gay is fine. There's nothing wrong with gay. I'd be gay if it were the only way I could have sex. So. Well then. All right, boys. It's been real!"

I smiled and shook my head as she started off with her cart, calling to Jefferson over her shoulder, "Thanks a lot for the Declaration of Independence, Tom. Nice work. So well written. Too bad you boys couldn't free all those slaves but, hey, I know, I know, not so easy. You can only do so much."

Jefferson faked a smile but his face flushed and his eyes flashed. "That is your neighbor?"

"That is my neighbor," I said.

"My heavens. Quite a boisterous woman."

"She's fun. She takes getting used to, that's all."

I gave him a section of the backyard to grow vegetables. Of course he needed an assistant, so we found him an Ecuadorian man named Victor from the landscaping crew that did my yard. Late every day he came to dig and weed and plant, under constant orders from Jefferson, who stood close by, wearing the straw hat Rachel had bought him, as if it were mid-summer in the Blue Ridge and the sun were blazing.

He couldn't get used to the phone. He kept holding it away

from his ear in the middle of conversations and looking at it with either fascination or frustration. The sudden interruptions and strange pauses annoyed Rachel, I know. After a couple of days with me, he made his call to Colonial Williamsburg about the job. I worried he'd be strange on the phone but he seemed to bear down on himself; he listened like an owl tracking a mouse and he spoke with an odd, proud formality. He was told they were reviewing applications and that interviews would be held in early May; that he should send a résumé, a photo, a video clip and a cover letter explaining his qualifications, his experience and why he wanted the job. If they wanted him to come down, they'd let him know.

I knew the video, if we did it right, would get him the job. The problem would come when he went for his interview. Jefferson called Professor Kant for advice and they talked on the phone for half an hour, Jefferson back to his tricks with the receiver, pulling it away from his ear and staring at it crossly. The next day we drove into the city so he could continue the discussion with Kant. Rachel came along. We had lunch at the Columbia faculty dining room. It became our summit meeting on what to do with our friend.

Kant told us he knew Rudy Powell, an old freedom marcher who'd become the longtime congressman from upper Manhattan. He'd developed a reputation for invincibility no matter what embarrassments appeared in the media about his condos and tax oversights. With a little help from his friends in Albany and Washington, Kant said, Powell could find a way to get Jefferson legalized.

No matter what Powell came up with, we agreed Jefferson should not tell the Williamsburg human resources people he was the man himself, as he'd taken to doing. He would have to present himself as the brilliant oddball hermit with money who'd lived off the grid for years — which Kant believed, or pretended to believe. He suggested the embellishment that Jefferson had grown up with another name and had changed it to Thomas Jefferson because he looked so much like him and he'd spent his lifetime learning every known detail about the man. He would tell them the only job in the world he had ever wanted was to play Jefferson full-time, day in, day out, in Williamsburg, but it had been filled so brilliantly for so many years by the great Bill Barker. And now that Barker was retiring, Jefferson hoped his dream could come true.

My bet was they'd find him irresistible no matter how freaked out they might be. But how would we establish where he was born and raised and other little bits of personal history that any real person would have?

"Tell them he had amnesia," Rachel said, "or was in an orphanage."

"Or find an abandoned identity and use it," Professor Kant said. "I have researchers who might help with that, including a fellow in Virginia. Let me look into it."

I was surprised. I hadn't suspected Kant to be the ends-justify-the-means type.

We rented a plain 18th-century outfit for Jefferson at a costume supply store in SoHo. He proclaimed the outfit dreadful. "I would not have been caught dead in this set of rags even in Williamsburg," he said. Too bad, I said. It was just for the video. We sat him down to practice in front of the camera in a book-lined corner of my study. With Rachel behind the camera, I sat just outside the frame to throw touristy questions at him after he finished a spiel about the Declaration and the Virginia Statute for Religious Freedom: Why didn't you free your slaves? Did you really have children with Sally Hemings? Why did you die broke? Did you run away from the British during the Revolution? What did you use for toilet paper?

Even though we'd gone over these things before, he flushed and turned icy when I bore down and really gave him the third degree: How did you keep your relationship with Sally secret? Weren't you kind of mean to your younger daughter Maria? Didn't you lie when you told John Adams you had never paid the press to slander him?

After answering several questions with extreme annoyance, he clammed up and glared into space. "This is ridiculous," he said.

"Thomas," Rachel said from beside the camera, putting her

hands on her hips, framing her growing belly. "This is the way it will be. It's all right to be a little annoyed. That will work. But you can't be furious about it. You can't refuse to talk. You are a job applicant here, not the master of Monticello or the president of the United States."

"The impertinence of it!" he said. "It's outrageous, discussing personal matters with those people in their sneakers and half-pantaloons draped across their vast buttocks."

"It will be like politics," she said. "Putting up with people you hate to achieve a worthy goal — in this case, *educating* them!"

That seemed to make him think. He flicked his brows, peered at the cheap fabric of his sleeve, resettled himself and said, "Very well, very well. Proceed, proceed. We'll try again."

She slept in the guest room but for all I know she snuck in with him in the middle of the night. In front of me, he was formal with her, as always. But in the morning, I saw him from my bedroom window in the vegetable garden, holding her hand as he showed off his flourishing patches of various beans, lettuces and asparagus.

Less than a week after we'd sent in his DVD and the rest of his application, he got the call for an interview.

He spent days studying my Williamsburg coffee table books, collected in the days when Pam and I were regular visitors. As he read, Dick perched on his shoulder, taking currants and raisins when Jefferson paused to offer them from his lips.

On the deck one evening, a couple of days before it was time for us to drive down for the interview, he told me, "I never liked Williamsburg, particularly. It had a superficial air of sophistication when the burgesses were in session," he said, "but many of them were nothing but gamblers and drunkards, and for the capital of a great colony, the town was a provincial little pile. Delightful dinners with the governor, I must say. Fauquier, I mean, of course. He was a good man of great learning. "

On a sunny day in May, he and I went to Rachel's graduation, making a detour to pick up Mr. Carter, whom I had called and convinced to go. He was civil and so was Jefferson, like family members with a bad history who made the effort to get along for a son or daughter's sake — as Ben and I had done in Pam's last days.

Kant was there, too. As we sat in the sun on the lower quad, waiting on our folding chairs, he leaned across me and told Jefferson that he had good news. Reaching into his jacket, he pulled out an envelope and handed it to Jefferson, who put on his glasses and opened it. After he'd read the papers it contained, he handed them to me without comment. They included a Virginia district court order allowing Jefferson to take the citizenship test as soon as he was ready.

Jefferson took back the papers, folded them and pulled a thumb and forefinger along the crease. "These were obtained fraudulently?" he asked.

"One would have to dig quite deeply to reach that conclusion, I'm told," Kant said. "No one will bother. And by the way, you have a friend in the Secret Service."

Kant had called Agent Turner, who'd turned out to be helpful, offering to advise Congressman Powell what he'd need to do to get Jefferson clearance through the Homeland Security Administration. "If he'd been brown, or a Muslim, it would not have worked out so well," Kant said.

Mr. Carter shook his head in disgust. "Aren't you too high and mighty for this sort of business?" he asked Jefferson, who ignored the question with a blithe gaze.

Kant said that Congressman Powell wanted Jefferson to become a citizen at Monticello, where the Thomas Jefferson Foundation hosted a big swearing-in ceremony every Fourth of July for people who'd passed the citizenship test. Powell wanted to be there with him for the photo op.

Jefferson looked at me with disgust. "So now my legal existence in this world depends on a corrupt congressman and his friends. And I will owe him a consideration."

Kant and I looked away while Mr. Carter smirked and chuckled. "Well, well. Nothing has changed all that much," he said.

Chapter 25

We were to be in Williamsburg for his interview Monday afternoon. That Sunday, Rachel called and asked Jefferson if he'd like another helper for his garden. He said there was not much left to do, except for weeding and putting in fencing. Then he listened and said, "Very well, Miss Carter, if you wish. I can always use another servant."

She arrived in her Saab two hours later with Pip. As I watched from the deck, they stood side by side outside the car, Rachel's arm over Pip's shoulders. Jefferson and his man Victor looked up from their work, Jefferson removing his straw hat, hesitating and then striding in his gangly way across the lawn.

Rachel gave Pip a gentle nudge. He walked a few steps toward Jefferson, who stopped and shaded his eyes with his hand. "Why, is that our Pip?" he exclaimed.

Pip, looking ashamed, went a few steps closer.

"Pip! You have come back!" Jefferson said.

Pip held still. "I didn't mean to lose your bird," he said quietly.

"Oh, Pip. Dick is back with me. Dick is well," Jefferson said.

"I know. Miss Carter told me that."

Rachel joined them, placing her hands squarely on Pip's shoulders. "He came to the apartment looking for you," she told Jefferson. "I've been taking care of him. That woman, I've talked to her. I've been talking to Child Services, too."

Jefferson stepped closer and kneeled before the boy. "I will not strike you ever again," he said. "You have my word on that.

But Pip, we cannot love a boy who runs away. You must not run away, Pip."

Pip hung his head and, in a moment, lifted it. "Can I stay with you and Miss Carter?" he asked. "Like before?"

Jefferson held him by the arms. "I think you are a stranger in this world, like me," he said. "You're a fine young fellow, Pip, a fine young fellow." He stroked the boy's head. "We would be glad for you to stay with us. We'll take care of you. Can you go to work? Are you prepared? Come along, then; this is Victor and this is my vegetable garden," Jefferson told him, guiding Pip into the rows of pastel green lettuce and bean sprouts.

Pip's presence gave me pause. He came from a world I'd never understand and, aside from that, I thought he was a little strange: immature and otherworldly, he seemed to go off happily in his own head. For a kid from the projects, he lacked street smarts, a tough hide, the required attitude. He was a blank slate for Jefferson to fill up with rules and admonitions and a sturdy, deliberate, carefully constructed love.

Rachel, shielding her eyes from the sun, looked up at me and waved. "Hi Jack," she said. I waved back, even though we weren't more than 20 feet apart.

Rachel and Pip spent the night, everyone in their separate rooms. I lay awake, listening, the house feeling full of life even though there wasn't a sound. For the first time in weeks, I dreamed of the well-dressed black man that night. He was caressing Pam, soothing her as she suffered. The terrible feel of that vision haunted me for days.

We left for Williamsburg very early in the morning, Rachel in the front with me, Jefferson in the back with Pip. The boy gazed out the window between bouts with a video game and a book about geography Jefferson had brought along for him.

Pip was supposed to be in school but we all felt he should come along on our visit to Colonial Williamsburg, where he might be living one day soon. He'd never been anywhere outside Manhattan and, after his long silence for the first 100 miles, he turned into a magpie: "What's this bridge? What's that river? Where are we now?" he asked.

Jefferson gave him impromptu commentary on the great river of commerce that was the New Jersey Turnpike and how the state and federal governments had cooperated to build it with borrowed money; the last farms of New Jersey holding out against suburban sprawl while factory farms in the West and all over the world produced our food; Delaware Bay, once bristling with British warships, and Philadelphia, just up the river, where he had worked so hard for our independence during the hot summer of 1776; and far below us as we crossed the bridge that carried I-95, the Susquehanna, the old pathway into the frontier, Canada and the Iroquois country.

After we crossed the Mason-Dixon line and he finished a lecture about the challenges of surveying a border through rough country, his stories turned richer, more personal — people he'd known, places he'd been on his travels and the strangers he'd met at taverns who never had any idea who he was, even after he'd served for eight years as the president.

After the six-hour drive, we parked in the commercial district called Merchant's Square, where Colonial Williamsburg's administrative offices are tucked away behind the brick storefronts. Jefferson had an hour until his interview so we walked into the restored area, azaleas and tulips blooming in bright neon splashes everywhere. He grew silent and grim. Rachel took his arm.

A group of tourists, three large, happy couples past middle age in sneakers, shorts and T-shirts of white and pink and yellow, approached us. "Mr. Jefferson!" one of the men said heartily. "You are out of uniform, sir! What the heck are those clothes you're wearing?"

Jefferson seemed to consider whether or not to send them away with some icy reply. But he smiled politely, bowed his head, and explained, "I wanted to try these modern store-made vestments. My friends here provided them to me. Very cheaply made, by paupers and very young brown and yellow children in the Orient, I understand."

The hefty bunch broke into laughter. One of the men said, "It's sad. We don't make anything anymore." Another stepped forward and extended a hand, which Jefferson shook with a hazy gaze. "I'm a real fan, a real fan," the man said giddily. Jefferson let his mouth fall open. "Ah," he said.

"No really. You're my hero. Religious freedom, equality, the rights of man and all that. States' rights, especially. The right to bear arms!"

There was a flicker in Jefferson's eyes and the corners of his mouth turned up. "I'm well pleased to know it," he said. "I know you will be a vigilant defender of the spirit of the Revolution."

As we strolled, he drew a lot of looks and smiles and more little groups stopped him to chat. A couple had us take their picture with a slightly befuddled and bemused Jefferson between them.

If he liked the attention and acceptance, it did not penetrate very deeply. When we reached the Palace Green, Jefferson seemed someplace far away from us. We walked slowly with him as he peered warily around. He stopped us in front of the Wythe house. "My God," he said. "It is the same. Here I studied law with a great and noble man."

He turned to look down the green toward the governor's palace. "How many nights I walked along here, a youth fresh from the Blue Ridge, headed for a night of brilliant conversation with the governor and Mr. Wythe and Dr. Small. If they had not admitted me to their circle, I don't think I ever would have gone on to achieve a thing except a law career to supplement my wheat and tobacco. I detested practicing the law. Drudge work. And people at you all the time."

He looked down at Pip, smiled and took the boy's hand as we walked on. "It is very, very strange to be here. It has both brightened and disturbed my spirits."

We had lunch at a table outside a gourmet sandwich shop that was choked with students and tourists waiting to place and pick up their orders. Jefferson had little to say. From there, he went off alone for his interview while Rachel and I looked through the shops of Merchant's Square with Pip, who helped distract us from our worry. We bought him a tricorn hat and a fife.

"Would a slave have a hat like this?" he asked.

We weren't sure. We didn't think so.

"What about a fife? Would a slave have a fife?" he asked. We didn't know that either and I felt unequal to the task of helping to raise this boy. Rachel and Jefferson seemed completely at ease with him but I wondered if they would do any better.

There is a bench in Merchant's Square on which Colonial Williamsburg has installed a life-size bronze of Jefferson, seated in his shirtsleeves, looking off in thought as he holds a quill pen over a document on a laptop writing desk — the Declaration, of course. Waiting, we sat on that bench next to the imitation Jefferson, Rachel and I anxiously silent, looking at our watches, as Pip peppered us with questions about the statue. He gawked at it, put his hand on its shoulder and swung around it as we explained that Mr. Jefferson was a very famous man, the kind of man people made statues of. "He be some good man to know," Pip said before settling down with a new game Rachel had let him install on her iPhone.

I thanked Rachel for never having brought up the journal. She looked at me with a mix of puzzlement and caution, her face slowly softening with a trace of happy surprise. She closed her eyes and gave me a tiny nod.

"There's really no need to talk about it," I said. "You were right to have me read it. But I have to tell you, they haunt me in my dreams, Pam and that man, and I think I've been expecting to see them come around a corner any time."

She reached for my hand and squeezed it. We hugged. I still must have been pretty raw because I had to fight back tears that had come up out of nowhere.

When we saw Jefferson coming our way across Duke of Gloucester Street, there was no reading his face. He looked serious, a man on a mission, like a lawyer marching to court. He gave the statue of himself a brief stare of surprise, reared his head in disdain, flicked his eyebrows at it dismissively and gave us a little bow and a crooked half smile. "Well, my friends: the position is mine," he announced, "on a trial basis, subject to letters of reference from you and Professor Kant. They don't seem to care about my vague résumé. Once they felt assured I was not an insane person, I think, they were quite charmed by me, if I do say so. My position starts next week, with my pay held in escrow until I can supply all the required identifications."

Rachel and I jumped up and congratulated him as Pip watched curiously. Jefferson hung there, wearing an odd, uncertain smile, while Rachel hugged him and I slapped his shoulder.

We had expected to head back that night. Rachel had to get Pip back in school, see her doctor and take care of things at the Claremont apartment. But Jefferson asked if I minded staying on for a day or two to help him reacquaint himself with the place.

I could see he'd wounded Rachel, thinking it was fine to let her drive home alone, a month before she was due. She tried to hide the injury with a chipper air, joking about us boys hanging out together in Jefferson's old haunt while the female took care of the chores. It was strange behavior for her.

I scolded him for wanting to dismiss her when she needed him. He clasped his hands behind his back, bent his knee, shifted his weight and looked at the sidewalk patiently until I had finished. "Very well. My apologies," he said. "As you say."

"You should go to the doctor with her tomorrow," I said, "and you should feel it as your obligation to do that kind of thing for her always."

"Oh really," he replied in a flat tone, just a note away from sarcasm.

"No, Jack," Rachel said. "This is important for him. I can manage. Pip and I will be fine."

"No. I want him to be with you. Humor me," I said angrily.

They relented, sensing the same thing I did, I guess: I seemed to have developed a raw nerve about their newly formed little family and it was best not to aggravate it.

On the drive north to my place, Jefferson lectured Pip again, which this time eventually put the kid to sleep. Rachel dozed, too. I switched on the radio and found NPR stations along the way. Jefferson sat up, listening to the news talk shows.

As it turned out, he developed a bad headache the next day and couldn't manage to go with Rachel to the doctor after all. I drove her into the city with Pip along. By the time we returned, Jefferson's headache had passed. The next day, Rachel and I bought him more clothes and found things we thought he'd want — his own camera, a backup drive for his laptop, a frame for a picture of the four of us, a jar of honey he liked from a farm stand near my home — and we packed him up.

As he and I prepared to head back to Williamsburg, I did not let myself consider it a momentous parting or a new beginning for Rachel and Jefferson. I figured he'd be back soon, before his job really got rolling, to be with her when the baby came.

"Call your father," I told Rachel. "Make up with him. Tell him to come stay with you for the night I'm away," I told her after she had sadly kissed Jefferson good-bye.

"Maybe I will," she said.

I don't know why I kept forgetting to tell her about Mr. Carter's box. It was a hectic few days and I guess there were a lot of other things on my mind. Somehow I had put the box in the same category as I'd put Ben's notebook. Maybe I really didn't want to know there were anything in the world that linked Rachel and her family to Jefferson. Maybe I did not want to be there when she showed him the box. One never knows what one is up to in the deepest reaches of one's mind.

Back in Williamsburg that night, Jefferson and I waited on the porch at Christiana Campbell's Tavern to be called in for dinner. That's when he casually mentioned he had no plans to return to New Jersey as Rachel's day approached.

"What? You won't be there?"

"I'll have duties here, I expect. She's young and healthy and your modern medicine has eliminated so many of the risks of childbirth. I've looked into that."

"Look, I'm sure they'll let you come back up for the birth of your own child. Even if it's just for a day. Just explain the situation to them."

When Rachel and her newborn were ready, I could send them down, he said.

"I myself," he went on, "would prefer she had the child in Virginia. She insists on New York. She knows the physician. Another one of Professor Kant's circle at the university. She has her friends nearby as well, and Pip can manage simple tasks for her. You'll be there for her, as well, Mr. Arrowsmith. She's a strong woman, not like my poor dear Martha, and I would be of no use to her. You'll bring her to me, won't you?"

I stared at him, dumbstruck, and roused myself to speak: "You should be with her, Mr. Jefferson. It's not right. The child is due soon. I told you it was yours. It's not mine or anybody else's. A miracle has occurred. You should come back for that."

"There are no such things as miracles. Miss Carter understands," he said. "We've discussed it."

"Jesus," I muttered. "You are cold."

"Oh, while you are in New York," he added, "can you give my measurements to a tailor? I've noticed the clothing they use for their performers here is quite shabby. Not at all what I would have been wearing in my days as a burgess. I can give you a list of the materials and colors."

I stared at him, trying to refocus. "Look. They'll give you your outfits," I said.

"Yes, but you see, my point is, I don't want their clothes."

Plodding history teacher that I was, I slowly realized he could not bear to be cast as a mere employee, a hired *actor*, no less.

"Mr. Jefferson," I said, "Think of it. You want me to buy you a custom-made outfit in New York when your girlfriend is about to have your child? While you hang out here in Virginia, remembering your youth?"

"Girlfriend? Is that the term?" he asked, unaffected. "Odd I have not picked up that colloquialism. My head is not filled with nostalgia for my days in Williamsburg, Mr. Arrowsmith. I am a very old man with a younger man's form. It is all wrong, all wrong. And, my dear sir, why do you insist it must be my child? Even if it is not yours, as you say, perhaps there have been others."

"Is that what you think?" I yelled. "What are you talking about? For Christ's sake, you don't know her at all if that's what you think! I thought we'd settled this, Mr. Jefferson."

Other people waiting on the porch gaped at us.

"Mr. Arrowsmith, I have many notebooks for you," he said. "I've actually completed the autobiography I started in 1818. A most tiresome business. But for you, Mr. Arrowsmith, I am pleased to complete the task. You have been my salvation. I will never forget it," he said, and he bowed, halfway.

He wanted to be done with me. He wanted his independence.

"Tell me," I snarled, "why is it so many people despised you? Washington once admired and respected you but, in the end, you turned even him against you. He and Martha came to hate you, with your sneaky politicking and dissembling and backstabbing. The same thing happened with the Adamses. Big friends who discovered what a weasel you could be!"

I couldn't believe what I'd said, even though every word was true. He didn't flinch. He looked down at the floor, nodded and looked out toward the reconstructed Capitol. His face remained a placid blank. "Please, Mr. Arrowsmith, let us not quarrel. General Washington was a great man, indeed, but he had no great mind. He was easily led. And Mr. Adams and his wife always were prickly New Englanders, even if they warmed to me for a short time. All that you refer to was a trifle. It was all mere party feeling."

The black woman in colonial garb standing behind the reservation stand called out, "Jefferson! Party of two!" Smiling faces turned our way. There was a murmur of laughter.

He smiled at me with a warmth that seemed strange in the context of the moment. "Jack, we must be friends," he said. "Our interests are the same. We both are concerned for Rachel and the child. As for history, I did the best I could."

I marveled at his perfect sangfroid, and let my head tilt back to emit a strange little involuntary laugh. We went in to eat. People stared and tittered as he went by.

Chapter 26

Rachel wasn't there when I got home. She had left a note saying she'd gone to the Claremont apartment one last time to make sure it was in perfect order for its owner. "Drive in and stay over with us. I want to spend the night," she wrote.

I suspected she missed Jefferson and felt closest to him there. She must have had memories from their winter in the city that I knew nothing about.

Finally I remembered Mr. Carter's box and brought it with me to the apartment, still pretending it was nothing important. After a cheery hello from Rachel, who was in the kitchen, and a surprising "Yo!" from Pip, who was on the floor drawing, I left it on the desk in its paper bag and looked around.

The place was all back in one piece, as good as new, except for the grandfather clock. It was in one piece again, too, but it didn't work, even though I'd hired some expert to fix it. He'd told me he'd succeeded but, every time I swung the pendulum, it stopped after a couple of minutes.

With Pip standing by to help, I took off the top casing, handed it to him carefully, studied the works and reached my hand inside the case. Rachel lay down on the couch with a book but instead of reading it watched me. I could feel the top of the pendulum shaft. It hung from some kind of cradle that connected it to the works of the clock.

I wanted to talk to Rachel. "Don't you have homework, Pip?" I asked.

"Nope."

"Well, listen, can you go out and get us some lemons at Mr. Kim's market?"

"Sure!" he said happily. I gave him the money and he looked at Rachel to make sure he had permission.

I waited until the door had clicked shut and his footsteps had faded down the stairs. Still fiddling with the clock, I told Rachel that I couldn't understand what she was doing with her life: We didn't know how long Jefferson would be in this world; she was too young for him and, on top of all that, I suspected he wasn't capable of the kind of love she deserved. He'd spent all that on his wife. He was a plantation master and a president, used to giving orders. Any love he had was purely the functional kind, intended to achieve an end.

"What end is that, Jack?" she said angrily.

"Companionship. Assistance. Sex. Things a privileged household slave — nearly white and a family relation, no less — might give him."

I stopped fiddling and turned to look at her, surprised at myself and a little ashamed. "I'm sorry. I had to say it."

She didn't answer at first. She turned a page in her book so hard I was surprised it didn't rip. All she said was, "You don't know him the way I do. Please don't lecture me about this. I've had enough of it from my father."

"Did you call him?"

"No."

I turned back to the clock and reached as far as I could into the case. I grasped the top of the pendulum and tried lifting it. The whole thing came easily away. Slowly I withdrew my hand from inside the case and stared at the pendulum, as if it were some organ I had dreamed I'd mistakenly removed from somebody's chest cavity. "Shit," I said. "I don't know what I'm doing."

"I'm really pissed at you, Jack," Rachel said with a thick, wavering voice. "You shouldn't say he doesn't love me."

"I'm sorry," I said. "I just want you to know your father is not the only one who thinks what you're doing is a mistake."

"You can be one cold bastard, Jack. With your distances,

your self-involvement: You are so damned cut off. You screwed up Ben with all your judging. And you must have driven Pam into her miserable affair with that psycho. You were so blind, Jack!"

I stood frozen, facing the clock. She cried quietly. After a long time, she said, "Shit, Jack. I don't want to be mean to you."

"Hey, hey, take it easy, take it easy now," I said, turning around, trying very consciously to imitate Mr. Jefferson's perfect sangfroid. "It's okay. I know exactly what you're talking about."

Rachel's crying stopped. I looked at the pendulum in my hand. I felt around behind the clock's face. Over and over again, I tried to fit the pendulum shaft to its cradle by feel, only to have it drop into the bottom of the case every time I gave it a swing. After a long time, by blind luck, the shaft clicked into some metal slot I had not realized was there.

"I think I got this," I said softly.

I held the pendulum at the top of its arc and let it go. This time it kept swinging. The clock ticked boldly, confidently. I stared at it. I'd brought it back to life.

After a long silence, Rachel said quietly, "Hey, don't hypnotize yourself over there."

I turned and went to the side of the couch and kneeled. "I'm so sorry," I said.

"They loved you, I know they did," she said, her eyes welling up again, sniffling as she stroked my bowed head. "What I said was wrong. They loved you." She looked over her shoulder.

"But I didn't love them enough."

There was a long silence. "I know you tried," she said softly, holding her palm against my cheek. "You're a good man Jack. Just as Thomas is a good man, no matter what anybody says."

I could not look up.

"So hey. What's that in the bag on the desk, Jack?" she asked.

"Oh," I said, gathering myself together. "Your father sent that to me. I kept forgetting all about it. You know, remember? That day you drove off with him waving after you? It's what he was trying to give you then."

"Hmmm. So he's turned whatever it is into a prop for your

intervention, I suspect," she said.

I got up, went to the desk, took the box from the bag and brought it to her.

"It's just stuff. From a long time ago. That's all," she said, studying the box.

"Right," I said.

I got back on my knees beside the couch. She stared at the box for a long time, took a breath and opened it, tilting it her way to peer inside. She lowered the box to me so I could hold it while she gently lifted out the inkwell, the spectacles and the buckle, one by one, without a word, and studied each in wonder before resting it carefully on her chest.

"I remember these," she whispered.

Her father had been a raging drunk long ago, she told me. His fights with her mother were a dim memory, all mixed up in Rachel's mind as just a few flickering images. But now she could see her mother on the floor, the box and its contents scattered around her — strange objects to a little girl. Carter had thrown them at her, Rachel now remembered clearly for the first time in her adult life, and seeing her mother go out the door that day was the last memory Rachel had of her.

She gazed blindly across the room, picturing it, stricken but dry-eyed.

When Pip came back with the lemons, he discovered the box and its contents. He inspected them while Rachel and I sat quietly at opposite ends of the couch. He asked what they were.

"Those were once Mr. Jefferson's," Rachel said. "So my father once told me a long time ago. They're very old."

Pip inspected them one by one, unimpressed, and went back to his drawing pad on the floor.

Chapter 27

Rachel gave birth on May 19 at Columbia-Presbyterian Hospital to a six-pound, seven-ounce boy. Mr. Carter, Professor Kant and I were there for the delivery, like expectant grandfathers. I studied the tiny face, red hair and blue eyes. Mr. Carter kissed his little feet. Kant gently laid his palm over his head. When I lost sight of him in a sudden flow of tears, Kant silently put his hand on my back and Rachel took my hand.

"Jack," she said. "It's all right, Jack."

She named him after me. He was John Arrowsmith Jefferson, to be known as Jack, and the birth certificate gave the parents as Rachel Carter and one Thomas Jefferson.

Rachel, the baby and Pip came to live with me after Rachel's professor returned from China. Her friend Sandra came too, accepting a summer job as Rachel's nanny.

I hired a lawyer to handle Pip's case; Rachel and Jefferson wanted to adopt him. Powell helped again and Kant dealt with the woman in the projects, his legal guardian, who required $25,000 on the side. I thanked God and Pam I had the money. Something hit me, something that should have been obvious all along: Pam would not have left me every cent if she'd hated me. That simple thought flashed like a burst of sunlight after a storm.

The baby was a marvel, good-natured and happy. He almost never cried. I lay awake at night and listened for him.

With a cup of coffee at the kitchen table, little Jack leaning against my chest spewing bubbles and Pip at the table across from me fixating on a video game, I tried not to make too much of the pleasure I took in their company — or in the sight of sleepy-eyed Rachel, wrapped in a bathrobe, her hair loose and tangled, as she reached up to feed Dick the mockingbird in his cage by the kitchen window.

Down in Virginia, Jefferson was becoming a phenomenon, according to the stories he told Rachel every evening on Skype. Little crowds gathered around him when he walked on Duke of Gloucester Street. In his tricorn hat and the custom-made blue suit and silk stockings I'd bought him, with his beribboned hair long again and tied in a queue, he posed for photos and told the tourists stories about his college days dining with the governor in the palace, dancing with Rebecca Burwell at the Raleigh Tavern and falling in with the wrong sort of planters' sons playing cards and betting on horses and cockfights.

He drew a crowd of people holding up cameras whenever he stood by the bench in Merchant's Square behind the bronze statue of himself. Another regular spot on his rounds was the doorway of the House of Burgesses chamber. As tourists gawked from the galleries, he stood there in the hall listening to the orations of Patrick Henry, as interpreted by a Colonial Williamsburg actor. A tour guide would let the tourists know who Jefferson was with an aside: "And there's Tom Jefferson at the doorway, learning the ways of revolution!"

They'd assigned him his own horse — he renamed it Gus, short for Gustavus — and he rode him up Duke of Gloucester Street at least once a day, doffing his hat and bowing to the crowds, like a politician. He was, in fact, already getting into the politics of Colonial Williamsburg, working with the domestic workers' union, which — he told Rachel — needed help fighting the "corporation and mercantile people" who ran the foundation.

His bosses seemed to love him anyway because he was a star attraction. The foundation sent out a press release on their amazing new Jefferson interpreter and the local paper, the Williamsburg Gazette, did a feature on him that we read online. It focused on how much he looked like the man himself and how "Jefferson" was actually his legal name. It glossed over the details of his biography, or the lack of them. So did the Virginia Pilot, the Norfolk daily, in a Sunday feature. I assumed Jefferson had been carefully vague and the reporters had let him get away with it. The Norfolk TV station picked up the story, which we saw on YouTube. It was pegged to the July 4 citizenship ceremony at Monticello. Jefferson would not only attend; he was to be one of the speakers.

"Williamsburg is pressuring him to do it," Rachel told me. "For the PR."

I stared into space. "Aren't you afraid of him going back there? What if he disappears into thin air in the middle of the ceremony?"

"Yes," she said. "I am very much afraid and I'm trying not to be."

* * *

In late June, we drove south, Rachel and the baby in the back seat of the BMW, with Sandra at the wheel and the mockingbird in its cage on the seat beside her. I followed with Pip in a U-Haul truck. In between long spells of video games or gazing out the window, craning his neck to watch people in other cars, Pip had questions: "Are we below Mason's and Dixon's line? Are we going to be able to see the Federal City from here? Where's all the red clay you're supposed to see in Virginia?"

I checked the rearview mirror often to make sure Rachel and Sandra were sticking close to us as the traffic shot by on our left, and I daydreamed about moving to Williamsburg myself one day, maybe getting a job there teaching just to be near the baby and Rachel and Jefferson. As daydreams go, it didn't work so well. It seemed sad to me, imagining myself hanging around like that.

When we got there in the late afternoon, we parked at the Williamsburg Lodge, where I had booked a room, and we walked up Duke of Gloucester Street, little Jack in a fabric carrier strapped onto Rachel's chest, Sandra and I on either side of Pip. As planned, we waited on a bench in front of the Ludwell-Paradise House, the handsome two-story brick townhouse in which Colonial Williamsburg had installed Jefferson. He was due off work at 4.

It was hot. Pip was bored. I took him to Tarpley's shop. As we came out, Pip pointed down the street. "There's Mr. Jefferson!"

He was standing in his blue suit, one knee cocked, before the bench on which Rachel and Sandra sat with the baby, a snazzy planter's straw hat in hand, the knuckles of the other hand pressed into his hip. Rachel was looking up at him like a star-struck girl, talking excitedly. If Jefferson had made a fuss over his new son, we'd missed it. As we approached, he turned and smiled warmly. I must have blanched because he now appeared to be a fresh and smooth-faced man in his early 30s.

"Why, gentlemen, what can be the matter?" he said.

"You look different, Mr. Jefferson!" Pip said.

"I merely look a little younger, Pip," Jefferson said, patting his head.

"How'd you get *younger?*" Pip asked, looking up at him.

"I don't know, Pip. Being here in Williamsburg seems to agree with me after all." He patted Pip on the back and stepped toward me, taking me by the shoulders with both hands. "Thank you, Jack, thank you for taking care of our little family so well. Little Jack looks to be a healthy strapping fellow."

"Any time," I said. "Did you know about this?" I asked Rachel, tilting my head toward the annoyingly young Jefferson.

She shook her head, still awestruck.

"Have your employers seen this?" I asked.

"Yes, yes, the women in the office accuse me of dyeing my hair and 'having work done.' What do they call it? *Botox.* Heaven forbid."

He held out his arms as if to gather us up and told us to come into the house. He led the way, unlocking the front door with a large brass key. It was dark inside, a little gloomy. Sandra, Pip and the baby would each have their own rooms on the second floor, he told us, leading the way upstairs and along a hall that ended at the master bedroom.

"I actually remember this house," Jefferson said. "I dined in it. The publishers of the Virginia Gazette lived here. Of course it has been greatly changed in its interior, with plumbing and electrical wiring and all your modern contrivances."

Pip, Sandra and I stood behind Rachel as she peered into the bedroom, holding the baby.

"Do you like it?" Jefferson asked her.

She looked a little worried. She entered the room like a nervous deer and stepped to a window to peer outside. "Yes, I do. I like this view out over the backyard gardens," she said.

"Very good, I'm well pleased," Jefferson said.

He offered us beer or cider and, after a chat in the drawing room, we all took a long walk up Duke of Gloucester Street to the Capitol and back again, continuing past the house all the way to Merchant's Square and on to the College of William and Mary. People stopped us so they could have their pictures taken with him. A group of women in wide, flowered colonial dresses encircled him to talk about a union meeting.

He had hired a black woman named Virginia to clean and cook for him part-time. She made us a ham dinner with fresh vegetables from the garden that Williamsburg workers tended behind his house.

At dinner, Jefferson talked about the politics of the Colonial Williamsburg Foundation, its departments, management and employees. He seemed to have studied it all closely. He also spoke about the inanity of the press — all the reporters he had met struck him as simple, lazy and dull.

That night, alone at the Lodge, I slept fitfully, and in the morning, we said our goodbyes and I left them to their new life together. I felt lonely and unsettled driving home. I thought there was an edgy arrogance to Jefferson and a hint of distance between him and Rachel, beyond his usual formality.

Back in New Jersey that night, I did something I'd always been careful to avoid. I had dinner with Nancy Steinberg at her house and got a little tight. We had some good laughs and I ended up spending the night with her. "So I guess you didn't go gay after all, Jack," she said.

Chapter 28

Rachel called me a couple of days after my return to New Jersey. There was something she hadn't been able to tell me before I'd left Virginia.

Their first night together in Williamsburg, she said, she presented Jefferson with the box containing the inkwell, buckle and spectacles, wrapped with a ribbon. She had gotten it into her head that it would be a way to show how deeply they were connected, even through time.

That struck me as strange, desperate thinking and not like Rachel at all, but then she had not quite been herself for some time.

When he opened the box, he was horrified. "Someone's been stealing from my rooms!" he roared.

She started to cry. He told her to stop weeping and explain where she had gotten those trinkets. She ran outside and sat on a bench in the back garden.

"I felt like everything was coming apart," Rachel told me, "that you and my father were right, that I was in a dream that was turning into a nightmare and there was no waking up. He never had been mean before. He always had been gentle and kind."

I thought of telling her that she should leave him, he was just a ghost. Other than that, I was stuck, paralyzed, useless to her.

"After a while, he found me out there, Jack," she said, "and he bent down on a knee, and he lay his head on my lap and asked me to forgive him. Then he asked very gently how I had come to have those things. I told him. I said my father had given them to me, that they had come down through my mother's side and she had left them behind when she left us. I did not want to tell him about remembering my father throwing them at her.

"His eyes went blank," Rachel said, "and he disappeared into his own head, and then he asked about my father, how much I knew about his past. I told him I knew very little, except for what I remembered from Emporia. All I knew from before was that his family had been domestics and sharecroppers and his parents were long dead and he'd had a hard life and had always worked to better himself.

"Thomas took my hands and held them. He said he'd been anxious and troubled, that living again in Williamsburg, where he'd been young and ambitious, confused him terribly. Jack, I really think that having to give a speech at Monticello was worrying him, too."

She stopped talking. I listened into the phone for more but slowly realized I'd heard the end of the story. What could I say? The miraculously reincarnated Thomas Jefferson was no more comprehensible to me than my own mysterious family.

"I'll be all right," Rachel said, filling up my silence. "He's okay. And I'll be all right. The funny thing is he seems so happy here, Jack. I don't care what he says about being confused."

Finally something that made perfect sense to me; I leapt at it. "Yes, yes, I think so too," I said. "And he seems to know exactly what he's doing."

But we fell silent again, the distance between us filled with the spirits and souls of our kin.

I asked how young Jack and Pip were doing. "Jack's great. Thomas carries him around singing Scottish songs to him. 'The Broom of the Cowdenknowes' and others. Pip is having some trouble, coming into school at the end of the year. I don't think it's anything serious. He says he can't understand anyone's accent. But he doesn't seem too troubled. He's so calm about things. I love him, Jack. I love Pip and Thomas and I love our Jack. If all this doesn't come crashing down in a heap, I'll be happy here."

After we said goodnight, I sat on my deck listening to the crickets. It was a hot night. Summer was coming in.

***

Agent Turner of the Secret Service and his crew showed up unannounced at my house in the black SUV the next morning. They wanted to know "every detail," he said, of how I'd come to know Jefferson.

"Didn't we go over that?" I said.

"No. We never asked. Now we want to hear if from you, from the beginning," Turner said. With a pleasant smile, he warned "just for the record" that I could be prosecuted if I lied about anything.

I told them the whole story again. One guy took notes while Turner listened. Once or twice the note-taker stopped, looked up at me, looked at Turner and started writing again. When my story was done, I opened my hands, raised my palms and said, "That's it. That's the deal. That's what happened, I swear to God. Waterboard me, draw and quarter me. That's all I can tell you."

Turner smirked. "We're not the ones who were waterboarding people," he said.

I asked if they had anything on Jefferson that I didn't know about.

"Only that some strings have been pulled for him to obtain a Social Security number," Turner said. He and the note-taker stood up to go.

"Okay then," Turner said. "So this is the story: A ghost is going to become a citizen at Monticello. You've spent the past year supporting this ghost. And this ghost has fathered a child with Rachel Carter, according to the kid's birth certificate. Or was it you?"

"For God's sake. She was my son's girlfriend. She's like a daughter to me." It was not true. She wasn't like a daughter to me at all. She was like a ghost, another mysterious spirit in the parade of souls that had taken over my life and all the memories of my past.

Turner smiled. "So tell me. The part of the story when he gets younger overnight; is that what ghosts do? Age in reverse? I never heard of that."

"I never heard of it either." I said. "It pisses me off. I'm slowly losing the hair on my head and growing it out my nose and ears and he keeps getting younger and better looking."

"Uh-huh," he said. "Funny." He wasn't laughing. "Well, Mr. Arrowsmith. We're not interested in pushing for a criminal case," he said after staring at me with that fixed smile of his. "That's not our job. We could let the chief law judge in Albany in on what we know about Mr. Powell and his string-pulling but we don't plan on it."

He asked for whatever records I had to back up my story. I gave him everything I could find from a drawer full of old receipts. I showed him emailed photos on my computer that Rachel had sent: the three of us at the Jefferson Memorial; Jefferson and me standing on the edge of the Coast Highway overlooking the Pacific; Jefferson and Rachel on either side of a redwood tree in Big Sur.

Watching them go, I had the feeling that he believed my story somehow. He didn't think Jefferson was really a ghost, of course, but he didn't think I'd been lying, either.

Mr. Carter called me the next day. Turner had paid him a visit, too.

"What the hell is going on?" he growled. "They wanted to know how I met him, what I knew about him, how my daughter met him. I told them I didn't know. She hasn't told me a damn thing and I haven't asked."

I said maybe Turner's renewed interest had something to do with the ceremony at Monticello, which I'd assumed Rachel had told him about. But Mr. Carter asked, "What ceremony at Monticello?" and I realized I'd blundered. There was nothing to do but tell him that Jefferson was to be sworn in as a citizen and speak at Monticello on July 4.

Mr. Carter greeted that news with dead silence. I was about

to ask if he was still there when he said, "And of course you all will be there for him, right? Huh. It'll be his big day. In more ways than one."

He asked if I'd give him a ride down. I couldn't think of an excuse so I said I would and, as soon as we hung up, called Rachel to apologize for spoiling her plan to exclude her father. She wasn't upset, just a little defensive. She blamed Jefferson. "He knew my father hated everything to do with Thomas Jefferson and Monticello," she said. Imitating Jefferson, she added in haughty whine, "Why impose on the poor man by trying to persuade him to come?"

"Well, he's coming," I said. "I'm driving him down. I couldn't think of a way to get out of it, short of declaring all-out war."

"It's all right," Rachel said. "Thomas has been trying to be good. He'll be okay with it."

I played golf that afternoon and later went next door to Nancy's and had a drink with some friends.

Chapter 29

Jefferson seemed close to panic in the days before July 4, Rachel later told me. He called in sick. He could barely eat. He had diarrhea and terrible headaches. He suffered from the delusion that his appearance would be a major national event. He told Rachel "the eyes of the world" would be on him once again, as they had been when he was president, but he lacked the power and the certitude of the man he'd been in those days. The Secret Service met alone with him for three hours in a room at the Williamsburg Lodge. He required several trips to the bathroom, Jefferson later told me, and an agent went with him and stood at the door, which he had to leave ajar.

On July 3, I drove down to Charlottesville with Mr. Carter. He seemed to have aged and had trouble catching his breath. Yet he was chatty on the way, telling me how much he loved the country around Monticello and how much he looked forward to seeing it again. That seemed odd; Rachel had told me he had vowed never to set foot in Albemarle County.

I tried to get some facts straight about him but he always chuckled and wheezed and sometimes fell into a coughing fit. What I did manage to learn was pretty thin: He was born in Albemarle, his father a white man and his mother a black household servant, and he'd grown up working for the same well-off family they had worked for, learning carpentry and later cooking.

"You sound like one of the Hemings men," I said. "Who was this family?"

He had a coughing fit, chuckled, and said he couldn't remember much, it was all so long ago. "Just rich white people. I quit, I quit that and went on my own," he said.

I asked how he'd wound up in Emporia. "One thing led to another. There's a mystery in there, though, I have to admit. Did a lot of drinking at one time, you know. Don't recollect much from those times." He shrugged and held up his hands. "I guess I woke up one day and finally figured out I had to find myself some work!"

I asked about his wife. He got grumpy and didn't want to talk about her except to say she "liked to pass for white and thought she was better than me."

Just past the ruined hotel for coloreds Rachel and I had seen on our first trip down to Monticello together, I stopped off Route 29 to call her from a grassy patch beside a big old oak tree. She reported there was a Secret Service man stationed at the house, Jefferson's guts were "in an uproar" and he was spending every minute that he wasn't in the bathroom working on his Monticello speech.

I told Mr. Carter that Jefferson was in some kind of distress.

"Yeah, I bet he is," he said with the usual wheezy chuckle that turned into a cough. He looked around and fixed on the big oak out his side window. "Now that tree there," he said, pointing, "that's a good hanging tree. I wouldn't be surprised if there were some hangings off that tree not too long ago. Look at the way that big branch comes right out sideways about 20 feet up. Just right!"

I looked at the tree like a dumb steer. Then I looked at him. "What?"

"A black man from the South always had hangings on his mind in those days," he said, gazing almost fondly at the tree. "I saw some of that myself."

"Really? When?" I asked.

He frowned and nodded slowly, his eyes on the tree. When I realized he wasn't going to say anything more, I started the car.

Back on the road, he spoke almost wistfully about slave magic; "hants," he called them. Women who turned into witches and rode men in their beds. People who turned into animals at night. He had never believed in it, he said. "That was for the field slaves," he said. "They'd get all worked up, telling each other stories at night."

"You knew field slaves?"

He looked at me with milky eyes. He seemed not to see me.

"Mr. Carter, are you all right?"

He looked back at the road. "Yeah, I'm all right," he said. "Don't mind me. I'm just a little misty. I believe in ghosts now, yes I do indeed. Those slaves were right. There's spirits all around the place. It's all just one big hant."

After we had checked in at the Cavalier Inn, he took a nap and I took a walk. I felt lonesome as I strolled up the hill to the sunny campus. It felt like the end of things, like the last day of school or of summer, when you realize everything has changed and the times you've been living through are already over. Our days had become memories that would only fade away, just like the spirits of all the people I'd loved and would never see again. I missed Rachel and Jefferson. I missed my family. I felt like a stranger in my own life.

Rachel arrived from Williamsburg in her Saab late that afternoon with Sandra, little Jack and Pip. I picked up the baby and kissed him. I shook Pip's hand. I said hi to Sandra and hugged Rachel, even though I felt as if I didn't know her so well anymore. Maybe it was all me, something in my own head, my own way of looking at myself and the world that was cutting me off. "I wish I had been more help to you," I whispered into Rachel's ear when I hugged her.

"We're doing okay," she said, resting a hand on my shoulder. She looked into my eyes. "Are you okay, Jack?"

"I'm fine. I'm taking things by the smooth handle."

She smiled and kissed my cheek.

Jefferson was still back in Williamsburg with the Secret Service. He was to come with them to Monticello in the morning. For his churning guts, he'd seen a doctor who'd prescribed Atavan and Immodium, Rachel told me.

Mr. Carter gave her a hard time from the moment he first saw her. "That man should marry you and treat you and that child with some respect," he told her, sitting on the foot of a bed in the room at the inn she was sharing with Sandra and the baby. I noticed Sandra, who was holding the baby, give Rachel a sharp look. I had the feeling she agreed with Mr. Carter and had been giving Rachel a hard time about Jefferson, too.

"Why did you come, Daddy, if you're going to be like this?" Rachel asked. "You don't even like the man."

"Well now, girl, it's not every day you get a chance to see the great Thomas Jefferson himself at Monticello," he said. "Been a long time coming for me. Here now, let me hold that child."

Sandra looked at Rachel to make sure it was all right then handed little Jack to his grandfather, who took him gently in his arms and bounced him on his knee. "Going to teach you how to ride!" he said. "Like a gentleman!"

Pip sat playing a game on an iPod. Carter had never met him so I asked him to stand up. "Pip," I said, "This is Mr. Carter, Rachel's father, and now he's going to be your grandfather. You should shake his hand."

Pip reluctantly stopped his game and got up. He shyly approached Mr. Carter and extended his hand. Carter took the hand and lowered his head to peer at him. "You look like somebody I once knew. What's Pip short for?"

Pip shook his head. "I don't know, sir," he said, "but my name is really Sam."

"Well, okay," Carter said grumpily. "He named you Pip?"

Pip nodded. "Yeah, Mr. Jefferson did."

"Damn strange," Mr. Carter said, "but no surprise. Mr. Jefferson likes to set things up the way he likes them, including people."

"He sure does," Sandra said. Rachel scowled at her.

Rachel and I escaped to dinner at Fleurie. Sandra baby-sat. Mr. Carter said he didn't feel well and went to bed in his own room.

Rachel barely ate. I tried to cheer her up. He was too real, I said, to disappear. He wasn't a ghost anymore because she'd given him his life back. "I could use some of that magic of yours," I said. "I'm envious. Or maybe even a little jealous, I guess."

A desperate look came over her. She struggled to speak. "I ... I couldn't have done anything else, Jack. If we could start this all over again, I'd still fall in love with him, no matter what it meant for me. I feel bound to him. It can be no other way."

I nodded because I thought I understood.

I found myself passing on the bits and pieces her father had told me about his past. She shook her head and repeated in a whisper, "I never knew that."

"Rachel, it started to cross my mind. Could your father be someone from another time? Could there be people all over the place from another time?"

She looked blankly at the table. "Well, that's just crazy, Jack," she said, lifting her eyes to mine with a tired half smile.

The chef appeared at the table, all smiles and chatter, telling us it was so good to see us again but where was our friend, Monsieur Jefferson? "We have seen him on ze news in Williamsburg!" he said. "He eez so famous again! Like two hundred years ago!"

We told him he'd be in town the next morning, that he was going to give a speech at Monticello.

"Ah yes? At ze ceremony! Zere eez talk, you know, rumors all over. Ze president will be zere. Maybe ee will meet ze president and zey can talk about ze pressures of ze job! Ha ha!"

Rachel and I looked at each other, surprised at ourselves for not having guessed it.

Chapter 30

Rachel, Mr. Carter, Pip and I waited 45 minutes in traffic backed up half a mile to get on the mountain for the ceremony. As always, the public was welcome, with no tickets required. There had been nothing on the news about the president coming to Monticello but everyone could tell something was up. A half-dozen state troopers and plainclothes cops had joined the guard at the entrance gate of Monticello; a couple of cruisers were parked off the side of the road with engines running and lights flashing. The troopers stopped everyone coming through to run a check on their plates and driver's licenses.

We all had VIP passes. When we showed them to the trooper, Rachel asked him if the president was really going to be there.

"Can't comment on that, miss," he said, leaning down to look into the car. He asked for all our IDs. "Who's that?" he said, looking into the back seat at Mr. Carter as we fiddled for our licenses.

"He's my father," Rachel said.

We handed him the licenses and Mr. Carter's Social Security card — he had no driver's license. The trooper handed them to the other trooper, who took them into the guard booth. The old guard squinted at us with his head hunched down.

"And who's that young fella?" the trooper said, looking at Pip.

"That's Sam Pip Quentin. He's 13," Rachel said. "We're in the process of adopting him."

"I'm going to be a Jefferson!" Pip declared with a tone of

annoyance, as if everyone was supposed to know it.

"That's why you're a VIP, " the trooper said.

"What's a VIP?" Pip said.

Mr. Carter grunted. "A Very Important Person, boy. And that's what you are because you're with the Great and Good Mr. Jefferson."

The trooper in the booth leaned out and signaled for the other trooper to come over. They huddled and peered at Mr. Carter. They huddled again. A plainclothes man joined in. Out of one of the cruisers popped a man in a dark suit with an earphone. They all huddled. The guy in the suit lowered his chin toward his lapel to talk into a microphone.

"Uh-oh," I said softly.

The trooper with Mr. Carter's Social Security card came to the car and leaned down to the window. "That's a fake Social Security card," he said.

"What?" Rachel said.

"That's a fake card. It's a crime to possess one and a crime to present one to a law enforcement officer. I can't let you take him up the hill."

Rachel turned and looked over her shoulder. "Daddy, what the hell? Why in the world do you have a fake Social Security card?"

"Humph. Ain't gonna matter."

"What?" Rachel said.

"Ma'am," said the trooper, "any other time or place, I could cut you some slack with this, but I'm going to have to take this man into custody. I could detain all of you. Now, I am not going to charge him but I am going to have to hold him in the cruiser until the ceremony is over." He opened the door of the car. "Ma'am, you're going to have to step outside so he can come on out."

Rachel looked at me and looked at her father. Her eyes narrowed.

"Daddy, what *is* this?" she said in a low voice.

"Come on, ma'am, please step out."

Rachel gave me an angry look as she stepped out of the

car. The trooper leaned in and lifted the latch on the side of the seatback and folded it forward for Mr. Carter. He struggled to make his way out. "This is going to be fine, this will still work just fine," he grunted. As he got out of the car, I looked at his face. The lines and the wrinkles had faded. His eyes somehow seemed larger, brighter.

"What the hell?" I said.

Rachel touched his shoulder. "Daddy, we will come and get you when the ceremony is over." She stopped and studied his face, too. "What is happening with you? Your eyes ..."

"I'm going to make that man do right by you, child," he said.

She was too startled by his face to listen. "Daddy, your skin, your eyes ..."

"Ma'am," the trooper said, taking him by the shoulders.

She stood staring as the trooper put him in the cruiser. Finally she got back in the car and closed the door. She looked at me with her mouth agape, speechless.

"What is up with his face?" I asked.

She turned her head and gazed straight ahead.

The trooper came back and leaned toward her open window. "I'll just hold him here," he said. "You can pick him up when you go by on the way back down. Does he have any medical issues we need to know about?"

Rachel stirred herself to deal with the trooper. "He hasn't been feeling well," she said. "And he doesn't look right. In fact he's looking better than he has in years."

"Any diabetes, heart trouble, history of stroke, asthma, any other breathing problems?" the trooper asked. The question made me realize I hadn't heard him coughing the way he'd been on the drive south.

"No, no, he's always been as healthy as a horse until just lately. Lots of coughing," she said.

The trooper asked us for a cell phone number. We gave him mine.

"Rachel," I said, "just how much *do* you know about your father's past? What's he doing with a fake Social Security card?"

"I don't know," she said, dazed again.

"And did you see ..."

"His face! He looked younger!"

As we walked from the parking lot with Pip between us, he broke our silence, bubbling over with questions about where the slaves had worked and lived at Monticello. When he started humming some tune Jefferson must have taught him, Rachel and I stopped, turned and looked closely at his face.

It was just Pip, not a ghost, nobody younger or older or dead. Rachel and I looked at each other with relief.

Barricades and police officers funneled everyone to the visitor center grounds, where there were three metal detectors at the top of the wide outdoor staircase that led to the shuttle stop. The lines moved quickly.

"Where's Mr. Jefferson?" Pip asked as we rocked along, heading up the hill in the shuttle. "I thought we was going to see him here."

"We are, Pip," Rachel said, putting her arm around his back as she anxiously watched the woods out the window. "He's here, up at the house, getting ready."

"We're going to his house? So, if he has this house here, why does he have the other house in Williamsburg?" Pip asked.

"This one really isn't his anymore, Pip. He designed it. His slaves built it. He lived in it. But he left it a long, long time ago."

"Why'd he leave?" he asked.

She looked at him and hesitated. "Well, everything comes to an end, sooner or later," she said. "Everything begins and ends. Everything changes. It's hard to realize that when you're very young, isn't it?"

Pip shrugged and turned back to the window. For no particular reason, I asked him how he was doing.

"I'm fine," he said. He grinned at me. "How you doin'?"

"Okay," I said. "A little weirded out but okay."

"Weirded out? What you weirded out about?"

"I don't know," I told him. "Just a feeling."

"That's weird," he said, eagerly looking back out the window again.

The walkway that went through a grove of trees to the east lawn and the front of the house had been roped off. Guides directed the crowd from the shuttle to the left, toward Mulberry Row, the long, straight path along which the plantation's utility buildings and slave cabins once had stood. We were to follow it past the house and then up brick steps to the west lawn, where the ceremony would take place.

Before heading off with the rest of the crowd, we three stood gazing at the house. For me, it had always been a sight for sore eyes — the beautiful one-of-a-kind home of a man in complete control of his life. Now it was even more of a wonder. "My God," I whispered. "We know the guy who dreamed up all of this."

Rachel took my hand. She looked very worried.

Like her, I feared for him, coming back to Monticello, not as master of the place or even its resident ghost, but as a mere visitor, a character playing a part in his own story.

Guides directed the VIPs — most of them relatives of the new citizens to be sworn in at the end of the program — to rows of folding chairs that had been set up on the lawn. The very first rows had been reserved for the prospective citizens themselves. Many were already seated: white, black, brown, yellow and red, but no Thomas Jefferson among them.

The west facade of the house had been draped in red, white and blue bunting. American flags lazily fluttered everywhere. A lectern had been set up on the right side of the portico. Two rows of chairs extended across the portico from behind the lectern, a bank of standing flags behind them on each side of the parlor doorway.

We took our seats out on the sunny lawn, behind the prospective citizens and their families. It was only 9 a.m. but the sun was hot. Rachel reached across Pip for my hand. I might have looked surprised. "Come on, Jack," she said. We clasped hands and rested them on Pip's knees.

"Not too hot?" I asked Pip.

"I'm okay. I like this place. I like it here," he said.

"Why's that, Pip?" I asked.

He shrugged. "I don't know. No whippins here unless you really ask for it."

Rachel turned her head and peered at him. "What?"

"They treated the slaves here pretty good," he said.

"And how do you know that, Pip?" I asked.

"I read it online. Mr. Jefferson showed me all about it online. He read things to me from stuff he found on some website."

"Ah," I said. Rachel offered a pained little smile. We gave each other a small shake of our heads and went back to scanning the scene, looking for Jefferson.

The members of the Charlottesville Municipal Orchestra fussed in their folding chairs under the big tulip poplar off the north side of the portico, the one in which Jefferson had been so interested on our first encounter. As the lawn seats filled up, the orchestra began to play Sousa marches. By the time every seat had been taken, they were playing "The Stars and Stripes Forever," and at its crescendo everyone was up on their feet, clapping, cheering, whistling and waving flags.

The parlor doors opened. A white-haired man in jacket and tie, followed by nine men and women in black judicial robes, emerged from the house to file onto the portico. The white-haired man took his place in a seat directly behind the lectern. The nine judges took their seats in a row above the top step. More people filed out and sat down, including the featured speaker, a British-born actress and comedian who'd become an American citizen herself.

Then came Jefferson, the last one out of the house, followed closely by Agent Turner of the Secret Service and Congressman Powell. They did not emerge from the parlor, like all the others, but from the south side of the house, where his own apartments — his *sanctum sanctorum* — opened onto the terrace. Wearing a simple, bluish-gray 18th-century suit and tricorn hat, Jefferson looked calm, steady and completely in control of himself.

"There's Mr. Jefferson!" Pip said, pointing.

"Yep, there he is!" I said, squeezing Rachel's hand. She did not squeeze back. She tensed up and watched him like a hawk.

A wave of chatter, laughter and a smattering of applause

rippled through the audience as Jefferson made his way onto the portico with Turner right behind him.

I 'd never seen his outfit before. I wondered if it might actually have been his, carefully preserved after he had died, first by his daughter, then by his grandchildren, then their children and eventually by the Thomas Jefferson Foundation. Maybe for such a special occasion, I thought, they might have taken it out of storage and let Williamsburg's marvelous look-a-like put it on for his big speech.

I leaned around Pip to Rachel and asked. She looked at me as if I'd lost my mind and shook her head. "That's from Colonial Williamsburg," she said.

"Oh. Well anyway. He looks like he's doing fine," I said.

"Yes, yes, I think so, I think he's going to be okay," she said with a hopeful look toward the house.

He bowed to his right and left before taking his seat near the lectern. There were two empty seats beside him. He crossed a leg, locking one knee over the other, and stared straight ahead without expression, feeling inside his coat for his speech, ignoring a fuss that Congressman Powell was making behind him. Apparently they wouldn't let Powell sit beside Jefferson. Apparently there was no seat for him anywhere on the portico. Somebody in a blue blazer and tie led him down the steps onto the lawn and left him standing with a red-faced scowl on the sidelines, near the orchestra.

Turner took a position standing just behind Jefferson. Five more men in dark suits appeared from different directions and took their places at the corners of the portico facing the audience. Immediately they began to scan the crowd. I realized there were more of them down on the lawn, spread out between the house and audience.

Rachel and I looked at each other. She offered a little smile. "This is so important to him," she said. "I just want him to make it through so we can go home."

"It's going to be fine," I said, knowing full well I had no idea what I was talking about.

The audience rustled and murmured. The orchestra came to

attention and, after the conductor raised his baton and swirled it in the air, broke into "Hail to the Chief."

Everyone stood up and began to clap and then cheer as President Obama, tall, fit, relaxed and confident, strode from the parlor doorway followed by two more Secret Service men.

He stopped at one of the chairs next to Jefferson and held up his hand to the audience in a motionless wave. People roared. His poll numbers weren't good but the people on the back lawn of Monticello on July 4 seemed to love him, at least for the moment. Jefferson, standing with bent knee, as usual, applauded politely for Obama with a pleasant smile.

"There he is! That's Obama!" said Pip. "He's the first black president ever! Man, he's so cool!"

The president shook hands with the judges, the actress, and the white-haired man, and took a seat one place removed from Jefferson. One of the agents who had walked out with him took the seat between them. The president leaned forward with a grin, turned his head to Jefferson, said something to him, and extended his hand in front of the agent. Jefferson smiled stiffly, bowed his head and reached over to shake the president's hand.

"Holy shit," I said to Rachel with a big grin. "I bet he got his wish. I bet he got to talk to him, right there in his own study, right before the show started."

I don't think she heard me. She was bouncing up and down, clapping madly with both hands raised in the air, her eyes all teary.

"Oh yes, yes, yes!" she cheered. "It is so cool, so cool!"

I couldn't help but laugh.

The MC waited for the crowd to settle down and then gave a formal, official welcome, listing everyone from the president on down to the prospective citizens, and when he mentioned Jefferson at the end, he turned and extended an arm toward him. "And that really is his name!" he said.

The primed audience roared again, this time with a mix of laughter along with the cheers. Jefferson's blank look cracked into a feeble grin and his face flushed. The president looked his way and applauded him approvingly.

"Wow," I said.

"Yeah, wow," Rachel said. "This has got to be making him happy. Oh, Jack. Be prepared for a big dinner bill tonight." She was talking to me but she couldn't take her eyes off Jefferson.

"It's a deal," I said. "I'm prepared."

President Obama, the first to the lectern, gave a short speech in which he said one of the founders of our country, Thomas Jefferson, had put a promise into words. "For all America's faults and problems, that promise still beckons people from around the world, " he said.

He held out his arms to the new citizens in the first rows on the lawn. "In joining us today as Americans, you make us stronger, you help us fulfill our great promise, and we thank you for it. It has made you one of us. It has made you Americans. May all your hopes and dreams come true."

A roar went up. People leapt to their feet. The Secret Service agents, like robots, didn't show the slightest response. Rachel held her hands over her face in tears. I got a little teary myself. Even Jefferson's applause and smile seemed warmer than usual.

Pip looked at us curiously. "What's the matter with you people?" he said.

I barely heard him over all the cheering and whistling. I just shrugged. "I don't know," I said. "We're happy. We're relieved."

It was more than he could understand, I knew, but he looked up at me calmly, as if pondering what I'd said. Into my head, from out of nowhere, came thoughts of the nigger chaser and the good-looking black man in the suit. I fought through them and gave Pip a rub on the head with my palm.

"Hey, what you doin' that for? Cut that out," he said, scowling and flattening his tightly curled hair, which I hadn't mussed at all.

"Oh, sorry," I said.

"Mr. Jefferson doesn't think Obama doin' a good job," Pip said. "He told me so."

"Really?" I was surprised. Every time the subject had come up, Jefferson had always begged off, saying it would be wrong for him to judge the man publicly. All he'd say was, "We do not have the true facts before us. Time will tell, time will tell."

Pip abruptly slapped both hands over his mouth. "Oops! Told me not to tell anyone he said it! I just remembered!"

"I won't tell anyone, Pip."

I happened to look off to the left, toward a stone-faced Secret Service agent under the big tulip poplar. Something in that direction had caught my eye, some movement high up in the tree. I looked up and thought I saw a man's face peer through the leaves and disappear into the boughs.

I was too distracted by what I'd just seen to pay much attention to the actress's speech. People laughed at whatever she was saying, even Rachel, who seemed to have decided nothing bad was going to happen that day. Pip told me he wished we'd let him bring his video game. I said it would be only another half-hour or so.

I kept glancing up into the tree and saw leaves shimmer and a branch shake high above the orchestra.

For the naturalization ceremony, all 70 or so prospective citizens stood in a group on the steps of the portico — including Jefferson — and took the oath administered by a judge. The moment he declared them citizens of the United States, the crowd offered up another roar.

The new Americans on the portico beamed, except for Jefferson, who turned around to study the ceiling above them, as if he had spotted something that needed fixing.

As the crowd settled into a loud murmur, the white-haired MC came to the lectern and explained that it was a tradition at the ceremony to invite the new citizens to say a few words, if they wanted to. When it was time for Jefferson to speak, the MC introduced him as the new re-enactor at Williamsburg who had come to be sworn in as a citizen just to resolve "an old paperwork problem."

The applause was halfhearted, with only a few cheers and a whistle or two. To the crowd, I guess, he was just an actor with a remarkable resemblance to the man they'd seen in pictures — and they'd grown used to him. Obama smiled warmly, though, and as Jefferson stood, the president clapped and leaned toward him to say something. Jefferson leaned Obama's way, smiled, nodded and said something back before taking his place at the lectern and taking his speech from an inside pocket. He unfolded it and, without looking up at the audience, began to read in a soft and earnest voice.

I could barely hear him. Even with the amplifying system, he spoke with such reserve that few words registered. People talked and moved around on the lawn in front of the Secret Service agents. No one seemed to pay attention to Jefferson. I ached for him. Rachel watched, heartbroken, her eyes wide and worried again, her fingertips pressed against her lips.

The MC came to Jefferson's side and interrupted him, leaning to the microphone. "Ladies and gentlemen, may we please have your attention. May I remind you we're all still up here and the ceremonies are not concluded."

Jefferson stood back from the lectern with a blank face. The crowd quieted down a little, the white-haired man nodded and withdrew, and Jefferson stepped forward and started reading again.

I gathered it was some kind of confession. He spoke about "the negro problem" — a very strange note for such an occasion — and how the nation had resolved it through civil war and a long struggle to establish the rights of the black man. President Obama sat up straight and listened to Jefferson attentively but no one else seemed so engaged, not even the judges.

I eyed Rachel. She looked back at me with a crinkle in one corner of her mouth, a fixed wince. I realized I had forgotten the tree. I quickly turned and looked up. This time I was sure. Leaves and branches shivered unnaturally. Then something else came into focus for me: a heavy rope wrapped around the base of a big branch, high up. The rope extended straight up and disappeared into the dense foliage of the tree.

"What the hell? Rachel! Look!" I whispered.

Jefferson was saying something about his critics being correct, that he had failed to use his power to lead the country toward a resolution of the slavery issue. Because he spoke louder and clearer all of a sudden, I distinctly heard him say, "I can offer you excuses, my friends, but to what purpose? My grand-children were left to resolve the problems I left behind, and they did so at great cost. Families and fortunes were destroyed. The South was ruined."

Nothing he said seemed to register with the audience. He was bombing big time.

Rachel looked where I was pointing. "I thought I saw something move up there," I told her. "Now I see a rope around a branch. Do you see that?"

"Oh God. I do, " Rachel said. "I *do* see that rope."

A brown face appeared in the high boughs, peering at us like some tree creature. Rachel gasped.

"Whoa! What the hell is that?" I said.

The face disappeared.

"That face! It looked like Daddy!" Rachel hissed. She looked at me in horror.

The great threat to the nation today, said Jefferson, was the overwhelming power of corporations and special interests to control the government as well as the minds and hearts of the people. "There has been a dangerous tear in the fabric of our society," I heard him say.

Then came a rushing sound. Branches heaved and leaves shook. A naked negro with a rope around his neck exploded from the crown and shot feet-first into the open air. When the rope snapped tight, he jerked upward like a rag doll, his neck snapping with a loud crack, his head slapping impossibly against his chest. The body floated in the air for a moment at the top of the bounce, then it fell again, bounced half as high, fell again, bobbed up and down a little, and then swung in a wide, lazy arc above the Charlottesville Municipal Orchestra, slowly rotating with its tongue protruding onto a shoulder from a monstrously distended purple face.

Rachel had frozen. She stared at Jefferson, who stared at the hanging man, his mouth open, his face twisted in horror. He wobbled and gripped the lectern, as if he might collapse. After what seemed a long time, but must have been no more than a second or two, the spell broke. Rachel stood up and screamed

"Thomas!" People turned to look her way. Two Secret Service agents in front of the audience pulled out weapons.

"Jamie!" Jefferson croaked loud enough for everyone to hear over the rustling and confusion of the audience. "Oh, Jamie!"

Rachel bolted from her seat and ran toward the portico. The Secret Service agents spotted her instantly. Weapons in hand, they headed onto the lawn to cut her off, showing no awareness of the hanging body. No one did. The crowd reacted only to Jefferson's strange behavior at the lectern and the commotion on the lawn.

As I stood, Pip looked up at me. "Why is everybody jumping around?" he said.

I realized he could not see the body either. No one could see the hanging man but Thomas Jefferson, Rachel and me.

"Rachel! Stop!" I called out. "Wait!"

She did stop and stood still, alone on the grassy aisle two rows away from her seat, just before the agents grabbed her. She was staring up at Jefferson, who was teetering at the lectern. Bringing a hand to his forehead, he pitched sideways and fell out of sight, hitting the slate flooring of the portico with a thud. The president half rose from his seat and reached toward Jefferson. Turner blocked him with an extended arm. With his other hand, he took a gun from under his jacket.

The agents on the lawn hustled Rachel away, up the far side of the portico steps and into the house through the parlor doors. Four or five others surrounded the president and seemed to lift him from his seat and float him into the house.

"Where they taking Rachel?" Pip said. "What's going on around here?"

"God only knows," I said.

I stared at the hanging body. It had stopped swinging but still it turned very slowly on its tether.

"Pip," I said, pointing, "do you see anything hanging from that tree?"

He scrunched up his face. "Hanging from the tree? That big tree?"

"The big tree, in the corner."

"I don't see anything. Is something there?"

"I thought I saw something. Maybe not."

A dozen state troopers formed a barrier in front of the house and scanned the crowd. Two people came from inside — Monticello staffers, I guessed — and stooped behind the lectern. Two people with stethoscopes around their necks joined the huddle. In a minute or two, two more EMTs showed up with a gurney.

The MC took the lectern and held his hands out at the chattering audience. "Ladies and gentlemen," he said. "Ladies and gentlemen."

I could not see Jefferson until they lifted him from behind the lectern and carried him into the house.

"Ladies and gentlemen," the man at the lectern said, "may I have your attention."

One of the people who had gone into the house with Jefferson came back out to the lectern and whispered in the MC's ear.

"Ladies and gentlemen, our friend Mr. Jefferson is all right," the white-haired man said. "He sends word he hasn't had to give a speech in 200 years and it proved just a bit overwhelming. He was never fond of making speeches, you know. And it's a hot day."

There was a ripple of laughter and a smattering of applause. The actress, leaning from her chair behind the lectern, said something out loud to the man. He laughed and turned back to the audience.

"And Ms. Ullman," he told the audience, referring to the former British lady, "says Mr. Jefferson should spend some time alone in the house with the president anyway — so Mr. Jefferson can give him some tips for his reelection campaign."

After another little wave of laughter, the white-haired man leaned to the microphone. "The president is all right, too. It was just a precaution for him to leave the portico. The young lady you may have seen being taken inside is fine, too. She is a friend of Mr. Jefferson. So! Ladies and gentlemen! Let's refocus here! Would you all rise for the national anthem, at the end of which our ceremonies will be concluded. And congratulations to all our new citizens and their families and friends."

I was the only one left who could see the broken-necked black man hanging dead above the orchestra as it struck up "The Star-Spangled Banner" — like a grotesque ornament brought in just for the occasion, for history's sake. I rubbed a hand across my face as I eyed the man, my other hand gripping Pip's shoulder.

As the crowd sang, the two Secret Service agents who had brought Rachel inside emerged from the house and resumed their places. Congressman Powell looked frantic, trying to get through the troopers to the house. He still wanted his photo op.

I looked at the contorted face and turned to look across the milling, chattering, oblivious crowd. I looked to the house for signs of Rachel. When I peered back up at the tree, the man and his rope were gone.

The thought came into my head that I had seen the hanged man because I was as dead as he was, pure dead weight at the end of a rope. Jefferson and I were dead and Rachel must have been dead, too, for all her youth and beauty and her life at school and her love for Ben and now this dead man Thomas Jefferson. We all were dead people walking the earth, imagining lives among the living.

I felt faint. I held my forehead and closed my eyes. I think I must have made a sound, some sad little whimper.

"Huh?" Pip said. "Hey Uncle Jack! What's the matter? Are you cryin'?"

I rubbed my hand across my face and tried to smile at Pip. "I just …"

"Where's Rachel? We got to go find her! Where's Mr. Jefferson?"

"We have to wait, Pip. They wouldn't let us through."

The anthem ended. The crowd began to break apart and spread over the lawn. The judges and the others on the portico stepped down to the new citizens, shaking hands with them as their families gathered around.

We walked toward the house, Pip pulling me along.

Chapter 31

They wouldn't let us into the house until the president's motorcade had gone down the hill. One of the troopers led Pip and me to a Monticello staff person standing nearby who told me to wait. She went inside and, in a few minutes, came back with another staff person. Together they led us up the steps of the portico, through the French doors into the parlor.

We passed people standing in little groups on the parquet floor, talking as if nothing out of the ordinary had happened. We followed the guide into the hallway that led to Jefferson's dressing room, where more people stood milling about. Beyond them, a man in a blue blazer, polo shirt and khakis stood by Jefferson's bed in the alcove, a stethoscope draped on his shoulder. On the edge of the bed sat Jefferson himself, his silk stockings removed, his feet hanging above a porcelain bowl of water and Rachel kneeling before him, washing his feet with a focused and determined look.

"Jack," Jefferson said with a half smile as I approached. "Hello, Pip."

"Why's Rachel doin' that? It ain't morning," Pip exclaimed.

"I fainted. It happens to me at moments of extreme agitation," Jefferson said.

Rachel looked up at us. "He was lying down on his bed when they brought me in," she said. "It was the nearest bed so they put him on it. I thought the worst until he opened his eyes and waved at me."

I put my hand on her shoulder. "Did he see? Did *you* see?" I asked.

"Yes, yes," Jefferson said before Rachel could answer. "Did you see, Mr. Arrowsmith? Did Pip?" Jefferson asked. "That vision had a violently convulsive effect on me. Yet no one else seems to have been aware of it."

"I saw, but not Pip," I said. "It's gone now. Poof. Like yourself that day last summer."

"Saw what?" Pip asked.

"We saw something in the tree behind the orchestra," I said.

"What did you see?"

I looked at the people who chatted around us. None paid any attention to our conversation, although a few here and there cast starry-eyed glances at Jefferson.

"Well, Pip," I said, "It was a man hanging from a tree. As if he'd hung himself — or he'd been lynched."

"What's lynched?" Pip asked, scrunching up his face.

"Lynched?" Jefferson said. "As in the term they used for the Tories in my state when they came before our zealous patriot, Judge Lynch, during the Revolution?"

"The term apparently came to mean something else after the Civil War," I said, "after the slaves were freed. It went on for a century in the South, right into my own childhood. Vigilante murders conducted by citizens, white supremacists, no doubt patriots too — but patriots of the Old Confederacy."

I knelt beside Pip and put a hand on his shoulder. "If they thought a black man had committed a crime, or even whistled at a white woman, a mob would run him down and string him up in a tree. Imagine that. In this country. Like something out of the Middle Ages."

Pip's eyes widened and he reared back. "Never heard of that where I come from," he said.

Rachel closed her eyes. Jefferson, propped back on his elbows with his hands flat on the bed, shook his head slowly. "Emancipation brought on new evils, I know. *Lynching.* Somehow I missed this term in my readings."

Rachel put her hand on Jefferson's knee. "It was Jamie,

wasn't it?"

"Yes," Jefferson said sadly, "I am certain. It was Jamie. Performing his tragical end for my benefit."

Rachel stared past Jefferson out a nearby window. "My father used to talk to me about Jamie Hemings as if he'd known him."

"Who's Jamie Hemings?" Pip asked. "Am I supposed to know him?"

Jefferson shifted on the bed to look out the window, toward Mulberry Row, as Rachel lay her head atop his knees. "I intend not to fail you, Rachel," he said. "A buckle, an inkwell and a pair of spectacles. That was all Sally could claim of me. And her brother; he received nothing from me, nothing but my impatience. He mistook it as an offense."

Rachel lifted her head. "Sally had her sons to remember you by — *your* sons, Thomas."

He blinked at her and slowly turned his head to look at the room and the people around us. I sensed he was seeing something else, something we did not see this time. He stared at one spot, off to the right side of the bed, and then dropped his head.

"What's the matter with him?" Pip asked.

"I don't know," I said. "I think, Pip, he's remembering his people, his family."

Jefferson took a kerchief from a pocket and blotted his eyes. "Indeed. That's so," he said quietly. "They are all dead and I belong with them. Why is it Jamie comes to me for my sins but they do not come to me for my love?"

After a silence, I asked if he'd talked with the president.

"Oh, yes, yes, I did indeed," he said, perking up. "In this very room! My room! Before the ceremony! He thanked me for my letters. He apologized for the Secret Service. He said he was 'a big fan.' He said, 'Wait for the second term. If we pull off a second term, it will mean the country just might be ready.'"

"Ready for what?" Pip asked.

"Ready for 'a real conversation about slavery,' he told me," Jefferson said. "It will be the year 2013, the 150th anniversary of Mr. Lincoln's Emancipation Proclamation. The president said the country would need to have some words to heal that wound once and for all. Perhaps I could write them, he said. I was most impressed with the man. He laughed when I told him I understood that he had no slave blood. Why would he laugh at that?"

My cell phone rang. It was the trooper at the bottom of the hill. There had been an "episode" with Mr. Carter. Everything was okay now; he was fine.

"What happened?" I asked the trooper.

Rachel and Jefferson fixed their eyes on me as I listened. The trooper said Mr. Carter had stopped breathing. Several ambulances had been stationed on the mountain so help came quickly. "They thought he was gone," the trooper said. "They got him breathing again and he's all back, he seems all right. Except for one thing."

I eyed Rachel as I asked what that one thing was.

"How old is he?" the trooper asked. "His face ... I mean, he seems older than he looked when we put him in the car. I've never seen anything like it."

I said he had a rare condition that affected his skin and appearance.

"Really? What's that? I never heard of that," the trooper said.

Rachel wanted to go to her father but first she helped Jefferson with his socks and shoes. He stood up and reached for his coat on the bed. The white-haired man who had hosted the ceremony came and shook his hand. A small crowd gathered around him. He talked quietly with them, thanking them for their concern, apologizing for the disruption, assuring them that he was fine now.

"Thomas," Rachel said, standing alone outside the growing little crowd. "My father."

He looked to her, vaguely surprised, then looked about the room and up to the skylight, which sent a shaft of sunlight angling onto the far wall. He seemed to lose himself in thought for a moment, smiled at Rachel and told his admirers it was time for him to go, he'd caused enough trouble. The group parted as he stepped toward Rachel, but he stopped and leaned forward for a close look at a little brass and black marble pendulum clock on a shelf over the foot of his bed. He'd had it made while he was in France, I knew. It featured two six-inch obelisks, with the clock suspended between them. "Oh, I must hear it," he said to himself, lightly fingering the pendulum to make it swing so the clock would tick.

"Oh! Sir! Mustn't touch!" the white-haired man exclaimed, lurching toward him to save the clock. Jefferson, turning his ear to listen closely, ignored the man and listened to the clock tick with a pleasant grin.

When we got down the hill, we found two van-size ambulances parked next to the state police cruiser with their lights flashing. Our trooper recognized my car. "He seems to be in pretty high spirits now," he told us as we climbed out.

Rachel walked ahead of us, breaking into a trot. "Where?"

"He's in that second ambulance, on the right," the trooper said.

She pushed into the little crowd of paramedics and police at the rear doors of the ambulance and climbed in. I followed while Pip and Jefferson stayed by the car.

Mr. Carter sat up on a gurney, looking entirely like his 70-ish self, wearing a nasal cannula and an IV attached to his arm. Rachel hugged him.

"What have you been up to, Daddy?" she asked. "What have you been up to all these years?"

"Where's Jefferson?" Mr. Carter asked grumpily. "I want to see him. I want to see his face." He broke into a wheezy chortle, gritted his teeth and glared at Rachel. "I ain't going to rest until he marries you and brings up that child right, like he never did for Harriet or Madison or Beverly or Eston."

Rachel nodded, as if it all made sense. I went to the car to get Jefferson. When I returned with him, Mr. Carter eyed him silently. He demanded that Rachel and I leave them alone.

We waited by the car. When Jefferson came back, his face ashen, he wouldn't tell us what Mr. Carter had said. Rachel started back for the ambulance but Jefferson put his hand on her shoulder to stop her.

"Your father is in a state like mine, it seems," he said. "He told me he would haunt me with such tricks for all the days I have been given to walk the earth again if I did not honor you and our child."

Rachel looked at the ground. Jefferson took her by the shoulders, studied her, tucked a finger under her chin to lift her face, smiled bravely and pulled her to him. She closed her eyes as they embraced.

Chapter 32

The wedding was in August, a hot, muggy time in Williamsburg, a year to the day after Jefferson had met Rachel.

She had landed a teaching job at William & Mary. Sandra worked nights at the Kings Arms tavern. During the day, she helped with the kids between the classes she was taking for her master's degree in history.

Mr. Carter, after a few days at the UVA medical center, came to Williamsburg to stay with Rachel and Jefferson. They gave me the job of closing up his place in Yonkers and putting it on the market. Rachel chose to keep the shuttered restaurant, at least for a while. She seemed to think she might reopen it one day.

Rachel later told me that Mr. Carter and Jefferson sometimes sat for hours behind closed doors in Jefferson's office, talking over old times, she supposed. Sometimes Mr. Carter cooked for them, shooing away the part-time lady, Virginia. He often made French dishes Jefferson had enjoyed in Paris and he helped with chores, picking up supplies for the garden, keeping Jefferson's violin in strings and in tune, joining the Williamsburg people tending Jefferson's plants and garden, keeping his mockingbirds — there were now two — fed and exercised. Sometimes he met with people as if he were Jefferson's secretary: political and union people, reporters, history students, mid-level people from the Colonial Williamsburg Foundation.

When I sent Rachel emails asking her to tell me about Mr. Carter — "Will you please tell me who and what your father is?" I finally wrote — she ignored them or forgot my questions in her replies.

She seemed happy and busy. I didn't want to push. I know how it can be for happy, busy people, people with careers or families or both. I would wait a while and try again and, sooner or later, I figured I'd get my answers.

Jefferson was busy too. Not only did he pretend to be himself for the tourists, at all hours night and day, but somehow — with letters, emails, personal visits — he turned himself into a trusted advisor to people from Colonial Williamsburg's various departments, even as he helped run the union. He offered guidance to the gardening and landscaping crews and often talked to the people who took care of the horses, the oxen and the sheep. The architectural historians valued his opinions. They had Wetherburn's Tavern repainted after he told them it had not been white but brick red in revolutionary times. They had gone back to their last paint analyses and found that a mistake had been made by earlier researchers and that Jefferson was right.

He traveled to speak at meetings and conventions. He did interviews on local radio and TV. National Public Radio did a weekend piece on him in which he hinted that perhaps he really was Thomas Jefferson — his idea of corny comic relief, they must have thought.

Every night, he read, wrote, Googled and listened to new music downloads, the bills going directly to him now, although I continued to send money to Rachel. I did it for her, the baby and Pip; he, meanwhile, was sending me checks, little sums that were intended to chip away at his debt to me.

Jefferson got up at dawn every morning and soaked his feet for 10 minutes in his bowl of cold water, delivered by Rachel. That was their time to chat. He skipped breakfast except for coffee to write long emails to a growing list of people who wanted his thoughts and his favor.

He found the time to take long walks alone, always in costume. He rode his horse, Gustavus, sometimes in the restored area, sometimes on trails to escape the tourists. He learned to drive a car and got his license. He was good at it, Rachel wrote. When they found the time, he took her and the boys on outings to sightsee, picnic and walk, Jack tucked into a carrier that either Rachel or Jefferson would wear.

He bought a bicycle. He was always hopping on it for last-minute meetings but preferred the horse for any errands within the restored area.

The local Democrats asked him to run for office. First came talk of a Williamsburg city council post but a state senator was retiring so they decided Jefferson could win that seat. In an email to me, he denied any interest in politics and wrote that he probably would reject the idea. After the "disaster" of his speech at Monticello, he wrote, he believed his reputation had been so damaged that he could have no future in public service. But he wasn't entirely sure; he considered it a duty for a man in his position to "take some responsibility for my city and state."

"Our friend Mr. Carter did more than play a mere trick," Jefferson wrote me. "His aim was to embarrass me, by rendering me incompetent during my appearance, in order to convince the public I was in fact no more than a frail oddity, unsuited for office. He has told me so himself with some glee. But he failed to consider the forgiveness of the people, or as he insists, their forgetfulness. My embarrassing collapse, it seems, was a minor matter to them."

A week or so before the wedding, the Virginia papers reported that Jefferson would be the nominee that fall for state Assembly from Williamsburg City.

Nancy Steinberg and I were doing well. I wouldn't call us a loving couple but we were getting there in our own way. She was a good golfer. I was playing several times a week with a foursome of my retired buddies and on weekends with Nancy in mixed foursomes. It was mindlessly pleasant. I was getting pretty good.

Nancy earned her real estate license and started working almost every day, sometimes in the office, sometimes from home. She did it "to keep busy," she said. She was an energetic woman. I liked her grown kids, too. They were easygoing, smart people. Uncomplicated, it seemed to me. They laughed a lot. Two had made money and become Republicans and I actually liked them in spite of myself.

I suppose I was relieved that Nancy didn't want to go to the wedding. "I think you'll have a better time if I don't go," she said. Nancy could have handled anything, I'm sure, but I never told her the truth about how Rachel and I had really met Jefferson.

He made me his best man so I had to be in Virginia early to take care of some things. One was picking up Elmer Kant at the airport in Norfolk. He would have driven down with me but he was too busy preparing for fall classes to spend any extra time out of town.

On our drive from the airport, Kant said he wouldn't be surprised if Jefferson ran for Congress or even the U.S. Senate one day. "He's so young," he said. "He has lots of time. He's made some connection with the White House, I've been told."

"He's over the hump. He's a real person," I said. "He's created himself and everybody's buying it. Amazing."

It was a slip. I'd forgotten we'd never told Kant the ghost story. He didn't bat an eye. "I think so. He's got the papers to prove it," he said, shaking his head. "How strange. No degrees, no work history. But rich, apparently. Rich helps."

"Right, right," I said.

"I'd like to see his place down here sometime."

"Place?"

"Yeah, you know, the little place where you and Rachel met him out there in Albemarle? Monticello?"

So he'd heard that part of the story, or some variation of it. From Rachel, I guessed, and she'd forgotten to tell me. "Right, right, we'll all go see it sometime," I said.

***

In the dead of summer, just before fall begins to show itself, a soft haze overtakes Williamsburg. Rough wooden fences on ragged back pastures, sloped fields close-cropped by horses and sheep, pocket gardens of hollyhocks and antique roses all bake in the smoky sweet air. Time stops and the flood tide of summer pauses before beginning its ebb toward fall.

After a dinner for the wedding party at the Fat Canary restaurant in Merchant's Square, Jefferson, Rachel and I sat in the light of his backdoor lantern on the steps overlooking his gardens and talked. He said I should move to Williamsburg. There was plenty of golf, I could volunteer as a guide or a colonial person in costume and we'd all be together. The idea appealed to me in some ways. I wanted to be someone in little Jack's life one day. But I really didn't want to hang around and play the aging uncle-in-residence. I felt a new life coming with Nancy and her kids' families. I didn't want to lose it.

Rachel's old friends and Jefferson's new ones packed Bruton Parish Church for the late afternoon wedding, a mix of black and white people crowding pews worn smooth by two-and-a-half centuries of polishing by the rear ends of Williamsburg's old WASP gentry. Rachel knocked them out in her strapless ivory gown with flowing skirts and a blue satin ribbon at the waist. The sight of her broke my heart a little, I have to say — it was a fatherly thing, I told myself, and Rachel on her wedding day made me think of Ben.

Jefferson was an all-modern groom, except for the queue with blue ribbon. He wore a lightweight gray suit from a good men's shop in Merchant's Square and a red tie with a bold, black pattern that turned out to be his father's famous map of Virginia, reproduced in a scale so large its roads, rivers, mountains and boundaries looked like abstract designs.

A fiercely proud Mr. Carter delivered Rachel to Jefferson's side and retreated to his place beside me and Pip. I thought I had never seen Jefferson smile so honestly as he gazed at her.

When the ceremony ended and they kissed, I could see that Rachel had spotted something on his cheek. She stole a moment at the altar to study it, her hand still on the back of his neck, her fingers lost in his queue and ribbon. My eyes followed hers to his sideburns. On their forward edges, I could see a slight fringe of white. She looked into Jefferson's eyes. Smiling, he cocked his head very slightly, as if to ask what was wrong. The church organ broke into a Handel recessional and, after an instant's hesitation, they turned to face the pews and the crowd, which by then had broken into applause, cheers, hoots and whistles.

Mr. Carter tilted his head toward mine. "People here love those two. I'd stick with them if I was you. It'd be a nice life. That's what I'm going to do, long as I got the chance."

"I don't know. I think I'd be a fifth wheel," I said.

"No way," Mr. Carter said. "You belong with us." Before I knew what I was doing, I gave the old man a hug. I couldn't help myself. "Take it easy, now," he said. "I'm not much of a hugger. I didn't think you were either."

The receiving line took close to an hour. Pip shook hands with elaborate ceremony. Jefferson had instructed him to say, "We're all so delighted you were able to come," which he did over and over again. Rachel pecked cheeks, giggled with girl-friends and listened with warm patience to worshipful men I didn't know. Jefferson shook hands robustly. He made easy small talk with everyone from the president of the Colonial Williamsburg Foundation and the mayor of Williamsburg to maids and groundskeepers in the union, black and white. If the man had once been a born-and-bred racist, you'd never have guessed it at his wedding.

The governor of Virginia, Bob McDonnell, was among the guests. I had the feeling when they shook hands that he and Jefferson were sizing each other up in a friendly sort of way.

They had invited Obama, too. He sent a personal note of congratulations and regret that he could not come. There was talk he'd show up anyway. That didn't happen but the rumor added a certain energy to the party even before it had built its own big head of steam.

We served 300 on the terrace of the Williamsburg Inn — it was just drinks and hors d'oeuvres under the two gigantic oaks that tower over the slate patio, out back between the inn's white-washed brick wings. I say "we" but Colonial Williamsburg gave that party. Mr. Carter and I gave the buffet dinner for 170 that followed at the Governor's Palace. Colonial Williamsburg's marketing people beamed along the sidelines at both the reception and the dinner-dance. Someone from The New York Times was there, taking pictures. So were The Washington Post and Entertainment Tonight. A porky corporate vice president told me excitedly that Colonial Williamsburg's admission numbers had been climbing steadily ever since Jefferson had joined them.

I drifted around the fringes, a glass in my hand.

"What are you shaking your head at?" some nice-looking woman in a green cocktail dress asked me on the terrace.

"Oh, it's too much to explain. I'm just a little bewildered, as usual."

"You mean how he looks? Just like Thomas Jefferson?" She was already a little buzzed.

"Yeah, that's it. Amazing, isn't it?"

"He's so charming," she said, unable to take her eyes off him.

"Oh yes, he sure is. I love that guy," I said, and drifted away to leave her to her reverie.

At 7 o'clock, the party shifted to the palace, about a half-mile away. Those who didn't want to walk could wait for the ox wagon, one of the elegant horse-drawn carriages or one of the Colonial Williamsburg buses that shuttled people over.

The cocktail crowd on the terrace was thinning when Jefferson, in shirtsleeves, trotted regally into view astride Gustavus from around the side of the inn. He slowed to a walk to make his way into the crowd, drew up beside Rachel and reached down for her. They must have practiced the move. She folded herself into his arm and hopped as he lifted and, in one smooth curve, twirled her onto the horse sidesaddle.

"Wow!" I had to say out loud to no one in particular. "That was fabulous!"

"Did you see that? They're like movie stars!" a guy next to me said.

Rachel laughed and stroked Jefferson's cheek, all thoughts of his white whiskers put aside.

We served dinner al fresco behind the palace, with guests free to sit in the garden or down the slope by the canal with its swans gliding along in the gathering dusk, or inside, in the ballroom, the doors of which had been left wide open to the garden. I spotted Rachel and Jefferson out there, in a little cluster of friends on folding metal chairs, under the trees at the far end. Mr. Carter, Pip and Professor Kant all waved and called for me to join them.

Jefferson was talking about the palace when he lived there as governor and the plans he'd made for renovating the place when the Revolution was over. It was wondrously strange how well his stories worked as modern dinner party chatter. No one batted an eye; they were all engrossed, except for Pip, who wanted to go see the swans.

"But you moved the capital to Richmond," Kant chimed in, "and you got in trouble over money because you rented a place to stay there as governor, right?"

"That is so, professor," Jefferson replied. "They called me 'Jefferson the spendthrift.' And as I'm sure you, of all people, know I was exonerated by the legislature."

"Well, of course you were," Kant said.

Jefferson talked, too, about local politics and issues, and sometimes people who I guessed were city and county officials drifted in and out of the group under the trees. As they came and went, and Jefferson chatted easily with them, I studied him. There were more strands of white in his hair and new wrinkles at the corners of his eyes. I glanced at Rachel, who was watching me watch him. She smiled and glowed, refusing to let me break the spell just yet.

The day's last light faded away and the tide of the party began to flow inside, slowly emptying the garden and filling the ballroom, where a small ensemble played Haydn and Vivaldi. The big room was almost unfurnished, with a bare wood floor, chairs against the walls, two huge portraits of William of Orange and his queen, Mary, and a "heating machine" taking up the middle of one wall — a massive iron stove stacked in vertical sections atop four legs.

When the crowd had filled even the edges of the room, the chandeliers were lowered and their candles lit. The ensemble shifted into tunes from the Great American Songbook. Rachel and Jefferson came in from the garden, stood side by side in the doorway and stopped for a moment to accept the applause.

They stepped together onto the bare floor and stood in each other's arms talking happily as the crowd spread apart for them and quieted itself. The orchestra played the introductory notes to "Long Ago and Far Away." When I heard a female voice begin to sing, it took me a while to spot her: a young woman in a slinky silver evening dress, holding a microphone in the corner of the room.

Rachel had taught Jefferson how to fox trot, it seemed. I was staring, somewhere between weepy and ecstatic, when I heard Mr. Carter say, "Mighty pretty couple!" I looked to my right and there he was, with a violin in hand.

"Oh!" I said. "Are you going to play?"

He nodded with a proud smile. "Yes I am. With old Master Jefferson. As soon as we get these young people's tunes out of the way."

A hot, sweaty two-and-a-half hours later, after the toasts, with candles casting the only light and doors and windows wide open to the steamy night, Jefferson announced that he and Mr. Carter wanted to play a reel. "At my request," he said, "Professor Elmer Kant has studied this dance especially for the occasion and he will be your caller tonight." Those who did not know the Virginia reel, he said, could "listen and observe, and join in when you can. It is not difficult."

Many people fell away from the center of the room but at least 20 stayed. At Kant's instruction, the men and women formed two lines with Kant before them at the front of the room.

I joined the line with Rachel's friend Sandra, who had been freed for the evening by a baby-sitter. Pip was in the lineup, too, way past his bedtime. He was Rachel's partner.

First, two people from the group demonstrated without music, as Kant went through the calls. Jefferson, in sweaty shirt-sleeves, watched serenely, his violin propped against his hip. When it was time for the dance to begin, he and Carter put their instruments to their chins, eyed each other sharply and started in with a lusty sweep of their bows to play the old Scottish tune "Money Musk."

There was chaos on the floor for a while but in time everyone started to figure it out, which inspired others on the sidelines to join in. After 15 minutes, we all had it down and we lost ourselves in the music and the simple patterns of the reel, laughing and sweating, hair sticking to foreheads, hands taking hands, elbows hooked in elbows, couples whirling.

Rachel was laughing her way through the line with Pip when I bowed out, leaving Sandra to go back to her own young man, a new boyfriend. I filled a glass from a huge punch bowl and stood watching Rachel, her golden skin moist with perspiration, her chin tilting up with every easy laugh, her sparkling eyes closing in pleasure.

I looked toward Jefferson and Mr. Carter, who seemed to be his old self, the wiry old man we knew from Yonkers; but even in the soft candlelight, I could see that Jefferson's face had grown thinner and craggier. Between numbers, he rubbed his wrists with a perplexed look. I glanced around for Rachel and saw her in the thick of the crowd, watching him, her smile gone.

At the next break, Mr. Carter asked for everyone's attention. He wanted to play a tune, he said, especially for Mr. Jefferson and his daughter, a tune that had become a favorite of Mr. Jefferson. "If you'd all make a little room out there for my Rachel and the groom," Mr. Carter said, pointing to the middle of the floor and swirling his finger, "I'd like them to have this dance."

Jefferson let go of his sore wrists and smiled, stepping forward, searching for Rachel a little desperately, I thought, his eyes instantly brightening as he spotted her coming out of the crowd with Pip in hand. Mr. Carter turned and spoke to the musicians. Rachel stooped and said something to Pip and pointed him toward me. I waved for him. He came over and took my hand. Together we watched Jefferson take Rachel in his arms when Mr. Carter started in with his "Ashokan Farewell" violin solo.

Rachel, I could see, had been busy; she'd taught Jefferson how to waltz, too. They turned elegantly in slow graceful steps to the bittersweet tune. The ensemble joined in, with a guitar that must have been brought along just for that number. Rachel rested her head on Jefferson's shoulder. I sensed she was letting herself have one last dream with him. All the guests gazed with rapt faces, as if they were dreaming too. No one but me seemed to notice the hint of stiffness in Jefferson's movements.

Rachel lifted her head and waved with both hands for everyone to come dance. Couples broke off from the crowd and quickly filled the floor, blocking my view of the bride and groom.

After a while, I was feeling quite alone when Rachel came beside me. She put a hand on my chest and whispered in my ear, "Jack, I think we have to go."

I wasn't sure what she meant. There had been no plans for a honeymoon. "You're going away after all?" I said.

"Find Sandra and give Pip to her."

"Okay. Why?"

"We have to go. The three of us. To Monticello."

I understood. I'd known it was coming all along and had managed to pretend otherwise. "Where is he?" I asked.

"He just went outside, out the front. He's waiting for us. He wants no one to see. He and I talked this through before. I'm so glad it's happening with you here with us."

"Oh Rachel," I said.

"It's okay," she said. "Out front, Jack." She stepped away and moved back into the crowd. They let her pass by in peace, granting her the privilege — as guests do on a bride's grand night — of conducting her own secret missions.

I found Sandra, whispered in her ear that Jefferson wasn't feeling well — he wasn't used to so much wine, I said — and that Rachel and I would be outside with him. I asked her to take Pip. She looked at me anxiously. "It's all right," I said. "We may not see you for a while. I think they're actually making their getaway and I've been recruited for service."

"Getaway?" she said. "Really? I didn't think they were going anywhere."

I shrugged, said, "Surprise," and squeezed her shoulder.

"Take care of little Jack."

I headed through the throng and out the open doorway into the garden, catching Mr. Carter's eye just in time. He nodded firmly at me once, as if he knew what was happening.

Outside, above the music drifting from the ballroom, the bell-like chorus of crickets filled the soft night. I walked around the palace and out the front gate, where I found Rachel and Jefferson on the edge of the road that curved around the end of the Palace Green. In the dim light of one old-fashioned streetlamp, they stood in a motionless embrace. I could see the glow of his hair, now nearly white. A few people strolled by but they were not guests from the wedding and they left the bride and her groom alone.

"Jack, my friend," Jefferson said in a raspy voice, turning to me as I reached them. "I believe our time together is running out."

I took his arm and gaped at him in near panic. "I'll get the car," I said.

"Jack," Rachel said. "There's a box on his desk in the study. You know it. Please bring it. I want him to have those things with him. That feels right to me. I don't want to look at tokens for the rest of my life."

At that moment she seemed strong and resolute, too focused on her mission for dread or sorrow.

"Wait here," I said.

I trotted across the palace green and up to the house, where I told the baby-sitter that Sandra would be home soon with Pip. I went into the master bedroom, cluttered with all the evidence of Jefferson's wedding preparations: hangers on the bed, shoe trees on the floor, bathrobe and towel in a pile on a chair, drawers hanging open in the dresser. I looked down at little Jack, asleep in his crib. What was to become of this child? I wanted to pick him up and hold him but there was no time for that. I found the box on Jefferson's messy desk, its lid open, as if he'd been pondering its contents.

With the box under my arm, I jogged back to the Palace Green and followed George Street past the Wythe house to the employee parking lot just outside the restored area. My hands shaking, I got in the car and fumbled for the key.

At the palace entry gate, I parked with the engine running and hopped out, looking left and right. I didn't see them.

"Here, Jack," Rachel called.

I turned and looked over my shoulder. Past the bend of the road, I spotted them on the steps of the Robert Carter house portico, the closest spot they'd been able to find a place to sit.

I got back in the car, thinking this was all happening too fast, there was no time to talk, no time to go over things, no time to say goodbye. I spun the BMW into a U-turn and pulled up as close to them as I could get.

"I'll get in the back," Rachel said as we helped the feeble old man off the steps.

"I apologize for this," he said. "The transformation has been extremely abrupt. I am relieved none of our guests noticed."

I tried not to let my expression melt into horror as I held him. He was the 82-year-old man I'd first seen on the lawn but now he lacked even the apparition's vigor. He was not only old but unwell.

After Rachel climbed in back, I helped him fumble into the front seat. He emitted a deep sigh as his head fell back against the seat.

"God!" Rachel cried in a high whisper, the only sign of panic I'd seen in her. She leaned forward and put her hand on his shoulder, a miserable, anguished look on her face.

I got into the car. "Are you sure about this?" I said. "We shouldn't just take him to the hospital?"

"He's sure," Rachel said fiercely. "He knows. He's sure. This is what he wants."

"Yes, yes," Jefferson breathed, "it's time for me to return to the time and place I belong. It was delightful, pretending that I belonged here with you." When she touched his cheek, he tilted his head against her palm.

As we drove off, Rachel fell back against her seat and began to cry softly. I could barely hear her over the rumble of the tires.

We headed for the interstate ramp only a mile away. It would take us all the way to an exit just down the hill from Monticello.

I felt the same thick sense of emptiness and pain that had numbed me when Pam and Ben had died. Jefferson dozed. Rachel, after repeatedly rousing herself to lean forward between the seats and peer at his face, slumped exhausted into her corner of the back seat and fell asleep.

He woke up now and then to ask Rachel and me if we were all right.

"We're fine, we're fine," I kept telling him, patting his knee and squeezing his hand.

"Good, good," he said in a hoarse whisper. "I want to be no further trouble."

He stirred as we neared Charlottesville. "I can feel we are close to home," he said. "Jack, I have more notebooks for you. Rachel knows where they are. I hope they will be of value."

"No, that doesn't matter, but I'll treasure them."

"I never rode in an airplane. I had intended to insist that we three take a flight one day."

He attempted to lift his head. "I hold a belief, Jack, that at last I will see my family. It grieves me so terribly to leave Rachel and you and the boys but I believe I will be at peace. You and Rachel and Jamie have freed me even though I have only pretended to understand your times. How wonderful it has been to visit your time and your country, joys and sorrows and all. And I fear not for my country. I fear not. There are forces at work against us but the spirit of freedom will not be vanquished. The mass of mankind has not been born with saddles on their backs, nor a favored few booted and spurred, ready to ride them legitimately, by the grace of God. The people will find their way. I'm sure of it."

I gripped the wheel and concentrated on the road. When I looked at him again, he had dropped back into his stupor.

In another hour, we were stopped, the engine idling, at the wooden drop-gate on the road that led up Jefferson's mountain. "We're here," I said.

Rachel sat up and touched Jefferson's shoulder. "Thomas," she said softly. "Thomas?"

He awakened slowly. "Yes, yes ... I'm here," he said weakly.

"What shall we do?" she asked.

His eyes were fixed. "We must reach the house," he whispered.

I looked at the gate, a single wooden slat, easy to break through. Rachel and I looked at each other. "Are there any night watchmen, Thomas?" she asked.

He had almost fallen back to sleep. "Night ... watchmen? Oh yes, I suppose."

I didn't see any evidence of an alarm system on the gate. "Can he walk, do you think?" I asked.

"It's such a long way up," she said and leaned close to his ear. "Can you walk at all, Thomas? Thomas?"

He did not respond. His breathing was labored.

"Oh God. He's dying!" Rachel cried.

I put the car in gear and drove through the gate, cracking it apart into pieces that clattered to the road. I expected the flashing lights of a security cruiser or the state police but as we climbed the mountain we were alone, all the way up to the visitor center. I turned off the headlights and slowed to a crawl. Under the dimmed lights in its parking area, I could see a pickup truck and an SUV with lettering on its doors. I checked the time. It was 3:30 a.m.

"He's buried in the cemetery. Shouldn't we take him there?" I asked.

"The house; he said it has to be the house, Jack."

I could just make out the road under the luminous glow of the pre-dawn sky. I turned off the air conditioning and opened the car window so I could listen — for what I don't know. Sirens? Someone shouting? We continued slowly the rest of the way to the top of the mountain and, when the ground leveled off, I made the turn toward the trees that sheltered the pathway to the east front of the house and shut off the engine. In the sudden silence, I once again heard those high-pitched Virginia crickets in their sweet, mindless song.

"Thomas," Rachel said, gently nudging his shoulder. "We're

back. You're home. You're at Monticello."

He didn't react but we could see he was breathing.

"We'll have to carry him," I said.

I opened the door, stepped out and folded the seat forward for Rachel. We stood together and looked around, Rachel holding the box of objects from Jefferson's first life. The sky to the east had begun to glow over the great plain of the Tidewater.

We went to the other side of the car. I leaned in, hooked his arm around my neck and lifted him out of the car. His head rolled. Rachel hooked his other arm over her shoulders.

"He's light as a feather," I said. "Where are we going, Rachel?"

"The west portico," she said. "Up the steps."

Jefferson moaned and tried to lift his head. "Are we home?" He seemed to rally and tried to walk. His legs mimicked the process, out of sync with our forward motion, but well enough so we did not have to drag him.

"We're at the east front, Thomas. We're almost there," Rachel said.

"I feel myself home," he said weakly.

We cut across the lawn to the side of the house, climbed the steps onto the south terrace and descended the opposite set of steps onto the west lawn.

"Did you hear anything?" Rachel asked.

"I thought I heard voices," I said, looking up at Jefferson's windows.

She glanced around fretfully. "I just want him to go peacefully. Please God, let no one bother us until he goes!"

We carried him up the steps of the west portico and lay him on its grass-bordered slate terrace. Rachel kneeled behind him, holding him up against her side and placing the box beside him. I sat down on the top step.

"This is what you said to do, Thomas. We're here," she whispered. "You are home."

We waited, I'm not sure for what. Merely death? We had been there for only a minute or two when I sensed movement. I looked to my right, off the portico, and jerked violently in surprise. Just where Jefferson had stood looking up at the poplar a year before stood a young black man, dressed in breeches and billowing shirtsleeves.

"It's Jamie!" Rachel gasped.

Without the grotesque twist of a hanged man's face, I could see Mr. Carter in his eyes and the shape of his face. He watched us silently.

I sensed more movement to my right and heard voices again. I turned and saw three people standing inside the French doors of the parlor, gazing wondrously at Jefferson. One was a woman — very fair and slight of build, with fine features and long, curly blond tresses — who wore an 18th-century formal dress of robin's-egg blue. She was perhaps 30. With her were two younger women, the older of the two tall and almost manly, with an angular face like Jefferson's, the younger one an even softer version of the lovely woman in blue.

"Do you see those people?" I asked Rachel, thinking I should have been used to all this by now, there was nothing new about seeing ghosts at Monticello or anywhere else.

She turned and looked over her shoulder. "I do," she said in an almost gleeful whisper. "It's Mrs. Jefferson and Polly and Patsy! It must be!"

"You know them?"

She rubbed her forehead, looking at the women and almost breaking into a smile as they looked back with happy yet somehow vacant faces, as if their patience were limitless. Before our eyes, more forms began to appear out of the darkness behind them — more people, men and women, young and old, all with the same benign, easy gaze. Right away I recognized the two young strangers I'd seen long ago in period dress at the cemetery, Jefferson's grandchildren George and Cornelia.

"Rachel," Jefferson croaked.

She leaned down and pressed her check against his. "Yes, Thomas, I'm here."

He barely lifted his head. "I believe I have committed no crime in loving you openly and freely. I broke no promise. My children were long gone."

"They're here for you now," Rachel said. "Can you see them, Thomas? Look!" She helped him turn his head. His milky old eyes squinted and brightened.

"Ah!" he said. "Oh, my darling, my darling! At last! At last!" he cried.

The gazing faces all broke into bright smiles, real ones. Rachel convulsed in a sob and covered her face. "Time wastes too fast," Jefferson whispered to her, trying to lift his hand to her face but failing. He made a soft noise, more an outflow of air than a vocalization, and his head fell back against her shoulder.

"Oh!" she groaned. "Thomas ..."

I took his hand. It was limp and cold. "I think he's gone," I said, looking up to the parlor doors. Their glass panes revealed only a faint reflection of the dawn sky. The people had vanished.

"Jack," she said, looking up at me with a mottled face, "he told me not to hold him now. He said to stand away."

I stared at her. "What? 'Stand away'?"

She gently moved from behind him and eased him down onto the slates, the little box of objects by his head.

"We're supposed to just leave him there?" I said.

She came down a step. I got up and stood beside her. A man's voice below us called to Rachel. It was Jamie. We had forgotten him. We turned. He was raising his hand in a salute. "Take good care of my little sister, Jack," he said, and just like Jefferson on the west lawn so many months before, he faded into vapor and vanished.

A breath of wind came up. We turned around and saw that Mr. Jefferson was gone, too. Only a slight powdery film of white dust remained, all around and inside his wedding suit, sloppily spread on the portico beside the box. A little gust blew against our backs and caught the dust in tiny swirls, lifting it up and over our heads in an expanding cloud that rose toward the fading stars.

The breeze fell away as suddenly as it had come. We heard only the crickets. I took Rachel's hand. She smiled at me, her eyes glittering with tears, before letting go to bend down and gather up his clothes. She stood up straight with them, holding them tightly against her chest as we walked slowly to the car. Down the mountain we rode in silence, as if we were ghosts on our own rounds, ghosts that no one in the world would see.

Epilogue

On our return to Williamsburg, Rachel learned that she'd lost her father, too. He had collapsed and died at the wedding, playing his fiddle for a reel. We buried him in Virginia, at a city cemetery in Charlottesville, as close as we could get him to Monticello. Professor Kant, Pip, Jack and Sandra were with us at the service.

We would have put him close to Sally, who was buried in Charlottesville by her sons, but there is no record of where and no stone to be found.

A man with an identity, a famous man, cannot just disappear. We had no choice but to report Jefferson as a missing person to the Charlottesville police. They suspected we were lying, of course, but they were never hostile. I think Rachel's demeanor — her calm melancholy, her lack of theatrics and the rare tear that spilled from an eye — made them careful and respectful. Maybe they thought Rachel and Colonial Williamsburg had been the victims of a con man.

It made the news. There were short pieces in The Times and The Washington Post about the missing Thomas Jefferson reenactor named Thomas Jefferson. There was something on Entertainment Tonight. Who knows where else? I didn't pay a lot of attention.

No one believed he wouldn't come back. Colonial Williamsburg needed him. The union needed him. So did the state's Democrats. They didn't think he was a crazy grifter.

The Thomas Jefferson Foundation announced that the inkwell, spectacles and buckle found on the west portico on the morning of his disappearance matched objects in the Monticello collection and may very well have belonged to the real Jefferson. They acknowledged they might have been the very same mementoes that a Sally Hemings descendant had tried to sell to the foundation back in the 1930s. People magazine ate it up. They did a feature on the mystery that focused on the old lady in California and her Hemings descendants. They barely mentioned the missing Mr. Jefferson.

The foundation made the most of it. Monticello visitors could take a special new "Insider's Tour" for an extra fee that included an exhibition of the objects in a room off the all-weather passageway under the house. Attendance at Monticello shot up 50 percent that fall.

A few reporters pestered Rachel for a while. She never made a public statement. Kant and I had some calls from producers and reporters, too. We wouldn't talk either.

Jefferson left me a dozen leather-bound notebooks, packed with his tight script wedged into the margins. Some of it seemed quite crazed until things began to settle into place for him in Williamsburg. There were some revelations — but so what? I have lost any interest in sharing them with the world. Instead I have told this story, which people can take as fantasy if they choose. The proof is in a lead box in the foundation wall in the all-weather passageway under their house, but I can't imagine they will ever allow it to be attacked with a pickaxe just because of some novel.

I love Rachel but we were not meant to be together, even for little Jack and Pip's sake. I would love to try again at being a father but it's too late for that. I see Rachel, Pip and young Jack whenever I can, driving down from New Jersey without Nancy to the old brick house on Duke of Gloucester Street that Colonial Williamsburg, for the time being, has been letting her keep. She's teaching just down the street at William & Mary. She has friends, including a young man who specializes in Jefferson studies. He is on track for a professorship, once he completes his doctorate on abolitionism in 18th-century Virginia.

I've picked up the boys and Rachel to take them to Monticello three times. Her young man never comes along. "Next time," Rachel always says. It's hard for Rachel and me, being at Monticello, but we want Jack and Pip to love it there. Pip has grown more quiet and serious. He reads constantly — anything he can find about Thomas Jefferson. I worry for him. I have gotten it into my head that Jamie Hemings is at work. But little Jack is an easy child. He smiles when we hold his hands and walk him through the gardens on the west lawn. He smiles all the time.

Just last year they cut down the big tulip poplar at the corner of the north pavilion. The insurance people said the big tree threatened the house even though it was perfectly healthy. After they cut it down, they counted the rings and found the tree had been old enough for Jefferson to have planted it himself.

I knew what Jefferson had said, that he had not planted it. Maybe he erred. Maybe he had simply forgotten, or had been unable to believe any tree from his day could have survived so unscathed. Who knows? It's just another mystery.

So the tree is gone and now you can buy pens and bookmarks made out its wood at the Monticello gift shop.

We have new lives, Rachel and me. I've come through the hardest time in my life happier than I've been in many years, even with Pam's black man standing in the shadows of my mind.

Mine is now an easy, simple, day-by-day happiness that comes from friends and a new family and Nancy's company. She came along the last time I went down to Williamsburg to see Rachel. Nancy was great. She helped clear the air and put our mourning aside. We had a big dinner by lantern light at the King's Arms with Rachel and her young man and two of their friends from the college faculty. There was nothing but good cheer and laughter.

Rachel and I caught each other's eye in the middle of it all, as one of those strolling troubadours in 18th-century shirtsleeves stopped by the table to sing a racy old Irish ballad. We smiled. It choked me up a little to see we'd made it through, we were going to be fine, we'd found a way to put our story to rest, even in its place at the center of our souls.

There will be no more great loves for Rachel or me. We are haunted. Everywhere we go, we are searching. I wait for Pam and Ben and we both wait for our friend, Thomas Jefferson.

Acknowledgments

I would not have kept working at this novel without the encouragement and support of my wife, Barbara, who loved the tale and whose suggestions, editing and proofing — not to mention cover and book design — kept me going through a long rewriting, revising and polishing process.

I am grateful to two friends in publishing who helped with the manuscript: Gabrielle Brooks, for her brilliant and hard-nosed critique of an early draft, and Lisa Higgins for her professional editing and guidance. Decia Fates and Jean Raymond each professionally proofed versions of the manuscript. Barb Pfanz of Main Street Media provided layout and typesetting expertise for the paperback edition through thick and thin.

This story was inspired by Thomas Jefferson and all his fascinating complications; his family's devotion to him; his enchanting homes near Charlottesville and Lynchburg, and by many books, including Dumas Malone's six-volume masterpiece, "Jefferson and His Time"; David McCullough's brilliant "John Adams," in which Mr. Jefferson vividly appears as a vexing figure; and by Annette Gordon-Reed's fascinating landmark history, "The Hemingses of Monticello," which brings Jefferson to life more vividly than any book I'd ever read — until this one.

Made in the USA
Middletown, DE
07 December 2019